P9-CCS-372

*New Orleans Legacy*

*Also by Alexandra Ripley*

The Time Returns
On Leaving Charleston
Charleston
Who's That Lady in the President's Bed?

*By Alexandra Ripley, Ninette Beaver, and Patrick Trese*

Caril

ALEXANDRA RIPLEY

Macmillan Publishing Company • New York

Macmillan Publishing Company
866 Third Avenue, New York, N.Y. 10022
Collier Macmillan Canada, Inc.

This novel is a work of fiction. Any references to historical events; to real people, living or dead; or to real locales are intended only to give the fiction a setting in historical reality. Other names, characters, places, and incidents either are the product of the author's imagination or are used fictitiously, and their resemblance, if any, to real life counterparts is entirely coincidental.

Library of Congress Cataloging-in-Publication Data
Ripley, Alexandra.
New Orleans legacy.
I. Title.
PS3568.I597N4 1987 813'.54 86-17935
ISBN 0-02-603520-0

10 9 8 7 6 5 4 3 2
Printed in the United States of America

*For John*

Day after day the young woman sat on the slope of the tall grassy bank beside the broad muddy river. A baby slept in a basket by her side.

From time to time the baby stirred, and the young mother bent over the basket to adjust the baby's coverings or simply to look at the tiny face and hands. Then she picked up the pen and paper she had set aside and resumed her writing.

"I can't believe I was ever that idiotically young," she told her baby, "but I was. I won't lie to you, never to you."

She was writing her own story for her child, so that the baby would never have to grow up without knowing what her mother was like. There was no reason to believe that she wouldn't be there to tell her daughter the story in years to come. But she had learned that life was full of surprises and that some of them were perilous.

At the bottom of each page she wrote, "I love you."

# Book One

# 1

The box was a mystery, and for that reason it was the most exciting gift Mary had ever received.

Her friends looked at it, then at one another, unsure of what they should say. "Open it, Mary," exclaimed one, trying to sound enthusiastic.

"Not yet," Mary said. She stroked the stained, battered old wooden box with her right hand. It was a gesture of love. Her left hand held the tantalizing letter that had accompanied the gift. The pages fluttered in her fingers, visible evidence of her emotion.

"Read it, Sue," she said, holding it out to her closest friend. "My voice is too shaky."

Sue snatched it from her, politeness overcome by curiosity.

"'My dearest Mary,'" Sue read aloud, "'this box is a gift from your mother.'" She glanced up at the other girls in the room. They looked as amazed as she felt. Everyone knew that Mrs. MacAlistair never even wrote to Mary. Gifts were unheard-of. It was her father who sent presents of expensive sweets and elaborately illustrated books, even though they were forbidden at the convent school. Sue returned hastily to the letter.

"'Dearest Mary,'" she repeated, "'this box is a gift from your mother, not from me. I have never seen what is inside. It is, she told me, the keeping-place for the secret treasures of the ladies of her family. She received it from her mother; her mother received it from her mother; and so on, for many generations. It is traditional that the eldest daughter become the owner on her sixteenth birthday and remain custodian until her own eldest daughter reaches that age.'"

Sue crushed the letter to the starched white linen bib of her school uniform. "I've never heard of anything so romantic," she said. "Aren't you going to open it, Mary? It's almost your birthday. You'll be sixteen tomorrow."

Mary didn't even hear her friend's question. She was lost in a daydream.

Mary daydreamed often. She was very young when she discovered that it was possible to live in a beautiful, happy world inside her head whenever the world around her was ugly and unhappy. In that private world, whatever she wanted was true, or would soon come true, and everything hurtful was forgotten, had never happened.

Now, in her imagination, she was opening the box with her mother by her side, eager to share its secrets with her. Her mother was the same beautiful, perfumed woman Mary had always worshiped. But she was not distant and disapproving. She loved Mary. She had only been waiting until Mary reached sixteen to demonstrate it.

Mary touched the box. It was no dream. It was solid, tangible. It was proof of her mother's love. She laid her cheek against it, caressed it with both hands, forgetting to hide her peculiar fingers the way she usually did, unashamed, for the moment, of the abnormality, the little fingers that were as long as the ring fingers on both hands.

Sue rattled the pages of the letter. "Mary!" She was practiced at calling Mary from her "silliness," as Sue called her dreams. "Mary, shall I read the rest?"

Mary sat up and folded her hands in her lap. "Yes, do. It gets better and better."

"'It is also traditional,'" Sue read, "'that no husband ever learns what is inside. I know your mother added her treasure before we were married. In case you might want to purchase a secret treasure for the box, I am enclosing a few banknotes. I promise never to ask what you used them for.'

"It's signed, 'Faithfully, your loving Father.'"

Sue looked in the envelope at the money; her eyes and mouth made circles of astonishment.

"Mary," she gasped, "you're rich! You've just got to open that box. It's probably full of diamonds."

The other girls joined in a chorus of demands to "open it, open it." The shouting broke through Mary's reverie.

It also brought Sister Josepha, with a frown on her normally serene brow. "Girls, girls," she scolded. "You may be graduating tomorrow, but today you are still bound by the rules. This is the hour for quiet and meditation."

"But Sister, Mary has a mystery..." Eight excited voices vied to tell the young nun about Mary's gift. She managed to hush them at last, but when Mary agreed to open the box, she joined in their soft cries of anticipation.

When Mary removed its lid, the box exhaled a scent of age, like dried rose petals. Something inside glowed richly in the sunlight slanting low through the window.

"Gold!" Sue exclaimed.

Mary lifted a heavy chain of twisted gold links. She held it up high so that everyone could see the big jeweled locket suspended from it. There was a chorus of appreciative "ooohs."

She waved away their pleas to show them more. The pearls and rubies on the locket made an intricate looped monogram. She looked closely at it, then shook her head. "I can't make it out," she said. "But I'm almost sure the pearls are an 'M.' Maybe my grandmother was named Mary, too."

"Ask your mother . . . show some more."

Mary carefully put the gold chain and locket down beside the box. She took a large fan out of it and spread it open with cautious fingers.

Even Sister Josepha sighed. The fan was a masterpiece of fragile beauty. It had sticks made of ivory, pierced into a delicate grillwork. They supported an ivory-colored arc of lace as sheer as gossamer, with a pattern of flowering vines. It was the largest fan any of them had ever seen, but it looked as weightless as a butterfly's wing. Mary held her breath while she folded it and laid it next to the locket.

"I can see more lace," said Sue. "Come on. Don't be so slow."

Mary held up two yellowed gloves edged with wide bands of heavy, knotted lace.

They were a hundred times more exciting to Mary than the gold. "Look," she whispered, "look how they're made." She slid her right hand into one of the gloves and smoothed it with her left. "Look," she said again. The little finger of the glove was as long as the finger next to it. She smiled at her friends. "I must have gotten my spider fingers from my grandmother, or great-grandmother, or even great-great-grandmother." Her wide dark eyes were gleaming, filled with happy tears. She kissed the ill-made glove.

"Show us the rest, Mary!"

Mary removed the ancient glove with maddening, slow carefulness.

The other things in the box were disappointing to her friends. They were curiosities, not beautiful at all. There was a small leather pouch that held an Indian arrowhead. It was no different from the dozens they had all found when they were children and considered arrowheads interesting. And there was a wad of stiff gray filaments wrapped in a piece of yellowed lace.

"That looks like the awful false hair we use for the beards in the

Nativity play," said Sue with a huff through her nose. "There must be something else, Mary."

"No, there's nothing more."

"Let me look." Sue edged Mary aside. She tilted the box so that the light could reach the corners. "Just dust," she grumbled. Then, "Wait. No, there is something. It's carved inside." She rubbed the inside of the lid with the corner of her apron. "M . . . A . . . R . . . It must be a message for you, Mary. Come see!"

Mary leaned close. She used her handkerchief to clear the embedded grime. "It says 'Marie . . . Marie Duclos.' It's French. I must be part French. I had a governess before I came here to school, and she taught me some French. She said I did well, too. It must be in my blood.

"There's more. 'Couvent.' Is that another name? No. I can see it now. It says 'Couvent des Ursulines,' Convent of the Ursulines, 'Nouvelle Orleans.' That's French for New Orleans."

One of the girls giggled. "Maybe your grandmother was a nun, Mary."

Sister Josepha gasped.

"Oh, Sister, I'm sorry," said the joker, horrified. "I forgot you were here."

"You will now devote yourselves to quiet meditation and prayer," said Sister Josepha. She was frowning again.

The sun was not yet up when Mary woke the next morning. She tried to go back to sleep, but she was too happy. She took the quilt from her bed, wrapped it around her shoulders, and walked silently past the sleeping girls in the long room to the open windows at its end. Although it was early June, there was a memory of ice in the air. The convent school was located on a high ridge in the Allegheny mountains.

She rested her chin on the windowsill and waited impatiently for the sunrise, crouched on the cold bare floor. Start, day, she commanded silently. This is the best day of my whole life, and I want it to begin. I'm sixteen now, grown up, and I'm through with school, ready for the world. Let me see it.

Her heart felt huge and warm inside her body. She put her hand under her breast to feel its strong beating and smiled at her foolish idea that it might burst from joy.

Only two days earlier, Mary had been afraid of her birthday and her graduation. The convent school was home to her, the nuns and the other girls her family. She had been there for five years, even during vacation because her father and mother traveled in Europe every summer. Christmas was the only time she left the mountain for the big stone house on the estate near Pittsburgh, and even then she was homesick for the convent because the house was always full of strangers, guests at the elaborate parties her parents gave during the holidays. Mary felt like one more stranger. The convent was where she belonged, and she had dreaded having to leave it.

Until now. Now, she felt nothing but happiness. Her mother would come to the graduation with her father; she was sure of it, because the box promised a whole new world of shared secrets and closeness. Her parents would be proud of her. She had won the prize for elocution; it would be presented at the ceremony. Her dress was the prettiest, too. Each girl had made her own long white frock as the final test of the skills the nuns had taught them. Mary's stitches were the tiniest and most even of them all, and her embroidered flowers were exquisite. She had also made handkerchiefs for her father and her mother. She hugged herself under the folds of the quilt, imagining their surprise and pleasure when she gave them a "graduation present."

As if to signal a confirmation of her hopes, the rim of the sun appeared over the mountaintop and the sky was streaked with rose and gold.

"I know they'll say yes," Mary whispered to the dawn. She had written to her father, telling him what she wanted for her birthday and graduation. "Please allow me to go with you and Mother to Europe."

Light filled the window and then the room. Mary heard the stirring and grumbling of the other girls as they woke.

"Stop fussing," she said, turning to smile at them. "It's a beautiful, wonderful day."

Mary thought nothing of it when Sister Josepha stopped her in the corridor after breakfast and asked her to come to the Mother Superior's parlor. It was traditional for each graduating girl to be invited for a short private visit with the head of the convent, to say goodbye and receive a blessing before the confusion of the day began.

"It's a beautiful day, Sister Josepha," Mary said.

The young nun suddenly began to cry. "I'm so sorry, Mary," she sobbed. She opened the door to the parlor.

"Come in, my child, and sit down." The Mother Superior was in the open doorway, her two hands held out toward Mary, her face unsmiling.

Mary felt a thump of fear in her chest; something was terribly wrong. "What is it, Mother?"

"Come. Sit. You must be very brave, Mary. There has been an accident, and your father is dead."

"No!" Mary cried. She refused to believe it, tried to retreat into her private world where such things never happened. She pushed away Mother Superior's hands, shouting, "No, no, no, no." Then she saw the gentle old woman's faded blue eyes in their wrinkled pouches, and the compassion that shone from them told her that the unthinkable was true and could not be escaped. She moaned softly, the weak cry of a wounded animal.

The Mother Superior put an arm around Mary's waist to support her. "God sends us the strength to meet our sorrows, child," she said. "You are not alone." She helped Mary to a chair.

The horsehair upholstery was held in place by large black metal buttons. One of them pressed against Mary's left shoulder blade. I shouldn't be noticing a little thing like a knob against my back, Mary thought, when my father is dead. What's wrong with me? Yet, in a strange way, the small, intrusive physical discomfort made it possible for her to listen to the Mother Superior's words, to hear and to understand.

The news had been brought by a messenger, a clerk from the office of Mr. MacAlistair's lawyer. He had arrived late the night before, bringing with him a bulging portfolio of legal papers.

Those papers, said the Mother Superior, were the cause of the delay in sending word to Mary. Her old face was pale and unnaturally grim as she spoke. Mary's father had, in fact, died six days earlier. He was already buried, without Mary's being allowed to attend his funeral. Those were Mrs. MacAlistair's orders.

The Mother Superior held Mary's hand in hers. There was more that Mary had to know, she said, something that was even more painful than the death of her father.

"The woman you thought was your mother is really no kin to you at all, my child. Your real mother died when you were born. Your father came to Pittsburgh after that, bringing his infant daughter, and a few months later he married again. Mrs. MacAlistair is your stepmother.

"May God forgive me for saying it, she is a cruel unfeeling woman.

She sent word that you are no longer welcome in your father's home. It is hers now, together with everything else he owned. I saw the will myself. It said, 'All my estate to my wife Alice, confident that she will take loving care of my daughter Mary.'

"You are a pauper, Mary, and homeless. We do not even know who your godparents are. You were baptized in whatever place you were born before your father moved to Pittsburgh. We do know that you must have been properly baptized. Your father told me when he brought you here that he was himself a Protestant but that your mother was Catholic and that it was her wish that you be raised in the Church. The Church must be your family, now, Mary. You have no other."

Mary's hand had grown cold and stiff in Mother Superior's grasp. Her face was like a carving made of stone, the eyes dry, staring at nothing. The elderly nun was alarmed. Perhaps she should have called for a doctor to be there when Mary was told. She peered anxiously at the silent girl.

Suddenly Mary smiled. The nun was shocked. "But I do have a family, Mother," Mary said. "My real mother left it to me; it's my legacy from her. All I have to do is find it."

"What are you talking about, Mary?"

"My box, my birthday gift."

"But your father sent that, Mary. Weeks ago. He asked us to keep it until the day before graduation."

"My father may have sent it, but my mother gave it to me. My own mother who loved me. I'm going to go to New Orleans. I have a home there."

# 2

"It's so romantic," sighed Sister Josepha.

"It's so foolish," Sister Michael replied. "Mother Superior did her best to talk Mary out of this venture, but that girl has always been hardheaded."

"Oh, Sister, don't be so harsh," the younger nun said. She waved one last time from the window at the disappearing wagon that was taking two nuns and Mary MacAlistair to Pittsburgh. "I would call Mary persevering, not hardheaded. She's always succeeded at anything she set herself to do. Remember her declamation, how hard she practiced. And her embroidery. She picked out some of the stitches a dozen times until she got the pattern right. She won't accept failure, no matter how hard she has to work."

"She'll find oratory and fancy stitches do her precious little good. Or her dreaminess, either. She doesn't know a truth when her nose is buried in it. This wild goose chase will get her in a lot of trouble, mark my words."

"God protects the innocent, Sister. He will take care of Mary."

The older nun opened her mouth to answer. She looked at the luminous young face of Sister Josepha and closed her lips tight to stop the words.

Mary saw Sister Josepha's waving hand, but before she could respond the road made a sharp bend and the convent was out of sight. I don't care, she thought, that's all behind me. I'm going to New Orleans. I belong there.

She laughed aloud with excitement, glancing at the two nuns, ready to share her exuberant emotions. They looked at her with reddened eyes filled with pain and apprehension. They were both going to Pittsburgh to have diseased teeth pulled. Mary made a sympathetic grimace, then turned her head away. I won't let anything spoil this day, she told herself.

For an instant she remembered the day of graduation and the anguish that had destroyed her hopes. But she forced herself to stop remembering. The pain was too raw. She looked at the wildflowers clinging to crevices in the mountain's exposed rock face and fastened her thoughts on the fantasy that shut out the memories. It was a picture of her mother.

Her name must have been Marie, like the name in the box, like Mary's own name, but in French. She was beautiful, Mary was sure, with fair soft skin and hair, and eyes of the clearest, deepest blue. She looked like the loveliest angel in the Nativity scene that hung on the wall of the chapel. And she was watching over her, Mary knew it, looking down from heaven, smiling gloriously, happy that Mary was going to her family, to where she should be, where her strange, spider fingers were a badge of belonging and not something to be ashamed of and to hide. The gloves in the box were the sign her mother had sent her. Mary held her hands together, loving them, proud of them. Lost in her dream, she didn't notice the jolting of the wagon or the discomfort of the bare wooden seat or the slow passing of the hours.

A touch on her shoulder brought her back to reality. The nun sitting next to her pointed at the landscape below the road. "Pittsburgh," she mumbled through the clove-oil-soaked cloth wadded in her cheek.

"Oh! It's wonderful." Mary leaned recklessly over the edge of the wagon to look down. She could see the wide bands of water, reflecting the bright sun in spots of light, and the convent school's geography lessons came to life. She murmured the rivers' musical names aloud: Allegheny . . . Monongahela . . . Ohio. There they were, ribbons of brightness through the green countryside, coming together in the center of a cluster of buildings and chimneys and church spires. "Oh!" she cried again. At the point of the rivers' meeting she could see a kaleidoscope of colors, the shirts and skirts and bonnets of tiny, doll-like figures, moving to and fro near the river and the toy-seeming boats that were sending up little dots of black smoke from gold-topped stacks.

"I'll miss my boat," she wailed. "We're still so far away. Hurry, please hurry."

But the wagon jolted along at the same rattling pace, and soon the city and the rivers were lost from view. Mary suppressed the urge to jump down to the road and run. She chewed on a corner of her lip and strained forward, her body willing the wheels to turn faster.

It seemed an eternity before the road emerged from between two massive rock formations onto the bluff that towered above the river joinings. The boats were still there, and the people. And Mary could hear the noise now. Shouting voices and whistles and the raucous hooting of poorly played horns making some unrecognizable tune. She drew a deep breath of relief and slumped against the seat back, shocked at the stiffness of her shoulders and neck; then she forgot the cramps in the overwhelming thrill of the moment. She was truly going; it was real now; one of those boats would carry her along the bright water of the river to her family, to New Orleans. And adventure. And perhaps even romance.

"We'll go with you to the boat, Mary," said the nun by her side when the wagon stopped at the entrance to the dock.

Mary shook her head. "I'm perfectly all right, Sister. You go on to the dentist and get that tooth drawn. You'll feel so much better once it's done."

"But Mother Superior said..."

"Mother Superior doesn't have a toothache. There's nothing I need help with anyhow. Please, I mean it. I'll be fine by myself."

"Are you certain?"

"Yes, Sister, yes I am." Mary's hands were already pulling at the straps that held her luggage on the back of the wagon. There wasn't much, just a tapestry valise that held her school uniforms, her graduation clothes, and her toilet articles. And her box.

"See, I can carry them easily by myself." The straps were loose, the luggage in her arms, and Mary on the ground near the wagon. "Goodbye, Sisters." She turned toward the flag-decorated entrance to the steamboat landing.

"God go with you, Mary," the nuns called. She turned her head to smile over her shoulder.

Why, she looks so pretty, thought one of the Sisters. Pretty was not a word generally associated with Mary MacAlistair. She was pleasant-looking, always neat, her nut-brown hair smoothly braided and wrapped into a knot at the base of her head, her nails clipped and clean. But she was rather short, and "sturdy" was more appropriate to her shape than "delicate," even though she was quite thin. She was shaped like a boy. The most noticeable thing about her was the bright color in her cheeks. At a time when extremely white skin was the ideal, Mary's robust rosiness was a definite drawback. Without it, her eyes might even have been attractive. They were round, large, and a very warm brown, the color of sherry wine. But the startling red cheeks were the only thing people saw when they looked at her. How strange, thought the nun, that they don't look too bright today. They seem just right with that happy smile. I'll be able to smile, too, when this tooth is gone and the pain with it. She gestured to the driver to move on.

Mary walked quickly through the gate, then stopped short, amazed.

I've never seen so much life, she thought. There was activity all over the huge landing. Buggies and carriages criss-crossed, drivers shouting, vying for position near the stone steps where passengers could step down. Carts and wagons were being emptied of crates and barrels or loaded with them. Three different bands were playing, and one of the steamboats was making even louder music with its shrill calliope. Near and between the music makers children and young men and women capered and danced. Mary stared at them, her feet moving in tiny pats, wanting to join in. She gaped at the lines of black men carrying cargo onto the boats and heaving enormous loads on and off the wagons. She had never seen a black person before, and she was fascinated and confused. Educated by ardently abolitionist teachers, she could not understand why the men were singing and laughing. She looked for their chains and shackles, but could find none. Then she saw a white man sitting on a horse near the freight wagons, a coiled whip in his hand. She shuddered and looked away.

Toward the boats. There were three, each larger and more dazzling than the next. Their smokestacks were topped with golden crowns, and gilding decorated the elaborate lacy wooden trim on their decks. The biggest was three decks high, with shining brass bells and rails, gold-edged doors, and a golden-towered city amid dazzling flowers of every color painted on the cover of its gigantic side paddle wheel. Gold letters named boat and painting *City of Natchez*.

It was too much to take in. Mary's head turned from side to side, trying to see everything. "Make way," came cries from all sides, from drivers, from men hurrying, from boys carrying luggage behind rushing people. "Make way," Mary heard behind her, and she was jostled to one side by a pushcart piled high with trunks and valises and hatboxes.

Her shoulder hurt from the blow, but she didn't care. This was life, color, excitement, gaiety, the world, and she was part of it. She adjusted her box more securely under her arm and entered the chaos on the landing.

"Please, where do I go to buy a ticket?" She tried to ask half a dozen people, but they all hurried past her, not hearing her small, polite voice.

I'll just get on the boat, she decided. They'll have tickets there. But she couldn't walk three steps before her way was blocked or she was pushed aside, time and time again.

I've got to do it, she told herself, so I will. The edge of the box was digging into her side, the bag dragged on her arm, and she was afraid that she might cry. Then she saw the small red clapboard building. Gold letters on a white board over its door said TICKETS AND BILLS OF LADING. It was not far away, and there was nothing in her path. Mary ran, her bag thumping against her leg, and the box wavering perilously under her arm.

Inside the building she blinked and squinted her eyes to accustom them to the dimness after the bright sunlight outside. There was a noisy crowd there, too, but it was more orderly. Three lines of people led to a tall counter in the rear. They were static amid all the activity in the room.

Along the walls there were low wooden benches. Mary saw a woman rise from one and walk away. "Thank goodness," Mary whispered. She put box and bag down in the vacant space and wiped her face and hands with a handkerchief from her pocket. After that she straightened the net mitts she wore on her hands, smoothed her rumpled skirts, and adjusted her bonnet to its proper place. She felt like herself again when she was tidy. She had been a goose to let the busyness outside fluster her so, she scolded herself. She selected the shortest line and began to walk to it.

"Better not leave your traps like that, Miss," said a woman standing nearby. "There's folks aplenty 'round here what steals for a living."

Mary hurried back to the bench. She reached down for her box, then suddenly sat next to it, her knees trembling. All her excitement and determination seemed to seep away. She felt alone and frightened. What have I done? she cried soundlessly. I never thought about thieves. I never thought about anything. I don't know what to do. I don't know how to manage anything. I've never been anyplace by myself in my whole life. Mother Superior was right; this is a foolish, ill-considered thing to do. I wish I were back at the convent. This place is Bedlam.

Clanging bells from the landing demanded attention. Mary looked frantically from side to side. There were people all around her: well-dressed ladies and gentlemen, hard-eyed, lean men with leathery skin wearing fringed buckskin clothes, men and women with bare feet and faded, patched garments, children of every age running free or holding fast to adult hands. All of them seemed to know what they were doing, to understand the confusion around them. No one looked frightened. Only me, Mary thought.

Then the bells rang again. Mary plucked at the sleeve of a stout gray-haired woman near her. "Excuse me," she said, "does the bell mean the boat is leaving?"

The woman turned to Mary, glaring. Then, when she saw the girl's terror-filled eyes and neat gray uniform and bonnet, her expression softened. "That's what they claim it means, but don't let it worry you. I've known 'em to rush everybody on board by eleven in the morning and then sit there loading freight until four in the afternoon. This your first trip downriver?"

Mary nodded, tried to smile.

"And all by yourself?"

"Yes, ma'am," Mary admitted. The Mother Superior's warnings came back to her. Older ladies could travel unaccompanied, although they rarely did. But young ones never. Only coarse females went about alone.

"My father just died," Mary hurried to explain, "and I'm going to my grandmother in New Orleans. She's all I've got now. My mother's been dead a long time."

"You poor lamb." The woman's voice was thick with sympathy. "You just stay with me, dear. Mrs. Watson's my name. I know the ropes of this river as good as any boat captain. And what I don't know, Mr. Watson does. He's up there at the desk, making sure we get the best accommodations. Give me your ticket money and I'll take it to him. He'll see you don't get shortchanged. Then he'll escort us on board."

"Thank you so much, Mrs. Watson." Mary fumbled in her pocket and drew out the folded banknotes her father had sent with the wooden box. She held them out to Mrs. Watson. "I don't know how much the ticket costs," she said.

"Bless your innocent heart, child, don't go around handing strangers all your money. The ticket's not nearly that much. I'll tell Mr. Watson to keep the rest safe for you."

A short distance away, a lavishly plumed woman turned her back in disgust. "A plump chick ripe for plucking," she grumbled under her breath, "and somebody got there before me."

# 3

Mrs. Watson put her arm around Mary's shoulders, and her brown, thickly fringed shawl was like the wing of a plump mother partridge.

"You just listen to what I tell you, dear, and you'll be just fine; I know how to guide a young girl. Why, I raised five of my own, and four boys, too. What's your name, child?"

"Mary MacAlistair."

Those were the only words Mary said for many hours. Mrs. Watson never stopped talking.

When she introduced Mr. Watson, she laughed and said, "Some folks call us the Sprats." While the tall, thin, silent man smiled at Mary, Mrs. Watson recounted Mary's sad situation and, barely drawing a breath, told Mary about Mr. Watson's successful general store in Portsmouth, Ohio, and about his shrewd bargaining with the wholesalers in Pittsburgh on the four trips they made every year to buy the most up-to-date merchandise for their shelves.

She held Mary's arm as they followed Mr. Watson's laden form through the crowds and confusion of the busy landing dock, shouting in her ear that she needn't worry about her luggage. "Mr. Watson's real strong and real careful. He can easy handle yours and ours, too."

Mary hid her chagrin when she saw that Mr. Watson was leading them to the smallest boat. Up close she saw that its paint was peeling and its gilding tarnished.

"We're taking the *Cairo Queen,*" Mrs. Watson bellowed. "The owner's a good friend of Mr. Watson's, so we'll get the best service. You couldn't pay me to go on one of them fancy new boats. Full of rich riffraff, and always racing each other. Only last month two of 'em blew up, and them that didn't burn to death was drowned. Now the good old *Queen* takes her time, but she'll get you where you're going all right. And sets a good table on the way."

Later, at dinner, Mary learned that Mrs. Watson's opinion of the "good table" was justified and that Mrs. Watson's appreciation was gargantuan. But before then, there was a nonstop, dizzying succession of marvels for Mrs. Watson to demonstrate and explain.

First she led Mary to the Ladies' Cabin, tested the mattresses, chose beds for the two of them side by side, showed Mary how to pull the curtains along the ceiling rods for privacy. She called attention to the soft pillows and quilts, the flower-patterned carpeting, the flower-painted bowls and pitchers in the adjoining washroom, the closet with a door to hide the closestool. The men's cabin was bigger, she told Mary, with thirty-five beds to the ladies' twenty, but it had no privacy at all. Mr. Watson had answered all her questions about it.

He had also told her what went on when the ladies retired after dinner, Mrs. Watson said, but Mary was too young to know about such things as drinking and gambling and smoking and the kind of stories men tell. All she had to understand was that in the morning, it was a good idea to take breakfast without too much talking or clattering of knife and fork.

Mary tried to imagine Mrs. Watson quiet, but couldn't. There was not time. The older woman was showing her the wonders of the saloon, the great central room where meals were served and passengers amused themselves. The tables against the walls were pulled out into the room for meals, Mrs. Watson said, and the groups of chairs in the center placed along the sides of the tables. "You'll see how elegant the service is, Mary. Silver forks 'most too heavy to lift, and silver platters served by boys wearing gloves. The chandeliers are all lit up, too, and they look like stars twinkling in all the mirrors. Just look at them, all gold and glorious. And the red plush hangings with the gold fringe. And the red rugs, thick as pasture grass. I'll bet you've never seen the like."

Mary never had. She was accustomed to the severely beautiful pristine atmosphere of the convent. The boat's plush was shiny with long wear and the gilt discolored. She blinked back sudden tears. What horrible mistake was she making? Maybe she should get off.

But a series of blasts from the smokestacks announced the boat's departure. Mrs. Watson rushed Mary onto the deck to see the dock seemingly move away.

Mary barely glanced at it. Her eyes were filled with the wonder of the giant blue paddle wheel in the stern. It was turning, lifting droplets of water and scattering them like diamonds, stirring a wake of white foam, moving the boat out into the center of the broad river as smoothly and regally as a swan. A breeze touched her flushed face like a caress and Mary laughed. In an instant, everything had changed. The tawdry boat had become a magic vessel, carrying her on a magic journey.

Her fears and sorrows seemed to be growing smaller, going away, like the river bank and the landing. She was really here, on her way, and it was right. She ran to the stern, held out her hands to catch drops of water from the wheel, brought them to her lips. The river, so wide, so beautiful, so powerful. It will take me away from everything wrong and hurtful. It will take me to my real family, the spider-fingered women like me, to my legacy. To New Orleans.

Mrs. Watson did not allow Mary much time to savor her new happiness. "Come away from there," she scolded, "you'll get soaked and catch your death."

Two hours later, walking the circuit of the deck, she was still telling Mary stories about the illnesses her children had had and their narrow escapes from death or maiming.

"Why are we stopping?" Mary managed to interject. The boat was moving very slowly and turning toward the tree-crowded bank of the river.

Mrs. Watson's conversation, too, made a smooth change of course. "We'll either unload something or somebody or else take on something or somebody or some of each. There's towns on both sides all along the river, and the *Queen*'ll stop at any one of them if there's any money to be made in it."

She grasped the ornamented railing and leaned across it, revealing sensible muslin petticoats and sturdy high-topped black boots. "Hoy!" she shouted. "You down there. What's the name of this place?"

A black man on the lower deck looked up. "I don't know, Missus. I just tote freight across the plank the same way every place. I don't ask the name."

Mrs. Watson was not discouraged that easily. "If you don't know, then ask somebody what does," she yelled. "I want to know the name."

The black man shrugged and moved off.

Mrs. Watson stood up, her face red from leaning over. "I don't know why I bothered to ask a nigger anything."

Mary was shocked. Never had she heard the word "nigger" spoken aloud.

Together with her shock, she felt a compelling curiosity to see a slave up close. When a voice from below shouted, "This here's Rochester, Missus," Mary stepped close to the rail and looked down.

The black man was very big and very black. Mary stared, forgetting her manners, eyes and mouth round with wonder.

He saw her, and he smiled. Mary, delighted, smiled in return. Her hand lifted slightly, beginning to wave. Then she remembered that the man was a stranger; she dropped her hand and her gaze, and her face flamed red with embarrassment. She fiddled with the wooden ball near her hand, one of the series that decorated the railing, pretending that she had meant it as the purpose of her raised hand. To her horror, the ball came loose when she turned it, and it fell, rolling, on the deck.

Mary chased after it, feeling clumsy and foolish.

"For heaven's sake," clucked Mrs. Watson, "what on earth are you doing, Mary? What happened?"

Mary was grateful that her compounded mistake had been unnoticed. She scooped up the ball and replaced it on its dowel. "I brushed against it, and it fell off, Mrs. Watson."

"I guess you'd best keep away from the rail, then. Stand back here. You can still see the landing if you want to. Rochester is the name of this town."

Mary stayed with Mrs. Watson for a few minutes. But curiosity soon pulled her to the bow to watch what was going on. The boat nosed to a gentle bump against an earthen bank. Heavy ropes with noose ends flew from the unseen deck below her into the hands of excited young boys on shore. They pushed and shoved one another for the privilege of dropping the nooses over waiting wooden pilings.

A crowd of men, women, and children were clustered near the river. They scattered out of the shadow of the two gangplanks as they were lowered.

Then a small pandemonium broke out. Shouts from shore, from the boat, bells ringing, a blast from the smokestacks, boys racing across the planks to and from the boat, the lowing protest of a prodded cow.

A mighty voice rumbled loudly above all the noise. "Hold up there. I is the cargo boss here, and I'll do the bossing."

The black man strode down one of the planks, two tremendous barrels held on his two shoulders by his ebony arms.

He was followed by a white man in a brass-buttoned jacket and billed cap who consulted a paper in his hand. "Hogsheads of nails for Hinkle. Step forward."

A man pushed through the crowd. "My mule won't pull the wagon next to that kicking cow," he complained.

"I don't blame him," the black man said. "Where's your wagon, Mister Hinkle? I'll put the nails in it."

The crowd parted to let him through.

He returned quickly and walked back onto the boat. Hinkle exchanged some silver coins for the paper in the uniformed man's hand.

Then the crowd's attention shifted to the balky cow. It would not step on the gangplank. The man in the uniform put his hands in his pockets and leaned against a tree, ignoring the excitement. Everyone else, it seemed, was offering advice, encouragement, or taunts. Mary giggled. Mrs. Watson gave, at length, her opinion of what should be done.

Men came from the boat after a while to join the onlookers. Mary saw the black man laughing with three other blacks.

She also noticed a trio of white men wearing fringed buckskins. She craned her neck to see. Yes, they were wearing moccasins. Mary sighed quietly. It was so romantic. Despite the nuns' disapproval of novels, she and her roommates had all read *The Deerslayer* and *The Last of the Mohicans.*

Mrs. Watson sighed also. "This is all very tedious. Come on, Mary. Let's go inside. The idea! Making people wait for a cow!"

"I'd like to watch a little longer, please," Mary said. "I'll join you later."

"What? Me leave a young girl all alone midst a lot of strangers? Not Muriel Watson. Nobody could ever say that I don't do my duty when I see it. Why I remember one time..."

Mary allowed Mrs. Watson's reminiscences to fade into the background of her consciousness; she was fascinated by the contest with the cow. One of the leatherstockings was trying to move it now. He fastened his arm around the cow's neck and closed it as he pulled.

"He's killing my cow," shouted a woman's voice.

The uniformed official stepped away from the tree. "Here now, stop that!" he yelled. "That's assigned cargo to be shipped, not killed for supper." He advanced toward the cow, and the buckskinned man released his hold.

"Works on Indians," he said. His friends laughed.

The official turned toward the black men. "Joshua," he called. "Come see to this cargo."

The big black man walked over to the cow. "Look here, cow," he said loudly. "You remember what happened at Jericho, ain't it? You don't want to go tumbling down, I reckon. So let's get moving."

He took the rope that was tied around the cow's neck and put the end between his teeth. Then he moved rapidly. Before anyone realized what he was doing, he was behind the cow, with his big hands firmly clasping the dangerous hind legs. He raised the cow's feet and started moving toward the gangplank, forcing the animal to walk in order not to fall. His grin was broad, the big white teeth firm on the rope.

"Like a wheelbarrow, look at that," said Mrs. Watson. "Well, I never."

The crowd laughed and applauded. Boys whistled and stamped their feet. Mary clapped her hands. The bewildered cow stumbled onto the plank, crying piteously.

A flash of light caught Mary's eye. Something bright was moving near the buckskinned man who had failed to budge the cow. He was running toward the boat, his arm raised. "Make a fool of me, will you, nigger?" he shouted. That's a tomahawk he's holding, Mary told herself. Look, it has feathers attached to the handle, just like in the books.

Oh, Lord in heaven, he's going to throw it at the big black man.

"Watch out, Joshua," she cried. Her hand found the ball decoration on the rail in front of her, wrenched it free, and threw it at the glinting tomahawk.

She heard a sickening thud when the ball hit the man on the side of his head. "Oh, no," she moaned. "What have I done?"

"What have you done, Mary?" said Mrs. Watson. "Come away quick before anybody knows it was you." She took Mary's arm and hustled her along the deck, through the saloon, and into the Ladies' Cabin.

"I didn't mean to hurt him," Mary sobbed. "He was going to throw..."

"Hush, child. Least said, soonest mended. We won't say a word, nor will anybody else. You'll just keep off the deck from now on. Let the lowlife settle their own quarrels.

"Come on and wash your face. It'll be suppertime soon, and we've got to pretty up." Mrs. Watson's chatter was soothing. She quizzed Mary about her wardrobe, declared that the graduation dress sounded exactly right, explained that all luggage was kept in a locker near the captain's office, marched Mary along the corridor to the locker, instructed one of the black maids to iron Mary's dress and her own and bring them to the cabin at once. "That's Mr. Watson's favorite dress of mine," she said; "I always bring it on these trips because it makes supper into sort of a party when you're dressed up. Now you carry your slippers, pretty little useless fragile things that they are. I'll help you with your hair, and you'll be quite the belle of the boat."

• • •

"Isn't she a pretty girl?" Mrs. Watson said loudly to the Captain. "An orphan, too, such a sad story. I've taken her to my bosom like Abraham's lamb. Mary, say how do to the Captain. I'm sure he'll want us to sit right next to him. An orphan on her first trip on the river... My, Captain, how elegant the table looks. Such fine heavy linen. Didn't I tell you, Mary? The *Queen* sets a fine table. My husband, Mr. Watson, he knows the owner of the boat... one of the owners, that is, I know there's a bunch... you remember, Captain. Me and Mr. Watson always travel on the *Queen* on our trips to Pittsburgh."

The Captain mumbled through his heavy muttonchop whiskers that he remembered Mrs. Watson very well. Then he concentrated on ladling a thick brown soup from the tureen in front of his plate. Waiters took the bowls from him and placed them before each of the twenty-six people seated at the long table in the center of the saloon. The *Cairo Queen* had less than half its full complement of passengers in the cabins. Most of its profits came from freight and from the passengers who found room for themselves among the crates and barrels and livestock on the cargo deck below, where passage cost only ten cents a day and people brought their provisions with them.

The food provided for the cabin passengers was, as Mrs. Watson had promised, very good and was served in overwhelming abundance. After the first twenty minutes of supper, Mary realized that nothing was going to be said about her throwing the ball. That must mean that the man wasn't hurt, she decided, and she enjoyed the chicken in gravy, mashed potatoes, fresh peas, carrots, corn muffins, green tomato relish, and milk.

She also enjoyed the conversation of the woman sitting next to her. "I'm eighty-seven years old," she told Mary, "and still have every tooth in my head. I heard about these boats and figured if I was going to ride one before I died, I'd better get a move on. So here I am. Got on at Rochester with my cow, and I'm going all the way to Crown City. Pretty near three hundred miles. I'll get to eat my fill by then, I reckon."

On Mary's other side, Mrs. Watson was silently absorbed in dedicated gluttony.

When the last crumb was disposed of, Mrs. Watson regained her voice. "Now we can socialize some, Mary. With the ladies, naturally. The men can hardly wait for us to leave so they can get to their seegars and other devilment." She rolled her eyes coquettishly at the Captain;

he smiled with difficulty, but stood with eagerness to pull out Mrs. Watson's chair so that she could leave the table.

Back in the cabin, Mrs. Watson introduced herself and Mary to the twelve ladies who were sharing the room. "A plucky little orphan girl," she told them, "going all the way to New Orleans to her grandmama, and she's never even met her."

The ladies responded with sympathetic little cries. Before Mrs. Watson could continue speaking, Mary seized the opportunity to ask if anyone could tell her what New Orleans was like. "I really don't know anything about it," she blurted. "I don't even know how far it is."

It was very far, she learned. So far that none of the ladies had ever been there or even knew anyone who had. They guessed at distance. The guesses varied from fifteen hundred miles to five thousand.

"And how far have we come so far?"

"Almost a hundred."

Mary was thunderstruck. I'll grow old on this boat with these old women, she thought. And Mrs. Watson will talk every minute of every day.

"Mr. Watson knows the owner," she was saying, "so we always travel on the *Queen*. We go to Pittsburgh four or five times a year. Mr. Watson owns the general store in Portsmouth, Ohio, you see, and..."

Later that night Mary lay awake long after everyone else in the cabin was sleeping behind the drawn curtains. She could barely hear bursts of laughter from the saloon, and she imagined that she could smell cigar smoke. Her father's clothes had always had a faint aroma of tobacco. She cried herself to sleep.

She woke abruptly, wondering what had wakened her. The rhythmic chuff-chuff of the smokestacks reminded her where she was. Then she heard music, in the distance, as insubstantial as a dream.

As she listened it grew louder. Mary got out of bed and padded past the sleeping women to the cabin's curtained window. She parted the curtains a crack and looked out. There was a bright moon that lit the rail of the deck outside and made the decorative knobs gleam like a row of lights. Beyond the rail she could see the river, black and mysterious with a silver path of moonlight leading to a distant bank of silver-tipped shadowy trees.

The music became more distinct and a magical apparition appeared.

It was the big white and gold steamboat she had seen in Pittsburgh. All the windows on its three decks glowed golden, and the light from them made the gilt trim flash and shimmer. As it passed the slow-moving *Queen* the music seemed to envelop Mary like an enchantment. She could hear laughter and see men and women dancing under brilliant crystal chandeliers.

And then, so quickly, it was past. Mary listened while the sounds grew dimmer and then faded away. She watched the moon-brightened white wake of the boat until it, too, was gone and the river was black again with only a single silver stripe.

The distant bank of silvered trees slid by, slowly, quietly, beautiful and strange. Mary sighed, moved by the wonder of it all, and she wished the journey might last forever.

Mary's life on board the *Cairo Queen* had a pattern unlike anything she had ever known or imagined. There seemed to be no time, no distance. Everything was without measurement. The river was always there, wide, moving, changeless despite the succession of bends and bluffs and islands and towns. She took possession of a bench overlooking the bow and sheltered by a deep overhanging projection from the pilot's cabin above. From there she watched the river, the other steamboats, the huge rafts of logs, the flatboats carrying barrels and crates and livestock and, sometimes, families with cooking pots and washtubs in use while the river took them to their destinations. She saw the signals when men on one bank or another waved a broad white flag to signal a request for the *Queen* to land and load, and she learned to recognize the three blasts that announced the *Queen's* intention to make an unloading stop. She never tired of watching the burst of activity on shore when the boat turned its nose toward the dock or landing, and she was soon able to predict when the boat would pick its own landing spot and send a crew member ashore to buy new wood for the boilers or food to prepare for dinner or supper.

When passengers left, she stood near the railing and called goodbye. When new passengers boarded, she looked at them with interest, trying to imagine what their stories would be, knowing that she would probably learn at least something about their lives because Mrs. Watson was sure to introduce herself and then Mary to them, always telling them Mary's "sad tale." And the ladies universally clucked sympathetically and promised to be adopted mothers for as long as they were aboard. So Mary always had company on her bench. And the lady always responded at length to Mary's polite questions about her home and family.

From them Mary learned that one side of the river was Ohio and the other side West Virginia. Pennsylvania was far behind them. Days and miles and bends and landings blurred together and then one side was Ohio and the other side Kentucky. And soon the Watsons left, Mr. Watson returning her money with a stiff bow, Mrs. Watson smothering Mary in a tearful embrace, leaving her in the care of Mrs. Ohlandt.

Stout, Wrightsville, Aberdeen, Higginsport, Neville, Cincinnati for a day and a night waiting for a big cargo of beef sides in hogsheads of brine.

Then a few hours and Ohio was gone, and one side of the river was still Kentucky but the other side was Indiana, with Rabbit Hash the first stop there. And Mrs. Ohlandt turned Mary over to Miss Dickens, "a spinster all my life and proud of my good sense for choosing it."

Towns came and went, ladies talked with Mary on her bench, at the table, in the cabin. But none of them had ever been to New Orleans or knew anyone who had.

Until Louisville. A family boarded there with five children under the age of seven, and the tranquil torpor on the *Queen* was shattered. "Yes, I took a flatboat all the way down to New Orleans once," said the harrassed father, "but I was real young then and what I saw of New Orleans ain't fit for your ears."

Two days later the *Queen* landed at Evansville. The family left, and all the people and animals on the boat knew a welcome return of peacefulness.

But it lasted too long. Long after the *Queen* had unloaded the family and the cargo consigned to Evansville, long after new cargo was aboard and secured, the boat stayed tied up. The smokestacks puffed gently, signifying that the boilers were producing steam to turn the great wheel. But the paddle wheel was still.

"What on earth can we be waiting for?" Miss Dickens complained. "It'll be dark before you know it. Supper should have been called an hour ago."

"I think we must be waiting for whoever is in that carriage," Mary offered. "Look, Miss Dickens. It's racing like the wind."

The carriage was black, as shiny as patent leather, pulled by tremendous white horses being driven at a full, reckless gallop. The driver was black, wearing a black top hat and a black suit, the neckline filled with white ruffles. He had to stand to pull in the horses at the end of the dock. Mary could see the reins cutting into his white-gloved hands.

Even after their pell-mell arrival, the occupants of the carriage seemed to be in no hurry to step out. The doors remained closed while the driver unloaded the valises and hatboxes stacked on top of the carriage. There was no movement until he had crossed four times to the boat and all the baggage was aboard. Then he opened the carriage door and bowed.

And the most elegant woman Mary had ever seen emerged. She was wearing a traveling costume, the color a sensible brown. Her gloves were black, also sensible because they would not show dirt. But her version of practical dress was incomparably refined. Her brown dress was made of silk, and the sunlight made the color shimmer and shade from the warmest amber to a deep shadowy coffee. The bodice fit closely, held by elaborate scrolled fasteners that ended at an impossibly tiny waist surrounded by a belt of the same twisted black silk that made the scrolls. Black silk ruffles edged the three flounces of her full skirt and the wide bell sleeves. The undersleeves were black silk gauze embroidered with tiny, thin brown scrolls. Their tight cuffs were tied with black silk bows. Her bonnet was brown straw with a neck ruffle of black lace and surprising wide blue silk ribbons tied under her chin in a big off-center bow. When she stepped from the carriage there was a brief glimpse of petticoats in five shades of blue.

She walked toward the boat, and another woman emerged from the carriage. She was wearing a gray silk dress with a lace-trimmed apron that was more for adornment than protection. Bright gold hoop earrings caught the slanting rays of the sun and glinted against her dark skin, which looked even darker than it was because she had a white turbanlike headdress on.

She waved off the driver's attempt to take the red leather case she was carrying and hurried to catch up with the woman ahead of her.

"Well!" said Miss Dickens. "I've seen fine feathers before, but never anything like that."

"Captain, I shall never forgive myself for keeping you waiting so long," Mary heard the elegant woman saying, when she entered the saloon with Miss Dickens.

"Neither will I," said Miss Dickens in a deliberately audible whisper.

Mary's face grew hot from embarrassment. The woman had turned to look at them with raised eyebrows.

The Captain cleared his throat. "Mrs. Jackson, may I introduce two of the ladies who'll be traveling with you. This is Miss Dickens, and the young lady is Miss MacAlistair. She's been with the *Queen* since the trip began in Pittsburgh, and she's going all the way to New Orleans."

Mrs. Jackson smiled at Mary and extended a hand in a perfectly fitted glove. "How nice to meet you, Miss MacAlistair. New Orleans is my home, too."

Mary shook the proffered hand with awkward excitement. "Oh, I'm so glad we waited for you," she cried.

# 4

"What a courageous young woman you are, Mary," said Mrs. Jackson. She had been polite but almost icily reserved when Mary bombarded her with questions about New Orleans after they were introduced. But later, when she learned that Mary was alone in the world, she began to thaw. And when Mary confided that she did not even know if her grandmother was still alive or what her name was, Mrs. Jackson took Mary's hand in hers and expressed her admiration again and again. Mary blossomed in the warmth of the older woman's approval.

"I feel so lucky to have you for a friend, Mrs. Jackson. You're so kind and so beautiful and so elegant. I wish I could be just like you."

"What a sweet thing to say, darling girl." Mrs. Jackson's voice was unlike any Mary had ever heard. It was slow and soft, almost liquid, with the consonants slurred or lost altogether and the vowels drawn out like notes of music. Her smile was slow, too, beginning with the slightest tremor of the lips then spreading, turning up the corners of her wide mouth, and finally revealing beautiful white teeth with a fascinating small irregularity, a slight overlap in the very front. She had fair hair and blue eyes, the brightest blue Mary had ever seen, deepset, with thick lids that kept them half closed until she spoke. Then her brows lifted and her eyes became large and round, hypnotically appealing.

Everyone on the boat had succumbed to her charm, even Miss Dickens. Mary felt uncredibly lucky when Mrs. Jackson made it obvious that she preferred Mary's company above all. After supper, when the ladies retired to their cabin, Mrs. Jackson asked Mary if she would like to go on deck with her instead. "It seems a shame to miss watching the sunset. The colors are so beautiful in the water."

Mary was sure that Mrs. Jackson was the most poetic woman in the world. I'll bet my real mother was like that, she thought. And beautiful, too, with the same music-voice. It's as if she wasn't dead at all, as if she had just been away for a long, long time and had come back to be with me and take me to her old home.

"Is New Orleans very beautiful?" she asked, confident that it must be if it was Mrs. Jackson's home. And her mother's.

"Like a fairyland. The houses are all different colors, with iron balconies like black lace. And every one of them has a secret, private garden filled with flowers the year round."

Mary gasped, "Wonderful."

"Yes, it is. You will love it. How I wish I could be with you to observe your pleasure."

Mary's heart plummeted. "But won't you be? Aren't you going to New Orleans, too?"

"Yes, of course. But not on this boat. It is too slow and too uncomfortable. It's about two hundred miles to Cairo, Illinois. And the Mississippi River. I'll change to another boat there."

"Oh. I see." Mary told herself she must not cry. Then Mrs. Jackson said the words she most wanted to hear.

"Why don't you change, too, Mary? Then we can travel together. I'd like that very much."

"I must be dreaming," Mary said. She turned to watch her skirts swirl around her, dizzied by her turning and her happiness. Mrs. Jackson smiled her slow smile. She had transformed Mary.

"You cannot wear that convent uniform, dear," she said. "It will be getting warmer every day as we travel south, and you'll perish. I'll have my maid alter one of my dresses for you. She's very clever and very fast."

The dress was a confection of gauzelike white handkerchief linen, tucked and ruffled and trimmed with stiff insets of lace over ruches of blue silk. Underneath it Mary was laced into a white corset with a corset cover of lace-trimmed white silk and three silk petticoats that foamed with lace ruffles. When she was dressed, Mrs. Jackson's maid brushed her hair and curled it with a crimping iron, then tied the ringlets in clusters above her ears with rosettes of blue silk ribbon.

"You look enchanting, my dear," said Mrs. Jackson. "Here are some white mitts and a parasol. Come say goodbye to the Captain and your friends. I feel the boat turning for the landing."

"God bless you, child," Miss Dickens said. She dabbed her eyes with a handkerchief. "I wish you every happiness."

"Thank you, Miss Dickens." Mary's eyes were damp, too. She said goodbye to each of the passengers in turn, then found the Captain on deck.

"We'll all miss you," he said. "You've been a pleasure to have aboard."

"Goodbye, Missus," the cabin maid said. "You look like a princess."

"I feel like one," Mary replied. "I've never been so happy in my life."

She followed Mrs. Jackson across the gangplank, almost running. Ahead was a magnificent steamboat, with flags flying and a calliope playing a merry tune. On the dock she turned to wave goodbye. The big black cargo boss saluted her. Mary grinned. "Goodbye, Joshua," she called. Then she hurried to catch up with Mrs. Jackson.

Mrs. Jackson touched the slender glass wand of the perfume bottle to each of Mary's earlobes. Then she laid her cheek next to the girl's. "I've always wished that I might have a daughter," she murmured, "a sweet girl just like you, Mary. Since you have no mother of your own, would you like to be a daughter to me?"

Mary threw her arms around Mrs. Jackson. "More than anything in the world," she whispered.

Mrs. Jackson kissed Mary on both cheeks, then freed herself from the embrace. "That makes me very happy, dear. And we'll have delightful times together. You will live with me in New Orleans and we'll find your family. Before we get there I'll teach you to be a real Southern girl. To begin, I want you to call me 'Miss Rose' instead of 'Mrs. Jackson.' Rose is my given name."

"I might have guessed," Mary said. "You're just like a rose, so pink and sweet-smelling."

Mrs. Jackson chuckled. "So are you, my dear. It's wonderful what a little perfume will do, and you have such a fresh natural color in your cheeks. Still, we might just rub a tiny little bit of rice powder across your forehead and chin to take away the shine." Her fingers moved expertly.

Mary gave herself over completely to Mrs. Jackson. She had already given her heart.

The *Memphis Belle* was a wonderland for Mary. It was one of the newest steamboats on the Mississippi, and its fittings had all the luxury of the "floating palaces" that were the pride of the river. Passengers had private cabins with huge four-poster beds draped in fine mosquito netting under tasseled silk canopies. Silk curtains draped big windows that opened onto the wide polished decks, and deep carpets felt like velvet underfoot.

There was a saloon two hundred feet long, with dazzling gilt mirrors that soared to the twenty-foot ceiling and gas-lit chandeliers with crystal swags and cascades of glittering prisms. Dinner was at eight, seven courses on silver dishes with five different wines in ruby glass goblets. A white-gloved black steward stood behind the brocade-covered chair of each passenger to serve the food and anticipate every conceivable need. Men wore dinner clothes, their shirts studded with pearls or jewels, and women were bare-shouldered, their throats and ears sparkling with gems. During dinner a string quartet played softly. After dinner the tables were moved away and an orchestra played for dancing. There was no need for the ladies to retire. A series of rooms for gaming, smoking, or billiards was available for gentlemen on the upper deck.

"I've never danced," Mary confessed. "Mayn't I just watch?"

"Of course, dear," said Mrs. Jackson. "We'll sit on this settee and enjoy the music. Tomorrow I'll arrange for you to practice with one of the officers." She looked at Mary with warm approval. A lace fichu covered Mary's shoulders and bosom. She had felt too bare in the evening gown Mrs. Jackson gave her.

Three days later she was wearing a pink muslin gown with tremendous puffed sleeves that began at the very tips of her shoulders, and her feet were tapping in time with the music, eager to dance. Miss Rose was teaching her how to be a real New Orleans young lady. Mary fingered the black lace fan that she had learned to use to hide her blushes and felt very worldly.

Across the room a man bet his friend a hundred dollars that he couldn't get "the little girl in pink" to dance with him.

His friend refused to wager. "I've seen what a dragon the mother is to anyone under seventy. Besides, innocent misses bore me, and that one's the greenest I've ever seen. I'd rather try the mother, but she's not exactly come-hither, is she?"

Mrs. Jackson was staring at them with a chilling haughtiness. "Brrr," said the first man. The two friends laughed and wandered off.

Mrs. Jackson smiled at the Captain. He walked toward her. "Mary, dearest," she said, "I believe the Captain is about to ask you for a waltz."

Mary fanned herself strenuously. She had danced often enough with the Captain to know that she wouldn't have trouble keeping step with him, so there were no nervous blushes to hide. She was trying to cool her face and neck. The temperature had been rising by the hour as the boat moved south from Illinois into Tennessee then on into Mississippi.

She confided in the Captain while they were dancing that she had never felt so warm in all her life. "I know it's July already, but I always spent the summer in the mountains before, you see. It's a surprise to feel what real summer is like, and I worry about being so much trouble to Miss Rose . . . Mrs. Jackson. She had to get her maid to curl my hair four times today."

The Captain smiled. Mary's artlessness was a novelty to him. Young ladies in the South were usually accomplished coquettes long before they reached her age.

"Suppose I ask Mrs. Jackson if I might be allowed to escort you ladies for a stroll on the deck?" he said. "There'll be a pleasant breeze over the water; we're doing near twenty miles an hour."

Mary nodded emphasis. "I'd like that very much, thank you, Captain."

Mrs. Jackson accepted the Captain's invitation, but with an amendment. "It's easy to take a chill after dancing," she said. "Run along to our cabin, Mary, and fetch us each a light shawl."

When Mary was gone, Mrs. Jackson smiled at the Captain. "We're making good time, it seems," she said. Her voice was brisker than usual. "How much money would you lose if you went straight through to New Orleans?"

"And not stop at Natchez? It's out of the question."

"Captain, I have a special engagement for the evening of July Fourth. It's worth an awful lot to me if I can keep it."

The Captain looked at Mrs. Jackson and laughed. "I'm a greedy man, ma'am."

She laughed with him. "You surprise me, Captain. Now astonish me. Name your price."

Her eyebrows soared when he did. "You were supposed to astonish, sir, not shock me to death. Four boats this size couldn't hold a cargo that would earn you that much. I'll offer half your figure."

The bargaining was brief and amicable. Before Mary returned with the shawls, the deal was made. Miss Rose and the Captain look very pleased with themselves, she thought. Wouldn't it be nice if they were falling in love? I could be a bridesmaid at the wedding. Her romantic young heart found it very sad that Miss Rose was a widow and said she'd never marry again.

When they were walking on deck, Mary moved ahead a few steps so that the Captain could be alone with Miss Rose.

Then she forgot them altogether. It was a moonless night, and the stars were thick in the sky. Mary had never seen a sky like it. "They look so close," she said aloud, "and so different. Soft and glowing, not hard and bright."

Mrs. Jackson put her arm around Mary's waist. "You're in the South now, darling girl. Everything is different. And more beautiful."

The following morning, Mrs. Jackson woke Mary much earlier than before. "Dress quickly. I want to show you something. We're having coffee on deck."

Mary never drank her coffee. She was too enchanted to bother with anything as ordinary as breakfast. The *Belle* was in a channel that ran close to the river bank, riding on clouds of swirling mist, gray-golden in the early daylight. Gray clouds hung from the nearby trees, too, swaying in the tendrils of mist that were rising from the river. There was an overwhelming sweetness in the air, sweet music from thousands of invisible birds, and a sweet perfume from thousands of tiny starlike flowers that wrapped the tree trunks and carpeted the ground between them.

Mary clung to the rail. She felt dizzy; all her senses were battered by the beauty. She could taste the sweet air, and it felt soft and foreign on her skin.

The star-filled trees ended; there was a clearing and a wooden dock, its boards silvered with age and gleaming with damp. Beyond it a wide white road drew Mary's gaze. The road was edged by tall trees heavy with glistening leaves of dark green and white waxy flowers of a size too big for belief. At the end of the road was a temple, white, with thick columns that rose up to a peaked dark roof above a wide arc of window, like a golden fan, shimmering with morning light.

"That's a plantation house," Mrs. Jackson said softly, her lips close to Mary's ear, "and the trees are magnolias, the vines honeysuckle, and the gray shawls Spanish moss. This is Louisiana."

"I love it," Mary whispered.

# 5

Mary refused to go inside. She stayed on deck all morning, straining unconsciously toward the river bank and the beauty there. Even when the channel led the *Belle* to the middle of the river and the banks were mere ribbons of green a half mile distant, Mary looked from one to the other, her eyes narrowed against the bright reflection off the water.

Mrs. Jackson tried to persuade her to come into the shadowed saloon for lunch, but Mary begged to be left outside. "This is what I need, Miss Rose. I feel like I'm getting to know my mother this way, by taking in all I can of where she came from."

Mrs. Jackson compromised. If Mary would put on a wide-brimmed hat, if she would sit in a chair in the shade, if she would drink a lemonade and eat a little piece of cold chicken while she watched, then Mrs. Jackson would leave her alone. "You'll ruin your skin, but I suppose it's for a good cause."

Mary lost all sense of time. Bells rang and the stacks hooted at other boats, but she heard nothing. She was in a dream world. The boat approached land, and she raised her chin, inhaling the perfume of Louisiana, then the river bend circled the promontory, and she lost the sweetness until the next bend. And the next. And the next.

The sun began to move lower, and a breeze made ribbons on the water. It brought the perfume of the land to her, stronger, warmed by the long heat of the day. Mary shivered. She was feverish with happiness.

Mrs. Jackson was just coming onto the deck. She hurried to Mary's side. "Are you all right? Do you feel ill? You might have got sunstroke." She put the back of her hand on Mary's forehead, then her cheek. Suddenly her head turned, and she ran to the rail, shaded her eyes with both hands to look at the river bank.

"We're turning," she said. "Making a landing. This won't do. I won't have it." She dashed off without a glance at Mary.

A landing. Mary hurried to the bow. She would be able to see the trees and the flowers and the land up close. She was trembling with excitement. The smokestacks blasted the signal for landing, and the vibration ran through her like a fire. She wondered briefly if she did have sunstroke. She didn't care if she did. All her senses were acute as they had never been before, and it was bewildering, new, and thrilling.

The boat neared its landing. There was no clearing; instead a slanting, tall, grass-grown wall rimmed the river as far as Mary could see. The top of it was as high as the deck where she was standing. When the *Belle* bumped gently against it, Mary was no more than twenty feet from the man standing atop the wall.

Beyond him in the distance she could see a plantation house like the one she had seen before, white, columned, glimmering amid lush green flower-strewn trees. In the dimming light, it was indistinct, like a mirage, a dream. The man was part of it. He looked as if he had come from the same dream of magical beauty. He was exactly what the person who lived in that house should be.

He was dressed in riding clothes; a black linen jacket fitted his wide shoulders and narrow waist, then flared over white broadcloth jodhpurs. His stock was gleaming white and his tall boots glistening black. As black as his thick curly hair and his eyes. His eyes met Mary's and his full, molded lips parted in a smile as white as his neckcloth. He touched his forehead with his whip in a salute, then bowed. Mary could not return the bow. She was transfixed.

The gangplank began to drop, and the creaking of the ropes brought her back to reality with a shock. I'm staring, she thought; I must look away, move away. But she could not.

The man looked away, watching the plank descend to touch the grass near his feet. Before it was still, he leapt on it and ran down it to the deck below the one where Mary was standing.

His disappearance broke the spell that froze her. Suddenly she was aware of everything. The breeze lifting the tendrils of hair on her forehead, the overpowering scent of flowers, of grass crushed by the gangplank, of water lapping the hull of the boat. She heard Mrs. Jackson's voice, and she turned guiltily, ready to apologize for her rude behavior, but she was alone on the deck, and the voices were lost in the sound of horses neighing and men shouting. Mary ran for the door from the deck to her cabin, running away from the excessive, frightening emotion she had felt.

Mrs. Jackson's voice had come from the lower deck. She was berating the Captain, demanding that the boat back out into the river at once and resume its journey to New Orleans.

The man boarding laughed when he reached the deck. "We won't be long, Rose. I'm just going to have my men bring two horses on, and then we'll be on our way."

Rose Jackson turned from the Captain to the new arrival. "Good day to you, Mr. Saint-Brévin." Her teeth were clenched in anger, the words brittle. "I am a private citizen on this boat, like any other lady. Kindly address me as Mrs. Jackson." She glared at the Captain. "If I do not reach New Orleans by the hour you promised, sir, your bonus is forfeit." She pushed Saint-Brévin aside and walked stiffly to the stairs.

The stiffness was gone, and the anger, when she entered the cabin. "My dear child," she cried, "why are you all huddled up like that in the shadows? Are you having a chill again?" She sat next to Mary and put her arms around the girl's shoulders. "Here, now," she whispered, "lean against Miss Rose. I'll take care of you. Tell me what's wrong."

Mary relaxed gratefully into the safety of Mrs. Jackson's embrace.

"There's nothing wrong, Miss Rose. All of a sudden I just felt peculiar."

Mrs. Jackson stroked her brow. "It was the heat, dear. You're not used to it. It takes people funny until they get accustomed. You don't have any fever, thank goodness. I'll just get a cool cloth and bathe your face, and then we'll go have a little light supper."

"Oh, no, I couldn't." Mary thought she'd rather die than risk facing the beautiful man from the plantation. He must think her the biggest fool on earth.

Mrs. Jackson laughed, hugging her close. "But we must, Mary. My maid has to come in and pack our things. We're almost there, only a little further now.

"Besides, you really need to eat something. You won't have time after we get to New Orleans, and you've barely had a mouthful all day. A girl can't have a good time when she's thinking how hungry she is. And you're going to have the best time of your life. I didn't tell you till now because I wasn't sure we'd get there in time, but now I know we will. Today's the Fourth of July, in case you've forgotten. And in New Orleans, the whole town celebrates all day and all night. Fireworks. And dancing in the street. And parties everywhere. I have one every year. The house will be decorated, and all my friends will be there. The servants know how to make all the preparations.

"I can hardly wait to show you off, Mary. I'm going to tell everybody,

'This is my own special girl that I found up north.' Everyone will love you, Mary, and welcome you to your new home."

Mary forgot her embarrassment, her fears, her unsettling emotions. A new home. New Orleans. New friends to welcome her. Like a family.

"I'd better wash my face," she said, and she returned Mrs. Jackson's hug. "I love you, Miss Rose."

There was no regular dinner so soon before the end of the trip. An array of hot and cold dishes was set out on a long table against the wall, and passengers filled plates with whatever took their fancy. Then they sat at small tables scattered around the saloon. Everyone could eat and drink when and if he chose.

The arrangement was a novelty to Mary. She hovered over the dishes, unable to make up her mind.

She was so occupied that she didn't notice when Saint-Brévin walked by with two other men. He bowed to Mrs. Jackson. She inclined her head and looked away.

The three men paused at a table holding a huge silver bowl filled with ice and bottles of champagne. "We'll take glasses and a bottle," Saint-Brévin said to the steward behind the table. "Let's go up to the smoker and have a drink," he suggested to his companions. "Then I'll accept your invitation for a few hands of cards."

"There's no time for a game, Monty. We can't be more than thirty minutes from New Orleans."

Valmont Saint-Brévin raised dark eyebrows. "More likely fifteen or twenty. But what has that to do with anything? The boat is going nowhere after we land. The champagne is going nowhere. We play until we get bored and wish to leave... or until I have won all your money." He bowed with a flourish, ushered his two companions toward the stairs with the hand holding the champagne bottle.

No one watching could have mistaken the trio for anything other than what they were: two Americans and a Creole, one of the French-speaking New Orleans natives. Saint-Brévin's accent gave him away, even though he spoke English fluently. So did the dinner clothes he was wearing. He had changed as soon as he boarded the *Belle*. Creole gentlemen always dressed for the evening, and this Creole gentleman dressed even more elegantly than most. His shirt was silk, ruffled with lace, and his waistcoat was made of gold and white brocaded satin. A gold signet ring was on the little finger of his left hand; his sunbrowned hands were manicured. Tailoring, bootmaking, haircutting, shaving were all flawless.

The Americans were wearing the clothes they had worn all day. Expensive and fashionable, but without the style that marked the Creole's coat and narrow trousers as Paris-made. They looked raw next to his glossy perfection.

Upstairs in the smoking room they took chairs around a table. Saint-Brévin poured champagne, crooked his finger at the steward. "An unopened deck of cards for my friends to examine before I deprive them of their money belts," he said. He stretched his long legs out before him and lounged back in the deep leather chair. "Tell me, my friends, can I jump to the conclusion that you're going to New Orleans for the steeplechase on Sunday? I'm entering two horses. Would you like to make a wager? I'm feeling confident enough to give you odds."

"I saw those plow horses you brought on board," said the younger American. "Just how confident are you?"

"Wait a minute," said the other. "Before we get to that, I want to know something. Monty, who is that lady you bowed to in the saloon? I've been trying to make her acquaintance ever since Paducah, with no luck at all."

Valmont Saint-Brévin grinned. "Luck isn't what you need, my friend. You should have showed your bankroll. That elegant woman is Rose Jackson. She runs the fanciest house in New Orleans, which means the fanciest house in the country."

"A madam? I can't believe it."

"I'll take you to her house if you like. I'm a pretty good customer. She serves the best wine and has the best beds you'll ever see."

"What about the girls? The one she's got with her doesn't look like she knows anything but her catechism."

Valmont laughed. "That's the specialty of the house. All of Rose's girls look like the dew's still on them. But they're real artists at their trade. They know how to do things you've never even heard of. That's why they cost so much. You have the feeling you're the first and that you're the inspiration for all their little surprises."

"What's she charge?"

"It depends. Fifty dollars for a regular turn. On up if you want something special."

"I never heard of fifty dollars. The best whore in Kentucky never got more than ten."

The younger man had been silently smoking. Now he joined the conversation. "What do you mean by 'something special'?"

"Anything you want. You don't have to tell me what it is. It won't be anything new to Rose. She'll even get you a genuine virgin if you're willing to pay two hundred. I've never been interested myself."

Below in the saloon, Mrs. Jackson held out a glass to Mary. "Drink this, dear. We'll toast the Fourth, and New Orleans, and the wonderful new life you'll have there . . . You look charming when your nose wrinkles like that, Mary. Aren't the bubbles delightful? Champagne is an acquired taste; you'll soon learn to love it."

# 6

Long before the boat reached New Orleans, the passengers could see the Roman candles erupt up into the dark sky. They clustered on deck to watch. Stewards scurried around the boat extinguishing lights or drawing curtains so that the fireworks would be more distinct.

Mary squeezed Miss Rose's arm. "That's just the way I feel, like I could explode in showers of red and blue and white. I'm so excited."

Mrs. Jackson smiled. She watched the holiday display with a measuring eye, estimating the boat's speed and the best moment to go down to the lower deck so that she would be one of the first onto the gangplank. She noticed the shower of sparks falling continuously from the *Belle*'s stacks into the river. They should be there soon. The boilers were operating at full capacity and then some. The Captain had taken her warning seriously. She decided that she'd withhold the bonus she'd promised him. Even if they did make the promised schedule. Her smile grew wider.

Then she changed her mind. It would be better not to have the Captain as an enemy. Mrs. Jackson was, above all things, a businesswoman, and personal gratification had no place in business.

The arrival at New Orleans was a disappointment to Mary. She couldn't see anything from the place Mrs. Jackson had chosen on the lower deck. "Why is there a wall outside the city, Miss Rose?" Mary asked. She remembered overhearing some ladies talking about alligators.

"That's called a levee, Mary, not a wall." Miss Rose was less patient than usual.

She did not regain her customary kindness until they were off the boat and into the carriage that was waiting for her. Her maid took the seat opposite, and Mrs. Jackson settled herself by Mary's side. Then she kissed Mary on the cheek. "Welcome home, dear Mary." She reached past her and pulled the curtain to the edge of the window. "Look at New Orleans, darling. You can't see much in the dark, but the fireworks help some." Mary leaned out the window, avid for some air. Once off the moving boat and the river, she felt that she couldn't breathe. It was hot and airless and suffocating. But the window gave no relief. There was even greater heat outside, and crashing, howling noise. Pressing close to the window there was a mad kaleidoscope of faces, men, women, children, black, green, red, stark bright white in the hard light from the skyrockets. The streets were full of people. They all seemed to be laughing. Or singing. Their mouths were open dark holes in their garish faces. Mary shrank back in the corner of the seat.

Mrs. Jackson patted her hand. "I guess it is a little noisy. It's a holiday. Look over the heads. We're turning into our street now. Look at the balconies. Up, Mary. Stretch your neck and tilt your head. See?"

Mary gasped. Above the pandemonium in the street she could see a vignette of calm beauty. Candles in glass shades lit a table and the four people seated around it. There were two women, a man and a child. All were dressed in white. The fireworks overhead bathed them in pastels and brightened the baskets of flowers that hung from the corners of the curly iron balcony on which they were suspended.

Mary had only a glimpse, then the carriage rolled on. But the momentary vision was enough. She had seen a family, beautiful, happy. She was sure that she would find a family like that, a family where she belonged.

"Are you sure we have my box, Miss Rose?" Mary was suddenly chill with anxiety. Suppose she had lost her treasure, her proof of parentage.

"Yes, dear. Your box, and your money. They're safe. I'm taking good care of you."

Mary relaxed. "I'm so lucky," she said. "Thank you, Miss Rose."

The carriage slowed, then turned into an arched passageway. Cool air came through the carriage window. Mary breathed deeply. Then she cried aloud with astonishment. They had entered an enchanted garden.

"We're home," said Mrs. Jackson.

A beautiful young girl in a ruffled blue gown opened the carriage door. "Welcome home, Miss Rose," she said. "We thought you'd never get here... Hello, who are you? My name's Annabelle."

"This is Mary," said Mrs. Jackson. "Climb out, Mary."

Mary stepped down and looked around her. She was in a courtyard, a serene square of patterned brick with a splashing fountain in the center and flickering gas lights in hanging lanterns that illuminated masses of flowers and green trees and vines. There were young women in flowerlike colored gowns moving around the fountain and among the potted trees. "Miss Rose," they called, and their voices were like flutes.

Mary turned to Annabelle. "I'm sorry," she said. "I was rude. I was just so surprised by everything being so cool and peaceful so suddenly. How do you do? My name is . . . "

"Later, Mary, later," Miss Rose interrupted. "All my friends will want to meet you. It's time to dress now. Lucy, take Mary to your room and find her something pretty to wear. She's never been to a New Orleans party before."

There was a slight stress on the words. The girl named Lucy nodded her understanding.

"Come along, Mary. You must be worn out. I'll show you where you can have a nice cool bath and a refreshing cool drink."

Mary didn't like the lemonade. It tasted bitter, and it made her head swim. But Lucy insisted that she drink it. "Later, you'll have champagne, and that will take away the taste. I guess they forgot to put sugar in it."

Her voice sounded blurred to Mary. She thought it must be Lucy's accent. Southerners talked like music, Mary said to herself. Then she giggled loudly. "What's happening to me?" she said. "I feel very odd."

"You're getting the party spirit, that's all. Hold up your arms and put them through these sleeves." Mary obeyed, like a puppet. Lucy's face seemed to grow very big, then shrink away, then balloon again.

The garden was full of people when Lucy led Mary downstairs. They were laughing and talking, and there was music coming from a shadowed corner. Lucy took Mary's hand to steady her. Mrs. Jackson came to Mary's side and took her other hand. "How lovely you look, dear. Come have some champagne. Then there's someone I want you to meet."

"I feel very strange, Miss Rose," Mary said. But the words would not come out right. Her tongue was thick and lax.

Mrs. Jackson smiled. "Here, my sweet, drink this. It'll solve all your troubles."

The bubbles stung Mary's nose and made her eyes water. Miss Rose dried her cheeks. Then she seated her at a small table near a heavily scented shrub. A silver bucket was on the table with a napkin-wrapped bottle in it. Mrs. Jackson lifted the bottle and filled the half-empty glass in front of the man who was sitting at the table. He took the cigar from his mouth to say, "Thanks, Rose."

"This is Mary," said Mrs. Jackson. "I don't think she should have any more champagne for a while."

The man rolled the cigar across his wet red lips. "Do you mind the smell of cigar smoke, Mary?" he said.

"No, sir. My father always smoked cigars." Her words were clearer. Mary smiled with relief.

"That's a pretty smile you've got there," the man said. He looked up at Mrs. Jackson. "You always come through, Rose. I'm ready now."

"Don't you want to enjoy the party for a while? Mary's a good dancer."

"I got an appointment. I was on my way out when your message got to me." He heaved himself to his feet. He was a big man. Tall and corpulent. A heavy gold chain glittered across his big-bellied yellow vest. He wrapped his hand around Mary's wrist. A big diamond ring glittered on one finger. It was surrounded by curly black hairs. "Come on, honey. I got something to show you."

Mary looked at Miss Rose. She didn't understand what was happening. Mrs. Jackson's smile looked different. Her face was harshly lined in the light of the gas lantern. A rocket burst overhead. Its blue explosion was reflected in her eyes. Mary felt cold.

The man pulled her up from her chair. Mary tried to resist, but he was too strong. She stumbled. Mrs. Jackson steadied her. "Shy, huh?" said the man. "Just what the doctor ordered." He pulled Mary onto his chest, her arm twisted behind her back in his grasp. Then he fastened his wet lips on her mouth, grinding his teeth against hers. He kept the cigar between his fingers and rubbed her breast with the palm of his hand.

Mary fought to get away. She tried to scream, but her mouth was covered by his.

Mrs. Jackson made a clucking noise of disapproval. "Not out here, you barbarian," she said. "You know the rules. The patio is my drawing room, and everyone is civilized. Take her to the room by the kitchen. You'll never get her up the stairs."

The man's mouth moved from Mary's. He took his hand from her breast and clapped it over her lips. The tip of the cigar burnt the end of a stray wisp of her hair. The sharp acrid smoke filled her nostrils and suddenly cut through the fog that clogged her mind. I've got to get away, she realized. And there is no one to help me. She heard him arguing with Mrs. Jackson, but she paid no attention. She was concentrating with all the feeble power of her drugged brain. She made herself go limp.

Her body sagged heavily, falling. The man's grip on her mouth and wrist was loosened by the surprise of her weight.

"What the hell?" he shouted.

Mary scrambled to her knees, then her feet. She ran for her life, stumbling and whimpering, crashing through the thorny branches of a group of blooming rose bushes. Two men were entering the garden from the archway. Mary pushed between them. "What is this," said one, "a new game? Is everybody playing tag or something? Hey, Rose. Who's 'it'?"

Behind her Mary heard Mrs. Jackson's voice, soothing and laughing a tinkling, brittle laugh. Then she plunged into the noisy confusion of the street.

There was a man with an accordian and a melee of men and women dancing and singing. "Join the reel, honey," said a bare-chested youth, but Mary could not understand his words. He was not speaking English. He put his arm around her waist, spun her across the dusty street. Mary sobbed and screamed and beat her fists against his face.

He sent her spinning with a slap that brought blood gushing from her nose. She fell against the wall of a building and mewed like a frightened kitten. The dancer loomed over her, his hand raised to strike her again.

"Ça suffit." A tall man in dark clothes stopped and spoke. He held out his gold-knobbed cane to stop the blow.

The angry youth pulled a knife from his waistband, crouched, snaked it toward the tall man. There was a click, and a gleaming swordpoint slid from the tip of the cane. It came to a stop a hair's breadth from the knifer's throat. The young man spread his arms and shrugged. Then he ran away.

"Mademoiselle." The Good Samaritan held out a silk handkerchief to Mary. She looked from it to the man's face. It was only a shadow among shadows.

At that moment a white skyrocket tore across the sky. Mary recognized the man from the plantation.

"Oh, thank you," she whispered. She took the handkerchief from his fingers and held it to her bloody face.

Valmont Saint-Brévin had recognized her, too. "You're Rose's girl from the boat," he exclaimed. "What are you doing out here with the rabble? Come on, take my arm. I'll see you back to the house."

Mary cried out. She dropped the bloodstained silk square and ran away.

She was buffeted by revelers, assailed by noise on all sides, terrified by the green- and blue- and red-lit faces with gaping mouths that had frightened her before. She felt blood wet on her face, salt-warm in her mouth, choking her when she gasped for air. But she ran, more afraid to look back than to go on.

Then she heard a new noise amid the other noises. Bells. Church bells. She stopped and looked for their source. There were tall doors, open, with the sound of an organ flowing out. Thank God, she cried soundlessly, and she pushed frantically through the people around her.

Her strength was born of terror. When she staggered into the cathedral, the familiar odors of incense and burning candles overcame her. She was safe. Her hand trembled, her arm was too weak to lift it for the sign of the cross. She sobbed once, then fell unconscious in the aisle.

# 7

The elderly nun tapped with her fingertips on the door, then opened it.

"Forgive me, Mother, I did not know you had someone with you," she said when it was open wide. She began to back away.

"No, Sister, do not go. Enter." The Mother Superior of the Convent of the Ursulines beckoned. She turned to the woman sitting near her desk. "You permit?" she said.

"But of course," the woman replied. All of them were speaking French.

The nun bent her head near the Mother Superior's ear. "I have the young person who was found in the cathedral last night, Mother. She was brought to us, and I have heard her story. I believe you should hear it, too."

"Can it wait?"

"She is distraught, Mother."

The woman in the chair gestured. "I am in no pressing hurry, Mother," she said. She was an angular woman with pale skin and pale lips barely discernible behind a thin black veil. She was wearing mourning, a severe black dress, black bonnet, and black gloves. Her name was Celeste Sazerac, and she was a tireless worker for the charities sponsored by the Convent. When they were interrupted, she and the Mother Superior were making plans for some renovations to the orphanage operated by the Order. Celeste had offered to organize a subscription of donations. She would, of course, contribute handsomely herself. The Sazerac family was one of the wealthiest in rich New Orleans.

"Here she is, Mother." The nun returned with Mary at her side. The girl was horribly bruised on the face; her eyes were discolored and swollen almost shut, her nose misshapen. Purple marks around her lips showed where brutal fingers had covered her mouth. Her left wrist was heavily bandaged.

The Mother Superior rose from her chair. "Ma pauvre petite," she cried.

"She speaks no French," the nun said.

"Then we shall speak English." The Mother Superior touched Mary's cheek briefly with gentle fingertips. "My dear little one, what can we do to help you? There is room in our hospital..."

Mary shook her head. "I don't need nursing, Mother. I heal fast, and I'm not hurt as bad as I look. I came to you for help in finding my family."

"You cannot find your family? I don't understand."

"It's a long story, Mother. May I tell it to you?"

"Of course you may. Sit down, child. Here, close to my chair so you won't have to strain your voice."

Mary grasped the arms of the chair and lowered herself into it. Her movements were awkward and stiff, guarding against pain. But her back was straight, and she did not wince or grimace. The stern, loving training of the convent school had not permitted self-pity or dramatics. The bruises on Mary's face testified to her brutal experience; her expression was controlled. So was her voice. She began her story calmly.

"Thank you... It all began with my birthday. My father gave me a box. It was about this big." Mary outlined an imaginary box with her hands. "I opened it, and inside the lid I saw a name and address carved in the wood..."

Mary continued with her story. From time to time she had to stop, when tears filled her throat and spilled from her eyes. Her long training in self-control was not equal to the desperation and despair she was feeling. But she managed to tell everything. Her father's death, the lie he had sustained about her mother, her stepmother's rejection, the decision to come in search of her real mother's family, her meeting with Mrs. Jackson, and the terrible happenings at Mrs. Jackson's party.

"... I got away all right," Mary concluded, "but my box is still there, and all my money. Now I have no place to go and no one to help me get them back. Can you tell me how to find my family?"

Celeste Sazerac stood up. "Forgive me, Mother," she said in French. "As you know I do not speak English very well, but I understand it well enough. I am appalled by the treatment this unfortunate girl has suffered. If I may be permitted to suggest... the woman Jackson must be punished for this. And she must be made to return the girl's possessions. I could go at once to my attorney and instruct him to initiate proceedings. This is a sordid affair and unsuitable for the Order to deal with."

"You are very kind, Mademoiselle Sazerac."

"I am always grateful for an opportunity to be of service. I will return with a report on what I am able to accomplish." Celeste hurried from the room, her silk skirts crackling at the movement. Beneath the veil, her features were rigid with determination.

"I don't understand," said Mary.

"Mademoiselle has gone to help you," said the nun.

"She is a lady who always succeeds in her efforts," the Mother Superior commented. She had a smile on her lovely old face. "She will recover your money and your possessions, my child. I shall be very interested to see your box, as you call it. I am almost sure I already know what it is. We call it a 'casket.'"

"'A casket?'" Mary began to cry. "Is everything I learn going to be about people dying?"

"Shhh." The nun gave Mary a fresh handkerchief.

The Mother Superior took Mary's free hand in hers. "Forgive me; it is the eternal problem of language. the French word is *casquette.* It means small coffer, box, as you say. In English it has come to be called casket. It is not about death, this casket, but about life. And bravery and hope. It has a wonderful history, your casquette. You will be proud to know it. Shall I tell you?"

"Yes, please."

"There, dry your eyes. We will have a coffee and a *beignet.* In New Orleans we drink a great deal of coffee, and the beignet is a delightful hot pastry that we particularly enjoy with it... Sister, if you will be so kind?"

"I'll bring them at once, Mother." The nun exited quietly but quickly. She returned in a few minutes, carrying a tray. The room filled with appetizing aromas.

Mary was surprised to find that she was very hungry. The nun filled a big cup with a mixture of hot milk and very black coffee, stirred in three spoonsful of sugar and put it on a small table at Mary's side. Then she smiled and unfolded a tremendous white linen napkin. "Put this across your knees," she said, "then let the sugar fall where it will." She put a plate next to the cup. It was piled with steaming brown pillows of dough, coated with a thick layer of white powdered sugar.

Mary's mouth was watering. But she had an even greater hunger. "If you could tell me about the casket, Mother..."

"I will talk while you eat. Be careful; everything is very hot...

"It was more than a hundred years ago, in 1718, that the French first settled New Orleans. There were no more than fifty men, and they did little more than make a clearing among the trees. But by the time three years had passed, there were three hundred men, streets were laid out, and a church was built. Two years after that, the population was nearing two thousand.

"They were mostly men. Soldiers of the King, and trappers, and men eager for land and a new life in the New World. There were women, of course, a few. Wherever there are soldiers there are women. You have learned what kind of women they are.

"The life was hard and dangerous. The colony had a church, but no priest. The soldiers built a hospital, but they had no nurses. So they applied to King Louis, the Sun King. He answered their petition like a loving father. In 1727, he sent a priest, and a party of ten Ursuline sisters, to nurse the sick.

"We want wives, too, said the soldiers. We want to raise families, build a civilization. So the King sent them strong, Christian girls to be their wives and the mothers of their children. Throughout all the towns and villages of France priests talked to the families of girls who would be suitable. They had to be very brave, because they were going to cross the great seas in small ships on a long journey to an unknown land filled with danger and privation. And they would be saying goodbye forever to their parents and grandparents, brothers, sisters, cousins, friends.

"A few of the most courageous agreed to go. As a gift to honor their spirit, the King himself gave dowries to these girls. They were small; there was little room on those old ships. There was linen, collars and caps, a frock, and some stockings. It all fit neatly into a wooden casquette.

"The first girls arrived in 1728. Every year afterwards for twenty years, a few more came, sometimes two groups in a year. And each girl had her dowry from King Louis, in a small wooden box. They have been known forever after as the 'casket girls.' They were the mothers of the children and grandchildren and great-grandchildren who became the people of New Orleans."

Mary had forgotten to eat. "I am proud," she said.

"And hungry," said the Mother Superior. "Your breakfast is getting cold."

Mary smiled for the first time. Then she drank deeply from her cup. "It's the best coffee I ever tasted," she exclaimed. A beignet brought a delighted reaction and a ravenous bite from a second. Then a third.

Mary's bruised lips were white with sugar and color returned to her cheeks. "My casket had the Convent as the address, Mother. Why is that?"

"All the casket girls came to the Convent. The sisters took care of them until they married. They helped select the husbands, too. There were many suitors for each bride."

Mary's eyes filled with tears again. But this time they were tears of happiness and relief. She knew, from her years at school, that convents kept meticulous, detailed records. As soon as the lady in black returned with the casket, she would show the name in the lid to the Mother Superior and then she would learn who her family were.

"I have come on behalf of the young lady who traveled on the *Memphis Belle* with Mrs. Jackson," said Mr. Carré. "I am a lawyer. Take me to your mistress."

Mr. Carré was a powerful man conscious of his power. He radiated authority. "Mrs. Jackson, she is still resting," said the manservant, "but I'll send word you're here."

"Show me into the drawing room," Mr. Carré ordered, "and bring coffee while I wait."

"For two," said Celeste Sazerac. She was behind her lawyer.

Mr. Carré frowned. He had advised Celeste against coming with him. A brothel was no place for a spinster lady to visit. But Celeste was determined, and when she was determined, he knew, no advice, no authority could sway her. He stepped to one side so that Celeste might walk in first. She was a lady and his client.

Mrs. Jackson's drawing room was sumptuous but not vulgar. Mr. Carré was surprised. He said as much to Celeste. She held up a hand to quiet him. She was standing near the door, listening to the hushed voice of the manservant somewhere in the house.

She nodded abruptly. "Wait here," she said, and she left Mr. Carré alone.

Celeste walked quickly to the stairs, mounted one flight, and came up behind a maid who was speaking urgently through a slightly open door. She pushed the maid to one side, opened the door, entered the room, and closed the door behind her.

"I have come to do business with you, Mrs. Jackson," she said. Her English was harsh, heavily accented.

"Who the hell are you?" said Rose. "Get out or I'll have you thrown out."

Celeste had crossed the room while Rose was speaking. "I don't believe you," Celeste said. She pulled on a cord; the curtains parted, and bright light poured into the room. It was cruel, revealing the pouches and dark circles beneath Rose's eyes and the sagging flesh under her chin and bare arms. Celeste regarded her with cold eyes.

"You won't eject me because you know that Mr. Carré could destroy you. I'm sure you bribe the police, probably half the city government as well. But they can't protect you against Carré. Or my family. My brother is Julien Sazerac."

Mrs. Jackson did not bother to acknowledge Celeste's threat. "What do you want?" she said crisply.

"I want the belongings of the young woman you foolishly brought to this house last night."

"What belongings? What young woman?"

Celeste Sazerac laughed, and for the first time in many years Rose Jackson was genuinely frightened. There was too much pleasure in the laughter, an edge of excitement. The woman is mad, she thought. What should I do? Her brother is owner of the biggest bank in the city; one word from him, and I could be jailed. Whores have no protection other than what they buy, and he already owns every official I pay bribes to.

Celeste's next words stopped Rose's scurrying thoughts. "I am willing to make a compromise with you, Mrs. Jackson. You agree to return the girl's possessions to me, and I will arrange it so that there is no prosecution."

Rose was immediately suspicious. The compromise was too generous. "How will you arrange it?" she said.

"I will, first, send Mr. Carré off with an easy mind. Then I will see to it that the girl leaves the city at once. Without her witness, there is no crime."

Mrs. Jackson's eyes were hard and cautious. "And why would you make this helpful arrangement? If, as you say, there was a crime. I deny any such accusation, you realize."

"I realize. And I also realize that you are a liar. However, my interest is not in punishing you. My concern is for the girl. I would avoid scandal. She is an orphan, and she has come under the protection of the Ursuline sisters. To save embarrassment, it is better that she leave. She can have a decent life under the roof of a suitable family, and she will not be reminded of her degrading experience by seeing the site of its occurrence."

You do-gooders love to arrange other people's lives, thought Mrs. Jackson, with an inner sneer. Aloud she said only, "I agree."

"I will send for the box and the valise. Have them ready. Good day." Celeste Sazerac was smiling when she left the room. If Mrs. Jackson had persisted in her denial, she would have eventually been convicted of abduction or something similar. But the box would have been lost forever. The priceless casket. No other was known to still exist.

She made her expression solemn when she joined Mr. Carré. "We are wasting our time," she said. "The girl was mistaken. She said it was dark, and she was driven from the dock to the house in a carriage. It could be any house. The woman here tells me that Jackson is a common name for her sort to adopt. She personally knows of at least a dozen others. It is a perpetual shame, Monsieur, that you men allow these conditions to persist. There is not one block in the old city that does not have at least one brothel, sometimes more. It would not be possible were it not for the disgusting appetites of you men. Do you know who was here last evening? Three members of the Municipal Council. A fine thing it would be if they had to serve as witnesses for this woman's testimony against an innocent girl."

Celeste's carriage was waiting outside. It took Mr. Carré to his office. Then the driver waited for instructions. She told him to return to the house they had just left and collect a valise and a box while she waited in the carriage.

The driver was gone for less than a minute. He put the luggage on the seat opposite to Celeste. "Now drive me to my cousins' house on Esplanade. The Courtenays."

Celeste drew the curtains across the windows. It made the interior of the carriage even hotter, airless. But she did not care. She had succeeded. She had the casquette. Her fingers slowly traced around its four edges, rubbed a smudge of oil, smoothed a scratch.

Then she tore the gloves off her hands and placed her palms flat on the top of the casket. She bent forward and kissed the dirty wood in the space between her hands. "Mine," she whispered, her lips moving against the box. Her hands slid across the top, down the sides, then, with a sudden spasm of motion, she seized the box in her arms and pulled it against her body in a passionate embrace. Her head was thrown back, her eyes closed; she laughed, an eerie, cracked sound.

And she cradled the worn, dirty casket in her arms like an infant. "Mine," she muttered, "all mine." Her dark eyes gleamed with triumphant possession. "My fan, my gloves, my locket, my arrowhead."

Celeste did not have to open the casket to know its contents. She remembered the thrill of seeing them when she was a child, when her mother told the stories of the women who had owned it. She had known who Mary was from the moment the girl sketched the dimensions of the casket in the air. Those were the fingers of Celeste's grandmother. And her great-great-grandmother. At that instant Celeste had vowed that she would make sure Mary never learned who she was. "Her mother got everything," Celeste confided to the burden in her arms. "My sister, how I hated her. She was the beauty, the talented one, the one everybody loved. She got all our mother's attention, all our father's affection. She got the man I loved. And then she went away with the other one, taking you with her. Now you're mine. You'll be my secret treasure. No one will ever see you. No one will ever see that girl, my sister's daughter. I'll burn her clothes and bury her valise. And the money . . . I'll contribute it to the orphanage."

Her body rocked with laughter.

# 8

Why don't I feel anything? Mary wondered. My last hope is gone. I have lost it all. My life is destroyed, and I don't feel anything. There should at least be pain, but even the hurt in my face has stopped. It's as if I were dead but still able to walk and talk and see and hear.

The numbness had begun even before Celeste Sazerac returned to the Convent. The Mother Superior shook her head when Mary said that the name carved in the casket would lead to her family.

"I am sorry, child, but that is not true. All the early records of the Convent were lost in the fire that burned the city in 1788. It was a sorry chapter in our history. The sisters wanted faith. When it was clear that the fire was going to consume everything they took the record books and carried them to the big square in front of the cathedral. They would have a chance of surviving there in the open, they thought.

"They should have placed their trust in God. When the flames neared the Convent, they remembered that. They carried the statue of Our Lady toward the fire, singing prayers for succor. God sent a change in the wind, then, and the fire retreated. Our convent was the only building in New Orleans that survived. But the record books burned."

Mary felt then as if she, too, were being consumed by flame. What have I done, she cried internally. Coming to this place where no one knows me, where even the language is different. I've been living a dream, and it's turned into a nightmare. Despair burned her heart.

And then all feeling stopped.

When Celeste reported that there was no chance of retrieving her belongings, Mary did not care.

She had no reaction to Celeste's words. They went on and on. Mary heard them, but they had no meaning for her. Even if Celeste had not been speaking French, Mary would not have been able to react. Her mind would not pay attention, or her heart feel anything.

". . . So I went at once to my cousin, Berthe Courtenay, Mother. I knew she was in the city for her grandfather's birthday celebration on the Fourth. 'Berthe,' I said, 'this unfortunate young woman needs a home. What better place for her than your plantation? She can be a companion to your Jeanne.' You remember, Mother, that Berthe's children were all taken by the fever, all save Jeanne. She has kept the girl in the country ever since for fear of losing her, too. Montfleury, the plantation, is terribly isolated. It's a lonely life for a girl. Young Mary here will be a godsend for Jeanne. And it will also remove Mary from the threat of taking the fever herself. People unused to our climate always seem to succumb so easily.

"She'll be like one of the family with the Courtenays. Berthe needs young life to fill the ache she still feels for her lost children."

The Mother Superior said that Celeste's plan was the answer to a prayer. "What a good Christian you are, Mademoiselle Celeste. Mary will be very happy there."

Celeste urged haste. Her cousin was ready to leave for the plantation. Mary accompanied her without a word. Her movements were jerky, puppetlike. She was barely able to summon the words to thank the Mother Superior for her kindness.

Everything around her was blurred, it seemed. A shimmer of heat rose from the brick pavement. She walked through it with Celeste Sazerac to the carriage, but her feet did not feel the heat that was blistering their soles through her thin silk slippers. She looked blindly at the floor of the carriage during the ride, at the brick walk to the Courtenay house when they arrived.

She didn't notice Berthe's shocked expression at her appearance, nor did she feel the compassion in the plump, pretty woman's touch when Berthe took her hand. She was not aware of anything.

It was many hours later that sensation returned to Mary. It came back as sharply and suddenly as it had left. They were deep in the country, jolting along on a narrow road covered with crushed shells. A long banner of Spanish moss was torn from a tree by their passing. It fell through the open window of their coach and landed on Mary's lap.

What is that gray thing? Her brain woke. I know this strange substance, she thought, and her hands crushed the spongy tangled curls of the moss.

It was in my box. I remember how odd and ugly I thought it. But it is beautiful. Look at it, like soft shawls on the trees. And the trees. So straight and tall, so heavy with green. And the flowers. Even my swollen nose can smell the perfume.

I love this Louisiana. From the first moment I loved it.

I was right to come. My heart knows this place even though I still have to learn it with my mind. This is my home, whether I can ever prove it or not. I know it in my soul.

And I'll learn.

She touched Berthe Courtenay's arm with a timid pressure. "Please," Mary said, "can I learn to speak French?"

# Book Two

# 9

"Montfleury" was the name of the Courtenay plantation. Like so many things about the plantation, the name confused Mary. There was no mountain, flowery or otherwise, not even a hill. The land stretched out to the horizon, flat as a tabletop except for the grassy bank of earth that separated the river from the immense lawn.

The house was not what she expected a plantation house to be. It was squat-looking, not tall and white with massive columns like the ones she had seen. It had only two stories on a high foundation, and it was very wide, with one tremendous room after another, all with doors onto wide porches that she learned to call "galleries."

The house had columns, but they weren't classical. Thick square brick piers supported the lower gallery, and the same brick construction reached to the roof of that gallery to support the gallery above it. The upper gallery was covered, too; its ceiling was held up by relatively thin round wooden uprights. Its roof was the house roof as well. It had a low pitch and was made of wood shingles that had aged to a soft silver-gray. It gave an impression of wide-reaching, comforting shelter.

And it gave shade. Mary understood very quickly why the galleries had such deep overhangs. She walked behind Berthe from the carriage to the gallery through the sunlight. Only a few paces, but enough to be grateful when she stepped onto the gallery. There was an illusion of coolness in the deep shade with the sun blazing outside. She even thought she could feel a breeze from the river.

Berthe led her into a wide shadowy hall that ran through the house to a gallery on the opposite side. She pulled a tasseled silk rope. "We have coffee," she said. "Jeanne will come." She struggled for the words, a worried frown between her eyebrows.

I must learn French right away, Mary told herself, I must. Suppose my grandmother speaks no English. Evidently most people in New Orleans don't.

She spoke urgently. "Madame, are there any dictionaries or grammar books that I could study?"

Berthe held up her hands and shook her head to indicate non-understanding.

Mary dug into her memory for her childhood French lessons. "Parler français," she remembered. Berthe smiled and nodded, opened her mouth to speak. Mary shook her head. "Moi," she said. She could remember nothing more that would help her. "I want to learn," she said desperately. "I want to learn."

"Yes," Berthe said. "You will learn. Jeanne will teach you French. You will teach Jeanne American. Jeanne will come."

"Who is Jeanne?"

Berthe's smile was radiant. "Jeanne is my daughter."

She had hardly finished speaking when Jeanne rushed in and embraced her, then began chattering in a torrent of French.

Mary had never seen anything as lovely as Berthe's daughter. She was the same height as Mary, but there was no other similarity. Jeanne was already a woman in appearance. She had full rounded breasts and a tiny waist, emphasized by the tightly fitting riding habit she wore. Its black linen jacket and white stock tie set off her dark hair and eyes and her gardenia-white skin to perfection. Her face was heart-shaped. A deep widow's peak defined the top of the heart. A dimple in her softly pointed chin decorated the bottom. Her full-lipped mouth was almost the same shape. Most beautiful of all was her slender neck. It was long, but not too long; it made Mary think of a flower stem, with Jeanne's exquisite animated face as the blossom.

Jeanne listened to her mother with her head tilted to the side like a curious bird. Then she clapped her hands and ran to Mary. The heavy train of her skirt billowed from the speed. "May-ree," she cried. "You will be my friend, no?" To Mary's astonishment, Jeanne grabbed her shoulders and kissed her loudly on one cheek then the other. "Papa has send me so much American teachers, but all old and dry. I learn very bad. You will teach me very good because of friend, yes?"

"Yes," Mary gulped. She would have agreed to anything Jeanne said. She was enchanted by the girl's liveliness and beauty and instant affection.

Jeanne chattered at her mother; Berthe nodded. Then Jeanne took Mary's hand and started toward the staircase in the hall, pulling Mary behind her. Mary had to jump to one side to avoid stepping on Jeanne's train. Jeanne giggled, stooped, and scooped it up with her arm. "Come," she commanded. "We find you a pretty frock. What you have is very ugly."

Mary looked down at her dress. She had not really thought about it before. The Ursuline nuns had given it to her. It was a dark, shapeless shift with long loose sleeves and a black cord for a belt. It was, she admitted, rather dreary. She hurried in Jeanne's wake up a long flight of wide stairs along a wide hall, open at both ends like the one below, and into a bedroom that could belong to no one but Jeanne.

The immense four-poster bed had hangings of shell-pink cotton tied to the posts with rosettes of blue-and-white-striped silk ribbon. The mosquito netting inside the hangings was looped up onto carved and painted garlands of roses; the same garlands were embroidered on the pink counterpane and were repeated in the needlepoint rug that covered the floor. A small mountain of lace-edged and lace-covered pink pillows filled the top quarter of the bed. Similar pillows were arranged on a chaise longue and slipper chairs covered in blue-and-white-striped silk.

There were stacks of illustrations ripped from fashion magazines, a small shelf holding novels by Alexandre Dumas, the *Fables* of La Fontaine, and a collection of fairy tales. Two wax dolls shared a chair with a box of tangled embroidery silks. A delicate fruitwood desk held an English grammar book, a silver inkwell with dried ink caked in the bottom, and a large crystal bowl of rose-scented potpourri. The dressing table was covered with a fragile white lace cloth; lace swags topped the enormous gilt framed looking glass. It reflected and was reflected by a gilt pier glass near the opposite wall. A riding crop hung from one corner of it. All four corners of the room were filled with large armoires painted with bouquets of flowers. Jeanne opened them all in turn. They were filled with clothes.

"This one," she said, thrusting a dress into Mary's arms, "and that . . . celle là et puis . . . non . . . this . . . cette horreur . . . that one for certain . . ."

At the end of an hour the room was a shambles of dresses and skirts and shirtwaists and slippers and petticoats and dressing gowns. Jeanne had changed her clothes three times before settling on pink organdy. Berthe had decided that four of the cotton dresses would do very well for Mary with tucks in the bodice to make the bust smaller. Mary was sitting on a bench near the open door to the gallery, nearly prostrated by the heat and stunned by the rampant femininity.

She followed Berthe and Jeanne out onto the gallery and into the room that was adjacent to Jeanne's. "You sleep here, May-ree, yes?" Jeanne said.

"Oh, yes," said Mary. She loved the room at first sight. It was very plain, almost austere, compared with Jeanne's bedroom. The tall pine bed was narrow, and its only canopy was the *barre* from which the white mosquito netting hung. Its counterpane was white cotton, candle-wicked in a pattern of vines. Crisp white linen cases covered the two square pillows. There was a simple pine wardrobe and a pine table with a small wing chair beside it. The floor was bare. Mary could imagine her bare feet on the glossy waxed boards. It would feel cool, she thought.

Cool.

At that moment a gust of wind rushed through the open door to the gallery. It billowed the net hangings on the bed and chilled Mary's sweaty body. She turned toward it, holding her face upward to be cooled. She saw what looked like a wall of water beyond the gallery railing.

Before she could recover from the shock of it, it was gone; heavy runnels of water dropping from the roof overhang were the only evidence that it had ever been there. That and a refreshing cool dampness in the air.

It was her first experience of a New Orleans summer rain, and it was unlike any rain she had ever known. But everything in New Orleans was unlike anything she had ever known. She had much to learn.

Jeanne smiled brightly and said, "Voilà, May-ree. You have your room and your dresses and Maman will find for you a hairbrush. You need only a maid now to take care of you. Do you prefer old or young?"

"Do you own slaves?" Mary asked. She hadn't thought of it before. Everything had been too fast, too strange. But Montfleury was a plantation, and plantations meant slavery, Mary knew that. Chains and inhuman cruelty. Before Jeanne could answer, Mary shook her head furiously. "I won't permit myself to profit from the misery of a downtrodden, mistreated fellow creature," she said proudly.

Jeanne frowned. "I do not understand what you say, May-ree. Such big words so fast. Is it that you want not to have a maid? Is that the way of Americans? Who dresses you and undresses you?"

"I dress myself."

"What a curiosity." Jeanne shrugged. She looked extremely French. "You must do what you like, May-ree, of course. I hope Clementine will not take offense."

"Who is Clementine?"

"She is maid for Maman. And she is how do you say—*directrice* of all maids. I will ask her to forgive you."

Mary tried to understand, but she couldn't. How could a slave forgive a white person for anything when white people were the cause of slavery?

How could a slave owner be worried about offending a slave? Everyone knows, Mary said to herself, that they beat and starve the slaves and sell the children while the mothers beg for mercy. She felt terribly guilty. She liked Jeanne and her mother, but she shouldn't like slave owners.

Her confusion was further complicated by the entrance of a frowning woman. Her skin was light brown, not black. And she had clearly never known starvation; she was very fat. She shook her finger at Jeanne and scolded her. In French.

Later, Mary realized that it was perfectly logical for slaves to speak whatever language was spoken around them, just as free people did. But that was later. Now it was the final, overwhelming surprise after a steady succession of surprises. Mary sat abruptly in the wing chair and began to giggle. She didn't know why she was laughing; there was nothing humorous about what was happening, as far as she knew. Her laughter was as bizarre, perplexing, unreal as everything else. And she couldn't stop.

Everyone stared at her. Then Jeanne began to giggle, too. The contagion spread until they were all laughing, without knowing why.

That was how Mary met Miranda, Jeanne's maid and ruler. Soon after, she met Clementine, Berthe's maid, and ruler of all the female servants in the house. And Charlotte, cook and tyrant in the separate building that housed the kitchen. And, most powerful of all, Hercule.

Hercule was a black man of awesome dignity and polish. He was so thin that Mary might have believed the Courtenays starved him had she not already revised that expectation when she met Miranda. He was the butler, the supreme commander of all the servants. He spoke for the master, and his word was law.

Late that afternoon she met the master himself. By then she was dressed in a lightweight cotton frock and had already begun to study the French grammar that Berthe had found for her. Mary was feeling very happy about her temporary home.

She smiled and curtseyed to the impressive white-haired gentleman when she heard her name in Berthe's rapid spate of words. She thought he looked irritated when he first saw her, but she expected that he would be as kind as the rest of the family when he heard her story.

He spoke briefly then walked away.

Berthe tried to translate what he had said, but she abandoned the effort. She turned to her daughter for help.

Jeanne was giggling. "Grandpère says he detest Americans. He says only French in his house so you be silent unless you learn."

Berthe took Mary's hand. "Please," she said, "forgive him. Grandpère is an old man. He likes old ways."

I was going to learn anyhow, thought Mary. I'll learn twice as fast, just to show that mean old man. I won't say a word, then, when I'm leaving, I'll rattle off French so fast he'll have to beg my pardon. I'll show him what Americans can do. I'll be going soon anyhow, as soon as Mademoiselle Sazerac finds out who my family is. I'll be glad to see no more of him. And his old ways, whatever that means, besides insulting people.

She learned that evening about the "old ways." Berthe's husband, Carlos Courtenay, arrived during dinner. He had come to see what kind of person his wife had taken in to be a companion to their daughter.

His first view of Mary was a young woman with a swollen, bruised face, scarlet cheeks, and eyes blinking to hold back tears. She was chewing and swallowing with concentrated determination; she obviously was unaccustomed to the hot, spicy seasoning characteristic of New Orleans food. But she ate everything on her plate. Carlos Courtenay liked that.

After dinner he took Mary aside to talk to her. His English was stilted but fluent, and she learned a great deal in a very short time. About the family, about the plantation, about New Orleans.

He was very young, he told her, when New Orleans, all of Louisiana, became part of the United States. He grew up accepting the fact. But his father's generation still resented the changes the Americans had made. They wanted New Orleans to stay as it always was.

The Americans wanted to change it, to make it American. They refused to learn French ways or the French language.

The Creoles like Grandpère refused to give them up.

Now, said Carlos Courtenay, New Orleans was not one city, but two.

There was the original city, laid out in squares within a greater square. Its streets were straight and narrow, its buildings side by side. Like all old cities it had once been surrounded by walls, and space had to be used efficiently.

Then there was the new city, where the streets fanned to meet the bends in the river, and houses sat alone amid broad lawns and gardens.

One old, one new; one French, one American. They were divided by a street with a green parklike mall in the center. It was known to both French and Americans as "the neutral ground."

"The language of war," he said. His smile was rueful. "It's madness. We French are going to lose, and we know it. But there are many like my father who will fight every inch of the retreat. They won't face the inevitable. The Americans have more people and more money. The French will be swallowed up.

"I learned to speak American because I'm a banker and Americans do business with my bank.

"I want Jeanne to learn because American is the language of her future.

"My father calls it the language of the barbarians. He sold his house in the city and lives year-round at Montfleury so that he need never hear it. Gallant, foolish old man. As a Creole, I love him for it. However, we argue all the time.

"He considers me a traitor," said Carlos. "Not only do I consort with the enemy but, worse, I prefer being a banker to being a planter. I like business, and I like Americans because business is all they live for.

"Montfleury will be mine some day, because I'm the eldest son. But I shall never run it. My son Philippe will be the Montfleury Courtenay. Eventually the plantation will be his.

"He'd like to be here now, but my father won't let anyone else have any authority. He won't even have an overseer. So Philippe lives with one of my brothers on his plantation. He's learning how to be a planter from Bernard. One of Bernard's sons works in my bank. I'm teaching him to be a businessman. Families are very useful."

Mary grabbed at the opening. "I'm looking for my family. That is, Mademoiselle Sazerac is looking for me. I wonder if you could tell me how soon I should expect to hear from her."

"Your family is in New Orleans? What is the name?"

"I don't know... It's a very long story."

"Then I'm sorry but I won't be able to hear it tonight. Another time, if you don't mind. I want to be with my wife and daughter for an hour before I return to the city... There is no hurry. No one is in the city in the summer, save for businessmen like me and a few eccentrics. If your family is to be located it will have to be done in the autumn, when everyone returns to town.

"Don't be downhearted, Miss MacAlistair. Only a few months remain of summer, and you will find life at Montfleury very entertaining. I'm delighted that Jeanne will have such a well-educated, intelligent companion. I'll tell Madame Courtenay how pleased I am."

"Thank you, Monsieur."

"Well said, Mademoiselle."

Mary stayed at the end of the gallery when Carlos went to join Berthe and Jeanne. Even though she couldn't understand, it would be wrong to be there when he was praising her to them. What a nice man, she thought. He makes up for the nastiness of his father. Even he doesn't seem quite so awful now that I understand why he hates Americans so much. It's lucky that my family didn't hate them, too, or my mother and father would never have been married.

Carlos Courtenay lit a cigar, and the smell of the smoke drifted toward her. Mary thought of her father, pushed the thought away, concentrated on her mother and the family that would be hers in the autumn.

Strange about family traits, she mused. Mr. Courtenay has a cleft in his chin exactly like his father's. Jeanne has it, too, but on her chin it's a dimple. All those paintings in the dining room . . . so many have that chin. Unconsciously she touched her little finger. She heard "Mary" in Berthe's voice and smiled. How kind they all were. She'd have to find some way to repay them when she moved to her family home.

"But Mary has no family," Berthe was saying. "Celeste Sazerac told me all about her. She was left as a baby at the door of a convent in Saint Louis. One of the nuns talked to her about New Orleans, and the poor child invented a history for herself. In time she came to believe it. We must pretend that we believe it, too. Her imaginary family is the only thing she has. Celeste said that she must have walked for weeks to come from Saint Louis. She was all bruised and nearly mad with hunger and her clothing was so ragged that the good Sisters had to dress her from the skin out."

# 10

Mary's first day at Montfleury had been too busy, too emotional, too crowded with shocks and surprises and things to learn. She fell into her new bed with a groan of pain and exhaustion.

Without the stimulus of new people and new surroundings to occupy her full attention, she could no longer avoid recognition of the position she was in. She was alone . . . frightened . . . helpless . . . wounded in heart and body. She touched her cuts and bruises gingerly, testing the degree of pain. She ached from head to toe.

How could everything have turned out the way it did? So wrong. Hot tears seeped from the corners of her eyes and rolled down her face. She forced her fingers into her battered mouth to muffle the sound of her crying.

Everything was lost. Her father was dead. Her mother was not her mother, and her real mother was dead. Her money was gone. Greatest loss of all, her gift from her mother, her box, was gone forever.

She was too tired and too hurt to shut out her memories as she usually did; they filled her mind, wounding her more painfully than any physical blow. She saw the convent, the nuns, her friends, and she longed to be back in time to when her life was simple and orderly and safe. The Mother Superior's face came before her then, and her words, "Your father is dead . . . your father is dead . . . your mother is dead . . . you have no home . . ."

The saintly gentle nun's face changed in her mind to the features of Miss Rose, soft, pretty, smiling . . . becoming hard and cruel and cold. Mary writhed, turned her head from side to side, crying a silent no, no, no against the hazy memory of the drugged moments in the deceptively beautiful garden. She smelled her own hair burning, a cigar burning, the heavy sickening sweetness of flowers mixed with strong perfumes. She couldn't breathe, something slimy was covering her mouth, and there were explosions and colors and monster faces, red, blue, green, white, purple, with black holes in the center and noise and falling and the taste of blood in her mouth.

There was a taste of blood, real blood. Mary took her bitten fingers out of her mouth and sobbed into her pillow.

A breeze stirred the moonlit netting around her bed. Somewhere in the distance an owl hooted. Mary crept out of bed and tiptoed onto the long gallery. She could see the outlines of tall trees, the ghostly gray of Spanish moss hanging from their branches, the silvery globe of the moon, and a scattering of moon-faded stars. Everything was sleeping except her, and the owl. The house and the land were drenched with peaceful silver silence.

The peace entered her heart. I won't think of any of it ever again, she promised herself. This beautiful country is my birthright, this house my home until I find my people. I'm going to be happy.

She tiptoed back to her bed and sleep.

Mary was wakened the next morning by Miranda with a tray holding a cup of coffee and a freshly cut rose. There was a drop of dew on the flower, and a thin light at the window. She wanted to ask what time it was, but she couldn't remember the words in French. She said "Merci" instead.

While she drank the strong black coffee, she studied her borrowed French grammar book. There was no time to waste if she hoped to be ready when she found her family. When Jeanne poked her head around the door between their rooms, Mary was able to say the words she had looked up. "Good morning. It is a lovely day. I slept very well." In French.

"May-ree, but how quick you learn so good," Jeanne exclaimed.

In the days and weeks that followed, Mary continued, in Jeanne's phrase, to quick to learn so good. She had always had the gift of determination and a willingness to work hard. Now she had the added spur of her conviction that soon she would be in the very center of a Creole family.

The early childhood lessons with a French governess had prepared her better than she knew. Her progress in learning the language was amazingly quick so good.

With the language came the ability to ask questions and understand the answers. Also to read. A boat stopped at Montfleury's landing twice a week with goods that had been ordered from New Orleans, including the daily newspaper *L'Abeille, The Bee.*

It was interesting and entertaining. And bilingual. The two big pages were printed in English on the outside, French on the inside. Mary tried to read the inside, looked on the other side of the page when she got stuck. She grew more proficient in French and more intrigued by

New Orleans with every edition. She learned which purveyors had received which cheeses from the ship *Normande* just in from Havre; which dry-goods shop had a new stock of handkerchief linen suitable for summer shirtwaists; which vintner received wines and brandies; which modiste had the very latest styles in Paris bonnets. All from the same ship.

Jeanne shared her interest in the advertisements of the ships and their latest goods. Mary had the newspaper to herself for the bulletins from Washington, Paris, New York, and the California gold fields.

She persuaded Jeanne to correct her pronunciation when she read aloud the chapters from the novel that *The Bee* was serializing. And she nagged until Jeanne read aloud at least one short column of news in English. That was the most she could manage as a teacher of "American."

"May-ree," Jeanne explained, "I am very lazy. I like to dance and I like to ride. For the rest of the time I am only an ornament."

The Creole girl infuriated Mary. She also charmed her and fascinated her. Everything about Creole life and Creole history fascinated her. She believed she was getting to know her mother as she learned.

Her dream picture of her mother altered radically. Now Mary saw her as a dark-haired, dark-eyed beauty with skin paler than milk. Like Jeanne. Like the portraits on Montfleury's walls.

Perhaps she had lived on a sugar plantation, too. The idea was romantically appealing. The plantation was like a dream world. The beauty of the lawn, the gardens, the grassy levee, the great, wide river was unlike anything Mary had ever known, even in the books she read.

And the orderly beauty of life on Montfleury was like an idyll. Gleaming silver bowls of flowers were reflected in polished mahogany tables in every room. Airy lace curtains at tall windows moved like dancers at every breeze. The air was always sweetly scented. By the gardens, by the bowls of flowers, by the sachets in drawers and cupboards, by the toilet water that Jeanne taught her to splash on her wrists and temples to cool herself when the breeze vanished in the heat of midday. Mary imagined her mother surrounded by sweetness, smelling sweet, smiling sweetly, rocking in the big chairs on the galleries, and sipping coffee, as Jeanne did for most of the day.

Or else she pictured her balanced gracefully on her sidesaddle, with the train of her skirt sweeping nearly to the ground, riding through the mysterious swampy woods or along the top of the levee, as Jeanne did after breakfast and before dinner every day. Jeanne tried to teach Mary to ride, but in this instance Mary's determination was not enough. She went out with Jeanne and the attendant groom every morning, but she disliked riding more each time.

She begged off from the afternoon ride with the excuse that she was going to help Jeanne's mother with one thing or another. In truth she was little help to Berthe Courtenay. But Berthe's kind heart was touched by Mary's eagerness to learn everything about Creole life, so she found things for Mary to do with her.

Berthe was always busy, whether it was necessary or not. She was seemingly indefatigable, even in the sultry heat. Mary trailed along behind her while she bustled from counting sheets in the linen press to inspecting the supply of straw-wrapped ice in the cool house to bothering the cook and other servants in the kitchen building that was on the opposite side of a yard outside the back door.

Mary tried to enjoy the visits to the kitchen building, but she always felt uneasy there. The kitchen was the social center for the house servants. There were always four or five of them sitting and talking and drinking coffee at the tremendous table in the center of the room. They stood when Berthe entered, moved quickly to do her bidding, answered her questions about their families and their health with eager, often laughing, anecdotes. It was apparent that they respected and liked her.

But they were slaves. They'd have to do all the things they did even if they had hated her. Everything about slavery confused and upset Mary. It wasn't anything like what she had been told at the convent. It wasn't simple.

The slaves weren't worked like animals until they dropped from exhaustion. As far as she could tell, none of them worked as hard as Berthe, with her perpetual busyness, or Grandpère, who went to the fields every morning and every afternoon in every kind of weather, and then did the correspondence and record keeping every evening after dinner.

No one seemed to regard the servants as inferior beings. Miranda had control over Jeanne. Berthe consulted Clementine before making any decisions. Hercule's bedroom was next to Grandpère's, and they played chess every night before they went to bed.

And yet all the women had to wear bandanas on their heads. The *tignon* was required by law for all black women.

And Clementine had to carry a pass, written by Berthe, when she went to New Orleans to visit one of her daughters who lived there. She would be arrested and jailed if she couldn't show it to any policeman who might stop her on the street.

And not one of them, not even the mighty Hercule, had the power to decide to go to some other place. Or the right to stay at Montfleury if Grandpère should ever want to sell him.

Sell him. Like a horse or a barrel of sugar.

Slavery was wrong. Mary was sure it was wrong. She wasn't sure that anyone else thought so. Not even the slaves. It was very upsetting. And there was no one she could talk with about her confusion.

So she learned to push it to an unexamined corner of her mind. And she studied her French. And she gradually became accustomed to the plantation's routines and rhythms and Grandpère's "old ways."

He read the prayers every morning at six-thirty to the entire household, black and white, kneeling together on the low stools that were scattered around the drawing room.

Then he presided at the long table in the dining room for breakfast at seven.

And again at noon for lunch.

And at seven for dinner.

He sat alone in a big armchair next to the family's bench at mass every Sunday in the plantation chapel and trounced Father Hilaire at chess when the visiting priest walked over to the house with him for midday dinner after the service was over.

Every other Wednesday Doctor Limoux came to treat any illnesses in the family or the slaves. Then he checkmated Grandpère with astonishing speed and spent the entire time at lunch telling him what he had done wrong.

On Mondays Monsieur Damien came from New Orleans to give Jeanne lessons in dancing and the piano. He was entranced by her grace in the reel, the waltz, the classic minuet. He was in agony when she played the Chopin étude even more badly than she had the week before.

Monsieur Damien did not eat with the family. He always had urgent appointments that required his immediate return to the city.

Mary speculated that he was afraid of Grandpère. She couldn't believe that he objected to the Creole tradition that she liked most. On Mondays, dinner was always the same. A plain, lightly seasoned, mouth-watering dish of red beans and rice.

Mary learned to appreciate the infinite variety of Creole cooking.

She developed the Creole habit of drinking coffee at every opportunity. They were acquired tastes.

She became a gluttonous lover of red beans and rice with the first mouthful.

At the end of a month, she felt almost as if Montfleury were her home. Her French was so nearly fluent that Grandpère was teaching her to play chess. And the pattern of life seemed so natural to her that she almost believed herself a Creole. Full, not half. She hoped her family would be pleased.

The only thing she couldn't adjust to, try as she might, was the eternal suffocating heat. She could only grit her teeth and look forward to the end of summer.

In mid-August, Jeanne and Mary returned from the levee to find the stable yard filled with strange horses. "He has come," Jeanne cried. "My brother is here, with his friends." She leapt down and began to run toward the house without even draping the train of her skirt over her arm. Mary was more decorous, but she hurried, too. Jeanne had talked so much about Philippe that she was eager to meet him.

"He is so handsome, May-ree, and so charming. And how he can make one laugh. He is the most marvelous brother in the entire world. You will fall in love with him in an instant, you'll see."

# 11

When Mary approached the house, she could hear male voices and laughter. She stopped, suddenly conscious of her sweaty face and ill-fitting habit, a hand-me-down from Jeanne's wardrobe. She scrubbed her face with her handkerchief, then used it to brush at the dust on her clothes. When she was as neat as possible, she still did not move. She was frightened.

Don't be such a ninny, Mary MacAlistair, she scolded herself. They're only people. Besides, no one's going to pay any attention to you anyhow. Pick up your feet and march in there.

But still she did not move. Mary had met very few men in her life; she didn't know how she should behave. It's all Jeanne's fault, she thought, going on the way she does all the time about falling in love, about romance and admirers and love tokens; she's made me nervous. My knees feel like they're going to give out on me. If I don't walk up those steps and into that room right now, I won't be able to walk at all in a minute. If only I didn't look so hot and disheveled!

In spite of her fears, Mary's young heart was excited, yearning for admission to the world of flirtation, attraction, eyes meeting and recognizing some special, unspoken communication. Her left foot made a shaky, tentative step forward, then her right, and then quickly across the rest of the path and up the stairs onto the deep, shaded porch.

She hesitated outside the open French doors that led to the dining room, standing to one side before she entered. She moved her head cautiously to look in, wondering how many people were there, whether she might recognize Philippe from Jeanne's description, where Jeanne was. Mary could hear her laughter among the others; it was bright, tinkling, like the sound of decanter against glasses that also came from the room.

Her eyes found Jeanne, not too far away. Mary took a deep breath and stepped toward the doorway. Then she saw the man at Jeanne's side. Tall and slim, dressed in white jodhpurs and black linen coat. He had been leaning down to hear what she was saying. Mary's eyes fixed on him at the moment he straightened to his full height and threw his head back to laugh.

It was him. The man she had seen from the deck of the boat, the man who had saved her from the ruffian on the horrible nightmare night in New Orleans, the man whose face and form filled her mind whenever Jeanne sighed and talked about romance.

I must be imagining this, Mary said to herself. But his voice was distinct, the deep ring of it, the laughter barely concealed beneath its words. She heard it clearly; all the other voices in the room were merely a blur of noise. He had spoken only a few words to her, but she would know that voice for as long as she lived.

Mary pulled away from the window. She leaned against the wall of the house for support. I can't go in there. Not like this. I cannot let him see me dirty and clumsy and nervous. It's like a dream come true that he would be here, in the same house that I'm in. I'll be able to meet him, learn his name, hear him speak. But not like this.

She gathered up her skirts and ran, racing around the corner of the house away from the dining room, into a different door and up the servants' stairs to her room where she could wash, and change her clothes, and splash some rosewater on her burning cheeks.

She heard horses on the gravel in front of the house and thought for an instant that even more people were arriving. Then she heard voices, one of them his voice, outside. "No!" Mary said aloud, "I'm almost finished. Wait." She ran from her room to the upstairs gallery and looked down onto the scene below. There was a confused group of horses, grooms, and hatted men. Mary looked from one to another, unable to see anyone's face.

Jeanne was there, holding onto the arm of a man in a brown jacket. He shook his head and pulled away. Jeanne stamped her foot. He turned his back to her and mounted a brown horse.

The man Mary was looking for came down from the lower porch and walked swiftly across the gravel to Jeanne. His face, too, was hidden by the wide brim of a low-crowned hat, but Mary did not need to see it to know him. His movements were controlled, quick, lithe, seemingly effortless; he was more graceful than a normal man could be; he was like a powerful jungle cat. Mary remembered the lightning-fast appearance of the sword hidden in his cane, the way it moved under his command, faster than the eye could follow. She thought of his long springing stride when he boarded the steamer the first time she ever saw him. No, there was no need to see his face. There could be only one man in the world who moved like that.

She looked at him, luxuriating in the freedom of her unnoticed vantage point. Her eyes moved over his shoulders and his back, down his arms to his hands. He was wearing a ring on the little finger of his left hand, gold, with a flattened oval top. Mary's hand moved by her side, her thumb and middle finger reaching toward one another, making tiny rotating motions as if she were turning the ring, looking at it, her hand brushing his.

He extended his right arm, lifted Jeanne's hand in his, and Mary felt as if a fist had struck her heart. He bowed, raising Jeanne's hand almost to his lips. Mary clutched the wide railing of the porch so violently that she hurt her palms. Then he turned, accepted the reins offered by his groom, and swung himself up into the saddle in one flowing, rapid movement.

Mary turned her head so that she wouldn't have to see him go away. She felt a hot wetness on her neck and realized that tears were pouring down her face. She hated Jeanne Courtenay.

"May-ree, I've been looking for you everywhere. What are you doing in your room with the shutters closed? Why didn't you come in to meet Philippe and his friends? I missed you."

Mary covered her eyes with her arm against the light that came in with Jeanne when the door was opened. She wanted to cover her ears, as well. The girl's voice was too loud, too cheerful, too confident of Mary's friendship.

"Poor May-ree. Are you not well?" Jeanne sat on the edge of Mary's bed and stroked her forehead. "Shall I order you a coffee? I'll get you some ice, would you like that? A cold cloth on your eyes would feel good, would it not?"

Mary felt sick with shame for her anger and jealousy. It was not Jeanne's fault that she was beautiful and charming and happy. She forced herself to speak, despite the sour bile in her throat. "I'm all right, Jeanne, truly I am. I just needed a rest. You know how the heat upsets me." She lifted her arm, moved Jeanne's hand away. "Ring for coffee, that would be nice. We'll go out on the gallery in the fresh air."

I can do this, she told herself. I can act as if nothing is different, nothing changed between us. I can do it. I must.

The gallery was shaded, but hot and airless. For once, Mary was grateful. She fanned herself with a wide, heart-shaped fan made of woven grass. It hid her face while she listened to Jeanne's lilting chatter.

"Oh, May-ree, I'm heartbroken that you weren't there with me.

You'll never believe what happened. It was so wonderful. May-ree, I'm in love. I could walk on the air, dance with the clouds. You should have been there, May-ree, to meet him...

"Valmont Saint-Brévin. He's the most romantic man in the entire world and so rich, May-ree. They say he's the richest man in Louisiana. ... Of course, this isn't the first time I've fallen in love with him. That was two years ago, at Philippe's coming-of-age celebration. I was allowed to stay up for the ball, but only to watch. Valmont had just come back from Paris, and everyone was fussing over him. But even so, he asked Maman for permission to partner me in the reel. He's such a perfect dancer, May-ree, and so handsome. Naturally I fell in love with him. But I was only a child. It was only infatuation.

"Today was different. Today I truly fell in love. And he likes me. I could tell. He remembered the reel. He asked me if I still enjoyed dancing. He said that I had become a beautiful young woman."

Jeanne touched her face, her lips, her throat. "It's true, isn't it, May-ree? I am beautiful. I see it in my looking glass. And I have become a woman." Her hands caressed her body. "See how full my breasts are and how small my waist. A man could hold my waist in his two hands; he could fill them with my breasts. I am ready to be loved, May-ree, and I love him. Oh, how happy I am."

She leaned toward Mary with a pleased, naughty, conspirator's smile. "I will confess something," she whispered. "When we go riding on the levee, I always take us in the same direction, in the direction of his plantation. I have been doing that for two years, ever since I first met him. I hoped that he would be riding, too, that we would meet again, that he would notice me."

Jeanne laughed, clapped her hands. "All those miles on the levee, and I never saw him. But now it has happened. We have met again. He has noticed me."

Mary moved the fan back and forth until her arm ached. Then she shifted it to the other hand. Jeanne retold her story a dozen times. Each time she discovered greater significance in every look and every word of Valmont Saint-Brévin.

That evening at dinner, Mary met Philippe Courtenay. Jeanne had spoken so often about her brother's dashing good looks that Mary could hardly believe that she was at table with the same man. Philippe looked older than his twenty-three years. His thick black muttonchop whiskers could not disguise his plump cheeks and slight double chin, and his corpulence made him look like a settled, middle-aged man. His elegant dinner clothes were inadequate to disguise his narrow chest, and his brocaded waistcoat only emphasized his little paunch.

He was not at all what Mary had expected. She was relieved when he talked very little to anyone except Grandpère. She could be silently miserable.

Jeanne, however, was displeased and let it be known. "Philippe," she said when the meal was half done, "you haven't spoken a single word about anything interesting ever since you arrived. Cane, and cane prices, and how the weather will be for the cane crop. I think you're horrid."

"Jeanne," said Berthe sternly, "be quiet. Remember your manners."

Grandpère's frown was terrifying.

But Jeanne was undeterred. "Your sugarcane is spoiling my life, Grandpère," she said. She pouted, exaggerating the moue, and looked at the old man with mournful appeal.

He was impassive.

Jeanne persisted. "Please, Grandpère, tell Philippe not to be so mean to me. Today he snatched away all his amusing friends just when I was having such a good time. He dragged them off to look at the cane fields. And he wouldn't let me go along. It broke my heart, Grandpère."

For the first time Mary saw old Monsieur Courtenay laugh. It began as a rusty wheeze deep in his throat then grew in volume until it exploded from his mouth as a contagious burst of merriment. Philippe and Berthe were laughing, too. Mary even felt her own lips twitch, although she didn't know what they found so funny. She heard an undignified snort at her side and saw that Jeanne was holding her napkin over her mouth in an effort to keep herself from joining in.

"It's not funny," she said in a muffled croak. Then she dropped napkin and dignity and laughed with the others.

Later she explained to Mary that she had refused all her life to go anyplace near the fields. She was convinced that snakes and crocodiles were hidden in the tall green thickness, because the swamp lay just beyond them.

Philippe rode to the levee with Jeanne and Mary the next morning. When they reached the top of the high grass-covered bank of earth, Jeanne turned, as usual, to the right.

"I'm going downriver, Jeanne," said Philippe. "You can come along if you like. No cane fields, though, I'm afraid." He chuckled, then grinned at his sister.

Jeanne tossed her head and sniffed. "You can stop making fun of me, Philippe. You had your fun last night. I prefer to ride this way."

"Suit yourself."

Mary forced herself to speak up. "May I ride with you, Philippe?"

He raised his eyebrows in surprise. "I'm going several miles."

"Good. I'd like a long ride," Mary lied. She could not stand the thought of being with Jeanne in her search for Valmont Saint-Brévin. Suppose he was on the levee; she'd have to see the two of them together, and it would be unbearable.

"Come along, then," said Philippe. "Jeanne, don't you go tearing off." He motioned to the groom who always rode behind the girls. "Stay close to Mademoiselle, boy." Then he spurred his horse into a gallop.

Mary kicked her horse and prayed she wouldn't fall off. It set off in pursuit of Philippe as if the road were a racetrack.

# 12

"My God, young woman, you might have killed yourself, and then what would Grandpère have done to me?"

Mary had managed to keep up to Philippe's pace for more than ten terrifying minutes. Then she lost the reins and after that her balance. She tumbled from the saddle onto the edge of the road and fell somersaulting down the steep grassy incline into a clump of violently pink-flowered oleander shrubs.

She barely had time to pull down her torn skirt before Philippe was at her side. His anger triggered her own.

"You might ask if I'm hurt before you start shouting at me," Mary yelled.

He was immediately contrite. "I'm sorry, please forgive me. I'm a brute. How are you? Did you injure yourself?"

Mary felt guilty. It made her even angrier. "Of course I did. You fling yourself down that hill and see how you feel."

Philippe started to remove his jacket. "Let me make a pillow for your head. I'll go get a cart and take you home. The doctor isn't far away."

It was Mary's turn for contrition. "I'm sorry, Philippe. Truly I am. I don't think I'm hurt. Just frightened. And ashamed."

She stretched out one leg, then the other, rotating her feet, flexing her knees, checking to be sure she had not broken or sprained anything. Concentrating on her legs, she missed Philippe's frowning look of suspicion.

It disappeared slowly while he observed her matter-of-fact appraisal of her injuries. He decided that she wasn't trying to play a trick on him.

Philippe had found Mary pleasant enough at dinner the night before. He had even approved of her. Unlike most young women, she hadn't flirted with him or laughed too much at his pleasantries or tried to draw his attention in any way. He was accustomed to all those things and wary, as a bachelor had to be if it was widely known that a rich inheritance would one day be his.

But when she invited herself along on his ride downriver, his approval vanished. She was just like any other girl looking for a husband, he thought, only more brazen. Proper unmarried women never went anywhere alone with a man.

When she fell, he was sure that she was trying to trap him, expecting him to be all sympathetic and gallant. The next move would be to collapse weakly into his arms, perhaps even swoon.

Not shout at him like a shrew. And certainly not crash around enough to break her neck. Philippe looked at Mary's dirty, scratched face and wildly disordered hair. No woman would allow herself to appear that unattractive if she was trying to be enticing. He held his hands out to her.

"I'll help you to get up," he said.

Mary put her hands in his. "Thank you. I'll probably moan and groan. Don't pay any attention . . . Ouch!"

When she was on her feet, she pulled her hands away and began to brush the dirt off her clothes.

"Are you all right?"

"Yes. Black and blue, I suppose, and a mess. But sound in wind and limb."

"That's good. I'll go get the horses."

Mary groaned. "Do we have to ride? I'd rather walk."

"When you're thrown, the only thing to do is to get back on the horse immediately. I'll be right back." Philippe started to climb the hill.

Mary watched him with glum resignation. She couldn't even recapture her anger. It's my own fault, she admitted to herself. I asked to come. Now I'll have to see it through.

There was no more galloping. They rode side by side, at a walk. As they rode, they talked. Each of them was surprised by how easy it was to be with the other. The angry shouting had proved to be a kind of unmasking, a strangely intimate exchange without any undertow of sexuality.

"Why did you want to take a long ride?" Philippe asked. "You obviously don't really like horses."

"That's an understatement. I hate riding. I'm so bad at it, and I hate doing things I don't do well. I just picked the lesser of two evils. I didn't want to be with Jeanne when she met up with her hero."

Her candor astonished Mary, then gave her a warm pleasant feeling. It was a luxury to be able to admit the truth.

"Who's that?" Philippe wanted to know. "Jeanne didn't tell me she had a beau."

"It's your friend Valmont Saint-Brévin." Mary said the name easily, but her heart turned over from the pain and the sweetness of feeling it on her lips.

Philippe's laughter startled her. "Val?" he said. "Val doesn't have time for a little girl like Jeanne."

Mary felt a dizzying elation. But she was afraid to trust in it. "Jeanne isn't a child, Philippe," she said. "And she's sure that Monsieur Saint-Brévin is . . . interested."

"She flatters herself. No matter. She'll forget all about him by tomorrow."

Mary couldn't let the conversation stop there. Philippe's words were a balm to her aching, jealous emotions. "She's in love with him, she says, Philippe. You'd better take her seriously."

"That's ridiculous. Our father has Jeanne's future all planned, and it doesn't include being in love with Val or anybody else. Jeanne knows that perfectly well. She's going to marry a rich American. That's why she has to learn their language."

Mary was dumbfounded. Surely Philippe was mistaken. Grandpère was violently anti-American. Jeanne was totally occupied by thoughts of love. She was about to tell Philippe he was wrong when he reached across and took the reins of her horse from her. "We'll stop here," he said, "and walk the rest of the way."

"Where are we going?"

"To look at the levee and the patch. I want to see them up close. I wasn't here last May when the crevasse happened; Grandpère sent for me to make sure there's not another one.

"You don't know what I'm talking about, do you? Look out there at the river, Mary. It's a half mile wide, moving at eight miles an hour, always pressing against these pretty grassy banks. At spring flood tide, it's only a few inches below the top of the levee. The Mississippi is a living thing, not just a piece of scenery or a road for boats to travel. It's powerful, and it's mean.

"Look at the land over there. That used to be a rose garden with bushes higher than your head. All gone. Drowned and carried away. Horses and mules and cows and chickens, too. It's a miracle no people were caught. The river broke through a weak spot in the levee, you see. That's what a crevasse is, a breakthrough. It might have started with just a trickle that nobody noticed; then it became a wall of water. It came through and kept on coming, until finally people got the break closed up. By the time they did, the water had flowed—inside the levee—all the way down to New Orleans, and that's more than seven miles."

Philippe's round face had looked stark and drawn when he talked about the disaster. Now the worried frown vanished. He grinned. "Grandpère will tell you it was a sign from God," he said. "The French Quarter didn't get much muddier than usual, but the part of town where the Americans have their businesses was under nine feet of water."

He dismounted, then helped Mary down. "Would you like to sit up here while I go look? You must be feeling rather sore."

Mary shook her head. "I'd rather hobble along with you, if you don't mind. It's fascinating, this whole thing."

It was true. She was intrigued, eager to learn more about the river and the land. Every bone and muscle in her body ached, but she felt wonderfully well. She was free of the heavy weight of angry jealousy and envy, free to enjoy Philippe's comfortable companionship and to learn more about this strange, beautiful world of Louisiana, the kingdom that was her birthright.

"I could hardly tell where the patched-up part was," Mary admitted to Philippe when they were riding back to Montfleury.

"Nor could I. Val told me the new grass had covered it all, but I had to see for myself."

Mary's heart lost a beat. She had not been prepared to hear the name. Philippe continued to talk, unaware of the effect on Mary. "Val believes that the only thing to do is to add more depth and height to the entire stretch of levee along here, starting at his plantation, going along Montfleury and Pierre Sauté's place, where the crevasse was, and on past it all the way to the Soniats'. We're all in a line before the river takes a deep inland bend, and that makes us the most vulnerable. Val has already talked to all the owners. If Grandpère backs him, they'll have to agree."

Philippe chuckled. "Grandpère is a close-fisted old bird sometimes. I suspect he hopes I'll say no. We should have a good loud shouting match when I tell him what I think."

"I'm surprised he'd listen to anybody, even you."

"Oh, it's not me, really. It's me speaking for Uncle Bernard. He's the one who's training me, and he's Grandpère's favorite son. His plantation earns more money per acre than any other in the whole state.

Even Valmont Saint-Brévin's." Philippe was smiling. "When it's my turn to run Montfleury, I intend to give Uncle Bernard some serious competition. I'm not about to let a crevasse destroy my inheritance. Tomorrow I'll talk to Val, and we'll order up some Irish."

"What?"

"Irish. New Orleans has hundreds of them. They'll do the labor. We always use the Irish for that kind of work. Slaves are too valuable. That kind of labor takes all the strength from a man. He's half dead before he's thirty. If he hasn't already keeled over on the job."

Mary looked at Philippe's face. He wasn't joking. And he didn't look like a monster. She thought of her father. He had been just as unfeeling about the servants, she remembered. They were Irish, too. He had also been fiercely antislavery, denouncing the cruel plantation owners of the South.

Mary shook her head, trying to clear it. It was all too confusing, a mystery.

"Headache?" Philippe asked.

She was grateful to have a reason to stop thinking about slavery, inhumanity, master and man, the Irish.

"Just a little," she said, recognizing that it was true. "It must be the sun. I lost my hat when I fell, and the heat always bothers me. I'm not used to it yet."

"My God, I didn't notice." Philippe grabbed the wide-brimmed straw hat from his head and jammed it on hers. "What a rotten, blind creature I am."

Mary felt blind herself. The hat was too big for her; it came down to cover half her vision. "Take your hat back, Philippe," she begged. "I don't need it. We're almost home."

"Of course you need it. You could get sunstroke. Or worse, your skin might be burned. Berthe will have my hide."

Mary protested, but she kept the hat. Her red cheeks were bad enough. She'd despair if her entire face was red. And the headache was getting worse.

Two hours later she was whimpering from the pain. And she was burning with fever.

Everyone thought she had sunstroke. They put Mary to bed, darkened her room, stationed two little slave girls on each side to fan her, and Jeanne spent hours wringing out cloths for her forehead from the bowl of iced water on the table next to the bed. Berthe came to the room four times a day to put butter on Mary's scarlet blistering forehead and nose and cheeks.

Mary was unaware of all of them. She was conscious only part of the time and that consciousness was distorted and demon-filled by fever.

Her delirium frightened Jeanne. She begged her mother to send for the doctor. But Berthe wasn't alarmed. "Sunstroke just has to work itself out. Mary's not in any danger. Dr. Limoux will be here on his regular visit in ten days, but she'll be all well by then, you'll see."

Berthe was right. After four days Mary's fever went away and her mind cleared. She was weak and ravenously hungry.

Jeanne brought her some broth. "That's all you get for two days," she said. "I'm sorry, but those are Maman's orders. Philippe even went to the city for ice cream for you, but she won't let you have it. Do you mind if I eat it, May-ree?"

"No," Mary croaked. Her throat felt swollen shut, and her mouth was dry. She tried to swallow the broth Jeanne fed her, but her stomach rebelled. She shivered, gagged, then vomited. She wanted to apologize, she wanted to cry, but she was too weak for speech or tears.

Jeanne ran to find her mother, but Berthe was not to be found. The kitchen building was the last place Jeanne looked. When Berthe wasn't there, she burst into tears.

"Hush, now, child," the cook said. She put her arms around her and rocked from side to side. "Tell old Charlotte what's wrong."

"Mary's not well at all, Charlotte, and Maman said she would be as soon as she ate some broth. But she can't eat it. She was sick all over herself. Maman has to get the doctor, she has to. And I can't find her."

"She's sent for the doctor already, lamb. He'll be here before dark. And you mustn't worry your Maman about a little thing like a weak stomach. She's got more to think about. Old Hercule is dying. She and your grandpère are with him now. I hope the priest comes soon. He's been sent for, too." Charlotte crossed herself. "Please, God, let the old man die in grace and not make trouble in this house."

Jeanne stopped crying. "What kind of trouble, Charlotte?"

"Nothing that concerns you, chère."

"If it's in this house, it does. What is it, Charlotte? I'm frightened now. My friend is terribly sick and now you say some awful trouble is on the way. I'm scared. I want my mother. I'm going to find her."

"No, you are not. There's nothing to be scared of. Mary's going to be all well any day, and there's no trouble coming. Old Hercule was calling for his grandchild, that's all. And she's too far away for calling. That's all. No trouble."

Jeanne's eyes and mouth were wide open with surprise.

"You think I'm such a baby, Charlotte, but I'm not. There's trouble coming indeed."

"Don't you say nothing to nobody."

"I won't. Not a word."

Jeanne ran from the kitchen to the house and up to Mary's room.

"May-ree, you've got to get well fast. I just found out the most exciting thing. Hercule is asking for his granddaughter to come see him before he goes to God. That's a sacred wish; Maman will have to let her come.

"Oh, May-ree, you've got to be strong enough to come with me to peek at her. She's Papa's mistress that he bought the fancy house for in New Orleans. I can hardly wait to see what she looks like."

# 13

Mary was too weak to resist Jeanne's determination. But she was also too weak to help. A half hour later the younger girl had managed to get Mary only partially dressed. She was trying to lace Mary's corset when the door opened and Dr. Limoux entered, followed by Berthe.

"What are you doing, Jeanne?" her mother exclaimed. "Are you trying to give Mary a relapse?"

Jeanne dropped the laces and jumped away from the bed. "May-ree told me she wanted to get up, Maman. She said it would make her feel much, much better." She curtseyed quickly. "Bonjour, Docteur Limoux."

The doctor nodded his response. "Open the blinds for me, Jeanne, there's a good girl. Let me have a look at our sunstroke here."

Mary attempted to smile at the kind, lined face she saw in the candlelight. But when the shutters opened the sudden brightness made her eyes feel as if they were on fire, and she gritted her teeth against the pain. Dr. Limoux lifted one eyelid with his thumb. The touch made her cry out.

"Sorry, Mademoiselle," the doctor said. He lifted Mary's right arm, then her left, turning each to look at the purple bruises. "How did she get these?" His fingers rested on her pulse.

"She was thrown from her horse, poor child," Berthe said, "the very same day she got the sunstroke. She's had a frightful time."

Dr. Limoux placed Mary's hand gently by her side. His palm rested on her forehead for a moment. "Get this unfortunate young woman out of all these garments and into a loose comfortable nightdress. She'll need at least a week more in bed before she can get up. I don't see any signs of sunstroke. She's recovering from yellow fever."

Berthe Courtenay shrieked, an eerie, high-pitched primitive cry. Then she collapsed, senseless, on the floor.

"Good God, is everyone in this house going to need treatment?" said the doctor irritably. "Jeanne, get some smelling salts for your mother. And a maid to help me get her to her room." He turned to Mary and spoke in a soothing, quiet tone. "You'll be fine, child. I'll make up a laudanum syrup for the pain you're feeling. Make them put some cracked ice in a cloth to rest on your eyes. They'll start feeling better very soon.

"I'm not going to bleed you; you're past the crisis and on the mend.

Just rest and drink as many fluids as you can hold on your stomach. Tomorrow try to eat a little soup and, if you feel like it, some bread soaked in milk. I'll be back to see you tomorrow evening."

He bent over Berthe's sprawled body, then stood erect. "Nothing wrong with her that a tot of brandy can't cure. I don't know why you women insist on squeezing yourselves into those infernal corsets. You can't breathe; that's why you faint all the time." He was still grumbling when he followed the servants who were carrying Berthe from the room.

Mary followed Dr. Limoux's instructions, except for the laudanum. She tried one dose and woke from the drugged sleep feeling sicker than she had before. After that she refused it. By the time Dr. Limoux saw her again, she was sitting up against her pillows eating a rice pudding.

"Youth," he said. "If I could bottle it and prescribe it, I'd be the most successful doctor in the world. You won't need to see any more of me, young lady." He took Mary's hand and bowed gallantly over it; his old-fashioned bushy mustache tickled Mary's skin and made her smile.

A few minutes after he left, Jeanne tiptoed in. "May-ree? What, you're eating? How marvelous. Dr. Limoux forbade me to visit you till now. I was afraid I had made you worse with my foolishness. How do you feel? Can I stay a little while?"

"I'm much, much better. Do stay. Sit here on the side of the bed. I feel as if I've been away for weeks and weeks." Mary was overjoyed to see Jeanne. Her pleasure made her remember the ugly feelings she had had, and she was ashamed of herself. "I'm lucky to have a good friend like you," she blurted. "And your family is so kind to me. I should be more grateful."

"What a cracked egg you are, May-ree. We should all be grateful that you came to us."

"How is your mother?"

"As always. Hurrying around, worrying about every little thing. You must disregard her swoon. She was upset about Hercule's visitor already, and when she heard that you had the fever, it was too much for her."

"I understand," Mary said.

"I doubt that you do. Poor Maman, hers is such a sad story. You see, May-ree, I once had four brothers and four sisters. I was the youngest. The fever came and in two days all my brothers and sisters were dead. I alone did not get it. Maman brought me to the plantation, and she hasn't let me go to the city even once since that day. That was almost twelve years ago. She's deathly afraid I'll die of the fever too. They say Creoles and black people don't get it. But all my brothers and sisters did. It's strange to think that I'm almost as old now as the oldest one was when he died. How I would have loved to know them all." Jeanne's beautiful dark eyes brimmed with tears.

Mary touched her hand. "Don't be sad. You have Philippe. He didn't die."

Jeanne laughed. "May-ree, don't you know anything? Philippe isn't my true brother. Papa adopted him. He's really the son of my uncle François. When Papa's own sons were gone, his brother gave him Philippe. He was a bastard, but Uncle François legitimized him. Still, Uncle François's other children were not very nice to him; Tante Sophie was glad to get rid of him, too. No woman wants to rear the son of her husband got on another woman."

Mary was enthralled. She wasn't sure she could believe a word Jeanne said. The story was too much like the kind of novel she had been forbidden to read. But Jeanne was so calm about it. She sounded no different from when she explained the bloodlines of the horses in the stables. Still, it couldn't be true. Nice people didn't do things like have illegitimate children. Mary tried to laugh. "Jeanne, you are wicked. I almost believed you."

"May-ree, you wound me. Of course I am telling the truth."

"You couldn't know things like that. You were only two years old, you said so yourself."

"But Maman talks all the time about the lost brothers and sisters. She has miniatures of them all, with their names engraved on the frames. You may see them if you like. They were beautiful children."

"All right. I'll believe you had brothers and sisters who died. But I won't believe that Philippe is . . . that word you said."

"A bastard? But he isn't, May-ree. His papa made him legitimate in the law. And my papa made him his son in the law. People do such things all the time. Everyone knows about it."

"Who told you?"

"I don't remember. Maybe I heard it. I hear many things that people don't tell me. Like Papa's mistress. I'm not supposed to know. Oh, I do hope she comes to see Hercule. Dr. Limoux says that Hercule had an apoplexy. He'll live a little longer, but then he'll have another and he'll be gone. Maman and Grandpère were arguing about it last night. Grandpère wants Hercule to be granted his dying wish, and Maman says she won't allow that woman to set her foot on the floor of the house she lives in. It was a fine battle. Grandpère was shouting so loud that the chandelier rattled. He'll probably win. He usually does."

"Jeanne, I think I'll rest now. Go away for a while, please."

Jeanne kissed Mary's cheek. "You know, May-ree, sometimes I think you are many years younger than me. I heard Papa say exactly that about Americans. They are all children. Go to sleep, American baby." Mary could hear her giggle as she left the room and closed the door behind her.

Mary rearranged her pillows, closed her eyes. But sleep wouldn't come. Jeanne's revelations, the easy chatter about mistresses and bastards, had disturbed her. Mary and her friends at the convent school had giggled and sighed and daydreamed about love, about beaux and weddings and doll-like babies. One girl repeated what her married sister had told her about husbands and babies, but they rejected the story with horror. They had never talked about sexuality, beyond a chaste, romantic kiss. But Jeanne Courtenay's stories were filled with sexuality. Her personality, her curiosity, her vibrant nature were all heavily colored with sex. Because of her, Mary had begun to feel sensations and emotions that were unfamiliar and alarming and irrepressible, no matter how much she tried to tell herself that they did not exist.

She remembered Jeanne touching herself, caressing her breasts, talking about Valmont Saint-Brévin's hands on them. And she tentatively moved her own hands to her body. She was surprised by the softness of her own flesh, by the sudden stiffness of her nipples. There was a pleasure she had never before experienced, dual sensations of delight in the skin of her palms and in her breasts. She felt as though she had discovered a secret and lamented the lateness of her discovery even while she explored it. She opened the buttons of her nightdress with fingers made clumsy by eagerness. When her hands touched her bared breasts she gasped at the piercing ecstasy of skin against skin. Her hands moved to her shoulders, her throat, her sides, her breasts again. Warmth traveled along her spine, then tingling chills, then warm and cold mixed together, alternating, fluctuating, making her breath catch in her throat, bringing tears of unnamed emotion to her eyes.

The pleasure was too great. It became a frantic inner demand that twisted her body from side to side and brought involuntary moans from her throat. The intensity of her passions terrified her. Mary threw her arms wide, rejected her own touch and the sensations it released. She stared at the sheer white netting of her bed's canopy. Her legs and arms were trembling, her chest rising and falling with short greedy breaths.

In time her vision cleared. Her trembling subsided, her breathing became normal. She was very tired.

I don't understand what I felt, what I did, what it means, she thought, on the edge of sleep. I'll figure it out when I wake up.

"Psst, May-ree, wake up, hurry. Look, I've brought coffee with my own hands. With milk, nice and foamy and hot, just the way you like it, May-ree. Come on, wake up."

"What is it? What do you want?"

"Here. Take your coffee. Maman will be here any minute. Oh, May-ree, such excitement. The house is in a stir since dawn. Maman is going to visit her sister in Baton Rouge. She's had trunks brought down from the attics, and she's throwing gowns and shoes all over her room. She's in a fearful hurry. That can only mean one thing. Papa's mistress must be coming.

"I know what's going to happen. She'll be looking for me next to tell me to pack, too. But I won't go. I'm longing to see the woman.

"So this is what you *must* do, May-ree. You must beg Maman to let me stay with you while you are still so weak. I shall beg her, too. We can both cry, just a little bit.

"Then she won't make me go. I'm sure of it."

Jeanne was mistaken. A little before noon, she, her mother, two maids, the coachman, four horses, a buggy, two grooms, four trunks, and six valises were taken aboard a steamer that had responded to the hail from the levee in front of Montfleury. Mary waved goodbye from the upper gallery. Berthe Courtenay had agreed that Mary was too weak for a journey. And, Berthe thought privately, there was no shame or loss of dignity for Mary to be in the house when That Woman came. She was not a member of the family.

Mary went back to her room and her bed, as Berthe had instructed her to do. A maid brought her lunch, broth and a bowl of pudding and a pot of coffee. Mary was still hungry when it was all gone.

This is absurd, she thought. I don't feel ill, and I'm tired of being in bed. I'll get dressed and go down to the dining room. Grandpère will be eating, and there's sure to be enough for me, too.

She was weaker than she anticipated. It took her a long time to get her clothes on and her hair arranged. When she reached the dining room it was empty; the table was cleared; only a residue of appetizing smells gave evidence that there had been a meal. She decided to go to the kitchen in search of the remains.

The sunlight in the yard struck Mary like a hammer. She staggered and put her hands over her eyes. Go back in the house, go back to bed, she told herself. But she had made up her mind to get some food. She stumbled toward the glaring whitewashed brick building.

"Don't go in there, Mademoiselle." A slim arm reached out from the shadows under the fig tree. It caught Mary across the chest and blocked her unsteady progress across the yard.

"Who's that? Let me go." Mary peered into the shadows.

A young woman stepped forward. "You can't go in there," she said. "The old man is dead, and his people are grieving." Her voice was cold and stern. Her bearing and her expression were haughty, disdainful. She was the most exquisite creature Mary had ever seen.

Her thin short nose was like a model of perfection in planes. It drew the eye down its sharp clear ridge to a mouth with chiseled curved outlines surrounding lips that looked as if they were stained with the juice of strawberries. Her eyes were dark, nearly hidden by thickets of long tangled black lashes. Above them were narrow black eyebrows arched like rainbows. They were startlingly dark against her pale skin. It had the color and the sheen of magnolia petals, like rich cream turned into satin.

Until that moment, Mary had thought that Jeanne Courtenay was the most beautiful girl in the country. Now she knew that Jeanne was pretty. Beauty was grander, more regal; it was a degree of perfection that made one doubt its reality. Beauty was this young woman facing her now.

Mary was so shocked that it took almost a full minute before the meaning of the girl's words reached her understanding. "Dead? Hercule? I'm so sorry. He was very kind to me." She turned back toward the house. "Naturally I won't intrude."

Then she remembered. "Did his granddaughter come, do you know? He wanted so badly to see her. Did he get his last wish?"

The girl's extraordinary lips parted. But before she could speak her attention was diverted. Clementine and another woman were coming out of the kitchen. Both were weeping loudly. Clementine had to support the weight of the grief-stricken figure with her. "May God and all the saints and the Blessed Virgin forgive me," she screamed, "he asked for me, and I came too late."

"Does that answer your question?" said the girl to Mary. She glided quickly across the yard with her arms extended to embrace Hercule's stricken granddaughter.

She moves like tall grass in the wind, thought Mary, and her dress sounds like wind through the grasses. The deep rose silk was the same color as the girl's lips, she noticed, as were the soft leather slippers on her tiny feet.

Mary forced herself to look away from the scene of grief. She was ashamed of her longing to have a good look at Hercule's granddaughter and her disappointment that Clementine's sheltering arms hid her from view.

She was also embarrassed to realize that she was still very hungry.

Then a new thought drove her hunger away. I wonder if that girl is the daughter of the granddaughter. If she is, then she's the daughter of Jeanne's father; she's Jeanne's sister. She must be. She does look like Jeanne, only so much more beautiful. No wonder Berthe took Jeanne away. It would be terrible if the two of them ever met.

What kind of complicated world is this place, this foreign French tropic New Orleans?

# 14

Hercule was buried the following day. Mary attended the funeral at Grandpère's command. "We'll hold you up, Philippe and I. Hercule was a good man, and all the whites on Montfleury must be there to show proper respect."

Mary looked around the plantation chapel with quick furtive glances. The fantastic girl wasn't there, nor her mother. Clementine was the primary mourner, seated in the first pew together with men and women and children whom Philippe identified as Hercule's children, grandchildren, and great-grandchildren.

"Perhaps even great-greats," he whispered. "I can't keep track of all the connections among Montfleury's slaves."

Mary could understand. The small chapel was filled, all the pews, extra chairs, and every inch of floor where a person could stand. There must be three hundred people here, she thought. I had no idea there were so many. What do they all do? How big is Montfleury?

She asked Philippe later when they were back at the house. "I don't know exactly," he said. "Grandpère keeps all the books and records himself. He won't even have an overseer, and he's told me a dozen times that I can just wait until he's dead to see them. I'd guess it's about eight hundred acres, a thousand if you count the swamp.

"As for the slaves, most of them work in the fields. Sugarcane takes a lot of attention. There are some specialists, blacksmiths and such. A plantation is like a little country. It has everything it needs within its own boundaries. Except wine for the gentlemen and fripperies for the ladies. They come from France."

"Would you show it to me, Philippe? I'd like to know about it."

"Would you really?"

"Yes, I would. Like the crevasse. I like to learn things, see them for myself."

Philippe grinned. "Think you can stay on your horse?"

Mary made a face. "Think you can remember you're not on a racetrack?"

He stuck out his hand. "Deal."

Mary shook it. "Deal."

"I'll have to ask Grandpère, of course. Nothing happens without his permission. And ladies don't usually go far from the house. You know, Mary, that's what I like about you. You're not like a normal woman at all." He left her and walked over to the corner of the gallery where Grandpère and the priest were drinking a punch.

"I guess that's a compliment," Mary muttered. She didn't know whether she was pleased or insulted.

A few days later she decided that she was definitely pleased. She saw Philippe in the company of "normal women."

The hooting from the packet boat was the first warning that guests were arriving. Simultaneously two little black boys ran onto the gallery shouting, "A boat's turning in."

After that, all was pandemonium for more than a week.

The guests were Grandpère's son Charles and his daughter Ursule. And their families. Charles's wife was also named Ursule, and Ursule's husband was Jean-Charles. There were also nine of their children, four of them married, three of the four with children. Mary never did get all the names and relationships straight.

"You will have to take Berthe's place," Grandpère told her, "you're the lady of the house." Then he walked toward the levee and the arriving guests.

Mary ran to find Clementine, shouting "help!" Clementine did more than help. She took over. Within seconds servants were scurrying to put fresh linen in bedrooms, fill washing pitchers, cut flowers for bedside vases, and bring hams and bacon from the smokehouse, ice from the icehouse, wine and whiskey from the storeroom, milk and cream from the buttery.

"You put on a big smile, 'Zelle Marie, and greet everybody. I'll be right behind you to whisper where their things should go. Charlotte's got coffee making for sure, and there are plenty of those cat's tongue cookies. Don't fret yourself. This house knows what to do with company ... It sure misses Hercule, though. You ask Monsieur if he's fixed on somebody for butler yet. Nudge him in the direction of Christophe if you can."

The guests streamed up the allée like an incoming tide. Mary had to plant her feet firmly on the floor to keep from running away. They inundated her. She was kissed on both cheeks by the women, kissed on the hand by the men. "But look, Charles, she is just as Berthe described her in her letters ... So charming ... Such excellent French ... Not at all American..." Exclamations of delight and admiration pelted Mary from all sides. She had never in her life heard such enthusiasm and vivacity.

A half hour later Philippe strode into the drawing room where everyone was feasting on an array of cakes and sweet wafers plus innumerable tiny cups of black coffee.

"I just learned that you were here," he said. "Forgive me for being away when you arrived."

"Philippe!" everyone cried, and there was a maelstrom of embraces.

Eventually all aunts, uncles, cousins had been greeted. Philippe took a coffee and stood near a window. Within moments he was surrounded by a rainbow of prettily gowned girls. Mary watched them vie for his attention. They giggled, peeked over fluttering fans, made cooing sounds of admiration about his jacket, his boots, his whiskers, his opinions. How silly they all are, Mary thought, and how false. If that's what "normal" women are like, I'm glad I'm whatever I am.

She saw Clementine in the doorway, beckoning for her. "Excuse me," she said to the woman who was telling her about the teething problem one of her children was suffering.

"What is it, Clementine?"

"We got to make some plans."

"I've never been so tired in my life," Mary complained to Philippe that night at dinner. Silently she blessed Clementine for arranging that he sit next to her. She needed a friend amidst all these strangers.

"You'll get used to it very soon," Philippe promised. "After all, this is a normal Creole gathering. At Uncle Bernard's we're always twenty or thirty at table."

Mary looked down the long table. It looked more natural surrounded by people than it did with only one end occupied. Leaves had been added, she noticed. Now it filled the space in the huge room the way it should be filled. This was what the room had been built for, the colors of the ladies' gowns, the sparkle of jewels on their throats and hanging from their ears, the glowing light of candles in the tall, twelve branched candelabra, refracted in the ponderous crystal-hung chandelier, reflected in the massive gilt mirrors.

The room was alive with laughter, with animated conversation, the clink of silver forks and knives against porcelain, the pure, clear ringing of tall-stemmed glasses touched in a toast. These were people enjoying themselves, loving life, loving one another. Mary saw the Courtenay chin on face after face, dimpled in the women, cleft in the men, repeated again in the portraits that looked down on the gathering.

This is a family, a New Orleans family, Mary realized. Her heart leapt. Somewhere there was one like it, one that belonged to her. Perhaps they were all together around a table like this at this very moment. Perhaps they held wineglasses high with strangely elongated fingers, their badge of kinship like the Courtenay chin.

They are mine, she thought, and they're close by, I just know it. Soon I'll be with them. It's August now. Only ten more weeks, and the summer will be over, everyone will return to the city, and Mademoiselle Sazerac will find my people for me.

Celeste Sazerac caressed the painting with her mad eyes. It was a portrait of a beautiful woman in an elaborate gown of gold brocade. Her unusual fingers held a fragile lace fan.

It is mine, now, she exulted. Her tiny, possessive smile was inhuman. Mine, the fan that opened at the royal court, that spread its lace to fascinate a king. Mine, as it should always have been. Mine at last. My treasure, with all the other treasures of the casket. My treasure and my secret.

No one will ever know. That foolish American creature will rot at Montfleury with that imbecile Berthe who comes to the city only once a year. They were so easy to trick, so eager to do my bidding. Fools.

She covered her mouth with her hand. She must not laugh aloud. No one must guess at her happiness, her triumph. She had defeated her sister at last, taken her casket, destroyed her daughter. It was so sweet, sweeter yet after the years of waiting. God sent me this revenge, she thought, and despite her hand, a sharp, hawklike cry escaped from her mouth.

She removed it and spoke aloud. "It is mine, and no one will ever take it away from me. I would stop at nothing to keep it. Nothing."

# 15

"It seems so quiet now that they've gone," said Mary. "I wish they could have stayed longer."

"I don't. It held up the work on the levee. We couldn't do anything because of all the promenading and picnicking." Philippe was decidedly out of sorts.

Mary drank her coffee in silence. The leaves had not yet been removed from the table; she felt small and lonely when she looked at the expanse of polished wood. And useless. Managing the entertainment had been a lot of work, even with Clementine's direction, but it had been exciting. Now she had nothing to do.

She glanced at Philippe. She'd like to ask him if he knew when Jeanne and her mother might be expected to return from Baton Rouge.

But he was reading a newspaper. He probably wouldn't know anyhow. She should have asked Grandpère. But he had left the table when breakfast had barely begun, anxious to check the cane after the hail-bearing thunderstorm that had come in the night.

Everybody has business to attend to. Except me.

She stole another look at Philippe. There was a tiny triangular patch of stubble on his chin that the razor had missed. Mary wondered what it would feel like to touch it. Her fingertips prickled at the thought.

What's wrong with me? Where do these strange ideas come from? She knew she had been dreaming a lot, although she didn't remember the dreams. Once she had waked up with her hands cupping her breasts. And, much as she scorned the flirtatiousness of the cousins, she had tried using a fan the way they did, watching herself in the looking glass, finally giving up because she was sure she looked absurd.

Philippe likes me, I know that, Mary said to herself. I wonder how much. Does he want to kiss me? Would I like it? She peeked at him again. His mouth was plump, like the rest of him. It would be soft. She touched her fingers to her lips to test their softness. They were chapped. She'd have to rub ointment on them.

"Mary." She started at the sound of Philippe's voice. Could he have guessed what she was thinking?

"Stop woolgathering, Mary. I'm talking to you."

"Well, then, say something. What is it?" She couldn't look at him.

"I'm riding over to the sugar house. Would you like to go? You look as if you're bored to death."

"I'd love to." All the unsettling thoughts evaporated at the prospect of something to do. "I'll run up and put on my riding things. I'll only need a few minutes."

"Take your time. I'll be at the stables having a smoke."

After that, Mary was too busy for idle, disturbing speculations. Grandpère had agreed to let Philippe show her the workings of the plantation, and every day was a new experience, a new education.

And if she dreamed, she wasn't aware of it.

The sugar house was at the far end of the plantation. To get to it, Philippe and Mary rode along the "street" between the slave cabins, and through the fields of cane.

Philippe nodded to the group of old black men and women who were sitting on rocking chairs under the shade of a huge, moss-hung oak tree in the middle of the street.

"And the filthy abolitionists say the blacks would be better off if they were free," he said to Mary. His voice was almost a snarl. "Those slaves haven't done a lick of work in years, but they still get fed and clothed and doctored. They'd starve to death on their own."

Mary was careful to stay quiet.

And then she saw the cane, and she couldn't have spoken if she wanted to. It was like a green wall ahead of them at first. As they drew nearer, she could see over the top of it. It seemed to go on forever, to her right, her left, ahead of her. It was awesome.

"This way," said Philippe. "Keep a tight rein; horses hate the cane, watch out yours doesn't try to bolt." He led the way into a narrow opening between the tall stiff green growth.

As soon as they had gone a few yards, Mary felt like bolting herself. Their passage made a rustling, rattling sound amid the cane on each side. It surrounded them, as high as their shoulders. Insects flew upward from the leaves, agitated by their intrusion, and Mary felt near panic when they touched her face and neck. She blew puffs of breath through her nose to keep them away. The horses' hooves sunk in the wet soil, made sucking sounds when they lifted. Mary thought wildly about quicksand. Overhead the sun blazed in a cloudless sky. The cane seemed to capture the heat, hold it, surround her with it, fill it with moisture from the earth, turn it to clinging invisible steam.

Philippe called back over his shoulder. "Isn't it magnificent?"

"Oh, yes," Mary answered.

And then she realized that it was, in truth, magnificent. The growth was so thick, so vast, so luxuriant. It was the embodiment of vigor, of living.

It excited Mary. She felt part of it. She blew away the insects and wiped her steamy, sweaty face on the sleeve of her jacket. "Magnificent," she shouted, laughing with the joy of being young and alive and in Louisiana.

The sugar house was disappointing. After the vitality of the cane fields, it seemed dead and clammy. It was a big brick building with a tall chimney, set in the middle of a big uneven square of hard-packed earth made slippery by rain.

Mary looked around her at the great empty space of the brick-floored storage room and shuddered. "It's lifeless," she said. "I think I'll go outside."

"'Lifeless'? You're crazy," Philippe said. "This is the heart of the plantation. Look here." He caught her wrist and pulled her into the adjoining room. "Look at those kettles. Come autumn they'll be full of cane juice, boiling and making the air hot and sweet. The press will be turning, crushing the juice out of the cane, and men will be hauling cane in one side of that big room and more men will be bringing it out this side and feeding it to the press. Night and day, crushing and boiling, first one kettle then another and another until it's so concentrated that it will granulate when it cools. Tons of cane and thousands of gallons of syrup. It's like a beehive, men working until they drop and singing, dancing while they work. How can you call it 'lifeless'?"

"Sorry." Mary's voice was meek. She looked at the immense kettles, each big enough to hold four people, and at the tremendous cylinders that rolled against one another to crush the cane. "Everything is too big, Philippe. I can't imagine people in connection with all this. It's sized for giants."

"I forgive you. You'll have to come again when the people and the cane are here. Then you'll see. There's nothing like it. And when it's all over, the whole building rocks with the celebration. Master and slaves and their wives and children. There's feasting and music, dancing, shouting. It's a sight to see."

"I'd love to see that. When will it be?"

"Every plantation is different. It depends on how big the harvest is and how fast the machinery works. We all start cutting cane in October. Uncle Bernard generally finishes sugar making by Christmas. Grandpère usually aims for mid-January, I think."

"It takes that long?"

"You saw the fields, Mary. There's a lot of cane. It has to be cut, then stacked, then brought on wagons to the sugar house. And then processed. It all takes time, even if nothing goes wrong, and there's plenty that can go wrong. It's a wild time. I love it. You will, too, if Grandpère lets you see it."

Mary nodded, smiled. Privately she thought: I won't be here to see it. I'll be with my family. It does sound exciting. Maybe they have a sugarcane plantation too. I'd like that. I'd like to see the wild time.

"I've seen what I came to see," said Philippe. "Let's go. I have to find Grandpère in the fields to report to him. You ride on back to the house."

"Can't I go with you?"

"No. This afternoon you can go with me if you like. I have to see the cooper about making some new barrels and hogsheads. You might be bored."

"No, I won't. I promise."

And she wasn't bored. Not at the cooper's, not at the smithy and the carpenter's shop the next day, nor at the wheelwright's, the tanner's, the nail foundry, the gristmill, or the brick kiln on subsequent days.

For the first time, she felt a sympathy for Grandpère. If she were ruler of this fascinating kingdom, she'd refuse to give it up, too.

Then, all at once, it was over. The adventure of discovery and learning, of riding with Philippe, talking and laughing and listening to his plans for changes and improvements when he became master of Montfleury.

Grandpère was having a toddy on the gallery when Mary and Philippe walked from the stables. "Christophe," he shouted, "bring some coffee. Sit down, you two. The mail packet came an hour ago. There's a letter for you, Mary, from Jeanne. She'll tell you that she's coming home tomorrow. I received one from her father. He's bringing Berthe and Jeanne back from Baton Rouge."

He shook a finger at Philippe. "As for you, my fine young fellow, you'd better get back on your horse. While you were out taking inventory of my property Saint-Brévin came looking for you. The Irish have arrived at his place. Better get over there before they're all too drunk to use a shovel."

"Hurrah!" Philippe shouted. He dashed down the steps and away.

Mary barely noticed that he had gone. In an instant she forgot the happy hours with him. They were erased when Grandpère said the name Saint-Brévin. He was here, Mary cried inside, and I missed him. This time I would have spoken to him, thanked him for rescuing me from the brute who hit me. I could have done it, I know I could. I would have been the lady of the house, just like when the family was here. I would have poured coffee and offered little cakes. Then I would have said, "Pardon me, Monsieur, but I must tell that we have met before. You were my knight"... no, that's wrong... "you were..."

"Mary," said Grandpère. "Are you going to take this letter or not? I don't propose to hold it out to you forever."

"May-ree, I am so happy to see you." Jeanne ran down the gangplank from the steamer and threw her arms around Mary's neck. She kissed her on both cheeks, then again and yet again.

"Did my letter reach you? I'm sorry it was so short. I meant to write pages and pages with all the marvelous news, but then one of my cousins came and dragged me away to a party. Baton Rouge is like a dream, May-ree, always some gaiety, and I was such a success. My aunt Matilde says that the earth must be covered with broken hearts when I leave.

"Come. Let's go to the house and tell secrets. Did you miss me dreadfully? Were you horribly lonely? Did you quiver when Grandpère growled? Did you fall madly in love with Philippe? Did he with you? Why don't you speak, May-ree? Don't you love me anymore? Why are you laughing at me? It isn't kind."

"You haven't given me a chance, Jeanne. Baton Rouge hasn't changed you at all, except to make you prettier than ever."

"Do you really think so? I do too. I'm sure it's because I bloom in society. I don't belong in the country, cooped up with dull old people ... Grandpère! How much I've missed you. I'm so happy to be home again."

After she received her grandfather's stately kisses, she beckoned to Mary and darted up the stairs to her room. "Aaagh, help me get out of this hideous travel costume, May-ree. It is so sensible. I despise it."

Her voice was muffled for a moment in the folds of her dark blue dress, but Jeanne did not stop talking. Mary had never seen her so exuberant.

"It's like a dream come true, May-ree, and all thanks to you. Imagine, Papa came to Baton Rouge in a fury. Maman had sent him a most terrible letter saying that she would live ever after with her sister because Papa shamed her by allowing his mistress to go to Montfleury. He was going to drag Maman home by the hair, I believe it.

"They had such a quarrel. I didn't even have to put my ear to the door, they were shouting loudly enough for the whole house to hear. I learned so many delicious things! When Maman took me away from New Orleans because of the fever, she told Papa that she wouldn't give him any more babies because she couldn't bear to see them die. And he told her that he didn't care because Amarinthe—that's his mistress—would give him all the babies he wanted and that she cared more for him than Maman ever had or ever would. They dragged the whole thing up again, breaking the china ornaments in Aunt Matilde's best visitors' room and making as much noise as a steam whistle. It was thrilling!

"You never thought of me at all, Papa said, you only wanted someone to father your children. And Maman said that wasn't true, that she loved him more than life itself and that all those years on the plantation were hell—she said 'hell,' May-ree—hell for her because he hardly ever came out from the city and she knew that he was with That Woman.

"Then Papa shouted louder than ever. 'What did you expect when your door was always locked?' And Maman started to cry. It wasn't locked since three years, she said, because she'd had her change.

"What does that mean, May-ree, her change? Do you know? No? I don't either. I'll have to find out... Anyhow, after that Papa bellowed loud enough to rattle the windowpanes. 'You always cry. I can't talk to you when you cry.' And Maman boohooed like a banshee. 'I was writing you a letter,' she said, 'telling you that at last I saw the error of my ways. I was asking you to let me come back, to live in the city again, to be husband and wife.'

"Papa shouted 'What?' and Maman cried harder than ever and said she'd stayed up all through the night writing the letter but before it was finished she learned that Papa's mistress was on her way to Montfleury. So she burned the letter and trampled the ashes into the hearth rug.

"Then Papa said 'What?' again. 'What was in the letter?' And Maman said what she'd said before. Then he started to boohoo just like

Maman. There was a lot of 'darling heart' and 'dearest love' and kissing noises, but they weren't shouting any more, so I couldn't hear it all. I did hear the best part: Papa promised to whip Amarinthe and leave her forever. And I heard the part about you, May-ree. Maman said that when she learned you had the yellow fever, she understood that she was wrong to hide me from it because it could always find its way if it was meant to be. So you see, May-ree, it's because of you that Maman and Papa are together again. Wait until you see them. They hold hands and sigh at one another. Old people like them. It's very touching.

"And now we'll move to New Orleans in time for All Saints' Day. I'll be introduced to society; Maman is writing to Paris to order my gown. If Baton Rouge was so delightful, imagine what New Orleans will be like! I'm the happiest girl in the whole world, and you did it all, May-ree. You're my special personal angel!"

# 16

September, to Mary's surprise, was even hotter than August. Everything slowed down. Birdsong was only sporadic, as if singing were too great an effort. Animals and men moved sluggishly, and their moods were irritable. Even the mighty river looked as if its current had succumbed to the general torpor.

In contrast, the rainstorms were more active than ever. The clouds built up in the faded blue sky with startling rapidity. Then they darkened, flashed with light inside themselves, and burst in an abrupt torrent of water and barrage of lightning and thunder.

The relief from the heat was momentary. The storms ended as suddenly as they had begun, leaving the air saturated with moisture that the sun quickly heated.

Even Mary gave in to the demands of the climate. Her French dictionary became mildewed, and she made no effort to continue Jeanne's lessons. She found that it required the strongest effort of will to move at all, even to lift an arm. She felt like crying all the time, and she began to believe that summer would never end, that every month would only be more oppressive than the one that preceded it. Jeanne fussed at her and teased her and tormented her. "Stop being such an American," she said. "Pay no attention to it, and the heat won't bother you." Mary tried. She forced herself to ride with Jeanne to the levee once.

But she wouldn't go again. The sight of the Irish laborers depressed her too much. There were men of all ages, their bare backs red from sunburn, their faces set and determined under the knotted bandanas that protected their heads. They stepped away from their work to let the young women and their groom ride by. Mary could hear their labored breathing in the few seconds rest that the interruption gave them. "No one should have to work like that under this sun," she said. "I can't bear to see it."

Jeanne was not bothered at all. She continued to ride every day. The levee was Valmont Saint-Brévin's project, she reminded Mary. "I'm bound to meet him there sometime."

Jeanne's only interest was romance. She talked incessantly about the hearts she had broken in Baton Rouge, the number of beaux she would attract in New Orleans. Her self-absorption got on Mary's heat-jangled nerves.

Occasionally she talked about romance for others, and that irritated Mary even more. Jeanne was determined to make Mary and Philippe fall in love. She prattled about how handsome he was and how rich he would be someday and how much he admired Mary. When Philippe was there, she praised Mary to him with the same extravagant disregard for truth. The result was that the easy relationship that Mary and Philippe had enjoyed was ruined. They became stiff and embarrassed in one another's company.

In mid-September he left to return to Bayou Teche. He wasn't needed for the levee work, he said, and he was needed for the cane at Uncle Bernard's.

Mary was relieved to see him go. Then she missed him. She blamed Jeanne, and became even more short-tempered. It was difficult to keep herself in check, especially when there was quarreling all around her.

Grandpère and Jeanne's father Carlos turned meals into battles. The old man stormed that bankers were parasites who drained the planters of their profits. Carlos responded with accusations that the world didn't begin and end at the boundaries of Montfleury where the eighteenth century was still hanging on. Berthe tried ineffectually to soothe both of them.

Soon Carlos, too, took his leave. "I look forward to seeing you in New Orleans," he said. He kissed Mary's hand and called her his "benefactress" for restoring his daughter to him. In spite of the daily quarreling, Mary was sorry to see him go. He had been very entertaining company, when he wasn't with Grandpère. Carlos Courtenay was a good-looking man, seemingly much younger than his fifty-four years. He had graying thick hair and laughing dark eyes and a slim, elegantly dressed and booted form. He was something of a dandy, with heavy lace ruffles on his sleeves and carved sapphire rings on his manicured fingers. He liked to gesture when he talked; he was an excellent raconteur, and he knew it. In the afternoons, he took coffee on the gallery with the ladies. His jewels and lace made graceful languid arcs while he amused them with drawling monologues. He told stories about his youth, the escapades he had led his brothers into, the near-disastrous consequences, their narrow escapes. He recounted the tamer gossip of the city: the flamboyant competition between the fencing instructors, with matches on the street for all to see, and to make wagers on; the races between steamboats that terrified their passengers and four-footed cargo; the two brothers who fought a duel over which had the better tailor; the exploits of a troupe of Italian acrobats who were the stars of the theater in the American sector until it was discovered that they were also the thieves who entered houses over the rooftops. He made Jeanne and Mary laugh, and his wife looked on with adoration. She cried when he went onto the packet boat and continued to cry until it was out of sight.

Then she dried her eyes, blew her nose, and led the way back to the house. "There's a great deal to do if we're going to be ready to move to town next month," she said. "I've got to see if the trunks need airing, and the rugs all have to be brought down from the attic and beaten before they go back down. The sewing room must be gotten ready for the dressmaker next week, and I've got to find those pearls and send them to be restrung. Then I have to remember to..."

"Maman never changes," Jeanne whispered to Mary.

Berthe's energetic preparations for the move were like a trigger for a change in the entire household. With October approaching, Grandpère was out at dawn, inspecting the cane fields and all the equipment and supplies for the upcoming harvest. He returned, elated, for breakfast, with the announcement that the yield would be the best he had ever seen. Every added day in the sun made the cane sweeter. It seemed to have the same effect on him.

On them all. Mary was sure that the heat was less oppressive, although the thermometer registered the same. She was preoccupied, as were Berthe and Jeanne, with daydreams of New Orleans.

Berthe pictured the tremendous amount of work involved in redecorating the big townhouse from top to bottom, and her lips curled in a happy smile of anticipation.

Jeanne saw herself in the center of a circle of handsome men, all pleading to be allowed to put his name on her dance card, and she hummed a joyful waltz tune.

Mary's imagination drew pictures of herself in dozens of variations of her meeting with her family and their loving welcome.

On October second there was a thunderstorm with a crisp edge to its winds. When it ended, the sky was bluer, and a steady cool breeze set the leaves of the bougainvillea dancing.

Mary felt like dancing herself. For the first time in many weeks, she was able to believe that there really would be an autumn and that her family would be found.

The Courtenays had been like a family to her, she realized, and she had not even thanked them for it. You're rude and selfish and ungrateful, Mary MacAlistair, she said to herself. Change your ways at once.

I will, she answered herself. I'm going to be different. In the fresh, cool air, everything seemed possible.

She thanked Berthe for her many kindnesses, she apologized to Jeanne for her surliness, and she threw herself wholeheartedly into the interest that occupied both of them to the exclusion of all else: Jeanne's début into society.

It wasn't difficult for Mary. She was confident that she, too, would be presented by her family as soon as she found them. It didn't matter that all the gowns, the pearls, the attention, everything was for Jeanne. Her turn would come. Until then, like Jeanne, she could listen for hours to Berthe's descriptions of what was going to happen.

"We'll take you to the Opera. All New Orleans will be there. Everyone always goes to the Opera. We'll have a box, of course, and there'll be a servant in knee breeches standing in a rear corner next to a table with champagne and wafers. We'll arrive in good time before the curtain rises. Then we'll take our chairs. You will be in front with Papa. Everyone will see you, so beautiful in your white Paris gown next to your father, so handsome in his evening clothes. That is the presentation for young ladies of the best French families.

"During the intervals, we shall receive visitors in our box. Friends and family who usually visit know they are not to come until the fifth or sixth interval, at the earliest. Because the beaux will be there, beginning at the first instant of the first interval.

"Your Papa will meet each one at the door to the box and offer him a glass of champagne. Then he will present him to me . . . and then to you."

Berthe smiled at her memories. "There is such excitement. Men hurry from box to box, everyone looks to see who is calling on whom, how long he is staying, how many beaux are calling on each girl. You, my darling, will be like a flame for the moths. A beauty of the finest family who has never been seen in town before. We will present you on the opening night of the opera season. No need to wait for an evening when no other girls are making their débuts. Opening night is for the girls who are vying to be known as the belle of the season. You are certain to win."

After one of Berthe's most ecstatic reminiscences of the Opera, Jeanne got out of bed near midnight and tiptoed to her mother's bedroom. She opened the door very quietly and entered with her finger crossing her lips in the universal signal for silence. When she had closed the door carefully, she ran to her mother's bed, climbed up on it and hugged her violently.

"I'm so very happy, Maman."

"I, also, my baby."

"Only . . . two things."

"Tell Maman."

"My dress isn't here yet, and the Opera is only three weeks from now."

Berthe brushed Jeanne's soft cheek with her fingers. "Three weeks is a long time, my angel. It will arrive. Don't worry. I promise you. What is the second thing?"

"It's May-ree. Can she go with us to the Opera?"

"Oh. Oh, dear. It hadn't crossed my mind."

"She believes that she's going, Maman. I don't know what to tell her."

"In that case, we'll have to take her. She's a sweet girl; it would be nice to give her a pleasure. We just won't take a maid. Mary can sit in the back in her place."

"Thank you, Maman." Jeanne kissed her mother and climbed down from the high bed. When she got to the door, she turned and came back to Berthe's side.

"Maman, what's going to become of May-ree?"

"I don't have time to think about that now. She can make herself useful in the house. There'll be invitations to answer and write, things like that. Later I'll see about finding her a post as companion or governess, just as she is here. She's a clever girl. She'll soon see that life is much more formal in town, and she'll learn her place."

# 17

The day had come at last. A perfect autumn day, too, with a warm sun and cool, nippy air. A great day for a journey, even a journey in the old-fashioned carriage that Berthe preferred to the packet boat. Mary and Jeanne were too excited to sit still. They bounced with the lurches of the carriage, caroming off the quilted padding with childish giggles. When they grew tired of the game, they began to sing. First the French songs that Jeanne had taught Mary, then the English songs that Mary had taught Jeanne. When the songs were over, the carriage was entering the narrow streets of New Orleans.

Ignoring Berthe's protests, the girls hung their heads out the windows, Mary on one side, Jeanne on the other. They wanted to see everything.

"Look . . . oh, look . . . ," they called to one another. They exclaimed over the houses, blue, white, green, pink, and over the rich aromas when they passed the open inviting door of a coffee house, and over the women on street corners selling candies or cakes or fruit or coffee. The carriage turned onto a broad tree-lined double avenue, and they marveled at the handsome mansions of stone and brick on each side. With a crack of his whip the driver turned the horses, and they rode into the dimness of an arched stone tunnel in the middle of an imposing brick house.

"We're home," said Berthe.

In the parklike strip in the center of the street, a black-draped figure scuttled into the deep shade of a tree opposite the Courtenay house. Celeste Sazerac steadied herself against the thick trunk until her heart stopped racing. The sight of the carriage turning into the porte cochère had surprised her; Carlos seldom entertained and never used a carriage. When she saw Mary MacAlistair's face at the window, she became ill from the shock.

How could it be? The miserable girl was supposed to be out of sight on the plantation forever. What should she do? There must be some way to protect herself. Protect the casket.

She stood as still as stone, thinking, for several minutes. Then she walked briskly to the corner, turned, walked, turned another corner, continued through the old streets in a pattern that led her eventually to an alley that few people dared enter. She crossed herself hastily and stepped into the dank, noisome pathway.

What a goose I was to be nervous, even for a second, Mary thought. There's nothing to be afraid of. Everything is wonderful, more wonderful than I could imagine.

Her first view of the Courtenay city house had frozen her with remembered terror. Directly ahead of the tunneled entry was a garden, and for an instant she was back, on the Fourth of July, arriving with Miss Rose.

"Come on, May-ree," Jeanne had called, and the grip of memory was broken. This courtyard was bright with sunlight and color and friendship. Mary ran to it, exclaimed at the beauty of the mossy, splashing fountain, the great clay pots holding trees covered with immense pink hibiscus, the mounds of ferns that grew at the base of the rosy brick walls.

The curving staircase from the courtyard to the floor above was under the roof of the house but open on one side to the scents of the garden, separated from the sweet air only by a waist-high tracery of arabesques in wrought iron. It invited and welcomed Mary to the heart of the house, with its high ceilings and windows, crowned with scrolls and waves of white plaster highlighted by gleaming gilt. Everything was fresh and airy and beautiful.

There was a balcony, too, like the one she had glimpsed with the beautiful family on it. A maid served coffee there, and Mary became part of the scene that had so stirred her. She smiled at Jeanne and Berthe, at the street below, at the carriages passing, the people walking, the charcoal vendor who offered his wares with a song:

Charbon de Paris
De Paris, Madame, de Paris

After coffee Berthe instructed Jeanne to put on her bonnet and pelisse. They had to go, she said, to the cemetery to prepare the family tomb for All Saints' Day.

For Mary it was as if a cloud had passed over the sun. This was a day for celebration and joy; there should be no thought of death, no talk of tombs. Yet still, she asked to go along. She wanted to learn everything about New Orleans.

And she found that she had been silly again.

The cemetery was like a busy, cheerful village. Mary stared, unbelieving. There was no sadness here. The tombs were like little houses, set on streets; the streets were full of people, mostly women, who were talking and laughing as if they were at a party. "I don't understand," she said to Berthe.

"It's our custom here to visit our departed loved ones on All Saints' Day, Mary. We bring flowers as gifts that symbolize eternal life; we also make a gift of the labor of our hands. Before that day, we clean and whitewash the tombs. It makes a more beautiful resting place for the flowers."

Berthe smiled. "It also gives everyone who's been away all summer a chance to see friends and catch up on all the news."

A woman who was coming out the gate looked at Berthe, then looked again. "I cannot believe my eyes," she cried. "Is it really you, Berthe? I haven't seen you since last year this time. Is it true what they're saying? Are you moving back to the city? My dear, embrace me. I'm so delighted." She kissed Berthe on both cheeks, then called back over her shoulder. "Hélène, just see who's here. It's Berthe Courtenay. She's come home."

Berthe turned to Mary. "We're about to be engulfed," she said. "You understand, Mary, that only the family washes the tombs. Would you like to go back to the house with the carriage?"

"Thank you, Madame, I'd rather stay and look at everything. I'll walk around if I may."

"Of course. We'll meet back here at the gate when it begins to get dark. The carriage will be waiting then... Hélène, how beautiful you look. And how is your dear mother? Is she with you today? This is my little Jeanne... Madame Desprès, Jeanne, your father's cousin's wife... Agathe, hello..."

Jeanne waved goodbye to Mary. Then she disappeared into a cluster of ladies.

Mary wandered, looking at tombs, looking at faces, looking always at the gloved hands of the women scrubbing, weeding, whitewashing. Perhaps she would see hands like her own. Her grandmother might be the woman over there, with the lace apron covering her black silk gown ... or that one, who looked as if she had been crying... or the white-haired lady on her hands and knees humming a bit of Mozart.

Some children playing tag came racing around the corner of a gleaming white marble tomb, like a miniature Greek temple. They bumped into Mary, begged a hasty pardon, and ran on. She smiled at their high-spirited laughter, at the fat black nursemaid who was trying to catch them.

She had no idea that she was standing only a few inches from the tomb where her grandfather was buried. SAZERAC was carved on the pediment above the Ionic columns. The tomb needed no cleaning. Celeste tended to it weekly, as if every Sunday were All Saints' Day.

Mary noticed the name, and she thought of Celeste. She must have already been here, all the tidying is done. She must have seen friends, talked to them, just as Madame Berthe is doing now. She may have already found out who I am!

A radiant smile brightened her face. While she continued to walk through the busy old cemetery, many people smiled in return. It was a rare, inspiring experience to see happiness incarnate.

Mary was puzzled by many things she saw while walking around the cemetery. On the way back to the house, she asked Berthe to explain them.

"Why is there a fence dividing the cemetery, Madame Berthe? Why are there no regular graves and grave stones?"

"The Protestant tombs are separated from the Catholic. And there is a section just for black people. But everyone has tombs above ground. Think about the river, Mary. It's higher than New Orleans sometimes. And the swamps are all around us. If you dig a hole more than two feet deep, the bottom will fill with water. I've been told that in the earliest days the settlers did bury their dead; they had to put stones in the caskets to stop them from floating. Tombs are the only sensible answer."

"They're very grand, though. What do poor people do?"

"They use the ovens. Didn't you notice the walls around the cemetery? They're really tiers of small tombs. Families can buy them or, if they really have no money, they can rent."

Mary shuddered. "Why 'ovens', Madame? Surely the dead aren't burned in them."

"Not usually. They're put in as in any tomb, and the entrance is bricked up. At the end of a year, the bones are pushed to the back of the oven, and the old coffin is burned. That makes room for the next burial. Of course if the tomb is rented for a year and then the renters don't lease it again, the contents are burned altogether. The new renter doesn't want to bury his dead with some stranger's bones. But that's not why we call them ovens. The opening is shaped like one; that's where the name comes from."

Jeanne spoke for the first time. "I think it's horrid to be talking about dead people and tombs and graves. I hated going to that awful place. I don't want to die, ever." She was whining.

Berthe was uncharacteristically stern with her only child. "We all die, Jeanne, according to God's plan for us. For the living, it is important to be able to remember the dead and to do something for them. It makes up for all our failures while they were with us. Tomorrow we will finish the cleaning. And the following day, we will make our tombs beautiful and we will pray to all the saints to make eternity a paradise for those we loved and lost. You'll concentrate on your prayers for the souls of your brothers and sisters instead of pouting the way you did this afternoon."

"But Maman, my gown hasn't arrived from Paris. How can I think about anything else?"

"You can, and you will, and I'll hear no more about it." Berthe turned away from her. "What else did you want to ask, Mary?"

"There were inscriptions on many tombs that said, 'Dead on the field of honor,' and 'Killed in defense of honor.' Were there wars with the Indians, or did the men of New Orleans fight in wars in Europe? I know that the American Revolution didn't involve Louisiana because it was French."

Berthe shook her head and sighed. "Men are not practical like women, Mary. Especially Creole men. Their tempers are as touchy as gunpowder. The 'field of honor' is the dueling ground. I know of young men with everything to live for who have lost their lives in a quarrel over an accidental spill of coffee on a sleeve. I will never understand it."

Jeanne interrupted, her voice back to its normal brightness. "Philippe says that Valmont Saint-Brévin is the best fencer in all New Orleans. He's been the victor in lots of duels since he came back from France. Philippe says that everybody goes to watch, that it's better than the horse races."

"Philippe shouldn't be filling your head with such nonsense... Thank goodness, we're home. I'm going to lie down for a while before dinner. The smell of whitewash always gives me a headache."

Mary heard the suppressed tears in Berthe's voice. She felt a tightening in her throat. What must it be like to know that eight of your children were buried behind the stones you were washing?

"Madame Berthe," she said quietly. "I admire the ladies of New

Orleans greatly. You all have servants, but the hardest work you do with your own hands for your family."

Berthe patted Mary's knee. "Thank you, my dear. Now let's go inside."

Carlos Courtenay was waiting for them in the drawing room. "Welcome home, my dearest Berthe."

Mary saw sorrow fall from Berthe like a discarded cloak. Her head and shoulders lifted, and her step became light and gliding when she walked to greet her husband.

Jeanne ran to him. "Papa!" She threw her arms around his neck.

Carlos staggered. "Such exuberance," he said. He kissed her cheeks. "You must have guessed what I brought home. All that joy can't possibly be caused by seeing a tired old banker."

"Oh, Papa, is it here at last? Where? Where is my gown? I have to see it at once." Jeanne rushed to her mother. "I was a wicked girl, Maman, and I apologize. I'll be ever so much better now. Tomorrow I'll pray until my knees are raw. May I try on my gown now, Maman? This very minute?"

There was no resisting her.

It was the first Paris gown Mary had ever seen. She understood at once why Paris was the Mecca for women's fashions.

It gave an impression of artlessness, of youth and innocence. The wide skirt was a floating cloud of white silk gauze as weightless as gossamer. Beneath it were petticoats, layered so cleverly that they gave body to the skirt but not an added millimeter to the tiny circle that was the waist. Each petticoat was edged with white horsehair for stiffening, and each was an individual work of art. The top one was made of lace, as fragile as a spider's web, in a design of lilies of the valley. Beneath it was a shimmer of delicate satin, and below the satin a waterfall of wide crinoline ruffles. The bottom ruffle of the crinoline was covered with the same lace as the topmost petticoat.

The lace was used again for sleeves, round as globes, puffed by brilliantly designed folds of sheerest silk organdy, and for a ruffle that edged and accentuated the deep curving neckline and the soft rounded shoulders it bared. Appliqués of lily of the valley covered the silk bodice, making diagonals with their leaves to emphasize a tiny waist and glowing with the gentle richness of the pearls that made their flowers.

There were also white silk stockings clocked with tiny embroidered leaves and silk slippers with fans of lace on the instep held by a narrow buckle of seed pearls.

An oval box covered in white brocade held a comb for the hair. It was a bouquet of lilies of the valley, the leaves of minute green beading and the flowers pearls suspended, quivering, from silver wire.

Jeanne was, for the first time in her life, unable to speak. She looked at the gown and its accessories with an expression of awe. Then she looked at her mother. There were tears in her eyes.

Berthe embraced her daughter for a long wordless moment.

Then, Berthe rang for Miranda, sent her to fetch warm water, and said, "Tell Clementine I want her, too. Both of you, wash your hands thoroughly before you come in."

She smiled at Jeanne. "You, too, Missy. Don't touch anything until you do."

Jeanne was herself again. She snatched the comb from its box and danced to the looking glass. "Will I have a hairdresser, Maman, to make me look beautiful?" She tucked the comb into the braid that crowned her head.

"Of course you will, but you won't wear the comb. Perhaps a white ribbon, nothing more. We'll take off the flowers and use them in the center of your fresh bouquet."

Jeanne pirouetted. "Mary, is that not the most dazzling gown in the history of the world? Are you sick with envy? Can you forgive me for owning it? I would never, never forgive you if it were yours."

"Truly, Jeanne, I'm happy for you, not jealous, although it is without question the most beautiful gown, and you will be the most beautiful woman in all New Orleans."

Mary was completely sincere. She was sure that she'd find her family at any moment now, and she was so happy that she wanted Jeanne—and everyone else—to have her heart's desire, too.

"I am magnificently, exquisitely, perfectly happy," Jeanne sighed.

"I wish I were dead and in that horrible tomb," Jeanne sobbed. "I've never been so miserable."

The gown did not fit.

"My darling," Berthe said, "it's not the end of the world. Just look, everything is perfect except the waist is a little too large. We'll let out the lacing on your corset, and..."

"And I'll look like a cow," Jeanne wailed.

"May I see?" Mary asked. "Stand up straight, Jeanne, and hold still."

"Why should I? My life is ruined."

"Because I think it can be taken in, but I have to see for certain."

Berthe wiped her eyes. "I thought of that at once, Mary, but it's no use. There's only one woman in New Orleans who could do it, Madame Alphande, and she's much too busy with the gowns she is making."

Mary peered closely, walking around Jeanne. "I could do it," she said. "I learned fine embroidery from the nuns."

"Oh, May-ree! You are the best friend in the world." Jeanne wiped her streaming eyes with her palms. "Aren't we lucky, Maman, to have May-ree with us in our time of need?"

Berthe didn't know what to say. She didn't believe that Mary could do such delicate work, but she didn't want Jeanne to despair. She played for time. "We are lucky indeed," she said.

Her agreement was an absentminded response. She was thinking about the amount of money that might be enough to persuade Madame Alphande.

The next morning both Berthe and Jeanne were astonished. The gown was fixed, the alterations invisible, the embroidery indistinguishable from the artistry of the Paris specialists. Mary had done it during the night.

"I cannot believe my eyes," Berthe said. "You're more skillful even than Madame Alphande, Mary." Jeanne showered Mary with kisses and gratitude.

Mary's smile made the shadows under her eyes barely noticeable.

But not to Berthe's motherly eye. She sent Mary off to bed.

It took only a few seconds for her to plunge into a deep, satisfied sleep. She heard nothing when the shouting and keening began in the courtyard.

Carlos stalked out to the stair landing. "What is the meaning of this?" he shouted. "Stop it at once."

The servants were huddled together, several on their knees, praying loudly with entreating hands raised toward the skies.

"Felix, come here at once," Carlos said. He walked down the first four steps.

Felix, his valet, ran stumbling to stop him. "Stay, Michie Carlos, go back." Felix's voice was hushed and quaking. "Gris-gris," he said.

Berthe had come to the top of the stairs behind her husband. She put her hand to her heart, and she fainted.

Gris-gris was the visible token of a voodoo curse.

# 18

The young woman walked as if she owned the sidewalk, or, as it was called in New Orleans, the *banquette*. She did not look down at the uneven bricks; her head was held high and proud, and her eyes looked straight ahead. Her lithe body adjusted smoothly to the treacherous footing, never lost its distinctive seductive movement; rolling hips and thrusting breasts belied the demureness of the simple blue chambray dress that buttoned down the front from her throat to its hem at her ankles.

Her face was striking. Light brown skin gave evidence that there was a preponderance of white blood in her veins. High cheekbones and a bronze undertone bore witness to at least one Indian ancestor. Her lips were sensuous, full, naturally red. Her gray eyes were startlingly pale.

She wore large, heavy gold hoop earrings and a bright red tignon. Observant watchers could see that it was folded and knotted to make seven points.

And there were many watchers. But they looked at her furtively, with quick sidelong glances, or not at all until she had passed, when it was safe to watch and admire her.

Because she was Marie Laveau. The seven points were the badge of dreaded royalty. She was a voodoo queen.

Her mother's name was also Marie Laveau, and she was *the* voodoo queen, recognized by all as the high priestess of the ancient religion, the sorceress who received power directly from Zombi, the snake god. And yet, there were those who said that her daughter's powers were even greater, that when she led the secret rites in the secret place, the presence of the god was stronger, more terrifying, more maddening in the wild orgiastic ceremonies that transported all the devotees to the realm of the god.

And so, when Marie Laveau approached, people moved out of her way and only the boldest looked. The banquette was hers as she covered the blocks of Rampart Street.

When she turned onto Esplanade Avenue, her walk did not alter, but the reaction to her passage was different. The black men and women still made way for her with deference and fear. So did some whites; one woman quickly took her child's hand and crossed to the opposite side of the street. But several white women stared curiously, and two white men looked at her with open appreciation and lust.

Marie Laveau ignored them all. She walked to the Courtenay house and rang the bell.

She smiled at Firmin, the butler, when he opened the door. She had beautiful, even, very white teeth. "Your master asked me to come," she said. Her light eyes were amused.

"Naturally I don't believe in any of that sacrilegious nonsense about voodoo spells," said Berthe to the friends she was entertaining. "I was quite irritated with Carlos when he said he intended to actually call on the woman. But, as he said, the servants were in such a state that we would probably have been served cold coffee and burnt bread for days if we hadn't done something to calm them down. They're all so superstitious, you know."

"What did she do, Berthe?" "What did she say?" "What did she look like?" Berthe's guests were all leaning forward eagerly, while their coffee cooled in their cups.

Berthe laughed uneasily. "She picked up the gris-gris. None of the servants would go near it or let any of us touch it. But she just picked it up and put it in the cotton drawstring bag she carried. Then she took out a bunch of twisted papers and went from room to room, opening a twist in each room and scattering different colored powders in the corners. I suppose I'll have to clean them up myself."

"What did the gris-gris look like?"

"Nothing at all. It was just a black ball. It looked like wax."

There were nine women calling on Berthe, all of them middle-aged, all with the characteristic look of Creole aristocracy. Three of them fumbled in their reticules for vials of smelling salts. The other six touched the crucifixes they wore on chains around their necks.

Berthe, too, knew that a ball of black wax was one of the strongest of all gris-gris. Purportedly, it always contained at its center a piece of human flesh. But it was important to maintain the universal pretense that no white Catholic placed any credence in the heathen beliefs of the blacks. She spoke quickly, and she laughed, even though the laugh was nervous.

"There's always a silver lining," she said. "I hate to think what Carlos must have paid the woman, but at least I'll be getting his money's worth. I persuaded her to do Jeanne's hair for the Opera. Even out at

Montfleury, I heard that she's the best hairdresser in the city."

"Berthe, you are clever!" "I tried to get her for my Annette, but she said she was busy." "Have you heard about the new soprano this season? They say she had thirty curtains at least every time she sang in Paris..."

The conversation veered into normal gossip. Outside the door Jeanne gently closed the crack she had opened and ran up the stairs to the room she shared with Mary.

She tiptoed in. Mary was getting dressed.

"Good! I'm so happy you're awake, May-ree. It has been so exciting here while you were asleep. I'm bursting to tell you all about it."

Jeanne's eyes were bright, almost feverish. She related the events of the morning; the discovery of the gris-gris, her father's abrupt departure, the arrival of Marie Laveau.

"She's so strangely beautiful, May-ree, not like anyone I've ever seen. I do believe she's a voodoo, no matter what Maman says. Her eyes are no color. I'll just bet they turn red or green or anything she wants. And she knows everything. She knew my name, and yours, and the names of all the servants. That just has to be magic.

"Best of all, she's going to do our hair. I'll bet you she puts some magic oil or something in it; I'm going to ask her to make mine a kind of irresistible perfume so that all the men will fall in love with me. You'll talk to Maman for me, won't you, May-ree? You occupy her while I whisper to Marie Laveau."

Mary was shocked. "Jeanne, you'd better pray before the altar right this minute. It all sounds like blasphemy. Magic and devils and gris-gris and voodoo. Shame on you."

"Pooh, May-ree, don't be so American. Everybody believes in voodoo at least a little bit. Miranda has told me stories..."

"Miranda's just a poor, ignorant slave."

"She's just as Catholic as you or me. She knows other things, too, that's all. Besides, I whitewashed my fingers to the bone while you were asleep. Maman and I were hours at the cemetery. We'd barely got home in time to change clothes before Maman's friends started pouring in.

"You know, May-ree, there's always a bad side to the good things. I'm dying to be presented so that I can be courted. But the minute I'm in society, I'll have to call on those old ladies and receive them with Maman. I'll probably go crazy from boredom."

"Maybe their sons will come with them."

"I hadn't thought of that. Of course they will. They won't be able to stay away because of the magic spell in my hair."

"Jeanne! I'll pray for you to all the saints tomorrow."

They went first to the cemetery and then to mass. And they went on foot. Mary was overwhelmed. "It's as if the streets were rivers of flowers," she cried. Everywhere, on every street, people were walking just as they were, with arms holding massive bouquets of white chrysanthemums. They formed irregular processions, all going to New Orleans's ancient cemeteries and their sparkling, freshly washed tombs. The currents of flowers merged at every intersection, becoming fuller, spilling out eventually onto the banquettes that led to the cemetery gates, themselves a sea of flowers in buckets and baskets and the hands of black women offering them for sale.

What a beautiful, magical place is this New Orleans, Mary thought ecstatically. My home. The devoted dressing of the tombs, the beauty of the soft creamy white flowers on the hard whiteness of marble and stucco, the dedication of the people to the memory of their dead—everything combined to erase the shock she had felt when Berthe Courtenay spoke so easily about the necessary disposal of old bones to make way for new.

Saint Louis Cathedral was crowded, colorful, joyful, and reverent with music and incense and candles. Mary could barely keep her mind on her prayers; she was tempted to look over her shoulder, to be sure her eyes weren't playing tricks. There were black people, men and women and children, worshiping together with the whites. Not in a gallery or in the rearmost pews, but throughout the cathedral. And no one behaved as if this was an unusual event. Only she. She couldn't stop herself from looking all around her.

Surely this was what God wanted, what was meant to be. And it was normal here. She remembered the things she had been told, had heard from the nuns, from the abolitionists at her father's dinner table, and she wished they could all be in the cathedral. New Orleans is different, she wanted to tell them. New Orleans is heaven on earth. There's no injustice here, only beauty and kindness.

Everything is a surprise, a happy surprise. One after another.

When mass was over, Mary found more surprises waiting for her. Outside the cathedral the air was filled with the scent of coffee and a mouth-watering aroma she couldn't identify. There were black women on the wide banquette cooking on gleaming copper heaters filled with glowing charcoal. Coffee. Bubbling, frothing milk. And the source of the delectable smell.

"Calas," sang the woman who was making them. "Belles calas... tout chaud... tout chaud... tout chaud... belles calas..."

Carlos Courtenay touched Mary's shoulder. "They're rice cakes, and they're delicious. We'll all have some." Again Mary observed that she was the only person who seemed to find it unusual to stand and eat in public after mass. At least half of the people leaving the cathedral went at once to the women with the stoves.

While they ate and drank, they talked; groups formed, dissolved, formed again with different members. Berthe was greeted by group after group of friends who were happy to see her in the city again.

The only person who was not caught up by a cluster of friends was a woman with bright red hair who walked too quickly to respond to anyone with more than a nod. She skirted the crowd and strode to a windowless and doorless brick building opposite the park that was directly across from the cathedral. The buzz of conversation faded; everyone was watching her. When she disappeared into the building, the buzz recommenced, more animated than ever.

"Who was that, Papa?" asked Jeanne.

"That, my dear, is the most fantastic woman in all New Orleans. She is the Baroness Pontalba."

Mary and Jeanne stared at the doorway that had swallowed the red-haired woman. Nobility and titles were only found in novels, they had thought.

Carlos Courtenay told them nothing more about the Baroness Pontalba. He knew her history; everyone in the French Quarter knew all about her. But he didn't think the story suitable for the ears of innocent young women.

# 19

She was born Michaela Leonarda Almonester in November 1795. Her father was Don Andrés Almonester y Roxas, a nobleman from Andalusia who had come to New Orleans twenty-five years earlier as an official of the Spanish Royal government that then owned the Louisiana territory. Wealthy when he arrived, Don Andrés multiplied his fortune many times over in the colony.

He was generous, and he loved his adopted city. When the great fire of 1788 destroyed the cathedral, he paid for the rebuilding and for a new building next to it, intended to be a home for the clergy. On the other side of the cathedral the city wanted to build a home for the government. Almonester lent the money for it and supervised the work.

He also built a chapel for the Ursuline nuns, a retreat outside of town for lepers, and a new Charity Hospital when a hurricane severely damaged the old one.

During the fifteen busy years of increasing his fortune and improving his city, Almonester was too busy to devote much attention to his personal life. Then he realized that he was sixty years old and had no family. He married the daughter of a French colonel. Ten years later a daughter was born. Michaela. Three years after her birth, Don Andrés died.

Michaela was the richest heiress Louisiana had ever known. It made no difference that she grew up headstrong and willful. Dozens of families made overtures to her mother about a marriage with one of their sons. But Almonester's widow was more ambitious. She made a marriage contract for her only child with the only child of a French nobleman who, like Don Andrés, had served in the Spanish government in Louisiana and had multiplied his fortune there before returning to France. The name of Michaela's husband was Joseph Xavier Celestin de Pontalba. He was known as "Tin-Tin," and he was the adored and dominated darling of his parents.

Tin-Tin and his mother traveled from France to New Orleans for the wedding in 1811. He was twenty years old. Michaela had just completed her education at the school of the Ursuline nuns. She was fifteen. The two young people had never met, but that was not unusual. The marriage united two great families and two great fortunes; personalities were irrelevant.

The voyage to France was their honeymoon trip. Both mothers accompanied them, and New Orleans believed that it would never see them again. Both families owned a great deal of property in the city, plus plantations outside it, but absentee landlords were common. Bankers acted as managing agents.

Word came from France from time to time over the years. Michaela and Tin-Tin's dramas gave New Orleans food for delighted gossip and speculation. Michaela didn't care for life in the Pontalba chateau, it was said. It was too isolated, deep in the country, far from the gaiety and excitement of Paris. It was easy for everyone to imagine the battles that the chateau must have witnessed. Michaela was accustomed to having her own way, and she had the temperament traditional to women with red hair.

Nevertheless, by all reports she was doing what a wife was supposed to do. There were three children, all boys.

But apparently motherhood did little to soften her nature. It was learned that Tin-Tin had left her. The men of New Orleans said that it was only to be expected: Michaela had never been a beauty, and she had a temper besides, whereas Tin-Tin was extremely good-looking and could surely find comfort elsewhere. New Orleans's women agreed among themselves that men were selfish, uncaring brutes. Michaela's mother had died years before, leaving the stupendous Almonester fortune to her, and now her husband was probably spending it buying jewels and love nests for pretty, empty faces while the mother of his sons languished in a dank stone castle.

Then there was a reconciliation.

Then Tin-Tin left again.

And again, they were reconciled.

And suddenly, in 1831, Michaela appeared in New Orleans. She had left him. It was rumored that she was trying to get a divorce, a scandalous idea. Callers descended in droves upon her cousin's house, where she was staying. They found that Michaela, now thirty-five, was even less pretty than she had been as a girl. But it no longer mattered. She was extremely chic, and her willfulness had become forcefulness. She was an impressive woman with wide knowledge of politics, art, literature, and business and strong opinions based on that knowledge. She was fascinating and terrifying.

No one was sorry when she completed her examinations of her holdings in New Orleans and left for a trip to Havana. Her energy was exhausting for everyone around her. It was much more entertaining to talk about her than to talk with her.

Many months later she was back in France; she and Tin-Tin were officially separated, and Michaela was at last living in Paris. She entertained lavishly and had a large circle of friends, reported people from New Orleans who attended her soirees when they visited Paris on trips abroad. Some of her friends were outrageously bohemian, they thought, but Michaela was obviously happy in her new life. The dramas were over, it seemed.

But the greatest was yet to come. Just before Christmas in 1834, her cousin Victoire Chalmette received a letter that was so shocking it could hardly be believed. It was written by a servant. Michaela was unable to do more than dictate it; she was bedridden, recovering from four bullet wounds in the chest. Her father-in-law had shot her. Then himself.

Michaela Almonester was now the Baroness Pontalba. Tin-Tin had inherited the title on his father's death.

And she was the most famous woman in all Paris. She recovered from the wounds in her chest, but she bore the mark of the murder attempt for all to see. The first finger of her left hand was gone, the third hideously mutilated. That was the hand she held up toward the Baron when she begged him not to shoot her.

Soon New Orleans could read about her attempt to divorce Tin-Tin. The affair was so scandalous that the Paris newspapers reported the details of her suit, Tin-Tin's countersuit, and the testimony in the many hearings that occupied the next four years.

The newspapers also carried long descriptions of the fabulous *hôtel particulier* she was building on the Rue du Faubourg Saint-Honoré. She had hired the most admired architect in France, and her demand for perfection was so extreme that she bought a mansion and had it demolished in order to use some of its wall panels for her new house.

Finally, in 1838, both her divorce and her house were finished, and the Baroness Pontalba vanished from the pages of the Paris newspapers.

The "library" on Royal Street regretfully returned its subscriptions to the number of copies bought in the years before the near-murder. The Baroness had increased sales more than six hundred percent.

New Orleans was reduced to occasional accounts of entertainments at the hotel when travelers returned from Paris visits. An entire generation grew up with no knowledge of the garish life of Michaela Almonester de Pontalba. Then, in 1846, her name was again on everyone's lips. She wrote to the Municipal Council. She intended, she said, to restore the Place d'Armes to the grandeur it deserved as the center of the Vieux Carré.

Her father had built the cathedral and the buildings flanking it. She, Michaela, was going to make the other buildings on the square equally imposing. The property belonged to her, and she would turn the crumbling shops and taverns and tenements into a unified architectural creation. She would also restore the square to the beauty that had eroded over the years. She would make a New Orleans adaptation of the Palais Royale in Paris.

If the city would agree to release her from taxes on her properties for twenty years.

In the French Quarter there was no thought of rejecting the Baroness's offer or her demand. The despised Americans were putting up bigger, grander buildings every year in the area above the dividing line at Canal Street. Here was an opportunity for the French to reestablish their rightful position as arbiters of taste and elegance, to prove to all that the heart of New Orleans was still where it had always been, at the Place d'Armes.

The Council replied at once, granting the concessions the Baroness wanted. The French waited eagerly for her arrival. All the old stories were resurrected, and, more than ever, everyone wondered what she was really like.

Their curiosity mounted for two years. And then she arrived. Still red-headed, but the red was unnaturally bright now. Still overflowing with energy, but the slim body was thicker and slower at fifty-four. Still fascinating, frightening, elegantly stylish, arrogant, forceful. She was even more than her legend. She attracted and repelled at the same time. She seemed capable of anything. It was even possible to believe now the rumor that everyone had rejected all those long years before: the old Baron had not killed himself at all, some whispered. The true story was that Michaela, with blood spurting from the four gaping wounds in her chest, had advanced upon him and wrested the pistol from his hand. Then she had shot him twice in the head.

Carlos Courtenay looked at his daughter's animated young face. She was such a child and so innocent. He thanked God for it.

"A real baroness!" Jeanne exclaimed. "Do you know her, Papa? Shall I be able to meet her?"

He smiled and shook his head. "I don't think so, my dear."

"Imagine, May-ree, a real baroness. I wish I could have seen her close up. Do you suppose a title makes a person look different? I do think it was mean of Papa to make us come straight home. We could have walked past the place she went in. I might have seen her."

"Maybe she'll be at the Opera."

"But of course she will! How clever you are, May-ree. I'll be too nervous to look for her, though. There will be lots of beaux, won't there? I'll be the prettiest of everybody, won't I?"

Mary had never heard Jeanne question her success before. It was a surprise to learn that Jeanne had any doubts at all. "You'll have armies of beaux," she said. "I'm absolutely sure of it."

"But will Valmont Saint-Brévin be in the armies, do you think, May-ree? If he doesn't come to our box I don't care about the others."

Mary was caught off guard. She hadn't heard that name for a long time, hadn't thought of Valmont. She would have said that she'd forgotten all about him. But when she heard his name so unexpectedly, her heart raced.

"May-ree!" Jeanne's cry forced her to collect her treacherous thoughts. She pushed away the pictures of Valmont's dark eyes and hair, the ring on his strong, graceful hands, his lazy smile...

"Monsieur Saint-Brévin is sure to come, Jeanne."

"I'll die if he doesn't. I know I'm a silly, May-ree, and my head is turned by every man who flirts with me. But that's all for fun. Valmont ... that's different. I love him, I truly love him. I always will, to the day I die. Even a silly can truly love someone. Do you really believe he'll be there? That he'll call at our box?" Jeanne had tears in her beautiful eyes.

Mary hugged her. "Your mother says that everyone in New Orleans goes to the opening of the opera season; he's bound to be there. And when he sees you in your Paris gown, he'll be the first one to come to the box."

Jeanne's smile was radiant, the tears gone. "You're right," she said. "I'm terribly beautiful in that gown. And you fixed it for me. How clever you are, May-ree, and the best friend in the world." She leapt up from the settee, ran to the mammoth wardrobe. "We haven't chosen a gown for you to wear to the Opera. Come see what you would like. Nothing that you have is elegant enough. How about this blue one? I've only worn it one time. Blue looks horrid on me, but it should be nice with your hair.

"Isn't it exciting, May-ree? We'll have a proper hairdresser to do wonderful things with our hair.

"Do you know, with the sun coming through the window on you, your hair looks almost red. Like the Baroness." Jeanne giggled. "I do wonder why Papa says I can't meet her. Do you suppose she's very, very wicked? If I were a baroness, I'd feel free to be as wicked as I liked. I know! I'll bet she's a fallen woman. I'll bet she has a lover.

"I'm being a silly again. All I ever think about is love. Why don't you, May-ree? Don't you want to fall in love?"

Mary smiled. "I am in love. I'm in love with New Orleans."

It's true, she told herself. And it's enough. I don't need to think about . . . him.

Valmont Saint-Brévin walked through the doorless door of the big brick building on the Place d'Armes. "Michaela," he shouted. "Where the hell are you? You're supposed to be giving me luncheon at your house, not inspecting your accursed real estate. You treated me a lot better in Paris."

# 20

The Baroness Pontalba poured coffee into a delicate porcelain cup and handed it to Valmont. "The decanter is at your elbow, Val. Pour yourself a *digestif* if you like."

"Just coffee, thanks. I like to leave my palate with memories of the excellent soufflé. As usual, a superb meal, dear Baroness."

"Yes, he does well, my chef. I had to pay him a fortune to leave Paris, but it's been worth it. I cannot abide the Creole cuisine."

"I confess, I rather like it. I used to have the spices sent to me in France, but I never found anyone who knew how to use them."

The baroness laughed. "I remember. You brought me a packet as a gift the first time you visited. You were endearingly provincial."

"I was young and homesick. You were very good to me, Michaela. But you never gave me gumbo." Val smiled, thinking of his first weeks in Paris. He was thirteen then, away from home for the first time, sent to the university by the grandfather who reared him after the steamboat explosion that killed his parents. Michaela's son Alfred was in the same group being tutored before taking entrance exams, and he took Val to meet his mother because she was from New Orleans. She had only recently returned from visiting there. It was 1832.

"In those days, dear Val, you would have spit it out. You didn't remain provincial very long."

"Every green youth should go to Paris. It's the ideal place to reach manhood. Rapidly."

"I do recall that you wasted no time. Alfred was terribly envious. His allowance wasn't large enough to keep a ballet dancer."

"It was an actress first, from the Comédie Française. I told my bankers I was taking lessons in Molière."

"Rogue."

The Baroness and Val exchanged nostalgic smiles. During the years Val was growing up in Paris his friendship with Alfred had gradually blossomed into an even closer friendship with Alfred's mother. Despite the twenty-year difference in their ages, Val had become the Baroness's equal in intelligence and sophistication. Her son had never reached that elevated level.

Michaela took Val's cup and refilled it. "I had a packet of letters yesterday. You can start making plans soon. Louis Napoleon has the Communists well under control, according to the people that know. We'll be able to go home to Paris next year. Personally, I think he should simply shoot the rabble and be done with it. I'll never forgive the idiots who let the revolution get started in '48. I had to run for London with barely a change of clothes."

"But you took your chef."

"My dear! One can always find a dressmaker."

"I escaped via Lisbon so that I could take my trunks. One cannot always find a tailor. Actually I rather enjoyed the revolution. All the shouting and shooting and banners waving. It reminded me of July Fourth celebrations in New Orleans. It reminded me that I was overdue to come back. I'm going to stay, Michaela."

The Baroness was not easily surprised, but Val had done it. She stared open-mouthed at him. Then she shook her head as if to clear it. "Why?" she asked. "You've told me you hate it here."

"I do and I don't. I hate the absurd pressures. Every hot-headed boy thinks he can prove he's a man by forcing me into a duel because of my reputation as the best there is. That means I have to keep up my practicing so that I can stay the best. I don't want to get killed. And I need all my skills to keep from killing them without humiliating them. It takes a lot of my time, and it's boring. There's no challenge.

"It takes a lot of time to keep away from the belles, too. I'm not a hermit. I want to go to balls, opera, dinners. But I'm too damned rich and eligible. The eager maidens flock around me, longing to be compromised so that I'll have to marry one of them. The fathers are worse. They can't decide whether they'd rather have me propose or find some insult to their daughters so that they can challenge me to a damn duel.

"There's hardly a place in this city where I can relax and feel comfortable, Michaela, save for your drawing room."

"Then go back to Paris, fool," said the Baroness. "Why stay here?"

Val stretched his long legs out in front of him. He stared at the tips of his boots as if he might find an answer there.

"There are things I like," he said. His voice was low, musing, almost as if he were talking to himself. "My grandfather died shortly after I returned, and I found myself the owner of a sugar plantation that had been deteriorating for thirty years. It's a challenge to repair the damages, to make it run the way it should. My God, Michaela, it's like being a king. I can decide what to do or not do. My word is the law. I can experiment with new ideas, new methods. It's the biggest battle I've ever been in, because I'm up against nature. I can be beaten by a hailstorm, a break in the levee, an early frost. I've gambled all my life, but never against such unpredictable odds. It makes my blood race. The tables at Baden Baden never excited me as much.

"There's something else . . . something I can't quite identify, something about the way people live here. In the French quarter, that is; the Americans are altogether different. The French seem to know how to live, they're aware that they're living, somehow. I can't explain it. It's as if they have a common secret, something they all know that makes life satisfying."

"My poor Valmont. You don't find life satisfactory?"

"Don't patronize me, Michaela, I beg you. I told you that I can't explain it. There's a mystery that I sense is worth discovering an answer to."

"Very intriguing. Of course you're mad."

Val grinned. "Perhaps. I enjoy it."

"Ah, well, as long as you are having pleasure. I've known you to enjoy lunacy before. Do you hear from the Baronne Duderant?"

Val's grin widened. "You are malicious, Michaela. You know Aurore hates to be called by her real name."

"My dear Valmont, how can one possibly know how to refer to her. 'Madame Sand' . . . 'Monsieur Sand' . . . a woman who wears trousers and smokes cigars and takes the name George for her sermons in praise of promiscuity . . . it is impossible."

Val was laughing. "They're novels," he said through his laughter, "and she defends a woman's right to independence, Michaela. You of all people should agree with that."

"Independence, yes, but one can be independent without being indecent."

"Aurore only does what a man is allowed to do. He makes no secret of his mistress, except to his wife. She has no husband, so she need not hide her lovers."

"There's no way to talk sensibly to you, Val. I suppose you're still in love with her. The revolution did you a favor, my friend. If you'd stayed with that hermaphrodite, you'd have been ruined for life. A laughingstock. She's twice your age. It was ludicrous."

"I was thirty-one. Aurore was forty-four. If a man has a woman who's ten years younger, even twenty, no one thinks it ludicrous."

The Baroness threw her hands in the air. "Pax," she said. "I don't like quarreling with you. I'm too fond of you. I should never have mentioned the name. I thought we'd share a smile, and instead we ended up at one another's throat. Pretend it never happened. Tell me about your latest amours in New Orleans instead. Surely we can smile about them."

Val laughed. "It's more amusing than you realize, Michaela. Everyone assumes that you and I are lovers. Now what do you say about an affair in which the woman is older than the man?"

The Baroness laughed until tears filled her eyes. "Isn't it interesting how a small shift in perspective can make everything appear completely different? I'm flattered beyond measure. Don't you mind what they think of you?"

Valmont kissed her maimed hand. "My magnificent Baroness de Pontalba," he said, "it is the greatest honor of my life."

Michaela kissed him briefly on the lips. "Chevalier," she said, "it is an obscenity against justice for a man to have so much charm and so much beauty, too. I thank you from the bottom of my cantankerous heart. What a pity that I'm not twenty years younger. No, all things considered, make that ten years." Her smile was wicked, worldly, and girlish at the same time. At that instant Val understood the legends that were told about her in Paris, of men committing suicide, writing poetry, climbing mountains all for love of her.

Then she was again a tired, slightly dumpy middle-aged woman with dyed hair and a sagging chin line.

"Much as I adore you, Valmont, I still must scold you. Do you know what kind of reputation you're getting? People are calling you a dandy, a fop, even a wastrel. I don't care if the rumors about your gambling and whoring are true. You've got more money than you can ever spend, no matter how profligate you are. And a man needs women. I understand that. It's unfortunate that America is so bourgeois, even New Orleans. There are no women skilled in the game of love who have convenient, understanding husbands. Still, you needn't be so distressingly public about your follies.

"You tell me you're serious about your plantation. Why won't you show that side of yourself to the world? You never invite people out there. Secrecy breeds talk. Some say you've got a harem of mulatto women. Others say worse, that you indulge in more depraved pleasures of savage whippings and even torture on your slaves.

"I know you, Val, and of course I don't give any credit to the rumors. But the people of New Orleans don't know you. Not even your own family. You've been away all your adult life, and in the two years since your return, you've made the wrong kind of name for yourself. I tell you this because I love you. Give up the ruffled cuffs and the Paris tailoring and the childish wagers on the number of minutes until the next rain shower."

Val's face had changed while Michaela talked. First it stiffened. Then he frowned. Now his expression was sardonic.

"Tut, tut, Baroness," he said, "to think that you, of all people, would urge me to become conventional. I should be bored to death or, worse, to a life in which every hour seemed a week because it was so boring. I have no interest in what people say, as long as they don't say it in my hearing. Then I have another exasperating duel on my hands."

Michaela shrugged. Then she laughed. "I cannot be angry with you, Valmont. I won't try to reform you any more. Just continue as you are, the most charming rake in this, or any other, country. Now, to my sorrow, I must leave you. I have letters to write. But you must stay, if you're not engaged elsewhere. Alfred and Gaston will be coming home soon, and they would be very happy to see you."

"I must be off, Michaela. This is sugar-making time at the plantation, and I like to be there every minute. If I hadn't had the obligation to dress the tombs with my galaxy of relations, I wouldn't be in the city at all today. I'm glad that I had to come in, though. Being with you is a tonic.

"I'll be back in four days for the first opera on Tuesday. Will you and your sons join me in my box?"

The Baroness laughed deep in her throat. "I'm afraid that would stop the rumors, dear. A woman who is involved in a passionate liaison would never take her sons with her to meet her lover. I have taken a box myself. We must bow very formally and stiffly to one another, then quickly look away. That will confirm all suspicions. I shall wear a multitude of jewels and paint my face brightly, à la Parisienne. Perhaps I'll allow myself one telltale simper when you first appear... I shall enjoy myself immoderately. Be off, now. I have business to attend to."

Val walked to the center of the open square and turned to look at Michaela'a building. She claimed that she was investing her money and her time only because she needed something to do while exiled, and that she expected to earn a handsome income. But Val believed that there were more important reasons, motives that she wouldn't admit even to a good friend.

The building was magnificent, a row of sixteen brick townhouses side by side that filled the entire block. The repetition of tall windows and chimneys and doors was like a rhythmic beat, repeated on the three levels, underscored by the iron columns that supported the two continuous cast-iron balconies, climaxed by three evenly placed pediments with central octagonal windows. The building was like music made architecture. Its ironwork was a lighthearted counterpoint to its brick and granite solidity. Valmont was certain that the beautiful curves of the iron were the secret reason for Michaela's return to New Orleans and her driven, perfectionist attitude to the project. The center of the design was an elaborate monogram: AP. Almonester-Pontalba. Again and again. Homage to her father, builder of the monumental side of the square. And triumphant competition with him. When the second building was finished, Michaela Almonester's imprint would be twice what her father's had been. Woman she might be, but her accomplishments were as great as any man's, even a man as great as her father.

It was no wonder, thought Val, that she had been so brutally disapproving of George Sand. The writer's affectation of men's clothing and men's habits held up women's independence as a charade to be mocked. While Michaela had paid for hers with bullets in the chest and a mutilated hand.

Still, Val remembered, Aurore had been an experience he would always be grateful for. What an exciting woman, in and out of bed. She infuriated him and educated him. And, he was afraid, spoiled him for ordinary women. They were too ready to surrender, too willing to agree with a man's opinions, to be dominated. There was no challenge, no intriguing game-playing, no wit.

Michaela was right, he thought sadly. If only she were ten years younger, what a delight it would be to persuade her to stay in New Orleans. He missed being in love, or at least playing at being in love.

A young girl passed him, escorted by a protectively glaring black maid. The girl's dark eyes met Val's, then dropped demurely to look at the path under her dainty feet. Her skin was very white, her waist very tiny. My God, these Creole girls are lovely, thought Val. En garde, mon ami. You'll find yourself on your knees asking for a soft little hand in marriage if you're not careful.

He walked briskly toward the levee and the boat that would take him to the plantation. A sharp wind scattered the dead leaves in the barren square, and he hunched his shoulders against it. He was painfully aware of his loneliness.

# 21

The four days before Jeanne's début were the most hectic she and Mary had ever known. The days were short, and every minute was put to use.

Miranda brought coffee to their room at first light; they drank it while they dressed. Then they accompanied Berthe and the cook to the Market to buy provisions for the day.

The Market was a long tile-roofed arcade near the levee, a pulsating mélange of sound and smell and color. Vendors called out the virtues of their wares, competing for the attention of customers. Caged birds with gaudy plumage cried shrill songs of agitation and fear. Tethered chickens, geese, ducks, goats, calves, and sheep added their squawks, honks, quacks, bleats. Noisy bargaining and argument was heard on all sides. California-bound gold prospectors inspected pickaxes and tents, howling at the inflated prices. Sailors from ships at the quay conversed loudly in a dozen foreign tongues. The chanting songs of the cargo loaders floated from the opposite side of the levee to make a musical background to the din.

The smell of roasting coffee beans and freshly cooked coffee permeated the air, mixing with the pungent odors of spices, long strings of peppers, garlic, herbs, onions. The scent of bunched flowers and leaves demanded notice near the slippery aroma of hot oil and the smoke of burning charcoal and the sweet richness of sugar-powdered beignets and calas.

Most of the vendors were black women, with skin in every shade of brown. Their crips tignons were blue, red, yellow, green, orange, violet, with stripes and swirls of every hue. Pyramids of lemons, oranges, plums, figs, pineapples, coconuts, guavas, and pomegranates gave testimony to the shipping that came to New Orleans from every corner of the world. Piles of game birds glistened with iridescent jewellike feathers on their limp necks and bodies; the scales of fish of every kind glittered from leaf-lined baskets; mountains of shrimp gleamed in pearly transparency; bright crayfish and crabs scuttled and struggled in tubs of water; crates of what looked like serrated rocks were stacked next to a table where three grinning black men wielded knives and pried them open to reveal delectable opaline oysters.

At the entrances to the Market, blanket-shawled Indians squatted with gourds full of *filé*, or powdered sassafras, the indispensable ingredient for the thick gumbo that appeared daily on Creole tables. Nearby a woman ladled bubbling gumbo into bowls for on-the-spot eating. The streets bordering the market were crowded with barrows and baskets and poles holding old clothes, hats, brooms, umbrellas, shawls, shoes, crockery, cooking pots,and every variety of cheap glass and brass jewelry.

Mary and Jeanne looked from side to side, overcome by the excess, while Berthe and her cook selected what they wanted and deposited the items in the baskets carried by the girls. "Lagniappe," each of the vendors said when Berthe paid for her selection, and gave her a small bonus with her change. A flower, a paper twist of herbs, a piece of candy. A small extra. A New Orleans custom. Berthe's thanks were graciously prolonged. Then she hustled the girls away. She continued to hurry them throughout the morning hours, leading them at a rapid pace along Chartres Street, plunging into one shop after another to examine their riches, occasionally choosing some delicate luxury of silk or satin or silver or intricate inlaid wood for Jeanne's wardrobe or the redecoration of the house. Here the lagniappe was more exotic, more foreign. The shops were like international Aladdin's caves. Every country contributed to the commerce of the port city.

The afternoons were less hurried, but for Mary they were equally strange and exciting. She worked on the dress Jeanne had given her, altering it to fit and adding an embroidered frieze of flowers to the square neckline. She sat on the iron-flowered balcony while she sewed, listening to Jeanne's ebullient chatter about their shopping and the approaching drama of her presentation at the Opera. From time to time Jeanne was interrupted by the sounds from the street, and she paused to listen with Mary to the songs of the street peddlers.

The cornmeal man had a brass trumpet hung on a red cord around his neck. At each intersection he stopped and lifted it to his lips to blow an attention-getting flourish before he sang his announcement of "Cornmeal, fresh from the mill."

A metal triangle was the instrument of the *gaufre* man. He beat it continuously as accompaniment for the minor-key scale in which he sang "Gau-fre." A shiny tin box strapped to his back carried the thin, sweet cookies.

Doughnuts and crullers were the specialty of the man with the crashing cymbals. A chorus of chirping was the song for the man who balanced a long pole on his shoulders with woven reed cages of birds hanging from the pole. "Romonez la chiminée," sang the chimney sweeps with their sooty brooms, and "Charbon de Paris," the charcoal man chanted.

"Candles" . . . "gingerbread" . . . "gumbo" . . . "crayfish" . . . "sharpen your knives today" . . . "calas" . . . "pralines" . . . "get your fresh cream cheese" . . . "water, fresh and filtered" . . . "potato cakes, Bel pam patat, Pam patat." One after another they passed by, men and women, all heavily laden, all smiling, all singing in the warm golden winter afternoon. For Mary every song was a love song in her romance with New Orleans.

Sometimes a carriage drove by or there were the footsteps of some man or woman. She craned her neck then, looking for them to stop at the door below. And often a lady did come to the house and knock, a caller for Berthe. Mary held her breath then, waiting for the summons that might come, the news that her family had been identified. When she could hold her breath no longer, she relaxed and went back to her sewing and Jeanne's prattle. It was early yet; the season would not begin until the Opera opened. She could wait a little longer.

Dinner was served in the courtyard with candles in glass columns on the table. The paving stones released the warmth they had stored from the day's sun and tempered the fresh, cool evening air. The fountain made music in the background. Carlos Courtenay grumbled about having to eat so early, but he chuckled when he complained. In his own way he was as excited about Jeanne's début as Berthe was. The reason for the early dinner was that Marie Laveau came before eight every night to dress Jeanne's hair.

"We will experiment with different arrangements," she told Berthe, "until we are sure which is the best. I'll apply pomade, too, to bring up a luster."

She did lesser treatments for Berthe and Mary, too. Following her directions Berthe had strong black coffee made and cooled. The voodoo queen added a dark powder to it—to make it penetrate, Madame—and rinsed Berthe's hair again and again until the gray hairs were blended into the black.

Mary received a massage that sent ripples of relaxation throughout her entire body. Marie's strong supple fingers dipped into a pot of greenish thick cream and rubbed the potion into Mary's scalp until it was all absorbed. "This will thicken and strengthen the hair, 'Zelle," she said softly. "Your hair is fine like a baby's." She murmured as she worked the cream in. The words were blurred, and a language that Mary did not know.

The days sped by, and suddenly it was Tuesday.

"We'll stay in today," Berthe announced. "Jeanne must be rested tonight. No drooping and no shadows under the eyes at the Opera."

Mary was relieved. She was feeling slightly ill. Her stomach rebelled at the mention of food, and she felt a strange lassitude, as if she was too weak to walk. It must be overexcitement, she thought, and she did the last bit of embroidery on her dress, holding it close to her eyes because there was a small blur to the edges of everything she looked at.

The bright sunny kitchen of the house on Saint Anne Street was redolent with spice. A black iron cauldron bubbled slowly over the coals in the big fireplace, blending the flavors of tender crab meat and sharp seasoning and rice. At a scrubbed table in the corner farthest from the cooling area, Marie Laveau hummed while she ground leaves and berries to a powder with a marble mortar and pestle. She smiled as she worked.

Another five days and the American girl would die. She was responding faster than expected. Marie's smile grew into a laugh when she thought of the gold pieces in the hiding place under the floor. The fool Sazerac woman had paid ten times the usual cost. Marie had set the price to punish her for going through an intermediary instead of coming directly to Saint Anne Street. Also for her arrogance. It was Marie's greatest pleasure to make the powerful submit to her greater power.

There'd be no difficulty convincing the Courtenay mother to hire her for another week. Marie knew all about the social season. By now at least a dozen invitations to balls, dinners, and musical evenings would have been delivered to the house on Esplanade Avenue. The daughter would want to attend all of them, and the mother would give the daughter anything she wanted. It was doubtful that the death of her friend would keep Jeanne Courtenay from a social engagement. Marie knew her type.

But the girl did have beautiful hair. Strong and silklike, it felt good in Marie's hands. Maybe she'd continue to dress it for the entire season. She didn't need to admire the head under the hair in order to enjoy working with it.

She gave no thought to the morality of what she was doing. She was a professional, with skills and secrets of herbal and mineral matter and other things that had been passed down from queen to successor queen for hundreds of years. People paid for her knowledge, and she healed many more than she hurt. It was all the same to her. Her secrets were the source of her power, and that was the only thing that was important.

She scraped the powder carefully into a jar of milk curds, then mixed it into a creamy paste. After she closed the jar she washed the mortar and pestle and the mixing spoon with great care. Then she cleaned her hands with strong soap and a stiff brush. She dried them on a spotless white cloth then dipped them in a clear solution that sealed the pores in the skin so that the poison would not enter her bloodstream.

It was half past three. Time to go. The opera began at six, and the débutante should be on display in her box well before the house lights dimmed.

She'd do the girl's hair in two falls of not-too-tight ringlets above her ears. That would bare the nape of her lovely long neck. Marie put two curling irons in her drawstring calico bag. She added a vial of oil impregnated with the scent of gardenias. That would do for the "irresistible potion" the girl wanted. She'd believe in it, and the belief would make it true. True enough, anyhow. Last of all she gently placed the jar of deadly cream in a padded corner. She piled her hair on top of her head and tied a bright red tignon over it with practiced motions. Her fingers adjusted the seven points to their prescribed pattern, and she left the house to take her proud walk to the Courtenay home. Her step was more like dancing than walking. The opening of the opera season was always exciting. She had her reserved seat, as she did every year. Tonight the performance was *L'Elisir d'Amore.* Marie Laveau preferred Donizetti to all other composers.

# 22

On the opening night of the opera season there was a line of carriages the length of the block on Orleans Street, where the theater was located. Usually people walked to the opera just as they walked to everything. In the French Quarter nothing was far away, and the narrow streets were easier to travel on foot.

But on opening night there were special reasons for the protection of a carriage. Débutantes dared not risk their white gowns on muddy or dusty streets; even the most elderly and infirm were unwilling to miss the opening; ladies wore their most elaborate and precious jewels and were nervous about the possible thieves in shadowed corners; visitors came from hundreds of miles around and had to trust hired coachmen to deliver them to the theater on its hidden street behind the Cathedral garden; music-loving or social-climbing Americans came from the uptown sector where they lived, a long distance from the center of the Vieux Carré.

All those who walked, as they always did, shook their heads at the noisy confusion, expertly stepped over and around the horse droppings, and congratulated themselves that they stood no chance of missing the overture.

In the Courtenay carriage, Jeanne was openly frantic. Berthe tried unsuccessfully to hide her worry. "Let's get out and walk, Papa," Jeanne begged. "It's so near, but we're not moving at all. I can't bear it if we're late."

"Sit still, Jeanne," said her father. "We have more than enough time for you to make an entrance. Berthe, stop fidgeting. You're as bad as Jeanne."

Jeanne began to weep. "Oh, chérie, don't cry," wailed Berthe. "You'll have runnels on your cheeks, and everyone will know I allowed you to wear powder. Wait, I have a handkerchief here someplace."

"I have one, Madame," said Mary. "Here, Jeanne. And feel! We're moving. Dry your eyes now; you don't want them to be red."

Jeanne sniffled once, then stopped. "Look, Maman," she said, "that's another girl being presented. See, stepping down from the carriage ahead of us. She's carrying a bouquet, and she's in white. Who is she?"

"Don't hang out of the window like that, Jeanne. Be ladylike."

Berthe took a discreet peek. "It's Catherine Desmoulins. My goodness. I thought she was presented years ago. I guess her father was reluctant to spend the money. He's such a miser."

"Berthe," Carlos growled. "Don't fill Jeanne's head with gossip and slander. She might repeat it."

"For goodness' sake, Carlos, she'll hear plenty of it from now on. We have dozens of invitations already. It's going to be a wonderful season ... Ahhh, here we go. Now, Jeanne, remember to wait for your father to get out and then hand me down and then you. Hold your bouquet in your left hand, take Papa's hand with your right. Be careful you don't tangle your ribbons. And don't stare around you. Little glances, but mostly keep looking down to see where you're putting your feet; the steps are very shallow and misleading." Berthe cut off the spate of instructions when the carriage door was opened. Then she smiled graciously at the doorman and extended her hand to her husband, who had already descended from the carriage.

Mary was amazed by the change in Berthe. As long as she had been fussing over Jeanne, she had been the same person, but in different clothes. Now she was metamorphosized. Quiet, moving slowly, with regal bearing, Berthe had become a woman of elegance, in fact and in appearance. She was wearing a low-cut gown of lavender watered silk with deep violet velvet bands on the flounces of the skirt and on the tiered bishop sleeves. Her evening cloak was made of the same velvet, lined and edged with ruches of the silk. Around her neck she wore a band of latticed diamonds from which hung a pendant of diamonds surrounding a tear-drop-shaped amethyst the size of a quail's egg. Smaller amethyst and diamond drops hung from her ears, and a wide diamond pavé chain circled her tightly corseted waist, held by an amethyst-studded clasp. A nosegay of hothouse violets was tucked in the elaborate chignon of her sleek, darkened hair, almost concealing the small diamond bar brooch that held them in place.

Mary had been impressed when she saw Berthe in her fine gown, amazed when Berthe opened one velvet case after another to remove her jewels. But she had secretly thought them excessive, inappropriate for the bustling, harried woman she knew. Berthe was more like herself when she fussed over the clasp of the simple pearls she fastened around Jeanne's throat and when she rummaged through a leather box of gold chains and brooches and pulled out a bow of twisted yellow-and-red gold and gave it to Mary to wear. "It's yours to keep," she had said, "as a thank-you for what you did to Jeanne's gown." All the attention then had been, as usual, on Jeanne. Berthe was mother, nothing more.

Now she was Madame Courtenay, fashionable wife of handsome Monsieur Courtenay, at home in the privileged society to which they belonged. She looked on with distant, queenly approval while Carlos handed his daughter down, then Mary, and while Mary made quick small adjustments to Jeanne's skirt and the long pastel ribbons that hung from her bouquet. Then she took her husband's arm and entered the Opera House at a stately pace, smiling, stopping and speaking to friends, nodding to acquaintances. All as if she did not know the meaning of the word "hurry."

Mary could hear Jeanne grinding her teeth with impatience. At least she thought that was what she heard. Sounds were clear one moment, muted and confused the next. She felt as if light and sound and vision were receding and returning in alternating waves, as if the floor beneath her feet were unsteady. She stumbled on the stairs; the press of people around her prevented a fall.

There were four chairs in the box, with generous room between them. Carlos Courtenay placed three in front and seated Jeanne between Berthe and himself. Mary was grateful to be alone and unobserved in the rear. She edged her chair into a corner and leaned against the wall. She was shaking from a debilitating chill. The lights began to dim, even more than they had been doing before; the sounds of conversation, rustling silks, rattling programs faded, then ceased; then all was darkness and quiet.

Blessed Jesus, she cried in her heart, help me. She thought she had been stricken blind and deaf.

Then the music began, swelled, filled the house, and the curtain went up, and light spilled from the stage.

Mary had never been to the theater, had never heard an orchestra, had never seen an opera. Within seconds, she was totally enthralled. She forgot her fear, her sickness, her companions, herself. With a hand spread flat against the wall for steadiness, she leaned forward as if to enter the glorious sounds and movement and color below her.

When the curtain fell at the end of the first act, she was still held in enchantment, unaware of the applause and the stirring in the box. Her throat filled with tears. She didn't want the magic to stop.

Damn, said Valmont Saint-Brévin to himself. The interval already. Now I'll have to start the rounds of the débutantes. If I don't pay my respects, a father or a brother or a cousin will call me out to avenge the insult.

He stood, adjusted his cuffs, addressed the friends who were sharing his box: "Gentlemen, it's the duty hour. Shall we go en masse to gladden young hearts, or should we spread our attentions more widely?"

"All for one, and one for all, d'Artagnan," said the youngest, a cousin named Jean-Luc. "You lead and we'll follow."

"But lead to my aunt Athalie's first, Valmont," added a stout perennial bachelor who suited his nickname, Max. "She'll have my head if I don't produce a rush for cousin Caroline."

Philippe Courtenay opened the door. "I don't care where we go first, but remember I have a sister to be called on. That takes precedence over a cousin."

"We'll see them all," said Val. "At least the champagne will be first-rate."

In the Courtenay box the first-rate champagne was already being poured. The house lights were barely raised when the first polite knock came on the door. Jeanne was a sensation, the most beautiful of all the débutantes. One, then a second, a third, fourth, fifth, sixth, seventh—the young beaux rushed to be presented. The hallway outside the box was jammed with eager admirers throughout the half-hour intermission. Twenty-six in all were received, presented, then replaced. There were still a half dozen waiting an opportunity when the lights began to dim for the second act. "Au revoir... au revoir... mes hommages...," said the lucky few inside the box as they bowed themselves out. "Au revoir."

"Maman," Jeanne whispered, "I'm a belle!" She took her seat and looked out over the thousands in the audience, offering her radiant face for them to admire.

Mary took her place in the corner, glad to be able to sit again. The rush of faces and names and talk, talk, talk had exhausted her. The Courtenays had punctiliously introduced each of Jeanne's beaux to her, too, referring to her as "Jeanne's friend Mary MacAlistair," but Mary knew that she was invisible to the eyes gazing past her to look at Jeanne. It mattered not at all to her. The opera was what counted, not the interval. She sipped the champagne Berthe had forced on her. It steadied her head, she had discovered. She'd be able to concentrate even better on the music, now. There were four more acts, according to the program. Mary sighed with happy anticipation.

When the curtain fell again, she applauded with the rest of the audience. She wished she had the nerve to shout "bravo," too, as many were doing. The flood of beaux began again, but it didn't bother her. She was still hearing the music in her mind; she made automatic polite noises and smiles without awareness.

"How do you do, Miss MacAlistair?" said a deep voice. Mary was jolted to attention. She had not heard anyone speak English for so long that it sounded almost foreign to her.

"How do you do?" she said.

"You may not have heard in all this commotion. My name is Will Graham."

"How do you do, Mr. Graham." Mary was surprised at how good English felt on her tongue. And by Will Graham's blue eyes. She'd almost forgotten that there were blue eyes in the world. Or hair that wasn't so dark it looked black. His hair was brown, like hers, but with touches of silver at the temples. He was a tall man with shoulders that stooped slightly as if he wished to make shorter men feel more equal. His face was long, his jaw square, and his nose had an upward tilt at the very end. Mary felt a kinship, even though she knew there was none.

"Are you enjoying the opera, Mr. Graham?"

"Since you're an American, too, Miss MacAlistair, I'll admit that I prefer a Stephen Foster song to any aria. I've never had enough time to learn much culture. I'm a businessman. Still, I believe the opposite of the old saying. I figure I can learn new tricks."

Carlos Courtenay replaced Graham's empty glass with a full one, put a glass in Mary's hand. "I was certain you will enjoy conversation with a countryman, Mary," he said in English. His accent was very French. "Like I say to you, Will, Mary is teaching my Jeanne to speak American."

"She speaks real well," said Will. He smiled at Mary. "You must be a fine teacher. I tried to learn some French when I came to New Orleans, but I didn't get much past 'bonjour' and 'merci.' I blame it on the teacher. That way I don't have to admit that my head's too thick to learn."

"But, Mr. Graham, you should try again. Just think of French as a new trick."

Carlos looked bewildered by the laughter of the two Americans.

Will Graham bowed to Mary. "A pleasure meeting you, ma'am. I'll consider having another go at parlez-vous." He held out his hand. "Carlos, thank you for inviting me." Mr. Courtenay shook the American's hand, with his second hand on top of the handshake.

"Your visit honors me and my family," he said.

Mary smiled at Mr. Graham as he left. Then her smile broadened. "Philippe!" she said. He entered the box as soon as Will Graham was through the door.

"Mary, my friend," Philippe said. "How are you? I didn't see you from in front. You must have been hiding... But you're very pale, Mary. Where are those rosy cheeks? You need a sunburn. Or at least some more champagne. Let me get you a full glass."

"Thank you, Philippe. But hadn't you better say good evening to Berthe and Jeanne? This is her début, after all."

"Dear Mary, my charming little sister would bite me with her lovely little teeth if I pushed aside one of her beaux to make room for me. Look at her."

Mary turned her head to see. She felt a stab of pain when she saw Valmont Saint-Brévin smiling down at Jeanne's upturned face. It was the scene that had wounded her heart at Montfleury, but this time the pain was even worse. She had convinced herself that she had gotten over her ridiculous obsession with him, that he was simply a symbol of a hero from all the romantic novels, that the man himself had nothing to do with her emotions. It no longer affected her when Jeanne talked about him, said his name again and again.

Or so Mary told herself.

But there he was. Tall and lean and muscular and handsome and strong and gentle. She could see that he was gentle by the way he was looking at Jeanne.

It was unbearable.

Mary turned back to Philippe. "I thought you were going to get me some champagne," she said. "I feel like celebrating. This is my first opera, and I adore it."

You will not cry, Mary MacAlistair, she said to herself.

"Don't be so cruel, Valmont. You will make me cry," said Jeanne. She looked to her right at Max. "Don't you think Valmont cruel?" she asked. "He's reminding me of things I did when I was a child, and he knows I'd rather forget them now that I've grown up." Her little pout called attention to the charming dimple in her soft chin and to the plump seductiveness of her mouth.

My, my, thought Val. Philippe's baby sister has got Max stammering. A hardened old bachelor like him. She'll have me stuttering in a minute if I'm not careful. What a lovely little minx she is, and knows it, too. She's the liveliest thing to hit New Orleans society since I've been back. It's almost a rule that young women be very pale and very pure. This little Courtenay is flushed from her triumph tonight, and she would, I'm quite sure, be extremely enthusiastic about ridding herself of her purity. He looked appreciatively at the silken-skinned mounds of Jeanne's full breasts and at her smooth shoulders and flawless white throat.

She was watching him, Val realized. Her breasts rose and fell with her quickening breath, and her pointed pink tongue moistened her lips.

She doesn't even know what she's doing, he realized. It was a shock. Jeanne was looking at him with the eyes of a woman approaching orgasm. Her pupils were immense. They made her eyes look black, bottomless, witness to the mystery of man and woman joined together.

Val forced himself to look away. He wasn't ready to accept the invitation. Not with all that went with it, courtship, marriage, children, the loss of his freedom. Not yet.

"We mustn't monopolize the most exquisite belle of the season," he said quickly. He cursed the hoarseness in his voice. "I retract everything I said about your childhood, Jeanne. It would break my heart if I made you cry."

"I'll cry if you leave so soon."

"But I must. There's a regiment of adorers waiting to meet you. Au revoir."

"Valmont! You'll call on us?"

"With the greatest pleasure."

He retreated in haste.

Philippe stopped him before he reached the door. "You haven't had any champagne, Val. In my expert opinion, this is the best yet." He was very slightly drunk.

Val wisely didn't argue with him. He accepted a glass, tasted it, pronounced it excellent.

"Have you met my friend Mary? Of course you have, at Montfleury."

Valmont looked at the pallid young woman at Philpppe's side. She was draining her glass.

Make me feel better please, Mary silently begged the wine. My insides feel hollow. There's a trickle of sweat running down my spine. My hands are clammy, my legs shaky, and everything is going and coming again. If I faint, I hope I die before I come to.

Come on, Mary, she told herself. This man is just a person like any other person. And you owe him at least a thank you for the time he saved you from disaster.

"We've met," she said. At the same moment Val said, "I'm sure we've never met."

Philippe blinked. "What is it? Yes or no?"

Mary spoke quickly. "Not at Montfleury, Philippe. Monsieur Saint-Brévin couldn't possibly remember me, but I remember him because he came to my aid when I was in desperate trouble. He may have even saved my life."

"That sounds pretty dramatic, Mary. What happened?" Philippe was listing to one side. "Fall off a horse or something?" He laughed uproariously. Valmont quietly held his arm to steady him.

"I feel extremely stupid, Mademoiselle," said Val. "I don't remember saving any young lady's life. But I'm pleased if I was of some service to you. If you'll excuse me, I think I should be of service to my friend Carlos Courtenay and escort his son back to our box."

Mary looked into Valmont's eyes for the first time. They were without reaction to her. "Yes," she said. Her voice was as leaden as her heart. "Goodbye, Philippe." Then something surged inside her, a fierce determination that Valmont Saint-Brévin admit that they were not total strangers, that their lives had touched, that he had held her in his arms.

"Before you leave, Monsieur, you must accept my gratitude. I feel an obligation to thank you. It was the Fourth of July, and a rough person had struck me in the street. You drove him away. I am in your debt."

Val's brow furrowed, cleared. "Was that you? My God! I made no connection with that brawl and . . . this gathering. How do you know the Courtenays? Through Philippe?"

"Madame Courtenay was good enough to give me a home. I went to the Convent for shelter, you see, and everything was arranged."

"I see." Valmont looked at Mary's feverish eyes and trembling hands. Philippe lurched against him. The house lights began their slow dimming.

"We must hurry," said Val. "Good night, Mademoiselle."

Just before the third act began, Jeanne ran to Mary and clutched her hand. "Did you see, May-ree? He came. He liked me, I think, he really did. Did you see, May-ree? Do you think he liked me?"

"Yes. Yes, I'm sure. I saw, and I'm very sure. Now be quick. Go to your chair; your mother's gesturing." Mary rested her forehead against the wall. Inside her skull, hammers were pounding. Inside her mouth her tongue felt swollen and spongy, and there was a bitter metallic taste.

Mercifully the music did its magic. She was able to forget her pains.

But during the next interval she kept to her chair in the corner, and she refused any more champagne. She was silent and very still, and she looked extremely unwell. Berthe and Carlos Courtenay agreed in a whisper to behave as if she was not even there. "Neither of us can leave to take her home, but she looks very sick. Let her be quiet."

Mary rested, with her eyes closed, and gave herself over to the music. It enveloped her and carried her through the attacks of dizziness and nausea until they went away. She was able to open her eyes in the middle of the last act and to watch the final dramatic scenes. At the end she was able to clap her hands for all seventeen curtain calls. And she was able to walk without obvious difficulty down the stairs and out into the reviving fresh air. By the time they were back at the house, she felt almost herself again.

I must have had too much champagne, she thought. I'll never again take more than one glass, no matter what.

Jeanne could barely contain herself long enough to get undressed. "Go away, Miranda," she ordered. "Take my clothes with you. I'll get into my nightdress by myself. Go on."

She tugged at the laces of her corset and pulled them into a knot. "Oh, no," she wailed, and began to sob.

"Shhh," said Mary. "I'll get the knot out. Just stand still. You've had too much excitement, that's all. Everything was just the way you dreamed it would be, Jeanne. You were the most beautiful, you had the most beaux, you'll be the belle of the season. There's nothing to cry about."

"Everything is ruined, May-ree." Jeanne was crying with the abandoned despair of a small child.

"No it isn't, Jeanne. It's just a tangle. I'll have it out in a second . . . there. Now I'll loosen the laces. You'll feel much better when the corset is off."

"May-ree, you don't understand. He was there. You talked to him, I saw you. I never believed it, but it's true. Papa is going to marry me to that American." Jeanne threw herself into Mary's embrace and wept hysterically.

Mary led her to the bed and sat her down on the side of it. "You're not making any sense," she said. "Your father can't make you marry anybody. Hold your arms up." She pulled Jeanne's nightdress on, guiding her arms into the sleeves and her head through the neck opening. It was like dressing a doll. Jeanne's tears subsided to shuddering sobs.

Mary dampened a towel and brought it to her."Wipe your face and blow your nose," she said. "You're getting all upset over nothing. You're making up nightmares."

Jeanne used the towel, dropped it on the floor. "May-ree, you don't know anything," she said tearfully. "Papa has always meant me to marry an American. He says they are winning, that New Orleans will be theirs before I am his age. And he can make me do it. If I go against his wishes, he'll refuse to give me a dowry, and no one will marry me. May-ree, you're not like me, you don't understand. I could never be an old maid. I'd rather be married to a monster than not to have a husband at all.

"If only Valmont had liked me more. I thought he did at first, but he didn't come back to the box again. I was sure that he would. I thought it must be meant. I love him so much, and Papa couldn't say no to him. His land is next to ours, and he's as rich as an American besides. I thought it was meant, May-ree. On All Saints' I prayed for it, too, just to be sure. But I thought it was meant. Maybe I didn't pray hard enough. I'll pray now."

She stretched beseeching hands upward. "Virgin mother," she cried, "Heavenly Father, Blessed Jesus . . . *please.*" It was a scream. And the wild, desperate sobbing came again.

Berthe came in, with her customary hurried step and worried expression. "What is it? My baby! Hush, now. Come to Maman." She took Jeanne and held her close, covering her bowed head with frantic kisses. "What's wrong, Mary, do you know?"

"She's afraid she might marry Mr. Graham, she says. I tried to talk to her, but . . ."

"Oh . . . Jeanne. Listen to Maman, my angel. I'm not supposed to tell, but I will. Papa got a message tonight, a note. An usher brought it during the last interval. It was from Valmont. He asked your father to meet him after the opera at the Curtius Club. He said he had something important and urgent to talk about with him."

Jeanne lifted her head. "Tonight? He wanted to see Papa tonight?" Her face was mottled and swollen. And shining with hope.

"Urgent and important, he said. It made me think of my début. Your father walked the banquette outside our house all night until my Papa was awake and he could ask for my hand."

# 23

"I can't bear it, May-ree. I have to know." Jeanne repeated herself a hundred times, vowed that she'd stay awake until her father came home even if it was all night.

But the outbursts of crying after the tension of the day and the excitement of her success all combined to wear her out. She plummeted into sleep in mid-sentence.

Mary had already slipped into a stupor that was half sleep, half faint. She was very weak.

Carlos Courtenay arrived home at 3 A.M. He woke his wife, and they talked in hushed, anxious tones for more than an hour. Valmont had warned him that his daughter's companion had once been one of Rose Jackson's whores.

The next morning breakfast was served in the courtyard. Jeanne was furious that her father and mother had not yet left their rooms. "It's cruel of Papa to sleep late like this, and Maman, too. They're torturing me. I can't bear it, May-ree. I have to know."

At last, Carlos Courtenay came down the stairs. Jeanne leapt up. Her chair tipped over with a crash. "Papa?"

"Your mother wants to talk to you, Jeanne. Go to her room."

"Oh, Papa! Mother-daughter talk. I'll run ever so fast. Oh, Papa, I'm so happy." Jeanne hugged her father and kissed him. Then she grabbed handfuls of skirt and lifted it so that she could race up the steps two at a time.

Mary sat very still. She had been preparing herself for the fact of Jeanne's engagement to Valmont ever since Berthe told them about the note. She was ready, she thought. She was in command of herself. Not for an instant would she show the searing disappointment and burning jealousy that raged inside her.

She was not prepared at all for what Carlos Courtenay said to her.

"Miss MacAlistair—if that is your name—be out of this house inside ten minutes, or I will throw you naked onto the street.

"Here is enough money to buy a steamboat ticket back to wherever you came from. My carriage will take you to the landing."

He threw an envelope onto the table in front of Mary. As he left, he spoke. He didn't look at her. "The servants are packing a bag for you. All the clothing that you have been given is yours to keep. I don't want even the ashes of it to be in my house."

Book Three

# 24

Mary stood alone and abandoned amid the hurrying crowds on the quai. I'm right back where I started, only worse. Her thoughts were bitter. So was the wind from the river. The sky was leaden with low gray clouds. It looked the way Mary felt. The New Orleans steamboat landing was even larger, noisier, busier than Pittsburgh's. Instead of three boats, there were dozens. The drays of barrels and bales for loading numbered in the hundreds.

This time Mary knew that she should hold fast to her belongings. She clutched the envelope of money, wrapped her arms around the valise she had been given. Behind her she heard the Courtenay carriage drive away.

I should have hit Carlos Courtenay, she thought, I should have spit at him. How dare he talk to me like that? And Clementine . . . she didn't say a word, she didn't even look at me, just grabbed my arm and marched me out to the carriage and pushed me up into it. Then she threw the valise and envelope at me. Not handed it to me, not put it onto the seat or the floor. She threw it, like a bone to a dog, or slops to a pig. They used me, then threw me away. Just like Carlos did to Hercule's granddaughter, his mistress. He's a monster.

The shock of her expulsion from the Courtenays' had acted on Mary's system like an injection of adrenaline. Her heart was racing, and the blood in her veins rushed through her body carrying the accumulation of poison that had been applied to her scalp by the voodoo queen. She felt as if her head were in a vise, being squeezed, pressed, with unbearable pain. Her stomach was knotted, stabbed with lances of fire. A spurt of sour liquid stung her throat and her nose, and she knew she was going to vomit.

She shoved the corner of the valise against her lips and ran toward the river with a shuffling, half-crippled gait, doubled over by pain. At the water's edge she dropped the valise and threw herself down on the muddy ground with her head hanging over the rim of the planked pier. Waves of sickness convulsed her body; she retched again and again, shuddering uncontrollably.

Passers-by detoured a few steps to avoid her. Some hurried, eyes averted; others slowed and stared. Mary was oblivious to them all.

When she finished emptying her sick stomach, she pushed herself up onto her knees, swaying and weeping quietly. Her body ached, and her mouth tasted foul. She found her handkerchief in a pocket, wiped her eyes and her mouth. The lace edge of the handkerchief snagged on the gold brooch at her throat, Berthe's gift to her the night before.

Mary's face twisted with ugly rage. Sweet words and gifts of unwanted clothes and trinkets, and she had been so pleased, so grateful. She thought the Courtenays were her friends. Fool that she was. Now she knew better. They had treated her worse than if she had been one of their slaves.

She stumbled to her feet and ripped the brooch off her dress. Anger gave her strength. Her right arm swung wide, back, then forward. The brooch sailed, gold glinting out over the river, then fell into the muddy, refuse-strewn water.

Mary heard a burst of deep-toned laughter behind her. She raised her fist and turned to attack the mocking intruder.

A giant of a man was standing there, still laughing. His teeth were startlingly white in his dark face. His skin was so black that it looked like shadows made human. Mary dropped her arm. She felt terribly aware of her vulnerability, her weakness.

"I'd know that throwing arm anywhere," said the man. "How you doing, Missy? Don't you remember Joshua?" He was speaking English; for a moment Mary had trouble understanding. Then the words made sense. Joshua. The first boat she took from Pittsburgh. The knobs that were loose on the railing. The cow, and the man with the knife, and the wooden ball hitting his head with that sickening sound.

She looked at the big black man as if he were a long-lost friend. He was part of the happy time when everything was fresh and exciting, when she was on her way to a new life with a heart full of hope and trust, when she had not yet been lied to and cheated and robbed.

"Hey, there, Missy, how come you're crying like that?"

"Oh, Joshua, everything is an awful mess. Can you help me?"

# 25

"You in a fine fix, Missy, that's for sure." Joshua shook his head. He had shaken it often while he listened to Mary's long account of her misadventures. It was a gesture of sympathy, understanding, dismay. But not disbelief.

"It ain't so bad as you think, though. We can find this lady what's looking for your grandmother. New Orleans ain't so big, not the Frenchy part. Anybody'll know where she lives."

"You'll help me?"

"'Course I will. Come on. I'll tote your valise."

It was only a five-minute walk to a corner where a black woman was selling calas, another five minutes, following her instructions, to the tall brick house on Royal Street where Celeste Sazerac lived. Mary brushed the dried mud off her skirt and took a deep breath, then lifted the heavy brass knocker and let it fall. At that moment, it began to rain. In seconds Mary was soaked.

The butler who opened the door was clad in antique-styled livery, with knee breeches and hose; a white-powdered peruke wig framed his brown face. He looked at Mary's sodden form without any expression. He might have been a statue.

"I would like to see Mademoiselle Sazerac," said Mary, in French. "Tell her Mademoiselle MacAlistair is calling."

The butler stepped back one pace, lifted a silver tray from a table, stepped forward again with the tray extended toward Mary. "Your card, Mademoiselle," he said.

"I don't have a calling card; just tell her I'm here. I'm very wet, and I want to come inside."

"Mademoiselle Sazerac is not at home," said the butler. He replaced the tray and began to close the door.

Mary held it open with her hand. Desperation made her bold. "When will she be in?" she said. "She will want to see me. I can wait for her."

"Mademoiselle Sazerac is out of the city for a week, Mademoiselle. I will tell her you were here." He closed the door.

Mary's courage was gone. She leaned against the door and cried.

"Here now, Missy, that won't do no good," Joshua said. "A week ain't so long. Maybe she's off someplace finding your kinfolks."

Mary wiped her eyes with the end of her shawl. What Joshua said made sense. If only she weren't so wet, if she didn't feel so sick, she wouldn't have despaired so easily. She forced a smile. "I'm sorry to act like such a fool," she said. "I don't feel very well."

"You got the emptiest insides on the whole Mississippi River, I expect. That's all that's wrong. Let's go back and get some calas on the corner." Joshua turned and walked slowly; Mary caught up with him, her steps wobbly. She didn't notice when a curtain was pulled to one side in a window of the Sazerac house.

"Jacques, who was that young person?" said the woman holding the curtain. She was dressed in widow's weeds, and she was extremely pale, not with the pallor of fashion, but with the bloodlessness of illness and depression. The gaunt planes of her face and the purple shadows under her eyes could not hide the beauty that had once been hers. She was like a macabre version of the glowing woman in the portrait behind her, a woman with the same features in the full bloom of youth and health, a woman gowned for a special moment, holding a fan of exquisite white lace spread half-open by her curiously misshaped, long, lovely fingers.

"She was looking for Mademoiselle Celeste, Madame," said the butler.

"I see," Anne-Marie Sazerac said. She let the curtain fall back into place, and the room returned to dimness.

"Missy, how much money you got in that envelope?"

Mary chewed the last of her cala, swallowed, spoke. "Thirty dollars." She felt much better with the hot rice cake in her stomach. Also, the rain had stopped.

Joshua shook his head. "At least they was going to get you a cabin on the boat. You can still go. The old *Cairo Queen* will be glad to have you. Who's to say I won't need you to conk the head of somebody who's out to get me?"

Mary's smile was genuine this time. "Thank you, Joshua. But I've got to stay. It's strange, but I've felt like this is my heart's home ever since I got here. I'll just have to go to a hotel until Mademoiselle Sazerac gets back. Do you know where one is?"

"There's a lot of them, from real fancy to worse than a jail. The trouble is, Missy, the fancy ones might not want a young lady all by herself; even if they do, thirty dollars might run out before that lady gets back.

"You ever heard of a boarding house? It ain't fancy like a hotel, but it's respectable. I know about one from one of the pilots on the *Queen.* His sister's there now. It ain't the kind of living you're accustomed to, but it's clean and the food's plentiful and your thirty dollars would last you a couple of months there. A widow lady runs it. She's Irish, named O'Neill."

"That sounds perfect, Joshua. Where is it? Let's go right now."

"It's uptown a ways. Not too far. But I can't take you there. It's in the Irish Channel, you see, the part of town where the Irish live. And they really hate niggers. I'd be a dead man if I tried to walk along Adele Street. I'll take you to Canal Street and find a policeman to go the rest of the way with you."

Mary had a sudden frightening thought. "Oh, Joshua, I've done you a terrible wrong," she cried. "I should never have asked you to walk me to the Sazerac house, to leave the docks that way. You can't put me in care of a policeman. He'd arrest you in a minute. You don't have a pass."

The big black man grinned. "What's a pass to me, Missy? I'm a free man."

"Here? In the South? I thought you had to go North to be free."

Joshua laughed. "New York itself can't touch New Orleans for free black men," he said. "Half the dark faces you see on the streets here are free."

Mary was still wondering if what Joshua said could possibly be true when they reached Canal Street. She had not really seen the street before. The boat landing at the end of it was totally unlike the rest of the street.

Canal was the widest avenue in America, a fact that Mary didn't know, but that she might have guessed. Broad sidewalks bordered with trees ran beside a paved street three times the width of those in the French Quarter. On the opposite side of the street was a wide allée of trees with grass beneath them and a pathway in the center. Beyond that, there was a second wide street, then another tree-lined sidewalk. Sidewalks and pathway were busy with well-dressed women and men walking and strolling. Smart carriages moved quickly along the paved double street. The handsome buildings looked fresh and new. It was nothing like the New Orleans Mary had seen with the Courtenays.

She remembered what Carlos had told her: Canal Street was the dividing line between the Americans and the French. That park in the middle must be what he called the "neutral ground," Mary thought. How lovely it is, especially for something with such a warlike name.

And how different this street is. It looks like New Orleans always has surprises for me. Good and bad. I'd better prepare myself for more.

In spite of her intentions, Mary was not prepared for the Irish Channel.

The policeman was very agreeable. He carried her valise for her and walked with her along a street that he told her was called Magazine. Mary told him when he asked that she was easily able to walk, but she soon wondered whether she would make it. Under a mile, he said. It seemed much longer to her.

At first she was intrigued by the shops and houses they passed. Then she was charmed. The neighborhood changed from solid-front rows of buildings to houses set amid large gardens. All of them were beautiful, she thought. Many had columned galleries; almost all had lacy iron gates, balconies, fences.

But at the same time the sidewalks changed from brick or paving stone to planks that gave a perilous footing. And the streets were slippery with mud and other things she didn't want to identify. Clogged shallow ditches bordered the streets for drainage; she had to jump over them sometimes to cross the street; even where there was a stone acting as a small bridge over the ditch, it was unsteady. And often the smell of rotting refuse was sickening.

When they turned off Magazine Street, the plank sidewalks disappeared. "Only five blocks more," the policeman said cheerfully.

Mary tried to smile. With every step it was harder to lift her feet. Her shoes were gathering mud that weighed like lead, and her feet kept trying to slide out from under her.

One block, then two. I can make it, she told herself; we're almost there. It's only the street that's bad. The houses are nice. Not very big, but nice. Three blocks, four. She heard a high-pitched animal sound, felt a blow on the back of her legs, and fell onto her hands and knees, too startled to cry out. She turned her head and stared at the small bearded face of a goat.

"Are you all right, Miss?" The policeman took her arm and helped her to her feet.

"I'm all dirty," Mary said weakly. She could contain her tears no longer.

"Here, now, no need for that!" The policeman was alarmed by his male helplessness. He hurried Mary along the street and deposited her and her bag on the doorstep of the only two-storied house on the block. "You'll be all right now," he said in a hearty voice. "Mrs. O'Neill will take good care of you." He touched his helmet with a two-fingered salute and made his escape.

Mary knocked on the door. She heard someone singing inside the house. Please be home, she begged silently, and please be nice to me.

The woman who opened the door was the tiniest adult Mary had ever seen. For a moment Mary thought she was a child. Then she saw the streaks of gray in the thick auburn braids that crowned the woman's head and the crows'-feet that edged the blue eyes when the woman smiled at the sight of her.

"And aren't you the most bedraggled sight I've ever seen? Come inside and tell me who you are. I'm the Widow O'Neill."

"My name's Mary MacAlistair."

"Come in, Mary MacAlistair. There's a fire in the kitchen and a kettle on the fire."

Mary had never in her life felt so grateful. "Thank you," was the only thing she could find to say; her heart was in the inadequate phrase.

# 26

Gratitude was not what the Widow O'Neill wanted as payment. As soon as Mary was seated on a stool near the fire with a cup of tea in her hands, the brisk little woman got down to business.

"You'll pay me three dollars a week. In advance until I'm sure that you're good for it; then you can pay me at the end of the week. I don't know you, Mary MacAlistair, so if you don't have the money now, you can drink your tea and be on your way."

"I have the money . . ." Mary began to fumble in her pocket.

"That's fine, then. You can give it to me later, after you've warmed and dried yourself. You'll get your breakfast at six and your supper at seven. If you're late, you get what's left over, and that generally means nothing. If you want me to fix your dinner pail, it'll cost you another dollar a week. Do you agree?"

Mary nodded. She wondered what a dinner pail was, but there was no time to ask. Mrs. O'Neill was talking too fast for interruptions. "You can take a bath here in the kitchen. I set the hour and provide the tub. You draw your water and heat it, and you scrub the tub when you finish. If I don't like the way you scrub it, you do it again. Use of the tub and towel is twenty-five cents. I provide the soap for the bath, but when you wash your clothes, you use your own soap. There's a washtub in the yard, and a clothesline. You can use my flatirons, too, and the table, but only when I'm not using them.

"I give you fresh sheets every second Saturday, and you'll not find a better pillow anywhere than the ones on my beds. See to it that your head is the only one that rests on it, or you're out. I have a parlor where you can visit with your man if you have one, and the door will be left open, if you please. This is a Christian house, and I'll have no sinning under my roof.

"If you're agreeable to those terms, Mary MacAlistair, I'll fill up your cup while you take out your money, and then I'll show you your room. Today is Wednesday. You can pay me a dollar thirty for the rest of the week or four twenty-five through next week. I collect rents on Saturday. You get your pay, I get mine."

Mary paid Mrs. O'Neill four dollars and twenty-five cents. In return, she got a narrow bed in a narrow room and an education.

At the convent school she had made her bed every day and, under the nuns' patient supervision, she had made her graduation dress. That was the extent of her domestic training. She didn't know how to do anything for herself.

After she washed her face, changed her clothes, and tidied her hair, Mary found Mrs. O'Neill and asked for help. "Will you teach me how to wash and iron my clothes? The frock I was wearing is dreadfully dirty."

The widow looked up from the potato she was peeling. "Teach you? What do you mean?"

"I don't know how to do laundry. It's always been done for me. I was always at school until I came to New Orleans. I'm looking for my grandmother..." She told the full story of her misfortunes to the widow.

Mrs. O'Neill peeled potatoes while Mary talked. Before Mary finished, the potatoes were all peeled, and Mrs. O'Neill began to slice them. When Mary's story was over, she continued to slice.

Her silence bothered Mary. She waited until the widow swept the white slices from the table top into a kettle. When Mrs. O'Neill busied herself with adjusting the kettle on a crane in the fireplace, still not speaking, Mary stood and walked to the woman's side. "What do you think, Mrs. O'Neill? Haven't I been treated shamefully?"

The tiny widow looked up at Mary. "What do I think, is it? I think you're the biggest fool ever set foot in this kitchen. Here. Hold this handle while I crank the crane higher." She grabbed Mary's hand and put it to work.

When the kettle was arranged to her satisfaction, she put her hands on her hips and looked Mary over from head to toe.

"You don't look afflicted," she said after the examination, "so you must be stupid. What did you expect from me, girl? Sympathy that you lost your box of trinkets? That your old dad didn't make you rich? That you never knew your mother? What I see is a healthy young woman who expects the good Lord to put aside all His important duties and see to it that she gets the world on a plate without lifting a finger. And that in spite of her throwing it away faster than He can deliver it to her. You've already had more than your share, Mary MacAlistair. It's time you did a little work for the rest."

Mary was thunderstruck. The Widow O'Neill had read her correctly; she expected sympathy, and she didn't know what to do when it wasn't forthcoming. "Excuse me, please," she said. "I think I'll go lie down for a few minutes. I don't feel very well." She heard the tremor in her voice and despised herself for it. I won't give this awful old woman the satisfaction of seeing that she made me cry, she promised herself. She left the kitchen with her head held high and her jaw clenched to stop her chin's quivering.

When she reached her room, Mary discovered that she no longer wanted to cry. She was too angry.

It was not yet noon, although it seemed to Mary that the day had already been a hundred hours long. There were more than seven hours before supper. Mary spent them sitting stiffly on the side of her hard bed, her growing hunger feeding the rage inside her.

She began with Mrs. O'Neill and her harsh words, moved on to condemn Joshua for sending her to this comfortless place, then to Carlos Courtenay, all his family, his servants, his friends. Even Jeanne. Especially Jeanne. She was getting what she wanted. She would marry Valmont Saint-Brévin. It made no difference at all, Mary told herself. They deserved each other. Both of them were shallow and vain and thoughtless. Valmont hadn't even been pleased when she made such an effort to thank him for his kindness on that first terrifying night in New Orleans.

That night when Rose Jackson betrayed her so foully. Mary pounded the bed with her fists when she thought of Rose. The worst of all the cruel people who had abused her so. Rose, who tricked her into admiration, even affection, who lied with honeyed words and honeyed accent, who stole everything she owned, including her family history, and who tried to steal her future by turning her into one of those creatures in her falsely beautiful garden.

Yes, Rose was the worst. She was dishonest to the bone. Every word she spoke was a lie, from the very moment Mary first met her. She lied by what she said and by what she didn't say.

*Just like my father.*

Mary tried to push the thought away. But the words rang in her head. She tried to recapture all the daydreams that had served so well in the past: he was too busy to write, visit, spend time with her in vacations; he proved he loved her by sending the expensive food baskets and sweets; he sent her away because her mother made him do it; he liked to show her off to his friends and therefore invited them all to the house at Christmas when he knew she'd be home.

None of them did any good. They had lost their magic. Or she had lost the trick of losing herself in them.

"My father was a liar." Mary whispered it aloud. Her mind leapt from memory to memory, trying to prove her words wrong, trying to retreat into the questionless love she had always felt for him. But that love was gone; it had never been real, because the man she loved had never been real. She had invented him.

I'm not even sad that he's dead, she thought. Now I don't have to try to earn his love because he's dead.

She's as good as dead, his wife. I'll never see her again, and I'm glad. She's a dreadful woman. I'm glad she's not my mother.

I never liked her. All those years that I adored her, I never liked her. She lied, too, calling me "our daughter," answering when I called her "mother."

They all lied, all of them.

*And so did I.*

Mary clapped her hands over her ears as if she could shut out the sound of the words she was hearing in her mind.

But they would not be stilled.

You lied more than any of them. Every time you made an excuse for your father, you lied. Every time you told yourself you were happy, you lied. Every time you lived in your daydreams, it was a lie. You believed their lies because you wanted them to be true, because you wouldn't look beyond them, because you were afraid of what you might see. Of all the lies, those were the worst because you were the liar, and you were lying to yourself.

Mary's mind was like a kaleidoscope that had been turned by an unseen hand. All the bright pieces of memory shifted, formed new patterns, and she saw everything fresh. The Widow O'Neill was right, she thought. I've been a fool.

The anger she felt toward everyone who had betrayed her grew even stronger; it was anger at herself, and her dreamy make-believe world.

On the wall beside the bed there was a small pocket mirror. Mary looked at her reflection, spoke to it. "You made yourself a fool, Mary MacAlistair. Now you make yourself different. Whatever it takes, you must learn to live without dreams. You have no one but yourself. Make that self someone you can trust."

She heard a bell ringing. She had been dimly aware of sounds in the house and from the street, but she screened them out. Now the sound of the bell was a signal for all the other sounds to crowd into her consciousness. There were voices, shouts, laughter, the noises of animals, of creaking wheels, of singing. And there were odors. Streets, mud, garbage, grass, animals, flowers, food.

Mary stood, stretched the stiffness out of her body. She felt a tingle of excitement. The world was all around her, waiting to be viewed with her newly found perspective. The world as it was, not the world as she wanted it to be. It would be different now because she would be different now.

She opened the door of her room and stepped out to meet it.

# 27

While Mary was taking the first steps toward adjusting to her changed circumstances and her new home, a storm was raging in the home of the Courtenays.

The name of the storm was Jeanne.

She had gone to her mother's room that morning expecting to hear that Valmont had asked for her hand.

Instead Berthe had told her that Valmont's meeting with her father was about Mary, about a secret in Mary's past that was so disgraceful that she was being sent away.

"May-ree? Valmont saw Papa about May-ree and not about me?" Jeanne threw herself onto her mother's bed in a fit of weeping.

Berthe tried everything she knew to calm Jeanne, but to no avail. When Marie Laveau arrived to dress Jeanne's hair for a luncheon party she found both mother and daughter in tears.

The cause, Berthe told her, was that Jeanne's friend had gone away.

"Mademoiselle's beautiful eyes will be disfigured," said Marie. "I will rub her temples to calm her. Then I will prepare a bath for her eyes. For yours, too, Madame." She lifted Jeanne easily, placed her in a chair and stood behind her, stroking her forehead with a strong circular motion, whispering strange words to the rhythm of the hypnotic spirals.

As she worked Marie thought about Mary MacAlistair. Her amusement was well hidden, but Marie was secretly laughing. The Sazerac woman would be extremely angry that her victim had escaped. That pleased Marie; she disliked Celeste, and she had no grievance against Mary. Now the girl would not die. A few headaches for a week or two, some weakness in the limbs for a few days, and then she would be all right. And Marie still kept the gold coins. An entertaining, most satisfactory outcome.

The little Courtenay was tranquil now. Marie nodded to the mother, held her finger to her lips to order silence, busied herself with vials of liquids she took from her bag.

"Soak a cloth with this, Madame," she said to Berthe, "and put it over your closed eyes for an hour while you rest. I will go with Mademoiselle to her room to wash her eyes and dress her hair."

Jeanne walked with Marie as if she were in a trance.

Her agitation returned when Marie was putting the finishing touches on her hair. "Look at me," she cried. She clutched Marie's arm. "Am I not beautiful?"

"Very beautiful, Mademoiselle."

"But why, then, does the man I love not want me? I am desolate. There must be something I can do. They say that you . . . help people like me . . . that there are spells . . . charms . . . potions . . ."

Marie removed Jeanne's hand from her arm. "There are such things, Mademoiselle." She tucked a small comb into Jeanne's hair to hold a long ringlet behind her left ear.

"I must have it, whatever it is. What do I do?" Jeanne's eyes were large and pleading.

"It is necessary to know the circumstances, Mademoiselle, the name of the man and his location. And such magic costs money."

"I have no money. Isn't there anything else? My pearls? My fur cape? My gown from Paris? It is sewn with pearls."

Marie looked at the velvet case that held Jeanne's string of pearls. They were, she knew, of the first water, perfectly matched, deeply lustrous. Worth thousands, worth more than the love of any man in her opinion. How foolish women were. And men, too. She had earned a fortune from such foolishness.

"There is a tree in the corner of the garden behind the cathedral," she said. "It shades the street outside where a cripple sells coconut cakes. In the trunk of the tree there is a hole the size of a hand. Tie the pearls in a handkerchief and drop it in the hole. I will bring what you want the following day."

"But I want it now. Take the pearls now."

"That is not the way these things are done, Mademoiselle. You must do as I say, or you will not succeed."

"I will. I will. I'll do anything you tell me to do. Only help me, I beg of you."

Marie stepped back to look at Jeanne's hair. It was perfect. She began to pack the lotions and pomades in her bag. "And the man's name, his address?"

"Valmont Saint-Brévin. He lives on a plantation upriver. It's called Benison."

Marie nodded. Jeanne searched her face for some expression of confidence, of apprehension, of warning . . . some hint of the possibility of success. But there was nothing, no reaction at all.

• • •

Marie waited until she was blocks away from the Courtenay house. Then she threw her head back and laughed until her sides ached. Even when the rain began and she scurried for home, Marie continued to laugh. She was drenched, but still chuckling, when she reached the house on Saint Anne Street.

The house was set back from the street, unusual in the French Quarter, and had a front yard crowded with unpruned green vines and plants beneath tall banana trees. A water-laden broad leaf released its burden of collected rain on Marie's head when she opened the gate in the sagging high picket fence. She cursed it amiably, smiling.

Nothing could dampen the humor of being hired to cast a spell on Valmont Saint-Brévin.

Almost no one knew it, but Val and Marie were close friends. The friendship was a curiosity, given their natures.

Val regarded young women as witless creatures, to be conquered and used if they were from a lower class, to be eluded if they were on his own social level. It was the common attitude of men, and he never questioned it.

Marie considered men easy prey to be manipulated and dominated for her profit and pleasure.

Yet each of them respected, admired, enjoyed the other. And appreciated the friendship all the more because of its unlikeliness.

They had met almost twenty years earlier, when Val was a youth of thirteen, about to leave for Paris and schooling there. The old black woman who had been nursemaid to his father and later to him had brought him to Marie's mother, the elder voodoo queen. She wanted a charm for him, a talisman to protect him in France and to bring him safely home again. Val was embarrassed, but amenable. He had a deep affection for his nurse. He followed all the voodoo queen's instructions, submitted to the anointings and dustings and ingestions of a long incense-heavy ceremony, and accepted the pouch of "powerful good gris-gris" with graceful expressions of gratitude. He lost his composure only once—when a wiry creature leapt down onto his shoulders as he walked between the banana trees on his way out of the house.

It was Marie, then four years old. She had heard what was said, that he was going to Paris. She begged him to send her a real French wax doll to play with.

Her mother freed Val from Marie's importunate embrace and cuffed the child. But Val promised the doll, and he kept his promise.

Marie learned to write so that she could send a letter to thank him. And to ask for new dresses for the doll.

Throughout the years the infrequent letters and gifts continued. As Marie grew older, her letters became Val's most accurate and entertaining source of news about happenings in New Orleans. And her questions about Paris and France made Val aware of things he would otherwise have neglected or ignored. He sent her books and sketches and newspapers. She sent him the ground herbs and spices essential for Creole food, with instructions for using them.

And, as so often happens, in these letters each of them revealed to a stranger thoughts and emotions that neither would have confided to a closer person. By the time Val returned to New Orleans the intimacy that had grown between them was so strong that even the shock of meeting face to face could not destroy it. And it was so cherished by them both that they avoided the potentially destructive added intimacy of a love affair. Instead they played skillful games with words and gestures that recognized all the possibilities that existed and denied their fruition at the same time. And added dimension to the friendship.

Marie knew Valmont's mind and heart even better than he did. It would be a superlative joke if she could voodoo him for the little Courtenay. But she also knew the limits of her powers. Strong as they were, they could not do it. She would have to settle for the trick she always played on women of Jeanne's class. If it worked, it would also trick Val. Even though she could never tell him about her part in it, she would be able to laugh about it for the rest of her life.

She went into the house and dropped her wet clothes in a heap on the floor. Smiling, humming, naked, and beautiful, she moved around her kitchen, gathering the ingredients for the love potion she would exchange for Jeanne's pearls.

Love was such a profitable commodity. Even more so than hate. Marie made a mental note to send word to Celeste Sazerac about the departure of Mary MacAlistair.

All in all, this day was one of the most satisfactory Marie had ever had. She began to sing while she mixed powders in a bowl. She sincerely hoped that the headaches Mary MacAlistair was having weren't terribly painful. Too bad she couldn't send her the antidote.

• • •

Valmont Saint-Brévin removed his hat when the rain began. The cold wetness felt good on his head. He had a pounding headache.

It was the inevitable product of a night with too much wine and no sleep, and he berated himself for his folly. Sugar-making season was too short to waste hours in gambling and drinking. He should have ridden out to Benison immediately after the opera.

Still, what could he have done other than meet with Carlos Courtenay once he had recognized the girl in his box? Carlos had to be warned that his daughter's companion was no fit company for an innocent girl.

The meeting left him with a nasty taste in his mouth, a taste of salaciousness, of petty gossip, of informing. So he had had some more champagne. And then a few hands of faro with some friends to put the whole episode out of his mind. A few glasses and a few hands became many, and an ill-considered joke provoked a challenge, so that at daybreak he was in the garden behind the cathedral for yet another duel. He meant to prick his opponent's arm and end the duel with one drop of blood. But he was drunk and he wounded the man in the shoulder by mistake. Wounded him seriously. God! The whole evening was nothing but a series of heavy-handed blunders, injuries that he inflicted on other people's lives. He was disgusted with himself and his life. Even the challenge of beating the weather and the clock was not enough to cure his malaise today. He couldn't concentrate on the task at hand. His headache got in the way, as did the distasteful recollections of the night before.

Carlos Courtenay had been like a wounded bull. He would have rushed out and killed the American girl if Valmont hadn't done the one thing that was sure to stop him, warned him of the scandal it would cause and the effect on Jeanne's reputation.

Jeanne's reputation must be a fragile thing already. Val couldn't help thinking so. The girl radiated sexuality, eagerness, availability. He had responded to it himself. Just remembering her unmistakable message of overheated desires gave him an unwanted stirring in his loins. By all the saints, it would be an experience to bed her! Even for a man as experienced as he.

She couldn't have learned that from the American whore. It was as old and as primitive as Lilith. Besides, the other girl had none of it. Funny that she seemed such an innocent. Rose Jackson trained her girls well. Val grinned at the idea that one of Rose's girls had somehow wormed her way into the ultraconservative shelter of Berthe Courtenay's protection. He had been right to expose her, but he couldn't help admiring her artfulness. She had almost pulled it off, too. He recalled Philippe Courtenay being very boring one night on the subject of the girl's rare virtues.

Rare, indeed. Nonexistent. Val wondered what had charmed Philippe so much. He hadn't observed any particular appeal.

Damn it all, he was wasting too much time thinking about women. He spurred his horse. There was sugar to be made, and the wagons were moving too slowly up ahead. After the work was done he'd go to the city and spend a week with a good whore in the apartment he kept at the Saint Louis Hotel. Maybe Rose's girl Annabel. She had a sense of humor. He remembered one time...

# 28

Celeste Sazerac was furious when she learned that Mary was gone. She tore Marie Laveau's note into a hundred tiny pieces then threw the pieces on the floor and ground them under her heels, moaning through clenched teeth all the while.

In the middle of her paroxysm, she abruptly stopped. She half crouched, hand to her mouth, head cocked, listening for sounds that were not there. Then she dropped to her knees and frantically scrabbled across the floor picking up the minute pieces of paper, certain that someone might find them and reassemble the message that tied her to the attempted murder.

When she had them all in a pile in front of her knees, she ate them.

Afterwards she went downstairs to her mother's sitting room for coffee.

"Did you enjoy the lake, Celeste?" Anne-Marie Sazerac asked vaguely.

"It was pleasant enough. Service at the hotel isn't what it should be."

"No one goes there in the winter. I'm surprised they were open."

"They opened a suite for me. Don't you remember, Maman? We own that hotel. Most of the family goes there in the summer. I don't know why. I don't like the lake in the summer; it's too crowded."

In fact Celeste didn't like the lake at any time of year. She hated to be away from the house on Royal Street where she ruled uncontested. But it was the only place she could think of, and she had needed to be away when Mary MacAlistair died and was buried. She was afraid her elation would be visible.

Now it was clear that the miserable ten days in the hotel had been unnecessary, wasted. Ten days of worry that someone might break the big lock on her wardrobe and find the casket. Ten days of being without it. Ten days away from her mother and the crumbs of attention she gave to Celeste. Ten days of waiting to be safe for all time.

Wasted.

Jacques came silently into the room and murmured to Celeste that a young person named MacAlistair was at the door.

Celeste let out a short scream.

Her mother looked up from the unread book she was holding in her lap.

"It's nothing, Maman." Celeste sent Jacques to the kitchen for fresh coffee to replace the untouched pot on the table in front of her mother. Then she hurried to the door.

"Good afternoon, Mademoiselle Sazerac," said Mary. "I'm so happy to find you home. Have you..."

Celeste didn't let her finish. "Go away," she growled. "You have no family in New Orleans. Go away from here and never come back. I'll have nothing to do with you, do you hear? Go away and leave me alone." She slammed the door with an echoing crash.

Mary winced at the noise. Then she walked away. At the house next door a maid was bargaining through an open window with the charcoal seller on the banquette. Both of them had stopped talking to listen to Celeste's tirade. They were looking at Mary with undisguised curiosity.

She nodded and smiled. "Somehow," she said, "I'm not really very surprised."

She had learned a lot during her week in the Irish Channel. One thing was, as a new friend had told her, always expect the worst and you'll never be disappointed.

Another was that it was neither a sin nor a crime for a young woman to walk down the street alone. She had no escort for her call at the Sazerac house, and the lack didn't concern her. On the contrary, being on her own, accountable to no one, gave her an intoxicating sense of freedom. Now that what she most feared had happened, there was a giddy relief. She needn't fear it any more. It was over. She could get on with her life.

She turned onto Dumaine Street and walked rapidly for two blocks to the market. It was after nine and the great rush of morning shopping was over. Mary strolled unimpeded by crowds, looking at all the things for sale. When she had seen everything, she went back to the seller whose gumbo smelled the richest. "Do you have crab in your gumbo?" she asked, with an approximation of the black dialect.

The man stirring the pot grinned mightily. "Much crab, 'Zelle, and many crayfish. This is the finest gumbo in Louisiana."

Mary held out the tiny coin called a picayune. In return she was given a deep brown pottery bowl of the thick rich mixture and a spoon. She ate it with relish; the Widow O'Neill set an ample table of solid food, but she scorned the seasonings typical of Creole cooking, and Mary missed them.

When her bowl was empty, she gave it back to the vendor with compliments on his recipe. He gave her a candy made of coconut and molasses. "Lagniappe, 'Zelle."

Mary thanked him and walked on, munching the sticky sweet. She had eaten a big breakfast and had no need of either gumbo or candy, but she wasn't eating for nourishment. Nor was it to make up for her treatment at the Sazerac house. It was, rather, a kind of celebration. Her future was in her own hands now, and she was celebrating the adventure of it by doing whatever she wanted to do.

She clambered up to the top of the levee and looked down on the river, the tall-masted ocean-going ships, the mountains of cargo waiting to be loaded, the purposeful chaos of men and animals and drays. It was a bright day; the wind off the river was cold, wrapped by the warmth of the sun; colorful flags from a dozen countries snapped atop ships' masts in the wind, bright against the blue sky in the bright day. Mary felt elated. Anything was possible in New Orleans. It was a place for excitement and adventure.

She walked next across the Place d'Armes, admiring the buildings of the fabulous Baroness. Some day, she promised herself, she'd find out why Carlos Courtenay had called the Baroness the most extraordinary woman in New Orleans. The second block-long building looked almost complete. Mary dawdled next to the cannon in the center of the square in hopes that the Baroness might come out. But no one appeared. No one at all. The buildings were lifeless, closed, except for one street-level door on the street to her left. Mary wandered over to take a peek inside.

The door led to a shop. Inside there were four counters made of glossy mahogany, a wall of shelves holding stands with bonnets, shirtwaists, shawls, capes, and a young woman who ran up to Mary and asked, in English, if there was something in particular that she would like to see.

Mary would have liked to look closely at everything, but she had no money to spend, so she shook her head and walked on to the Cathedral at the head of the square. It was shadowy inside after the sunlight. She stood for a moment until her eyes adjusted, then she blessed herself, genuflected, and slipped into a rear pew where she knelt and whispered to God.

"Thank you, Heavenly Father, for helping me find the happiness I feel today."

She started to rise, then knelt again.

"And please will you help me tomorrow when I go to look for work that will pay me wages."

When she left the Cathedral Mary walked up to Chartres Street, crossing from side to side, looking in all the shops. No one rushed to help her the way the woman in the Baroness's building had done. The shops were too crowded and busy. Mary was able to admire all the elegant and delicate and frivolous array of goods for sale at her leisure. It took her over three hours to walk six blocks.

Her pace quickened when she reached Canal Street. She was no longer just looking at pretty things, she was shopping. She looked for the place she had been told about, found it almost at once. Big letters on the side of the building identified it: D. H. HOLMES. It was, to Mary's eyes, enormous, like all the shops on Chartres Street put together under one roof. She walked from aisle to aisle, counter to counter, dazzled by the variety and the quantity of things for sale.

She had brought five dollars from her precious supply, and she spent it carefully. At three o'clock she emerged with a smiling face flushed with triumph. She was carrying a big paper-wrapped parcel that contained some sturdy black leather ladies' boots, brown wool gloves, five yards of chocolate-brown alpaca, two sets of white linen cuffs and collar, brown buttons and thread, and two needles. On her head she was wearing a new chip bonnet with a perky brown-and-white-striped taffeta ribbon tied in a bow under her chin.

It was the first time she had ever bought anything for herself by herself. She had found everything she was looking for. And she had sixty cents left over.

Enough to buy bakery cakes for her friends at the boarding house and to ride the streetcar home.

"Mrs. O'Neill, look what I brought for dessert." Mary put the ribbon-tied bakery box on the kitchen table. "I've had the most wonderful day!"

Mrs. O'Neill untied the ribbon, smoothed it flat between her fingers, and rolled it into a neat tight circle. She put it in a box she lifted down from a shelf and returned the box to its place. Then she opened the bakery box.

"Chocolate," she said. She touched one of the cakes with a careful finger and put a dot of icing on her tongue. "Real chocolate . . . It's been twenty years and more that I haven't tasted real chocolate." She sat down on the stool near the fire. "You found your grandmother, then, Mary, and she's as rich as you always believed."

"No. No, I didn't find her at all. Mademoiselle Sazerac slammed the door in my face. But it doesn't matter. I'm even glad in a way. I'd much rather take care of myself and make my own way."

The Widow O'Neill held back the words on her tongue. The girl would learn soon enough. To her great surprise, Mary was a good learner. In the week she had been in the house she applied herself diligently and with reasonable success to learning how to wash and iron, scrub and sweep, find her way around the neighborhood and the city. She had also made friends with the other boarders and had gone to confession on Saturday and mass on Sunday. Most amazing of all, she hadn't put on airs or told her poor-little-me-the-rich-girl-done-wrong stories at all. Mrs. O'Neill had grown almost fond of her. She'd be glad to have Mary stay as long as she had money to pay her rent.

"May I borrow your scissors, Mrs. O'Neill? I'm going to make a dress to wear tomorrow when I go to look for work. I bought some lovely material."

"Do you know how to sew, Mary MacAlistair?"

"Oh, yes. I've made a dress before."

"And you'll sew this one before tomorrow?"

"I don't mind working on it all night if I have to."

"I see. You'll be wanting extra oil for your lamp."

"Oh. I hadn't thought of that. Yes, thank you very much."

"Did you buy a needle for this sewing you're going to do?"

"Yes, I did. And thread and buttons and a very nice ready-made collar and cuffs that can be washed separately. I bought everything I need."

"Pins, too?"

Mary's elation ebbed visibly.

"No matter," said the widow. "I've a box you can borrow."

I must be daft, she said to herself after Mary dashed off to her room to start working on her dress.

One of the dresses that Jeanne Courtenay had handed on to Mary was a pale-green muslin sprigged with tiny pink flowers, buttoned from throat to hem with pink china roses. It was Mary's favorite because it was, she believed, the prettiest and most becoming of the five Jeanne had given her. It also fit her better than the others. Her plan was to copy the dress, with slight variations, using the muslin as a pattern. She could take out the stitches in the dress seams, cut out the pieces from the brown alpaca, sew the muslin back together, and have two favorite dresses, one for summer and one for winter. She needed a winter dress. Even in New Orleans it was chilly to wear summer frocks in November with only a shawl for warmth. And she needed something less girlish than Jeanne's hand-me-downs when she went looking for work. She had to look responsible and mature.

Her plan for the new dress was a good one. But carrying it out was not as easy as she had thought it would be. Jeanne's dress was well made, with strong small stitches that were difficult to see and to remove. Mary was still working on the first seam when daylight began to fade. She had only just finished it when she heard the familiar clatter of the other boarders returning home from work. There were four of them, three men and a young woman who was two years older than Mary.

The Widow O'Neill's house was the largest on Adele Street. Only one other had two stories, and it had only two rooms to a floor. The O'Neill house had four rooms, two on each side of a narrow center hall. Mrs. O'Neill's bedroom was on the second floor; the three men had the remaining three bedrooms. Mary and the other young woman had rooms on the ground floor. One of the four square rooms had been divided into two narrow rectangles, big enough for a bed, bureau, and straight chair. The bureau also served as a washstand; a bowl and pitcher sat on top of it, with a towel hanging on a peg above. Additional pegs on the back of the door were for hanging clothes.

The rest of the ground floor was taken up by the kitchen; the dining room, where meals were eaten and the boarders sat to relax and talk; and the parlor, the pride of the house. As far as Mary knew, no one ever went there except Mrs. O'Neill, armed with dust cloth and carpet sweeper. The kitchen was the heart of the house during the day, the dining room in the evening.

Mary's next-room neighbor tapped on Mary's door, opened it partway and stuck her head in. "How was the day?"

"Just fine, Louisa. I went to the Holmes store like you told me, and it was as wonderful as you said it would be. I bought some brown alpaca."

"Good. And boots; did you get the boots? Those things you're wearing are close to falling apart."

"I got boots. And a new bonnet. It's so pretty, Louisa, let me show it to you."

"Mary. You don't need a new bonnet. Yours has months left in it."

"I do need it. It makes me look..."

"Pretty. For Paddy Devlin, huh?"

"No, I'm not thinking about Paddy Devlin."

"But he's thinking about you. All the time. Night and day."

"Hush! Louisa, please. He'll hear you." Louisa winked and was gone. After a moment Mary heard the monotonous sound of scales being sung. Louisa practiced every night for two hours, one before supper, one before bedtime. She wanted to become an opera singer.

Mary was the only one in the house who didn't mind Louisa's scales. What she did mind was Louisa's teasing. Patrick Devlin was the first admirer in Mary's life, and she didn't know how to handle his admiration or any jokes about it.

When Mary was introduced to the other boarders at her first supper, Paddy Devlin's reaction was so extreme that even Mary knew that he was smitten. He dropped the bowl he was holding, knocked over a chair when he bent to pick it up, stammered and blushed whenever he was called on to speak, and gazed at Mary "like a moonstruck calf," as Louisa said later.

Mrs. O'Neill acted as if nothing unusual had happened, but the two other men were merciless to poor Paddy. "And why don't you pass Mary the butter, Paddy?... Mary's waiting for you to finish with the salt, Paddy... Did you happen to mention to Mary what a fine reputation you have as a dancer, Paddy?... Did you get a sunburn on this gray rainy day to make your cheeks so red, Paddy?" They roared with laughter at their own humor.

Mary was embarrassed, too, but she wasn't the butt of their humor; she could keep her eyes cast down because the Reillys weren't talking to her. They were a father and son and looked it, both of them burly, hearty, red-faced, blue-eyed, black-haired men. Next to them Patrick Devlin looked almost fragile and extremely young. He had the freckles so often found with fiery red hair like his, and he was deceptively slight of build. He was nineteen years old and as strong as an ox.

After that first supper the two Reillys were not as broad with their taunts. Mrs. O'Neill had spoken sharply to them about disrupting her supper table. But Patrick's adoration was undiminished, and he still blushed whenever Mary looked his way.

Mary found the experience rather heady. But she didn't like Louisa's teasing. Especially when she twitted Mary about the famous tempers that redheads had and speculated about the trouble her children would give her when she and Paddy were married and had a houseful of them.

Mary didn't want to think about marriage because that made her think of Jeanne. And Valmont Saint-Brévin. She particularly didn't want to think about him because her thoughts were so disturbing, so full of hopeless longing and bewildering bodily desires.

She was determined to concentrate on the euphoria of independence, to be happy, to carry out the bold plan she had made to find work.

She stayed awake very late sewing, until her eyes were bleary and her fingers were bleeding from needle pricks and the lamp was dull with soot. The dress was far from finished.

She sewed all the next day. And the next. On Friday afternoon it was done. She tried it on then, heavy with apprehension and fatigue. Her sore fingers trembled when she buttoned the front.

It was perfect. Mary returned the widow's pins and scissors, paraded around the kitchen to show off her handiwork, then went back to her room, hung the dress carefully on a peg, and climbed into her bed to sleep for thirteen hours.

She woke at five Saturday morning with a warm, tingling sensation of well-being and confidence. "Today I'll become a self-supporting grown woman," she announced to the still-dark, chilly room. "Nothing can go wrong now."

# 29

It was a day to inspire confidence in anyone, even those much less optimistic than Mary MacAlistair. Sunny, with an invigorating breeze that carried the scent of flowers from the warm sheltered gardens of the Vieux Carré throughout the narrow streets already rich with the aroma of coffee from the open doors of coffee shops and from the street-corner vendors with their shining copper cookers.

Mary stepped down from the streetcar in her perfect dress and gleaming new boots and brave new bonnet. She was smiling. At the day, at the adventure she was beginning, at the city she had made her home. Many people smiled in return, some gentlemen lifting their hats. Her pleasure in life was a pleasure to see.

Confidence carried her further than she knew. When she walked into the shop that Berthe Courtenay had talked about, Mary asked to see Madame herself. The clerk she spoke to thought Mary must be a new customer of great wealth; no one else ever got to see Madame. She ushered Mary through the shop and into the luxurious small salon where preferred clients conferred with the most exclusive provider of the most expensive gowns and accessories in the city, the legendary Madame Alphande.

Madame did not appear until after a maid had brought a silver pot of coffee and a silver tray of almond wafers and put them on a table near the chair where Mary was sitting. Mary had time to enjoy a cup of coffee and a cookie before Madame swept in with the costly whispering sound of silk skirts over silk petticoats.

Mary stood and smiled. "Bonjour, Madame."

"Bonjour, Mademoiselle." Madame was haughty but correct, her greeting carefully measured to intimidate the customer but not frighten her away. She gestured an invitation for Mary to seat herself again. Clusters of diamond rings on both hands glittered a warning of expense to come.

Mary remained standing. She was sure that employees were as polite to their employers as students were to their teachers; she had no other guideposts. "I've come to work for you," she said cheerfully.

Mary didn't know that only shock kept Madame Alphande from

shouting for someone to throw her bodily out the rear door. The Frenchwoman was incapable of speech.

But she could hear. Mary told her about the dress she was wearing, that she had made it in under three days, and she related all the details of the alterations she had done on Jeanne Courtenay's Paris gown, including the intricate embroidery.

Madame was familiar with Jeanne's gown; there was little she didn't know about the wardrobes of New Orleans's society women, and Jeanne's début had been the talk of the French Quarter.

"How much time did you spend on each lily of the valley?" she asked, her voice restored by cupidity.

"More than two hours. They were very complicated."

Madame thought quickly. Her best embroidery woman could not have done better. And the season had barely begun. She had more gowns already ordered than she could be sure of delivering. This impertinent girl was a godsend.

"This is not a convent school, Mademoiselle, it is a business. The work is demanding, and I brook no excuses for less than perfection."

Mary nodded eagerly. "I understand."

"The women in the atelier are here promptly at eight; they work until five, with a half hour in the middle of the day free for a meal that they provide themselves."

"Yes, Madame."

"The week is from Monday morning until Saturday evening. Sunday the workroom is closed unless there is an emergency that must be dealt with."

"Yes, Madame."

The girl looks strong, mused Madame Alphande, and the good Lord knows she's eager enough. I might be able to pay her less than the others, perhaps as little as two dollars a day instead of two fifty. "How much money do you expect you are worth, Mademoiselle?" she said.

Mary had thought about her wages for a long time. She took a deep breath and asked for what she thought was a fortune. "I would like to earn six dollars a week, Madame."

"Be here at eight on Monday. Use the rear door, on Toulouse Street. Speak to Mademoiselle Annette. I will tell her to expect you. What is your name?"

"Mary MacAlistair, Madame."

The Frenchwoman's lip curled. "American. Your French is surprisingly adequate. Here you will be Mademoiselle Marie Quatre. There are three other Maries. You may go now. It will be the final time you use the entrance on Chartres Street."

"Thank you, Madame." Mary curtseyed. "I'm very grateful, and I promise you, you won't regret..."

"Go. I have work to do."

Mary's new boots practically danced her out of the shop. Success. She had known nothing could go wrong. She would be rich! Six dollars a week, and just look at everything she had bought for only five when she went shopping. Including chocolate cakes for everyone. And she still had a little more than fifteen dollars left from the thirty she had started with. She hadn't a care in the world.

I'll walk down to the steamboat landing, she decided. Maybe the *Cairo Queen* will be in, and Joshua will be there. I'd like to tell him my good news.

The docks would be a maelstrom of activity, of course, loading and unloading, stevedores everywhere. Patrick Devlin would probably drop the load he was hauling if he caught sight of her in her new bonnet. Mary giggled, crossed the street, and set off, skimming along the banquette as if it were a ballroom floor.

She didn't look inside the coffee house across from Madame Alphande's shop, so she didn't see Valmont Saint-Brévin standing at the counter for the tiny cup of coffee known as a "small black." Valmont saw her.

Rose's little girl must have landed on her feet again, he thought. Shopping at Alphande's, she must have landed very comfortably. And is she ever pleased with herself. One can almost see the canary feathers at the corners of her mouth. I suppose I did her a favor removing her from the respectability of the Courtenay house. I wonder if she'd like to show her gratitude? There must be something extraordinary about her that I can't see if some man has set her up with a purse that can buy Alphande's wares. I'd like to find out what it is.

"Another small black," Val said. There were still ten minutes to pass before his meeting with his banker, a block away. He was annoyed by the message he had received from Julien Sazerac. It said only that Val must come to Sazerac's office at ten for a confidential meeting of urgent importance. It was too cryptic and damn near arrogant. The subject had better be extremely important and urgent to call him away from Benison during sugar making. If it was nothing more than another of Julien's investment schemes, Val thought he might change bankers . . . of course, Julien had made a lot of money for him with those schemes . . . he wished he liked the man better. Julien was a cold fish, in his opinion.

Time to go. Val stepped to the door, then retreated hastily when he saw Jeanne Courtenay with her maid on the other side of the street.

Another importunate note-sender. He had received three little scented missives from Jeanne in the past week, urging him to attend three balls that she was going to. Val had never before been pursued quite so openly. He couldn't decide if Jeanne was childishly artless or clever enough to appear that way. Nor could he make up his mind whether or not he wanted to risk responding to her overtures. He watched her from the shadowed interior of the coffee house. She was appealing, he had to admit. Beautiful. Delectably young and excitingly mature, a powerful combination. Imperious, too. She spoke sharply to her maid, left her waiting on the banquette, and entered the shop of Madame Alphande as if she owned it. Reckless. Young ladies were not supposed to be unchaperoned for as much as a minute, not even inside their dressmaker's place of business. Decidedly reckless. She might be dangerous, this one. Val was intrigued.

He left the coffee shop and hurried toward the bank; he would be late, and he prided himself on his punctuality. He was irritated with Jeanne now for delaying him.

He would have been much more annoyed if he had known that the reason for her visit to Madame Alphande's was to give another message for him to a maid there. The black woman was one of Marie Laveau's many accomplices and informers among the servants in New Orleans. She would pass the note on to another, whose identity Jeanne would never know, who would manage to put it into hands that would deliver it to Benison and Val. The delivery was expensive. Jeanne had started stealing money from her mother's purse.

She didn't like doing it, because she was afraid she'd be found out, but she had no alternative. She had to see Valmont, had to use the spell Marie had left in the hollow tree. There wasn't much time. Her father was encouraging the calls of the American, Will Graham. If he asked for her hand, her fate would be sealed.

Jeanne went at once to the salon for preferred customers. "I'd like coffee," she told the clerk. "Afterwards you can show me some white lace mantillas." The maid who brought the coffee was the one who took her letters. And what did it matter that she already had two mantillas? Lace tore so easily.

In slightly more than a week Jeanne had already learned the privileges that accompanied the social success of a rich man's only daughter. She bought two more mantillas and instructed the clerk to have them delivered. "You know the house. Send the bill to my father."

"Yes, Mademoiselle. Would Mademoiselle be interested in seeing the new chemises that arrived only yesterday from France? Or a lace cap for evening at home? There is one of such enchantment that only a face like Mademoiselle Courtenay's can do it justice."

"No. I'm never home in the evening. The season is too busy."

"For you, yes, Mademoiselle. All New Orleans knows that you are the reigning beauty."

Jeanne's rudeness melted away. She knew that what the clerk said was true, and she loved to hear it said over and over again. "Perhaps I will look at the chemises. And if you have a silk petticoat in pink..."

Maman will fuss, she thought, but not too much. And I do love the things here. Madame Alphande's is definitely the best shop in town.

"It's unquestionably the best shop in town," Mary said at the supper table that evening, "and I start working there day after tomorrow." She was glowing with pride.

Paddy Devlin's spoon clanged against his bowl then fell onto the floor. Mary bit the inside of her lip to keep from laughing. She didn't dare meet Louisa's eyes. It's a good thing that I didn't see Paddy at the landing, she thought. Who knows what he might have dropped on his foot... or on me.

She was sorry, though, that she hadn't seen Joshua. She said as much to Louisa. "Your brother's on the same boat. Will you ask him to let Joshua know how I'm doing?"

"Sure I will. At least he won't try to fix me up with a nigger. He's tried with every white man on the river who isn't already married. I tell you, Mary, families are a trial."

"I've learned that. It's much better to be independent."

"I've got to hand it to you, Mary. When you first came here I thought you'd never make it, not somebody from your class."

"What do you mean? This is America. There's no class system here."

"If you can say that, you're not as smart as I thought you were. But you'll learn."

Mary began to learn the next day.

When she left the house to go to mass, Paddy Devlin was waiting on the corner. "Is it all right if I walk alongside you, Miss Mary?" He was blushing, and looked more uncomfortable than ever in his Sunday suit. It was too tight in the shoulders with sleeves too long and trousers too short. There was an indentation across his forehead where his hat had pressed on his head until he removed it to greet Mary.

"I'll be happy to have your company, Mr. Devlin," Mary said. She was afraid she might be blushing, too. She hoped her normally bright red cheeks hid the flush she could feel. She was, in fact, glad to have company. Louisa was sleeping late, and Mrs. O'Neill had been to the earlier mass.

It was a long walk to Saint Patrick's, the Catholic church in the American sector. Six blocks from the boarding house to Camp Street, then another fifteen blocks along Camp. There was plenty of time to talk, but Paddy seemed unable to think of anything to say. Mary chattered to fill up the silence, commenting on the houses and gardens they passed, exclaiming at the speed of the horse-drawn carriages that went by, the shiny brasswork on them, the skill of the drivers, the amazing sight of a woman driving herself in a cabriolet with a footman no bigger than a child standing on the rear platform between the wheels. Paddy nodded vigorously to everything she said.

When they arrived at the door of the church, Mary spied a half-empty pew near the back on the left. "There's room for us over there," she said to Paddy.

"We'll sit together?"

"Yes, there's plenty of room."

Mary didn't see Paddy's face at that moment. He was not blushing now. He was pale with emotion.

When the mass began, Mary saw that Paddy took a rosary from his pocket and began to pray. She nudged him gently with her elbow. "Psst. I have my missal," she whispered. "You can share it with me." She had been in the same predicament herself once, forgetting to bring a missal, being unable to follow the mass.

Paddy shook his head. "I do not have the reading," he told her.

Mary looked down at the small book in her hand without seeing it. ". . . not have the reading." What did he mean? He didn't know how to read? She couldn't believe that. She concentrated on the service, found her place, gave herself over to the beloved familiarity of the ritual that was so much a part of her years at the convent school.

Nevertheless she was aware every minute of Paddy beside her, his rosary moving through his fingers.

When they were outside the church again, Paddy was the talkative one. "Next Sunday there will be a fine parade," he said. "I'd be proud to have you watch it with me, Miss Mary. In a year or maybe two I have hopes that I'll be one of the marchers myself."

He spoke easily, enthusiastically as they walked, telling Mary about his life and his ambitions. He had been in America for almost two years and a half now, and he was at last working steadily as a stevedore, instead of only now and then, earning good money and banking most of it. He worked extra hours, too, without pay, learning how to load cotton into the holds of the ships for overseas. There was a special art to it that not everyone could master. It demanded skill as well as strength to pack in the maximum tonnage. "Screwing in the cotton" it was called, and a screwman could make as much as five dollars a day. Screwmen were the elite of the stevedores. It was their Association that would be parading, in full regalia.

It would make his mother proud, Paddy said, to see him marching in a fine apron of blue silk with silver fringe and a band in front and blue banners with silver announcing that these were the screwmen, the best and the bravest on the waterfront. He was sure she would see him, looking down from heaven, and she would be happy that she had insisted on him going to America. He was the eldest and the strongest. He was to have saved his money and sent it back to Ireland to buy passage for the rest of his family. But there wasn't enough time. They were all dead in the famine before his ship reached New Orleans.

"My parents are dead, too," Mary said.

Paddy sighed. "Ah, the sadness of it... But you are alive and well, and I am too, and it's a fine day, the finest I've ever known.

"It will be news to you, Miss Mary, but you were no stranger to me when you came to the Widow O'Neill's. I saw you before, one time only. It was before I got taken on as a stevedore working steady, and I was shoveling dirt to raise a levee. All of a sudden the foreman shouted to us to move back, and along you came. You were riding a great beast of a horse, sitting up on his back, tiny thing that you were, making him do your bidding. You were a glorious thing to see, Miss Mary, glorious.

"When you sat down to the widow's supper table, it was like a princess had come in. I couldn't believe what I was seeing. Every night when I came home I thought you'd be gone, that you were a dream I was having.

"Then last night when you told us you'd got work, just like anybody else, I gave myself a talking to. 'Paddy, my boy,' I said, 'you've got only your own coward's heart to blame if you don't speak a word to Miss Mary.' So I waited for you to walk by me this morning, and I've never done a harder thing than when I said hello to you. The world has seen many miracles, Miss Mary, but none grander than that you should be walking out with Patrick Devlin. I'm a grateful man."

Mary was unable to say a word. Paddy's eloquence was a surprise and his adoration a shock. She smiled as best she could manage, and they walked together back to the boarding house and Mrs. O'Neill's big Sunday dinner. Both of them were silent at table, thinking about the hours that had just passed.

Mary was basking in her first experience of being courted. She didn't know that she had misunderstood the rules that governed the world she now lived in. When a young woman shared a sidewalk with a young man in the Irish Channel, it was a statement. To share a pew in church was a declaration. And sharing her missal was an act of breathtaking intimacy. Even if the sharing was offered rather than actual.

When Paddy Devlin said they were walking out together he meant that they were as good as engaged to be married.

Mary thought he meant no more than that they were taking walks.

# 30

On Monday morning Mary was awake before dawn. She waited impatiently for the day to begin, for her new life of independence to start.

She had to wait again outside the back entrance to Madame Alphande's shop. She arrived a half hour early.

At last a tall thin woman came along the banquette, stopped, took a key out of her reticule, and put it in the lock. She identified herself as Mademoiselle Annette before she turned the key and opened the door.

Mary followed her inside and entered a reign of terror.

A dozen women, thirteen with Mary's arrival, worked in a small, ill-lit room sewing for Madame Alphande. There was no heat and no ventilation; in the first hour of the day the room was chill and clammy, then the heat of the women's bodies warmed it, and by afternoon the air was hot and suffocating.

They sat on backless stools around a table covered with white padding to protect the fragile fabrics of the gowns they were making. Minute bits of lint from the padding escaped into the air and lodged in their nostrils and mouths.

Mademoiselle Annette was the tyrant in charge. She had come from Paris with Madame Alphande twenty years earlier, and she had never seen any reason to alter her contempt for everything in what she called "the colonies." No single piece of work, not even a single hem, ever measured up to her standards.

The women were not allowed to talk, but Mademoiselle Annette talked from morning to evening, spewing out a steady monologue of vituperative comment on the women's work, character, and general worthlessness.

It was she who assigned the tasks for each to do and allotted the time for doing them. There was no letup. She wore a black silk smock over her dress, kept a notebook and pencil in the smock's big pocket, recorded any waste in the notebook. A broken needle or bent pin or extra inches of thread at the end of a seam made her jubilant. "This will come out of your pay envelope," she crowed, brandishing her pencil like an avenger's sword.

The women called her "the bitch." Madame Alphande was "the big bitch." Her demands and her rages were even greater than Mademoiselle Annette's.

Mary was so frightened the first day at work that her hands were shaking and she could do nothing right. Mademoiselle Annette stood behind her, looking over her shoulder, and criticized every move she made. Mary could hardly see the work in front of her because of the tears that filled her eyes.

There was no relief until lunchtime, when Annette left to go upstairs to the dining room in the apartment she shared with Madame Alphande. Once she was gone, Mary learned about the unaffectionate nicknames for her and for Madame. She also learned that there was no sympathy for her from the other women. Mademoiselle Annette's concentration on Mary meant less attention to each of them; that was the only thing that mattered to them. There was no unity among the work force at Madame Alphande's; the women were jealous of one another, were convinced that the work was unequally distributed, each believing that her burden was the greatest. It was one of Mademoiselle Annette's management skills to maintain dissension among the workers so that they couldn't rebel as a group. Individuals could be fired and replaced.

Mary tried to make friends at lunchtime. Mrs. O'Neill had prepared a dinner pail for her; it was the same hearty meal she fixed for the male boarders, and there was much too much food for a young woman with a sedentary job. Mary offered to share with her coworkers. Inside of thirty seconds there was almost nothing left for her. The other women ate greedily, looking at Mary with hostile eyes, resenting her youth, her new dress, her lavish lunch. She didn't look as if she needed a job, whereas for each of them the weekly pay envelope was vital for survival.

"What's she doing here anyhow?" Mary heard Marie Trois say to Marie Deux. "Her with her lady way of talking and dressing. Who does she think she is, a duchess doing her tapestry work for her castle?"

The antagonism made Mary angry; her anger saved her job. In the afternoon she worked like a tireless, flawless automaton. She was determined to be as unfeeling and cold as the women who had rejected her friendship. Before the end of the day Mademoiselle Annette had shifted her attentions to a more responsive victim. Mary felt an ignoble sense of triumph and relief.

She dragged home that night more tired than she had ever been in her life. Every muscle ached from the cramped hours on the stool. And her heart was sore with disappointment at the death of her expectation of joyful adventure in her first job.

"Fine," she said with an effort at brightness when she was asked how the first day had gone.

"Fine," she said on every succeeding exhausted evening. As one nerve-wracking day after another went by, her body and her mind were becoming too numbed to realize how miserable she was.

The realization struck her only at the end of the week, on Saturday, when things got better. She was given an intricate piece of embroidery to do, a colorful burst of silk stitches that made up a tiny glowing hummingbird poised over a rich red poppy. It was the decoration on the pocket of an apron for a lady devoted to her garden.

Mary loved seeing the wings, the petals, the leaves take form under her skilled fingers. The tensions in the airless workroom faded away as she concentrated on the assignment that was more like pleasure than work. This was what she had expected the job to be. She didn't notice the angry stare of Marie Deux, who was the most skilled and highest paid of all the women. Her specialty was embroidery.

When it was finished Mademoiselle Annette could find nothing to criticize. Mary smiled for the first time since Monday morning.

"Wrap it up and deliver it," Annette said sharply. It was raining and cold outside.

She would have been chagrined if she had known how good the biting air and muddy streets felt to Mary.

It was only when she returned from her long walk that her elation evaporated and despair filled her heart. She couldn't face the fetid room and hostile women. I hate this job, she admitted to herself.

But she had to face them. At least the week is almost over, she thought. I can stand anything for another hour. She grasped the handle of the door as if it were a nettle and plunged into the thick unhealthy atmosphere of the workroom.

To discover that in her absence her scissors and pins had been sabotaged. The points were broken off.

She protested angrily to Mademoiselle Annette who berated her for carelessness and impertinence. And who took the notebook out of he pocket with a gleam in her eye.

When Mary got on the streetcar to go home she opened her small brown envelope and dumped her week's pay into her lap. There was five dollars and forty-seven cents. She had expected to feel a thrill of accomplishment at this moment. The only thing she felt was tired.

"Louisa, may I interrupt you for a minute?"

Louisa waved an invitation to enter while she completed the scale she was singing. "Lie down on the bed, Mary; you look terrible."

"I'm awfully tired. I wanted to ask you how you manage. You go to work every day but you still have energy to practice when you get home. Don't you ever get tired?"

"Sure I do. Playing the piano for that old fraud Mr. Bassington's School of the Dance is a terrible chore. But it gives me the money to pay for my voice lessons and to go to the opera, so I don't mind. I want to be an opera singer more than anything on earth. I can bear anything if it will help me to reach my goal. Why don't you come with me tonight? Have you ever been to the Opera?"

Mary massaged her sore cramped fingers. "Yes, I've been to the opera," she said. "It seems as if it was a long time ago."

"What's the matter? Do your hands hurt? Oh, the fingertips are all cut up. I'll ask the widow for some alum. You can soak them to make them tougher... Lord, Mary, what funny fingers you've got. Let me see..." Louisa took Mary's hands in hers and examined their curious structure. "Boy, if I had fingers like that, I'd be the best pianist in the world. Do they make you sew better than other people?"

Mary looked at her hands. Louisa's open curiosity didn't bother her. It seemed a century ago that she had tried to hide her fingers from view. How young she had been. Young and silly.

"Maybe they do help me sew," she said. It was an interesting speculation. She hoped that they were good for something besides making her daydream about a family that didn't exist where all the women had hands like hers. Hot tears spilled from her eyes.

"Oh, Mary, it can't be as bad as all that." Louisa put her arm around Mary's shoulders and patted her like a baby. "It's always hard in the beginning. You'll get used to it, you'll see."

"I'll never make it," Mary said. Her voice was dull. "Look." She took a brown envelope from her pocket, held it out to Louisa.

She had written on it with a pencil. The writing told a sad story:

| | |
|---|---|
| Rent | \$3.00 |
| Dinner pail | \$1.00 |
| Streetcar | \$1.80 |
| | \$5.80 |

"That's my pay envelope, Louisa. For a whole week. It had five dollars and forty-seven cents in it."

"Well, Mary, I can see that you're a great booby. You're not a stevedore hauling crates on your shoulders. You don't need a dinner pail. I always have a coffee and something from a street seller for lunch. That costs about five cents. And you'd do well to walk instead of taking the streetcar. You sit down all day while you're sewing. You just have to learn how to manage, that's all.

"Now come on. Wash your face. I'll treat to the opera, but we have to hurry if we're going to get there on time. We'll have supper when we get back. It'll keep; I can tell by smelling it that it's red beans and rice. Again. For the third time this week."

"I like red beans and rice."

"Good thing you do. We sure get our fill of them."

The opera had already begun when Louisa and Mary got there. The music faintly penetrated the walls of the staircase that they climbed to the upper gallery. Louisa's lips moved soundlessly framing the words of the chorus. She grinned at Mary. "*Barber of Seville,*" she whispered. "I know all of it, even the part for the basso profundo. Mr. Bassington gave me the score and libretto for my birthday."

For Mary the music was a magical escape from her worries and fatigue. She forgot where she was and who she was, until the interval. Then the house lights illuminated the little stages that were the boxes and the dramas within them. Mary saw Jeanne and Berthe Courtenay receiving guests in their box, and it was impossible for her to believe that only a few weeks earlier she had been down there with them. She had not even noticed the galleries when she was in the box. But it was not possible to be unaware of the boxes when sitting in the gallery.

It was also not possible to stop looking for remembered faces, to keep her heart from expanding with happiness when she saw that Valmont Saint-Brévin was not one of the men in the Courtenay box raising glasses to toast Jeanne. That meant that there was no engagement after all.

• • •

The music of the band that led the parade was very different from the music of the orchestra at the opera. But it was equally exciting in its own way. Instead of engulfing Mary and taking her away from the world, it infected her with its rhythm and joyousness and made her joy a part of the joy of the crowds around her. Her feet were tapping, like theirs, and her hands clapping in unison with the hands on all sides of her.

"I'm having such a good time," she shouted to Paddy Devlin.

After the parade passed by Mary and Paddy walked slowly in the crowd along Jackson Street toward the levee. Ahead of them people were stopping, gathering around a leafless tree.

"What is it?" said Mary.

Paddy craned his neck, stood on tiptoe. "Ah," he said, relaxing, "it's a death notice. Come on, Miss Mary, let's go see." He shouldered a path for them through the crowd.

A black-bordered paper nailed to the tree announced that Michael Francis Corcoran had departed this life for a better one on Saturday, November twenty-fourth. The remains could be viewed and last respects paid at the house on Josephine Street opposite the Asylum for Orphan Boys. Paddy asked Mary to read it aloud.

"Frank Corcoran finally drank himself to death," said a thin elderly woman. "I've been saying it would come." Her voice rang with satisfaction.

"It'll be a fine wake," a man said. "I'm for it." He pushed hurriedly past Paddy and Mary.

"What's his hurry?" said the satisfied old woman. "Kate Corcoran will still be cooking the ham, I'm thinking. There's plenty of time."

"She's right, you know," said Paddy in an undertone. "Let's have our walk on the levee like we planned. Then we'll go to the wake if you want to, Miss Mary."

"I don't want to. I've never been to a funeral, and I don't even know the Corcorans."

Paddy waited until they had walked away from the people near the tree before he spoke. "You don't know the wake, then, Miss Mary? It's not a funeral, like you said. The funeral is for later, for the family. The wake is for the departed and all who knew him. It's a grand, festive thing. Everybody will tell fine tales about Frank Corcoran and what a grand man he was. Lies, most of them, because he was a mean man who beat his wife and drank the rent money, but there's no harm in painting a handsome picture for the widow to remember. There'll be good food to eat and a keg of whiskey and some glorious fighting in the yard outside after a while. There's nothing that can match a wake."

Mary was horrified. "Why do people fight?"

"For the high spirits of it. It makes a man feel good to do some bashing."

"Have you ever been in a fight, Mr. Devlin?"

Paddy laughed aloud.

"Ever since I could walk. There's many a one owes the bend in his nose to Paddy Devlin. Don't you worry, Miss Mary. No one will ever give you trouble as long as I'm there to stop them."

Mary thought of Mademoiselle Annette. She'd love to have Paddy break her nose; she knew that wasn't what he was talking about, but the idea of it made her laugh. She didn't really believe Paddy's bragging. People argued, shouted, maybe, but they didn't hit one another.

Paddy smiled, believing that Mary was pleased by his protection. "Will you let me take you to the Corcoran house, then?"

Mary shook her head. "I'd rather not."

Paddy's smile widened. "No matter," he said. "The wake will go on for two or three days. I'll stop in tomorrow maybe."

They walked in comfortable silence along the levee on the wide path between the willow trees that grew on top of it. The cascading green limbs of the trees moved gently in the light breeze, and the river was dappled with sunlight. Mary thought about late November in the Pennsylvania mountains and luxuriated in the green trees, green grass, and warm sun on her shoulders.

"I don't care if I never see another snowflake as long as I live," she said.

"What?"

"Nothing important, Mr. Devlin. I'm just thinking about how happy I am."

"His name is Snow Cloud," said Valmont Saint-Brévin. "Isn't he magnificent?"

Michaela de Pontalba shrugged. "He's striking, I'll grant you that. A pair of whites in front of a black landau looks smart driving in the Bois. But for a race horse, my dear Valmont, there's something very vulgar about such a showy animal."

Val chuckled. "You're trying to buy him from me, aren't you?"

"I wouldn't think of it. I'm letting you know that I wouldn't be offended if you wanted to give him to me as a token of your esteem."

"Dearest Baroness, I esteem you more greatly than any woman in history. Flawless emeralds are yours for the asking. But not Snow Cloud. I've been after him ever since I saw him run in Kentucky. My brilliant banker learned somehow that his owner wagered him at the poker table and lost him to one of the riverboat professionals. God bless Julien Sazerac. He sent for me in time for me to meet the boat when it docked. I never would have gotten Snow Cloud otherwise. He's the fastest, smartest horse in America. I'm going to take him to Charleston in January and make my fortune."

"You already have ten fortunes."

"And you forty. Do you object to making another? It's the challenge, and you know it."

Michaela smiled. "That has become your favorite word of late, Val. 'Challenge.' I'm afraid you're suffering from boredom. You should fall desperately in love. Unrequited, of course. Then you would certainly bore everyone else but you would be fully occupied."

Val laughed. "I'd follow your advice in a minute, but I can't. I'm always requited even before I fall."

Now Michaela laughed. And kept on laughing. "If the gods heard you," she said after she stopped, "you will pay for your flippancy a thousand times, my foolish young friend. Now take me up to the house. I admit that your horse is superb, but I have admired him long enough. I want coffee and a brandy and then a magnificent meal. The air in the country always makes me ravenous."

"You haven't told me yet why you honored me with this visit," said Val when he poured the brandy. "Am I supposed to guess? To know?"

"I wanted to get away from the city. But you're right, I had a purpose. My buildings are not going well, Val. The second is almost completed and I have no tenants. Not even in the first building. I am there with my sons in one house, and a young portrait painter with his wife is in the house next to mine. Sixteen are still empty. It is an abomination." The baroness emptied her glass with one long swallow, held it out to be refilled.

Val poured a larger drink. "I warned you, Michaela. The old-guard French are losing control of the city. New Orleans is moving uptown. The Vieux Carré is too crowded, and it's easier to build in the Second

District or in a suburb like Lafayette than it is to tear down and then build as you have done. The businesses are almost all above Canal Street now, the big stores are on Canal, the brokers and factors are on Camp. It's been going on for years and now it's accelerating. There's a new generation of Creoles who learned English as well as French in school. They don't want to stay behind the invisible wall in the neutral ground."

"What a philistine you are!" Michaela raged. "Do you care nothing for beauty or tradition or charm? Did you learn nothing in Paris about civilized life? The Americans are creating a barren city dominated by business establishments. They think that big equals beautiful. My buildings are in the heart of New Orleans; I intended for them to give new vigor to that heart. The most elegant shops along the street, the most elegant living above in the apartments. When the construction is done I will redo the Place d'Armes, install parterre gardens and a fountain, so that the people from my buildings will have something beautiful to look at from their balconies and a beautiful garden to walk in. There is no such elegance above Canal Street. Why can't everyone see that? Why am I emptying my pockets and my heart to create pearls cast before swine?"

Valmont knelt by her chair. "Dear friend," he said quietly, "tell me what I can do to help."

Michaela stroked his cheek. "I will be calm," she said. "I needed someone to hear my anger. You are a dear creature, Val. I want you to have your portrait done by my little artist tenant, Rinck. That will make him chic, and the rest will follow."

Valmont rose to his feet. "All right. I'll even do that for you, Michaela. But, by God, now I wish you had asked for the horse. I'm going to feel like a fool."

"Not you, my dear. Never you. You have style, élan."

"I've said I'll do it. No need to sugar the dose."

The Baroness held out her hand. "Don't sulk. Come. Kiss me and say you forgive me."

Val raised her hand to his lips. "I will never forgive you, but I shall love you as long as I live."

While Val and Michaela were talking, a small, secretive figure had come to the house, darting among the shrubbery to stay hidden from view. It was Jeanne Courtenay. She ran up onto the gallery just in time to see Valmont with Michaela's hand in his and to hear his flowery laughing declaration through the half-open French window.

"No!" she shouted. She threw the window open with such force that the glass shattered. "You can't love her." Jeanne stamped across the fragments into the room. "You can't. She's old and ugly. I'm beautiful and I'm young and I love you, Valmont. You've got to love me, you must."

The Baroness was amused. "Dear Val, entertainment, too. What a perfect host."

Jeanne's little hands curled into talons, and she launched herself toward the Baroness. Valmont caught her around the waist from behind and held her fast despite the blows of her boots against his legs and her wild struggles.

Michaela stood with a sudden spring. In two steps she was in front of Jeanne. She caught the girl's hands around the wrist. "This won't do," she said calmly. Then she released her grip and, before Jeanne knew what was happening, slapped her face, snapping her head back against Val's chest.

"Drop her," the Baroness said. "I can take care of this." There was such assurance in her voice that Val did not for an instant doubt the truth of her statement.

Nor did Jeanne. She stopped flailing and squirming and began to cry. Valmont released her. "Go away, Val," said Michaela. "Order my carriage. I'll take this young woman home. It's Mademoiselle Courtenay, isn't it? Go, Val."

She looked at Jeanne as if the girl were an undisciplined house pet. "Sit down, Mademoiselle. We will have coffee together until the carriage comes. Val, I told you to leave us. Defeat is bitter; don't add humiliation to the girl's burdens."

Jeanne had buried her face in her hands. She didn't uncover it until she heard Michaela say, "He's gone. Now we can see what can be salvaged. You've made a fool of yourself, and that's very nearly fatal. But you did it with a touch of style and a great deal of passion, and Valmont is susceptible to both of them."

Michaela left a message on the table next to the coffee tray. "The matter is in hand. I am returning J. and her horse to her grandfather with an appropriate story that will protect everyone's good name. Such a pity. So dull. The impassioned young C. came armed with a voodoo spell that you would have been defenseless against, so you are more deeply in my debt than you realized. You will certainly be delighted to have an opportunity to defray at least a portion of it. See reverse."

Val turned the square card over. On the other side was a printed advertisement:

ALBERT D. RINCK
PORTRAITS # LIKENESSES
OILS AND WATERCOLORS
5 ST. PETER ST. # NEW ORLEANS, LOUISIANA

The border of the card was a replica of the graceful sinuousities of the iron galleries on Michaela's buildings. Including, at the center of the top, the elegant cartouche with her monogram. Val grinned at the imprint of her personality on her tenant's profession.

He laughed aloud at the scrawl in one corner. "Do you know the charming English play *School for Scandal*? There's a bit of doggerel that goes 'Here's to the maiden of bashful fifteen; Here's to the widow of fifty.' How delightfully apropos."

He put the card in his breast pocket. After he surveyed the progress of the sugar making Monday morning, he'd ride into the city and call on this painter. There was someone else he wanted to see, too. If the Baroness had not been at his house by chance, there might have been a scandal that he wouldn't have found humorous at all.

# 31

Was it only a week ago that I was so happy to be going to work that I got there too early to get in? Mary closed the door of the O'Neill house behind her and shivered. The sun was still barely over the horizon. It was gray in her heart and gray all around her. The low cottages along Adele Street had seemed cozy to her when she first saw them. Now they looked flimsy and cold. And squalid. The muddy, rutted street smelled rancid; a goat running free in the gutter was streaked with filth.

Mary squared her shoulders, raised her skirts above the ankles and set forth through the mud to walk to work.

You mustn't let things get you down, she told herself. You must not give in. You're strong and you're healthy and you have a place to live and friends who care about you. Why, even though you told Mrs. O'Neill you wouldn't be buying a dinner pail any more, she still fixed you something. Something you like, too. So what if it's Saturday's leftovers. Red beans and rice is one of your favorites. And it's Monday, isn't it? Everyone eats red beans and rice on Monday in New Orleans.

Twice? she asked herself. She knew they'd have a fresh pot of it for supper. Mary felt like crying. Or laughing. So she laughed. Her steps became firmer and faster. Madame Alphande's wasn't the only dressmaker in New Orleans. The thing to do was to keep her eyes and ears open, use her lunchtime to look around. Something better would come her way; all she had to do was be alert to recognize it. In the meantime she was learning a lot. Already she understood much more about constructing a dress than she had even known was out there to learn. Little tricks, too, that made a gown look better than it was, and shortcuts, and pitfalls to avoid. If she ever had the time and the money to make herself a dress again, she'd know exactly what to do. Before summer came she'd restyle the dresses that Jeanne Courtenay had given her, make them fit better, maybe change the trim on the blue one...

Her mind busy with possibilities, Mary walked quickly along the uneven banquettes, unaware of the distance she was covering. The sky changed from gray to gold to blue, and her shadow moved alongside her. When she neared Canal Street and the first shop windows, her pace slowed. Other people walking by saw a young woman smiling at the tempting array of goods for sale in the shop windows. Mary saw dozens of shirtwaists, chemises, aprons, corset covers, and dressing gowns that were less attractive and less finely finished than the work she did.

The room and the women at Madame Alphande's were as cold and unpleasant as usual. But Mary was in luck. She was given a job of interesting embroidery that would last for at least four days, maybe longer. It was an undulating pattern of wide scrolls, like cresting waves, around the hem of a ball gown. The stitches were done with silk thread, each stitch fastening a small iridescent bead, as clear and sparkling as a drop of water. The fabric of the gown was a pleasure to hold in her hands, a thick rich satin the color of the warm golden flesh of a peach.

Mary could feel the resentful eyes of Marie Deux on her; the older woman was working on a simple border of appliquéd leaves on a short cape. Her jealousy made Mary enjoy her own delicate task even more. May God forgive me, she thought, I'm becoming as mean-spirited as the rest of them. But her pleasure outweighed her guilt, and she ate all her lunch with relish, offering not even one bean to anyone else.

The sagging gate made an unearthly groaning noise when it was pushed. Unless one knew that it should be lifted slightly first. Valmont Saint-Brévin moved it easily; the hinges were kept well-oiled.

"Good day, Your Majesty," he said when the elder Marie Laveau answered his knock on the door. "It's Monday, and I'm hoping to be offered some red beans and rice."

The voodoo queen's laughter was hearty. "Come in," she said. "Marie is cooking, and I'm about to go out."

"I'm heartbroken. I came to see you."

She laughed again.

Valmont walked through the house into the big kitchen. Marie smiled at him. She was barefoot, with gold bracelets around her ankles and a huge ruby and diamond ring on one of her toes. Her curly black hair fell over her shoulders, almost hiding her flashing diamond earrings. A ruby necklace emphasized the coppery color of her skin. She was wearing a white blouse with a deep V neckline and a full, ankle-length skirt made of red silk.

"Are you dressed to match the beans and rice?" Valmont asked.

"Of course. Are you hungry?"

"Of course."

"Sit down, then. It's ready." Marie put a tray on the table near the window and began to load it with the bottles and jars that cluttered the table top. Valmont started to help, but she slapped his hand, so he stopped.

"What's in that collection, Marie? Do you really have powdered lizards and black cat bones and mandrake root?"

"Don't mock my spells, Michie." Marie's accent was thick *gombo.*

"I'm interested," said Val. "But if you'd rather play games..." His accent was clipped Parisian.

"Old habits die hard," Marie said, in perfect French. "You looked like any other white man. I forget what you look like when you haven't been here for a long time."

"It's sugar-making season."

Marie smiled. "Is that what you call it?" She moved the tray and put heavy earthenware bowls on the table. Aromatic steam rose from the beans and rice in them. "Are you going to let me see the monogram?" she asked. She had an expression of innocent inquiry, but her gray eyes were bright with mischief. "There's a question of whether you were just branded with the iron from the balconies or whether you had to be tattooed."

Valmont was caught with his mouth full, as she intended. He nearly choked when his laughter exploded.

When he regained control, he took Marie's hand and kissed it ceremoniously. "I'm honored by your jealousy," he said, his lips still touching her smooth fingers. He released her hand and began to loosen his neckcloth. "And your curiosity. I'll make it easy for you to satisfy it. You can search for the monogram."

Marie chuckled. "You flatter yourself as usual. Strip to the bone if you like, but you'll not get into my bed, Monsieur."

Val retied his neckcloth without speaking. Then he concentrated on eating.

So did Marie.

Their silence was comfortable, the eating a shared pleasure. The beans and rice were savory, and the sexual tension between them added a seasoning that both appreciated.

It was highly unlikely that Valmont would ever get into Marie's bed; both of them knew it. She took lovers, but never white men and always men she could dominate. Val was disqualified on both counts.

But highly unlikely was not the same thing as impossible. The possibility was a teasing idea for both of them, something to play with, to play games about, to appreciate even more because it was unrealized. It was one of the foundations of their friendship, though not the strongest. That was a mutual respect and admiration. Each recognized the strength of the other, the individuality and independence. Neither had to prove himself to the other. And so they were comfortable.

"More?" said Marie when Valmont's bowl was empty.

"Coffee, if I may. That was superlative."

"I'll put the pot on." Marie whisked the bowls off the table, put cups at their places, then took coffee beans from a tin and began to grind them. Her back was to Val.

"What expensive ingredients do you mix up for a love spell, Marie?" His voice was lazy.

Marie said nothing. Her shoulders were shaking with laughter.

"So it was you, dammit!" Val's tone was casual no longer. "What kind of friend do you call yourself? If you need money, I'll give it to you; you don't have to sell my future to some hysterical girl. Stop that grinding, damn you, and talk to me."

Marie looked briefly over her shoulder. "Just a minute. I want to get the coffee started."

"I don't want any coffee; I want some answers."

"I want coffee, whether you do or not. And remember that you're in my house, Monsieur Saint-Brévin. Act like a gentleman or get out." She busied herself with the coffee pot while Valmont fumed.

Then she took her chair at the table. Her eyes glittered with merriment and a touch of malice. "You've lost your sense of humor, Val. I'm disappointed."

"There's nothing funny about it, Marie. How could you send Jeanne Courtenay to my house with some spell? She made a grotesque scene; it was appalling."

Marie leaned toward him, her chin supported by her hand. "What kind of grotesque scene? I'm fascinated."

"Just take my word for it; it was grotesque. Why did you do this to me, Marie? I didn't believe it was you that sent her until you started to laugh your head off."

"Ah, Valmont, don't act so wounded. I meant you no harm. The foolish girl disobeyed instructions. I gave her the spell for overheated society virgins. She was to whisper it in your ear when you were in bed together. It always leads to marriage for her kind. If you took her to bed you'd have had to marry her; that's the rule in your world."

"You told her to go to bed with me?"

"I did not. I told her to whisper the spell when she was already in your bed. There's a significant difference."

Val stared at Marie's bland expressionless face. Against his will he began to chuckle. "Witch," he said.

"Thank you."

"Isn't that coffee ready yet?"

"It could have happened," Val said between sips of coffee. "If she had showed up when I was a little drunk, or lonely, or randy. She's a luscious-looking creature."

"You need a woman, my friend... No, not me. And not the little Courtenay. She'd bore you to death within a week."

"I know that. But when I'm near her, I'm afraid I forget it. She's very beautiful, Marie, and I have a weakness for beauty."

"Without brains?"

"There are no brains between a man's legs."

Marie smiled. "You're in worse shape than I thought. I believe I know the answer to your problem."

"Some of your powders? I don't want to be a eunuch." Val was irritated. First the Baroness, now Marie. Everyone thought he had a problem, and everyone wanted to tell him what to do about it.

Marie said the only thing that could cure his irritability. "Dear Valmont, the last thing I want in the world is for you to lose your manhood. I'm too selfish." Her look was charged with sexuality, with wanting him, with the almost-promise that one day she would be unable to keep the distance between them.

For an instant Val was almost frightened. Marie as friend was a cherished part of his life. Marie as lover would be... he didn't know, but a chill touched his spine.

"I will send word to you, Val," she said. "Soon. Trust me."

"Not too soon. The sugar is not finished yet. I shouldn't even be in town, but I promised a favor to a friend."

"The Baroness de Pontalba y Almonester."

"Yes, if you must know."

"But, dear Val, I do know. I always know everything. You forget that I am Marie Laveau."

"If you know everything, Marie Laveau, then you know if I'm branded with the Pontalba mark, so why did you ask?"

Marie's laugh came from deep in her throat. "Perhaps I was jealous, as you thought."

Valmont smiled. The familiar old game. The dangerous moment had passed. He slid his cup toward her for more coffee.

Michaela de Pontalba was being talked about by many people besides Valmont and Marie.

A half dozen women who were drinking coffee together discussed ways she might be persuaded to accept invitations to the balls they were giving in December.

Jeanne Courtenay sobbed like a baby in her mother's arms after confessing the escapade the day before. "How can he love that wrinkled old woman and not me, Maman? How could I have ruined everything the way I did? Now he'll never love me. I might just as well marry Papa's American."

Berthe's arms closed more tightly around the soft body of her only child. She knew that Carlos Courtenay's lawyer was already negotiating with Will Graham's lawyer about settlement and dowry.

"A messenger from the dock just arrived," Madame Alphande said to Mademoiselle Annette from the door into the workroom. "The ship is here from France. Send someone at once. The gloves for the Baroness are in the shipment. She has been screaming for them."

"Marie Quatre, your legs are the youngest." Mademoiselle Annette shook Mary's shoulder. "Move."

Mary tied the box of gloves with the lavender silk ribbon she had carried with her from the shop before she delivered it to the maid who answered her knock on the door of the Baroness's apartments. The ribbon was Madame Alphande's trademark on all packages from her shop, her lagniappe.

I ran all the way to the docks and then all the way here, Mary thought. I'm not going to rush back to work.

She looked in the window of the shop next to the door. It had changed hardly at all since she had first seen it weeks before. Nor had the interior. The same young woman was there, with the same look of anxious eagerness.

Mary's lips widened in a smile. This might be what she was looking for. She opened the door and entered the shop.

As she had done before, the young woman hurried to meet Mary, offering to help her.

"I think I can help you more than you can help me," Mary said. "I work for Madame Alphande. You can engage me to work for you, and I'll tell you all the secrets that made her so successful." Mary was proud of the firm boldness in her voice. Her knees were shaking.

The young woman's voice when she replied was as shaky as Mary's knees. "I wish I could, I really do. But you see, I don't have any money. There are no customers. I don't know how I'm going to pay the rent, and it's almost the first of the month."

"Oh, I see," said Mary quietly. "I'm sorry I bothered you." She backed out of the door and hurried to Madame Alphande's, afraid of losing her job.

# 32

I'll have almost three dollars for myself from this week's pay envelope, Mary kept telling herself. The walk to and from work was frightening. The dark came earlier every day, and there were no street lights after she left the business district. Often she had to take cover behind shrubs or trees when she heard the loud voices of a band of rowdies or the uneven shambling footsteps of a drunk. She was hungry, too; Mrs. O'Neill had no more leftovers for a free dinner pail after Monday.

Still, the days went by somehow. Mary was learning to shut out everything except the moment. One step and then the next until she arrived at Madame Alphande's. One stitch and then the next until it was time to go home, one step and then the next. Home was a plentiful hot supper, an hour of work on her summer dresses by the light of the dining room fire, then a few minutes in her cold bedroom to brush her brown dress, change the collar and cuffs, wash the used ones, wash her face and teeth, and then the warm oblivion of bed and sleep until the next identical day.

Monday, Tuesday, Wednesday, Thursday passed, and the week was half over. Mary looked with tired eyes at the glittering design on the yellow satin ball gown. She had just sewed on the final bead. It was a lovely gown; her embroidery made it exquisite, remarkable. It was a fine piece of work.

And she was glad it was over. She thought she would go blind if there had been even one more inch of the intricate labor.

She folded the protective white muslin cover around the delicate yellow satin and put her needle and scissors away. Almost three dollars, she reminded herself, but not if I take the streetcar, so I mustn't. She felt too tired to walk home through the terrors of the night.

"Finished at last, Marie Quatre?" Mademoiselle Annette's voice was sharp with criticism. "That gown was supposed to be delivered this morning. You made it late, and you will deliver it. Now."

Mary wanted to cry, to scream, to murder Mademoiselle Annette. Instead, she delivered the big box with its giant bow of lavender ribbon.

The address was on Rampart Street, only five blocks away. Mary walked across Toulouse Street, too tired to look around at the neighborhood even though she had never been in this part of the French

Quarter. After a block there was no longer any paving in the street. Her feet were heavy and clumsy on the uneven brick of the narrow banquette. For one terrible moment she thought she was going to drop the box in the rank filthy gutter, but she regained her balance and her grip on the box.

There was a warmly lit cafe on the corner of Toulouse and Rampart. It filled the air for half a block with the smell of fresh coffee and cooking food. Mary's empty stomach knotted painfully at the stimulus. She prayed it wouldn't take too long to find the house where the box was to be left. She used the light from the cafe to read the directions again.

"Mademoiselle Cécile Dulac. Next to Café des Améliorations. Blue shutters." It was too dark to see the color, but the small house next to the cafe did have shutters; that was enough to be encouraging. Mary opened the gate in the iron fence and walked up the short smooth brick path.

The door opened before she could knock. "Is that you, Marcel? You're late . . . who are you?"

The speaker was a woman with a low-pitched musical voice. There was a lighted room behind her, making a halo around her head and shadowed face.

"I'm from Madame Alphande," Mary said. She held out the box.

Mary was fully illuminated. She half closed her tired eyes against the light. Then they opened wide in surprise.

"I know you," the voice was saying. "Dogsbody for a dressmaker; is that what you've come to? I suppose Carlos Courtenay threw you out, too. Come in, whatever your name is. I'll give you a glass of wine to drink the damnation of the Courtenays with." She grasped Mary's wrist and pulled her inside.

Fatigue slowed Mary's mind, and she thought at first that she was looking at Jeanne. She puzzled thickly over why Jeanne was in this house, why she was so angry at her father. Then she realized that she was seeing a more beautiful Jeanne, and she remembered the crisis at Montfleury when Hercule was dying. This was the exquisite girl she had seen then. This was Carlos Courtenay's illegitimate daughter. This was Jeanne's half sister, the child of a shameful liaison between a white man and one of his slaves.

No wonder this Cécile Dulac hated Carlos Courtenay so much.

But Mary couldn't drink to his ruin. She refused the wine Cécile offered her. "I'm worn out," Mary said truthfully. "If I drink any wine I'll probably keel over."

"I believe you. You look like death. I'll ring for coffee. Would you like something to eat? No? At least a little piece of cake." Cécile issued orders to the uniformed maid who came in response to her tug on the brocaded bell pull by the door. In a few minutes Mary was looking at a tray piled high with assorted confections, sandwiches, and pastries.

There was something fantastical about the excess and contrast of it all: the warmth and light after the cold dark outside; the soft depth of the down-cushioned chair after the hard stool in the shop workroom; the lavish assortment of delicacies after the hungry hours; the richness of silk curtains and velvet upholstery and gilded mirrors and plush carpet and crystal chandelier and silver candlesticks and perfumed air and the extraordinarily beautiful young woman sitting opposite. Mary felt as if she were in a dream.

Dreamlike, too, was Cécile Dulac's insistent intimacy. Confident that Mary shared her outrage and desire for revenge against Carlos Courtenay, the beautiful young woman spoke with icy control over her mellifluous voice, telling a story that was, to Mary, too inhuman to be anything other than a nightmare.

Cécile was the product of a long-established system known in New Orleans as *plaçage*. Her mother was one of the women called *plaçées*, which meant that she was placed in a house by a white man where she lived for no purpose other than to be available for his pleasure at his convenience.

Carlos Courtenay had noticed Cécile's mother when she was fifteen; he wanted her. She was one of his slaves, and she had no right to deny him, but Carlos considered himself a moral man. He wouldn't use his female slaves for casual sexual activity. He saw nothing wrong, however, in making Cécile's mother his mistress. He took her off the plantation and set her up in the house on Rampart Street. To make her the equal of the placées in the other Rampart Street houses, Carlos gave her her freedom.

Freedom from official slavery, but not from the real slavery of her position. And from the slavery of love. Cécile railed against what she regarded as her mother's weakness. "Her name is Amaranthe, like the flower they call 'Everlasting,' and that name is like a curse. Because she gave her everlasting love to that man. She gave him a son because he wanted one. He allowed her to have a second child because she wanted a daughter, and she was grateful when I was born. There were no more children. He didn't want them. There were powders from the voodoo woman instead, and terrible pains and bloody beginnings of children expelled from her body into a chamber pot overflowing with her blood. For love of this man.

"For love of him, too, she kept us out of the way, my brother and me. When Michie Carlos came, he mustn't be disturbed by the noise we made when we played or when we cried. So we were locked in the room next to the kitchen until he was gone.

"Unless he wanted to admire what his seed had grown from my mother's womb. Then we were dressed up and put on parade for the great white god. How charming we were, how we smiled, bowed, curtseyed, recited the poems and sang the songs we had learned. We would do anything to please him because we could tell, even when we were very, very young, that it meant so much to our mother.

"Our beautiful, gentle, loving mother. She was always beautiful. Beautifully gowned and coiffed and scented because Michie Carlos just might come that day or that evening or that night. And because she lived in constant fear that he might find someone more beautiful, more youthful, more anxious to please, and then he would cast her everlasting love aside.

"I asked her, when I grew old enough to see what her life was, I asked her how she could bear it, the neglect, the fear, the slavery that was worse than slavery. And she hit me across the mouth for speaking ill of him. He was so generous, she said, to give her freedom, to give her two children, to give her clothes and jewels to make herself beautiful for him. Slaves, too, he gave her. To take care of the house and the furnishings he chose for it and to take care of her, to dress her hair and her body and her children, to prepare the meals that he might share if he chose to visit.

"He was so generous that he allowed my brother and me to go to school, and when my brother was ten, he sent him to France to be educated as a gentleman and to stay there forever because in France a drop of black blood is no barrier to advancement and acceptance. Such magnanimity, to tear away a child from the mother who gave him life. Almost as magnanimous as he was when he gave her the deed to the house and everything in it and a letter that guarantees that his bankers will provide her money every month. That's what he gave her for a farewell gift, when he told her that his wife and daughter were returning to the city and that he would not shame them by coming to this house again.

"That's when my mother died, when she told him goodbye and thanked him for his generosity. Later she took a knife and drove it into her breast. But she was already dead; it hardly mattered that she missed her heart and survived her wound. She's like a beautiful shell, with no life inside. Carlos Courtenay killed her."

Cécile looked at Mary with scorn and pity mixed. "You, too, you look like the walking dead. What did he do to you? How did he pull you down; what changed that fine young white lady at the plantation into a half-starved drab?"

Mary wanted to protest. She was not a pitiful, contemptible creature; she was an independent, self-reliant woman. Then she saw that the tray in front of her was empty. She must have eaten everything on it without awareness of her need or her actions.

"I don't know what happened," she said. Her words were intended to be an apology for her greedy eating. When she heard her own voice Mary realized that they were also an apology for her life. Something had gone wrong. Somewhere she had taken a wrong turning. She had believed she was making the right choices, following the path to happiness. But she was just what Cécile said, a half-starved drab, too tired to fight the description or the condition.

"I don't know what happened," she repeated. She reminded herself that Cécile was asking about Carlos Courtenay. "One night I was in a box at the Opera," said Mary, "and the next morning he told me that I wasn't fit company for his daughter. Clementine bruised my arm when she pushed me into the carriage."

Cécile snorted through her thin aristocratic nose. "Clementine! My dear loving grandmother. She loves the Courtenays more than her own daughter. She came running when my mother was taken to the hospital with the knife still in her breast, but when the danger was past all she could talk about was the need for silence, for discretion, so that no scandal would touch the Courtenay name."

"I'm sorry," Mary said. It was inadequate, but it was all she could say. She was profoundly sorry for this beautiful, hate-possessed girl.

Cécile laughed. Her face and body underwent a terrifying transformation. Her hands, balled into angry fists, opened and drooped gracefully from her narrow wrists while her shoulders changed from a constricted hunching thrust to a smooth flowing line that lifted her breasts and chin.

Her head tilted, she looked from the corners of her eyes through a thicket of downcast lashes; her mouth slackened, softened, invited.

"Don't feel sorry for this free woman of color," Cécile said in a voice like velvet. "I'm going to run my life a lot better than my mother did. I know how. A lot of white men will pay for Carlos Courtenay's sins. Maybe even Michie Carlos himself."

Mary shivered, chilled by the presence of a primal force and instinct too powerful for her understanding. "I wish I were more like you," she blurted. Cécile raised her eyebrows. Her smile became sardonic. Mary blundered on. "I don't mean beautiful like you. I wouldn't know what to do with it. I mean I wish I knew what I wanted and how to get it."

A knock on the door interrupted her. Cécile walked hurriedly to the door, moving with the eerie gliding sinuousness Mary remembered from their previous meeting. "Marcel," said Cécile, "you're late. Have you got it? Give it to me."

She turned toward Mary, something small hidden in her hand. "I must dress now . . . what is your name?"

"Mary MacAlistair."

"I must get ready for the ball, Mademoiselle MacAlistair. Marcel is our coachman. He will drive you home. Where do you live?"

"Adele Street."

"Good God, the Irish Channel! And Marcel is as black as soot. He'll drive you as far as it's safe for him to go. Thank you for bringing my gown. Will the other one be ready in time? I'm sick to death of that old woman Alphande and her last-minute dramatics."

Cécile had already dismissed Mary as spiritless, defeated. Worthless in her eyes. The American, she thought, was a poor thing, not even capable of resentment. A born victim, she deserved to be a flunky who delivered packages to her betters.

She was astonished when Mary suddenly came alive with energy. "Wait a minute," Mary said. "I want to know something." Her drawn face was no longer gray with exhaustion. Her cheeks flamed with color, and her eyes had lights in them. "Suppose you could find gowns as good as Madame Alphande's somewhere else. Maybe even better gowns. And guaranteed to be finished when they were promised. Would you buy your gowns at this other shop even though it was new, not yet fashionable?"

"What are you talking about? Of course I would. Anybody would. But there is no one in New Orleans like Alphande."

Mary clapped her hands. "I'll call on you again, Mademoiselle, if I may. I believe I'll have something to tell you that you'll be pleased to hear.

"Thank you for your hospitality. Good night." Mary pulled the door open.

"The carriage..." Cécile called.

"Oh, I won't need it. Thank you all the same."

Cécile shrugged. "A very strange young person," she murmured. "It might be interesting to hear what she has to say."

# 33

It was after nine o'clock when Mary got home to the Widow O'Neill's. Paddy Devlin was pacing back and forth outside the door. When he saw Mary approaching, he bounded forward. "Where have you been, Miss Mary? I've been half crazed with worry."

"I've been minding my own business, Mr. Devlin." Mary was excited and pleased with herself and pert.

Paddy stepped between her and the door to the house. "You've no call to worry me so. It's not safe for you to be roaming in the dark streets so late. I should go with you to protect you." He was grumbling more than speaking.

Mary felt impatient with his interference. But she knew he was right. She had walked on the opposite side of Adele Street from the Ocean Home barroom, but she had been nervous. The sounds from its door were rowdy: drunken singing and shouted curses and breaking glass. She had never before been out so late in the Irish Channel.

She put her hand on Paddy's arm. "The truth is I didn't notice the time," she said. "I was talking to a nice woman about going to work in her shop. I'm not very happy at Madame Alphande's.

"And I'm tired. Stand aside, Mr. Devlin. I want to go inside."

Paddy opened the door for her. Mary saw that he was scowling, but she didn't care. Nothing could dent her euphoria.

She had half walked, half run from Rampart Street to the anxious young woman's shop in the Pontalba buildings. "I'll bring you the customers," Mary promised her, "and you share the profits with me."

Hannah Rinck took Mary upstairs to the apartments where she lived. "You'll have to talk to my husband, too. We make all our decisions together."

Mary's enthusiasm and confidence easily convinced Albert Rinck. The three of them celebrated the bright future with supper and a bottle of wine. Albert drank most of it because his celebration was double. He had received a commission to do a portrait only a few hours earlier.

"Good God, Michaela," Valmont complained, "the fellow wants to paint me full-length and life-sized."

"You don't have to like it, my dear," said the Baroness. "You only have to say you do."

Mary's obvious happiness attracted the attention, and therefore the persecution, of Mademoiselle Annette when she went to work the next day. The older woman hovered, criticized, sneered, assigned the dullest tasks. And Mary didn't care. She kept her head meekly bowed over her work to hide the smile that kept sneaking onto her lips. The following day, Saturday, was more of the same. But it did, at last, come to an end. Mary accepted a lecture on her faults with her pay envelope and promised humbly to do better in the future.

"A lot better, you old toad," she said aloud when she was safely away from the workshop, "but not for you. For me." A woman near her on the banquette glared at her in response. Mary didn't notice. Her mind was busy with her plans.

Tomorrow is December the first, she was thinking. That gives us three months left in the social season. Maybe even three and a half. I'll have to find out when Easter is next year and figure out when Lent begins.

She stopped short, stood motionless in the midst of the crowds on the busy Canal Street banquette. I was thinking of business, Mary realized, and of Easter as a date to measure business days by, not as the holiest day of the year. I was looking forward to tomorrow, too, planning all the things I was going to do without remembering that it will be Sunday. The Lord's day. I'm becoming a heathen.

She began to walk again as abruptly as she had stopped, and her pace grew increasingly rapid. She had to get to Saint Patrick's, to confession. She needed to ask forgiveness for her worldliness and to pray for help in resisting the temptations of Mammon.

The priest who heard Mary's confession blessed her and gave her a penance of saying three Our Fathers. It confused her.

"I used to have to say ten for sins like thinking about breakfast during mass when I was at school," Mary told Louisa. "I don't understand."

Louisa was impatient with her. "You're not in a convent anymore, my friend. Your sins just don't weigh much in a place where there's drunkenness and murder and blasphemy as a normal part of daily living. He'll be a lot harder on me if I ever get up my nerve to go to confession.

I'm planning to change jobs, too, but not the way you are. I'm going to give up playing the piano for Mr. Bassington and start living in sin with him instead."

"Louisa, you can't!"

"Not for a while. I've got to wait until my brother's come and gone for his next visit. Otherwise he'll find me and beat the devil out of me and probably kill Mr. Bassington. Once Christmas is over, my brother will be going to California to look for gold. Then there'll be nobody to stop me."

Mary was sure that Louisa would come to her senses before Christmas. She told herself that Louisa was saying such outrageous things only because it was Saturday night and she had no money for a ticket to the opera. Mary would have liked to give Louisa the money from her intact pay envelope. But she needed every penny for her plan.

She needed every minute she could find, too. Paddy Devlin looked morose when she told him that she would be busy all day Sunday after mass. He had expected that they would spend the afternoon together. "We could ride the streetcar out to Carrollton," he said. "I hear there's a fine park there, and it's less than an hour away."

"If it was only ten minutes, I couldn't take the time tomorrow and I won't even be home for dinner. Don't be so gloomy, Mr. Devlin. It's too cold for the park now, anyhow. When spring comes I'll be happy to go. And I'll have Sundays free, most likely."

She added "more's the pity," under her breath. Spring would mean the end of the Season.

On Sunday the sky was a distant strong blue, and the temperature was so warm that Mary regretted wearing her wool dress. She hoped Paddy Devlin wouldn't point out that it was a glorious day for an outing to a distant park.

He didn't say that, or anything else. He accompanied Mary to church, bowed, and said goodbye on the sidewalk outside when mass was over.

"Sulk all you like," Mary muttered when she walked away. Then the promise of the day erased him from her thoughts. She felt that she was in control of her life after too long a time of being dependent on the whims of chance and the vagaries of other people. It was a good feeling.

• • •

Cécile Dulac took control away from her within five minutes of Mary's arrival at the house on Rampart Street.

"You intend to work for Alphande's six days a week and work for this Rinck business on Sundays and at night? That's absurd."

Mary defended her plan with angry passion. It was not absurd. She was young and strong and she could do it. Hannah Rinck had no money to buy what they needed to get started, but Mary's savings plus the extra from her pay envelope would take care of the costs for the first gown she'd make for Cécile. The profit from that would buy the necessary materials for the next gown, and so forth. After a month or six weeks, if all went well, Mary would be able to leave Madame Alphande for full-time work with Hannah Rinck.

"After a month or six weeks," said Cécile, "you'll be dead or so exhausted that your work will be no good. I will tell you what you are going to do."

Two hours later Mary set out for the short walk to the Pontalba buildings with her head in a whirl. She had two things to take to Hannah Rinck: a leather pouch full of gold coins and the news that the shop now had a silent partner, Cécile Dulac. Mary would never have to go to Madame Alphande's again.

"But who is she?" asked Albert Rinck. "What kind of woman has sacks of money like this?" The gold coins were spilled out on the table in front of them in a long, irregular curve of riches. Albert and Hannah Rinck stared at them as if hypnotized.

The table was the only furniture in the large, elegant room. It was covered with a length of faded green velvet to hide its scarred surface. Hannah had placed a white china bowl filled with green leaves in the center of the table in an attempt to beautify her home. Albert had painted the casks that surrounded the table for use as stools. Their brave efforts only emphasized their poverty. The gold was brightly incongruous.

"Who is she?" Albert said again.

Mary had been searching her mind for a simple answer, but there was none. "I told you," she said, "her name is Cécile Dulac, and she's a quadroon. Not really a quadroon, because her blood is much more than three-quarters white, but quadroon is what all the light-skinned women are called in New Orleans. We'll be making her gowns for the Quadroon Balls."

She repeated what she had learned from Cécile. During the season there were balls almost every night in the ballroom next to the Orleans Theater, where the opera was performed. There was an admission charge of two dollars, and only white men were admitted. The quadroons were chaperoned by their mothers or guardians, who were rigid about the protocol of the event. A man had to ask for permission to be introduced to the daughter, and he could not protest if permission was refused. There was strict decorum, unlike many other balls where the dancing partners were white women, and the admission price was a dollar or less.

The Quadroon Balls were more like the private, invitation-only balls of the Creole aristocracy. In fact, many of the men who attended them were the same men invited to the Creole festivities.

Because the ultimate goal of the Quadroon Ball was the arrangement of formal liaisons between these men and the beautiful young quadroons. The mothers negotiated contracts and settlements for their daughters to become the placées, the mistresses of the men. The balls were the marketplace.

Hannah Rinck was shocked by Mary's account. "That's the most immoral thing I've ever heard of," she said.

Mary nodded. "I thought so, too, Hannah. But it's no different from the marriage arrangements that aristocratic families make for their daughters, except that the quadroons don't have the same protection that marriage gives to white girls. Besides, it's the way things are here, the way they have been for generations. It's not up to us to change them. All we have to do is make the gowns. You can see why each of the mothers wants her daughter to look her best."

Albert began to replace the coins in the pouch. "You're asking my wife to cater to prostitutes, Mary. I won't allow it."

"No such thing, Albert," Mary almost shouted. "These girls are not prostitutes. They are brought up with every protection, educated in a convent school, and given to men who will take care of them. Exactly like a white girl from the finest family. They're faithful to their protectors, just like a wife is faithful to her husband. These are virtuous girls."

Hannah removed the pouch from her husband's hand. "Albert," she said calmly, "don't be a jackass. If they had horns and wore scarlet, it would make no difference as long as they bought the scarlet from us. It takes money to buy your paints and pay the rent."

She turned to Mary, tucking the pouch into the waistband of her apron. "How many ball gowns will Cécile buy from us?"

"None. She's already paid for hers by giving us that money. We'll use it to buy patterns and fabric and trimmings. The first gown we make will be for Cécile. When she wears it, it will be an announcement of what we can do. The orders will come from the other quadroons. They'll all want whatever Cécile has because she's the most beautiful and sought-after of them all."

"How do you know that?"

"She told me so, and I believe it. It's impossible that any woman on earth could be more beautiful than she is. She went to her first ball last Thursday, and her guardian has already rejected four offers."

"I think I'd like to paint her," Albert said.

Mary and Hannah exchanged smiles. They were in business.

That's enough for now, Mary told herself. The other things Cécile told me can wait until later.

She didn't quite know what she really thought about the new partner. She only knew that she had a chance now to make some money, perhaps a great deal. Her experience with independence had convinced Mary that having enough money was the most important thing in the world.

# 34

The Baroness de Pontalba did not, as a rule, take much interest in women. Men had wider interests, accomplished more, were more original and more daring, she believed. She had more in common with them and understood them better. Or thought she did.

But when the little shop in her building underwent a transformation into something quite extraordinary, she became very interested in Hannah Rinck. She had envisioned a row of exclusive shops on each side of the Place d'Armes; now one had appeared as if by magic from an ugly-duckling beginning. It could very well attract others, be the first step toward realizing her goal. She decided to encourage Hannah by patronizing the shop herself and by allowing the painter's wife a carefully remote friendly acquaintance. She invited the Rincks to a reception she was giving on the third Sunday afternoon in December, the fifteenth.

"You have to wear something splendid, Hannah," Mary insisted. "This may be the most sought-after invitation in all New Orleans, and you'll be seen by the most important people in the city. It could bring us dozens of new customers."

"Mary, we can't take care of dozens of new customers. We can't take care of the ones we have now. It's impossible for you to keep on working seven days and seven nights a week. I'm no help to you."

"That's not true, Hannah, and you know it. You work just as hard as I do."

But it was true, and Mary knew it as well as Hannah. Mary did virtually everything. She had been incredulous when she discovered that Hannah spoke no French. The shop was in the very heart of the Vieux Carré where most people spoke nothing else. So she began to help the few customers who wandered in out of curiosity. Hannah took care of the handful who spoke English; it gave her something useful to do.

Hannah tried to help with the sewing, but her work was so poor that Mary had to take out the stitches and do them again.

Hannah arranged the window, too, trying to include one of every item they had for sale. Albert told her it was a visual abomination. When Mary agreed with him, he instructed her in how an artist composes a still life. He also instructed Hannah to leave the window to Mary.

Hannah was left with the duty of keeping the shop clean and of running the errands and making the deliveries. There were a steadily increasing number of them after Cécile's appearance in the golden peach gown. She skillfully allowed the untruthful word to get out that the gown came from the Rinck shop, and the following day three mothers brought their daughters to place orders for ball gowns. Mary admitted to Hannah that she was more pleased to take credit for Cécile's gown made in Madame Alphande's workroom than she was when the gowns from their own shop began to be talked about. "Revenge really is sweet," she crowed, "even if Mademoiselle Annette doesn't know that I'm getting it." By working on the three gowns day and night, Mary finished them in less than two weeks. She was proud and astonished by what she had done.

In truth the gowns were even lovelier than those made at Madame Alphande's because Albert worked with Mary on the designs. He was responsible for the unusual combinations of colors and the striking, dramatic trims of laces, ribbons, plumes, flowers, and outsize embroidered and appliquéd patterns that became the signature of a Rinck gown, the name the partners chose for their specialty.

"It is all color and line," Albert said, "and those are my tools." He sketched the gowns with quick strokes of his brush on small canvas squares then gave them to Mary to use for samples to show the customers. It was Cécile who had the idea that made the shop famous almost overnight: secretly include the price of a portrait in the price of the gown.

"When it is finished, Monsieur Rinck can add the head of the owner to the sketch of the gown. The portrait will be the lagniappe. Never duplicate the design, and add that promise to the price, too."

The first three orders became a dozen. Every one of the quadroon beauties wanted to be immortalized in oils as well as glorified in silk and velvet. Mary and Hannah put a notice in both the American and the French sides of *The Bee* and hired two women to do plain sewing. Mary did the intricacies. She continued to work seven days and seven nights a week. Hannah continued to worry about her.

But she did agree to let Albert design a splendid gown for her to wear to the Baroness's party and to let Mary make it. Hannah was twenty years old, and she had never owned an evening gown nor gone to an evening party.

She was the fourth child in a family of nine, from a small Ohio town where her father operated a dry-goods store and livery stable. She had met Albert Rinck when he painted a new sign for her father's store, and had run away with him when the sign was finished and he left for the next town. They were married before her father caught up with them, and had been poor, peripatetic, and happily loving ever since. She always ran a little shop wherever they lived. Her earnings supported them while Albert tried to make his reputation as a painter of portraits instead of signs. Until New Orleans, the arrangement had worked well enough. Then it looked as if disaster was just over the horizon.

Now it looked as though the horizon hid imminent prosperity and security. Everything had happened so quickly that Hannah didn't understand the sequence. She didn't try. She was content to let Albert and Mary be the smart ones. She concentrated on enjoying the unexpected good fortune.

She explained her position to Michaela de Pontalba at the reception. The Baroness found Hannah's happiness extremely dull as conversational matter. I should have invited this Mary person, she thought briefly. Then she moved on to talk to someone else and forgot that she had ever heard of Mary MacAlistair.

Less than a week later she heard the name again, and this time she paid attention. Valmont Saint-Brévin was her caller. The sugar making was done, and he had moved into town to enjoy the Season.

"I'm so unspeakably virtuous, dear Baroness, that my first act was to go for a sitting for that accursed portrait. And who did I see but the agile Mademoiselle MacAlistair? Do you have any idea what a clever little cat you are harboring under your new roof? She always manages to prosper. And to move up in the world. First she was one of the girls in the best brothel in the city. Than she was a sort of honorary daughter to Berthe Courtenay. Now she seems to be proprietor of an extremely elegant fashion establishment. I'm impressed."

Michaela was impressed, too. She definitely wanted to meet this Mary person now. An adventuress is never dull.

Below, Mary fussed with the shop's window display. It was dramatically simple, almost stark, a long pink satin glove on a stand with its fingers bent around a half-opened fan of sequined black lace. There was no improvement she could make. On the contrary, her fussing threatened to destroy the delicately balanced arrangement.

But if she stayed near the window long enough, she would see Valmont when he left. Just a glimpse. She didn't dare hope for more.

Her sensitive hands touched the fragile folds of satin and lace with rough clumsiness because she was angry. Angry with herself.

How could you have made such a fool of yourself, Mary MacAlistair? When you went to Albert's studio and saw him there, why didn't you just back out? Or say good morning, like any civilized person, and then leave? Why did you babble like a maniac and show off like a clown and try to impress him with all that nonsense about the new sketches and the orders that had to be filled? Who were you trying to be? The Baroness? Madame Alphande?

Or were you just trying to find some excuse to stay a little longer, to look at the way his hair fits his head like a shining black cap and his eyes fit into the hollow under his brows and his legs stretch so long and springlike and his mouth turns down at the ends right before it turns up in that smile that knows you're making a spectacle of yourself, staying where you don't belong in hopes of seeing him smile.

Can't you stop? Do you have to make things worse, make yourself even more ridiculous? Can't you leave this window alone and go do any one of the hundred things that are waiting to be done?

Mary knocked the display over, looked at it with despair.

No, I can't, she answered herself. I can't. It's not fair, seeing him so unexpectedly. If I had known he was there, if I had been ready, then my heart wouldn't have jumped the way it did, my silly, stupid, hopeless wanting would not have started all over again. I was over that, recovered, as if I had gotten well after being sick.

And now it's worse than before. I can't even make myself take three little steps away from the window. I can't.

She picked up the glove stand and the fan and tried to reassemble the display.

I'll never get it back together the way it was.

She wanted to weep from frustration.

Outside the window two middle-aged women came into view and stopped, watching Mary's efforts. They spoke to each other, came into the shop.

"What is the price of that fan, Mademoiselle?" said one. "Do you have it in other colors?"

"This is the place where the artist's wife makes dresses, isn't it?" the second asked. "Can you show us some samples?"

Mary smiled gratefully at them. They were saving her from the folly she couldn't control. Her heart stopped its unruly pounding, and her mind abandoned its futile, disjointed self-accusations. She was able to concentrate again. Almost. With one last look out the window, she turned toward the interior of the shop. Hannah's gown had done its job. These were Creole ladies of unmistakable Caucasian respectability. The new customers were beginning to find the way to Rinck's.

Val looked through the shop window when he left Michaela de Pontalba's apartment. He didn't see Mary, nor did she see him. She was kneeling behind the counter, getting a box with yet another fan to show the new customers. The top of the counter had eighteen fans spread on it. Each had been examined, discussed, and rejected.

Val turned and walked away with a light step. It was good to be back in the city. His sugar was already in hogsheads on the levee, waiting for loading. It was time for amusement. He would sort through the piles of invitations waiting at the hotel when he went there at the end of the day, choose a ball or a dinner or a reception to attend that evening. Or perhaps all three. In the meantime, he had to call on a dozen or so elderly aunts, uncles, cousins. Duty first, then play. His feet tapped the brick banquette with the beat of a fast-paced reel. Yes, he decided, a ball for certain. He wanted music and dancing and champagne. He had to catch up with the rhythm of the Vieux Carré.

This would be the third time he had been in New Orleans for the Season since his return from Paris, but he was still amazed by the dizzying gluttony for pleasure that infected the old city. Beginning with the rather stately opening of the Opera Season in early November, the celebrations were a ceaseless, accelerating avalanche of music and food and drink and dancing and entertainment of all sorts. A pause for the reverent observation of Christ's birth gave a renewal of energy, and the festivities resumed with increased vigor, becoming more and more fevered, hedonistic, uninhibited until the final explosion of the entire city into the madness that was Mardi Gras.

"Some people are so pleased with their own company that they don't notice anyone else is alive." The woman's voice came from Val's left. His head swiveled quickly. Marie Laveau was passing him, going in the opposite direction. He turned, caught up with her.

"I beg your pardon, Marie. I was woolgathering."

"I can't stop," Marie said. "Go on to where you were going. Come to the Quadroon Ball tonight. I'll be there."

"I don't know...," Val started to make an excuse. But Marie wasn't there to hear it. She had gone through the gate of the house in front of him.

Val stood on the banquette, staring at the gate. He was puzzled. It wasn't like Marie to speak to him in public. Both of them recognized that friendship between a white man and the voodoo queen would be regarded with suspicion by her world and by his. And why had she given him orders as if he were one of her followers? And why, in particular, orders to go to the Quadroon Ball? He had been once, when he was first back from Paris; it had disgusted him, and Marie knew it. He had told her so.

Val frowned, retraced his steps, continued in the direction of his aunt's house. His feet were no longer dancing. Marie's unwonted behavior bothered him. He'd have to take her to task when he saw her next. He'd try to go by the house on Saint Anne Street before the week was out. But he was not going to obey her orders; queen or no queen, he wouldn't go to the Quadroon Ball to see her.

# 35

Mary stayed later than usual at the shop. She had promised Cécile Dulac that her new gown would be finished that day, and the Creole ladies had taken up almost three hours of her time. They had not bought anything, either.

She attached the final silk flower petal to the gown at a few minutes before eight, folded it carefully into a box, and put on her shawl and bonnet. She'd have to deliver it to the Rampart Street house on her way home. Perhaps Cécile would give her something to eat. She'd dashed out for calas and coffee in early afternoon and she was hungry. Tired, too. She rubbed her hands together to ease the cramps in her fingers.

When she crossed the intersection of Royal and Toulouse streets, Mary could hear music from the Saint Louis Hotel. The orchestra was tuning up for the ball that would begin soon.

I've never been to a ball, she thought. She felt like Cinderella with no fairy godmother. In all the hours she had spent working on ball gowns, and in arranging and selling the exquisite accessories for evening wear, Mary had never felt sorry for herself before. Now self-pity washed over her in waves. She wanted to be carrying a box with a beautiful gown for herself, she wanted to be going to a place with light and music and laughter, she wanted to step into a warm, padded carriage that would transport her unsoiled through the muddy streets.

She wanted to be bathed and perfumed and coiffed and gowned and beautiful. And dancing through the night in the arms of Valmont Saint-Brévin.

Cécile's maid took the box from Mary. Mademoiselle Cécile, she said, was in her bath. She made no offer of refreshments.

Mary trudged along Rampart to Canal and across Canal to the streetcar stop at Baronne Street. There was no car waiting. Out of some perverse desire to underline her self-pity she walked on for three more blocks until she was in front of the Saint Charles Hotel, the immense American competitor to the Saint Louis Hotel in the French Quarter. Here, too, there was music for a ball. She watched while carriages drove up and deposited men and women in evening clothes who entered the hotel, talking with eager anticipation of the pleasures ahead.

"Here now! What are you hanging about here for?" A policeman took Mary's arm and marched her roughly away from the hotel entrance. "Be off, or I'll take you before a judge."

She was too low in spirit to protest. Her steps were slow and heavy on the way to catch the streetcar.

Usually, riding the cars was a treat, a small adventure. From Canal Street the car was drawn by a horse for three and a half blocks to the car barn. Then she changed to a car pulled by a noisy, sparking steam locomotive for a zigzag route along Baronne and Howard to Tivoli Circle and then Nayades uptown, past the city limits to Jackson Avenue. She changed again to a horse-drawn car at Jackson for an eleven-block ride to the end of the spur line at the levee. And a walk of only two blocks to Adele Street.

When the car reached Jackson Avenue this unhappy night, Mary almost stayed in her seat. There were only two other passengers and the motorman on the car; she had half of it to herself. It would be nice to stay right here, she thought, all alone. Ride all the way to Carrollton, then back, then back to Carrollton again, and back, passing by all the places and all the people as if I were invisible, or a ghost, instead of a real woman who had nothing to look forward to except too much work and too little sleep.

But she did pull the bell to signal a stop at Jackson, and she did step down to wait for the horse-drawn car to arrive.

I'm dispirited because I'm hungry, she told herself. I'll stop at the grocery near Mrs. O'Neill's and buy something to eat; then I'll feel better. Her mouth quivered with sour humor. I couldn't go to one of those balls if I were invited. I don't have anything to wear.

The same lament was echoing in the Esplanade Avenue mansion where the Courtenays lived. Jeanne was having a tantrum. She grabbed the ball gown Miranda was holding and threw it on the floor. "I've already worn this twice," she shouted, and she jumped up and down on the frothing ruffles of the skirt.

Miranda went to find Berthe Courtenay. Let someone else try to deal with Jeanne, she thought, I can't stand much more. She's been a demon ever since they told her she was going to marry the American.

Berthe hastened to Jeanne's room, wringing her small hands and making little worried, bleating sounds. With a combination of sympathy, pleading, bribes, and promises, she managed to quell the storm and get Jeanne ready for the ball.

Then she scurried to her own room to finish dressing before Carlos was ready to leave. Clementine came in to help her and found her in tears.

"I hate all this upset," Berthe wailed. "Why can't things be nice and quiet and everyone be happy?"

Mary rushed into Louisa's room and slammed the door before she started to cry. "Why does everybody act so mean?" she wailed.

Louisa stared at her. "Well, well, poor little you," she said after a few minutes. "I didn't know you had that much feeling in you, Mary. You've been more like a machine than a woman lately. What's wrong? Did all your needles go dull?"

"You're just as bad as the rest of them," Mary sobbed. "I can't understand why everyone wants to pick on me all of a sudden. Mrs. O'Neill raged at me because I wasn't here for supper without telling her, and Paddy Devlin scared me to death by charging out of the barroom when I walked past. Louisa, he yelled at me on the street, screaming about how worried he was. He wasn't too worried to get drunk, I noticed."

"That's probably why he got drunk, because he was worried. You've been treating him shamefully, Mary."

"I? What have I done? I'm working myself half to death. Do I have to concern myself with Paddy Devlin, too? He acts as if he owns me. It's crazy."

"He wants to marry you, Mary."

"What?" Mary's question was a screech. "That's the dumbest thing I ever heard. Why, he can't even read. How could he think I'd consider marrying him?"

"Don't shout so loud. Everybody'll hear you. You're such a fool sometimes. Don't you realize that you and I are the only ones in the house who can read? For that matter, I read music a lot better than regular print."

Mary was shocked into silence.

Louisa pulled back the blanket on her bed, climbed into it. "It's late," she said. "Get some sleep. I'd be dead to the world by now except that I waited up for you, too. I have an invitation for you. My brother's in town. He's taking me to the Hibernian ballroom tomorrow night. If you have any sense at all you'll take some time off from the shop and come with us. Paddy can be your escort. You need to have some fun, Mary. You're turning sour."

"But I don't have anything to wear." Mary started to laugh. It was a long time before she was able to stop.

"Sometimes when I start laughing, I just don't seem to be able to stop," said the overly plump girl in pink. "You do say the wittiest things, Monsieur Saint-Brévin."

Valmont looked surreptitiously around the room to see if rescue was in sight. He had been trapped in a corner with the girl for what seemed an eternity. Surely she must have a brother or a father or a cousin who would save him. There were accepted, unspoken rules for the relatives of wallflowers.

He saw a young man with a martyred look making his way through the crowd. "You do me too much kindness, Mademoiselle," Val said with a smile. "It's your responsiveness that makes my poor conversation seem to sparkle."

The girl in pink giggled.

Valmont bowed with a flourish, relinquishing his chair to her brother.

Sometimes, he had to admit, his sympathy for the less fortunate got him into unanticipated difficulties. He had come to dance, not solace. He walked to the edge of the dance floor, looking for a skillful partner.

A stir of animation near the entrance caught his eye. Jeanne Courtenay was arriving on her father's arm; her beaux were flocking to ask permission to put their names on her dance card.

Valmont retreated a step; the memory of the scene at his house was fresh in his mind. He smiled inwardly at the commotion around Jeanne. Like moths to the flame, he thought. It was understandable. Jeanne radiated sexual promise. He remembered a friend in Paris saying, about a girl like Jeanne, "My friend, it would be nothing more than courtesy to relieve that unfortunate young woman of her unwanted virginity."

No, Val added, he wasn't doing Jeanne justice. Her appeal was more than that. She was extraordinarily lovely. Almost flawless. No, again. She was altogether without flaw.

He turned away quickly, aware of his dangerous response. That was one indulgence he could not afford. He wasn't ready to marry, and nothing else was allowable. It would be insane even to consider any kind of dalliance . . .

He turned again; Jeanne's eyes met his, inviting him to her side. He began to move toward her.

An elbow hit his arm. "I beg your pardon, Monsieur," said its owner.

And then, "I truly do beg your pardon, Val. For God's sake don't challenge me. I'm too bored to die."

The speaker was Val's friend from Paris, Alfred de Pontalba, the elder son of the Baroness. Valmont embraced him. "I haven't seen you for too many months, you villain. How are you?"

"As well as could be expected surrounded by all this colonial respectability. I was going to try my chances with the tearing beauty who just came in until I discovered that her brother was my host on the plantation I've been visiting. He's a good fellow, do you know him? Philippe Courtenay. He gave me some good sport down on Bayou Teche, shooting alligators. That's one thing I can't find in France."

"I know Philippe. Is he here?"

"He is." Philippe appeared at Val's side.

"I'm glad to see you, Val, even though I hear that you outproduced us in pounds per acre this year. My uncle is gnashing what's left of his teeth."

Valmont stopped a passing waiter and they took flutes of champagne. "To sugar," said Val.

"To sugar," echoed Philippe. They drained their glasses and exchanged them for full ones.

"I hope that concludes the agricultural report," Alfred said. "Shall we drink to something else, or shall we simply drink?"

"Drink to freedom," Philippe suggested with a grin. "I have been let off the leash by my esteemed father, so we can leave. He is of the opinion that I won't be needed to save my little sister from the corner of the wallflowers."

The three men looked at Jeanne's clamoring circle of admirers. "I think you can be spared," Val said. "I'll come with you. What are you planning? I'm sure the cockfights have started by now at the pit on Chartres. Or we could play a little poker at Curtius's place."

Philippe looked at Alfred. "Should we relieve Monsieur Saint-Brévin of his sugar profits? He must be deplorably rich."

"It would be an act of friendship, I agree. But one can gamble anywhere. You promised me a local specialty, a visit to New Orleans's demimonde."

"So I did. Come along, Val. We're going to the Quadroon Ball."

Valmont shook his head. Then changed his mind. He would like to know what Marie Laveau wanted to see him about.

• • •

The walk to the Salle d'Orléans was only a few blocks, but it was long enough for Val to regret the impulse that had made him come. After they were scrutinized at the door and allowed to purchase admission tickets, he tried to persuade Alfred and Philippe to go to one of the gambling rooms on the ground floor for a game of faro. They thought he was joking. Hats and cloaks taken by an attendant, they mounted the stairs to the ballroom and sounds of orchestra and musical laughter.

"Mon dieu," exclaimed Alfred. "This is what a ball should be." Tremendous cyrstal chandeliers suspended from the soaring ceiling splintered the light from their candles into shards of color that fell onto the white shirtfronts of men and the bright gowns of women in the center of the floor. The dance was a reel, a patterned meeting and parting, marching and twirling that served to exhibit each of the quadroons in turn to the nondancers standing along the edges of the floor. They were as beautiful as their legend promised; the subtle differences in the colors of their skins, from milky white to golden brown, made their loveliness exotic; the vivid colors they wore were like the overpowering blooms of tropical flowers; their decorous smiles contrasted with the wisdom in their lash-veiled eyes that promised a lifetime of training in how to please a man.

There was one exception, one woman who was not like the others, one who dared instead of promised, whose movements were like a tender sapling in a south wind, whose beauty made the story of Helen of Troy a reality.

Val felt Philippe stiffen with shock by his side, knew that his own body must be equally rigid, heard Alfred's long indrawn breath when he realized what the others had already seen. The woman was the distillation, purification, enhancement of Philippe's sister Jeanne.

"My friend," Philippe said to Val. "I cannot stay here. Yet I gave my word to Alfred. If you are my friend, say that you will stay with him. I must leave."

"I will stay," Val murmured.

No power on earth could have taken him away at that moment.

# 36

"I would give half my fortune to own that woman," said Alfred.

Val kept his anger in check, but his words were brittle. "This is not a slave auction. These are free people of color."

Alfred's eyebrows peaked. "Remember, Valmont, I'm only a visitor to your city," he said smoothly. "How does a stranger secure an introduction?"

Val clapped his friend's shoulder, wordlessly apologizing. "We must present ourselves to the tribunal on the dais over there. They are the sponsors. And the censors. Versailles under the Bourbons had no stricter protocol. Come along. I'm reasonably certain that I will know one of the ruling deities." His initial shock had subsided, and his mind was functioning again. He thought he knew now why Marie had commanded his presence.

As he expected, she was in the center of the half dozen women who directed the ball.

Valmont bowed, as he had done at other royal courts. "I beg your leave to present my friend, Alfred de Pontalba," he said formally.

Marie was regally gracious. She extended a splendidly jeweled hand for Alfred's kiss.

And, at his request, she beckoned when the reel was over. "This is my protegée, Cécile Dulac," she said when the girl responded to her gesture.

"Cécile, Monsieur Alfred de Pontalba, Monsieur Valmont Saint-Brévin . . . Monsieur Pontalba has asked the favor the next dance."

Cécile curtseyed, a lissome sinking into a pool of ivory satin skirts. She rose, rested her gloved hand on Alfred's arm. "You honor me, sir," she said. Then she smiled at him.

Val could see her hand move, shaken by the quiver that ran through Alfred's body. He led her onto the floor.

"And so, my old friend, you approve of my solution to your problem, do you not?" Marie's voice was warm, amused, tender.

"Tell me about her," Val demanded.

"As you can see, she is Carlos Courtenay's daughter. She cast aside his name when he cast aside her mother, and she calls herself Dulac, her mother's name before she became Courtenay's 'shadow wife.' Amaranthe, poor, foolish, gentle creature, has not yet recovered from the termination, so I am acting for her in Cécile's—shall we call it 'début'?"

"And you expect me to become her protector?"

"I have no expectations. She is willful. There have been offers, excellent offers, but she turns them all down. And you, dear Val, are the most peculiar of men. I confess I don't know what you want."

"I want a dancing partner, no more."

"That much I did expect. And I will admit that I am deliberately using you. There have already been duels. One fatal. I hope that your fame will prevent any more such incidents if it is believed that you're taking an interest in Cécile. She's vulnerable. There is jealousy. There have been threats, bad gris-gris on her doorstep. She is drawing attention that the other girls believe should be theirs."

Val laughed. "You're spreading it too thick, Marie. Who would dare voodoo your protegée?"

Marie shrugged. "The world never lacks fools."

The music stopped. Alfred returned Cécile to Marie's side with obvious reluctance.

"Monsieur Pontalba," said Marie, "may I present another partner to you? Monsieur Saint-Brévin has spoken for the next dance with Mademoiselle Dulac." She nodded at a striking girl in red velvet, signaled the orchestra.

Val offered his arm to Cécile. The music began, for that most intoxicating and intimate of all dances, the waltz.

Val put one hand behind her narrow waist, took her hand in his. Her fingers curved over the edge of his hand bringing their gloved palms together, and they moved as one into the sweeping circles of the dance.

Before the Saint Louis Hotel was built, all fashionable Creole balls had been held at the Salle d'Orléans. Experts were still bemoaning the change, although twelve years had passed, because the floor of the Orléans Ballroom was a marvel. Made of cypress, the indestructible pithy swamp tree, the floor was constructed in three layers, with a final layer of polished oak, like icing on a sponge cake. It had a buoyancy, an imperceptible springiness, that made even the most awkward dancer feel as if his feet were light and graceful; good dancers skimmed and floated like winged-slipper Mercuries.

Valmont Saint-Brévin felt as if he had thistledown in his arms. Cécile was weightless; her steps mirrored his; her body moved to his thoughts even before he led her into the pattern of the dance. He felt exhilarated, a part of perfection in motion. Neither of them spoke. Cécile's exquisite face was rapt, lost in pleasure. He knew that his was the same. He wanted the music to go on forever.

But it ended. "My thanks, Mademoiselle," he said.

"And mine," Cécile replied. "Will you take me down for a coffee?" She walked off, confident that he would follow.

The stairs in the rear of the ballroom led down to a flagstoned courtyard where small candlelit tables were placed among orange trees and sweet-smelling shrubs of tea olive. The floor and the brick walls held the warmth of the day's sun, while overhead stars were sharply brilliant in the black winter sky.

Waiters moved silently from table to table bringing champagne, absinthe, brandy, coffee, sweetmeats, and cigars. Music floated down from the ballroom, filtered by the bower of green leaves, and quiet conversations mixed with it from the secluded tables. There was private laughter and from time to time the clear, high ring of fine crystal goblets touching in a private toast.

"Will you take champagne, Mademoiselle?"

"Thank you, no. A small coffee, very hot."

Val searched for something to say. Opposite him Cécile was a glimmer of ivory skin and ivory gown, ebony hair and eyes. She was silent, and unconcerned by the silence between them.

Val let the warmth and scents and quiet seep into his unsettled spirit. There was no need for him to speak. Champagne released slow bubbles from the glass in front of him. There was no need for him to drink. Cécile sipped her coffee.

The cup made a tiny sound when she set it in its saucer. "Here comes the man to whom I had promised the next dance," she said.

Val looked up at the approaching figure. He knew the man, a cotton broker notorious for his rages.

"He will offer to kill me," said Val quietly.

Cécile said nothing.

"Will you be sad if he does?"

"No . . . nor if you kill him. Dueling is men's nonsense."

Val laughed. "In that case there's no point in dying. You astonish me, Mademoiselle. Tell me, do you have a heart in your ravishing corsage?"

Cécile smiled, and she was so beautiful that Val's breath stopped. "I have been told that I do not," she said.

The broker was at Val's side. "Monsieur," he said, "you have given me great offense." His voice was loud, a startling ugliness in the peaceful enchantment of the courtyard.

Val stood. "And you, sir, are offending a number of people by your noisiness. I shall be happy to give you satisfaction, for them as well as for myself."

"I demand that you meet me at once."

"So be it. My second is upstairs."

The small public garden behind the Cathedral was the most popular site for dueling. Daybreak was the most popular time. There was a spice of novelty for Val in fighting by torchlight. He flexed the rapier, one of a pair that Alfred had brought from the Pontalba buildings, only a block and a few steps distant. It was a superlative blade, made for the fencing master in Paris who had taught him and Alfred and most of the other elegant young men of Paris society. Too good to waste its mate in the coarse hands of the noisy broker. Val thought of those hands touching the satin skin of Cécile Dulac, and his mouth tasted sour. Like a tarantula on the petals of a flower. He was looking forward to this duel.

Everything was ready. The seconds withdrew to stand flanking the doctor, who had been roused from his home nearby. The adversaries saluted one another, blades glinting in the uneven light. Val added a salute to the torchbearers and to the balconies of the ballroom across the street where shadowy figures were crowded to watch the duel.

The broker lunged when Val was looking up toward the balcony. Val's insulting inattention added to his anger. His rage exploded when Val parried the thrust with negligent ease, and he launched an attack that surprised Val by its furious, unexpected skill.

The man was worth fighting.

Val concentrated on the swordplay, enjoyed the difficulty of the shifting shadows and the uneven, unseeable footing of paths and grass. He was excited by the thought of Cécile watching from the balcony with indifferent eyes, and he fought with unnecessary brio, laughing at himself for childish showing-off, laughing at his opponent's attempts to force a conclusion, toying with death, playing with the broker like a matador with a dangerous, maddened bull. He felt alive, involved, challenged by the half-seen rapier that sought his heart and by the heartless woman who sought the excitement of men killing for the privilege of a dance with her.

The broker was tiring, worn down by his own emotion-laden fighting. Val could feel the change in the rhythm of the clashing, sliding, circling blades. Should I finish him? Val wondered. He examined his thoughts with curiosity. It had been many years since he had killed an opponent. He had been young then and hotheaded and eager to prove himself a man. He was surprised that the notion of killing had entered his mind.

He put it aside. It would be too easy. Instead he executed a rapid series of attacks culminating in a twisting, spinning thrust that lifted the rapier from the broker's hand and sent it arching into the darkness. Then he held his swordpoint to his enemy's heart. "Do you yield?" He could feel the rise and fall of the broker's panting breath vibrate through the fine steel of the rapier.

The man sobbed suddenly. "For God's sake, draw blood, man," he begged in a whisper. "You've beat me. Don't shame me."

Valmont's lip quivered, almost sneering. The man was a craven. He might have begged to be finished, like a man of honor, and Val would have respected him even as he spared him. But to beg for a harmless wound to save face was the act of a coward. A coward who would have killed if he could.

Val's wrist moved, the rapier snaked upward, neatly sliced a millimeter of flesh off the broker's earlobe. Then he turned his back to the man and walked away.

Alfred brought his coat to him, took the rapier from his hand. "An entertaining duel," he said. "I trust the flight through the air, pretty though it was, did not affect the balance of the other blade. The servants are searching for it.

"What now? Shall we find some champagne and drink to your success?"

Val's smile flashed in the shadows. "Not yet," he laughed. "I believe I have just won a disputed dance with Mademoiselle Dulac."

"Are you sorry he didn't kill the cotton man?" Marie Laveau asked Cécile.

The girl shrugged. "I didn't want to dance with him. Now I don't have to. I'm glad."

"Don't play your games with me, Cécile. Remember who you're talking to. These duels you incite are becoming an embarrassment. You're like an overindulged child breaking her toys."

"And what am I to these men, Madame, but an expensive toy? I hate them all."

"Including Saint-Brévin?"

"He is a man."

"You disappoint me. I believed you were intelligent."

Cécile gasped as if Marie had hit her. "I'm sorry," she said after a long pause. "I am grateful for your kindness to me and my mother. I don't want to disappoint you... This Saint-Brévin, you are sure the Courtenay girl is in love with him?"

"He is the only thing she wants in life."

"I had hoped that the Courtenay son would be possible."

"I told you, never. He is a bastard himself. He couldn't bear to see another of his father's bastards on view, no matter how beautiful. There is also the repugnance of the incestuous."

"In that case, Madame Marie, I will have Monsieur Saint-Brévin. Please make the arrangements."

"Perhaps he will not be agreeable."

Cécile laughed. It was a genuine, youthful laugh of delight. She kissed Marie's cheeks. "I won't disappoint you a second time."

She left the balcony, just as Val reentered the ballroom, crossed the floor to meet him. "You fence as well as you waltz, Monsieur," she said. "My compliments."

Valmont bowed. "You do me too much honor."

"I think not."

Val smiled. "Will you do me the additional honor of granting me another waltz?"

Cécile put her hand in his.

Marie stood in the shadows of the balcony, looking at them. There were tears in her eyes. For an instant she wished that she could be other than who she was, that she could be a beautiful young girl with no powers other than the power to captivate and capture Valmont Saint-Brévin. To consider the world well lost for love.

Then she laughed deep in her throat at her sentimentality, and she felt her power strong in her veins. She had long ago chosen the world; she would never consider losing it. She was a queen.

# 37

It was absurd, Mary told herself, to let the idea of going to a dance change everything in her life. But the fact was that her gloominess had vanished the minute Louisa mentioned dressing up and going out. She had slept well, had dreamt something that she couldn't remember except that it was happy, had wakened with a smile on her face.

The day was as hectic as always, but nothing bothered her. Customers who demanded her attention even though they were "only looking," seamstresses arriving late for work, Hannah spilling coffee on a bolt of best crinoline—all the things that would have driven her mad the day before now seemed almost unimportant. Mary looked again at the length of silver lace she was going to sew onto the blue evening gown she had worn to the opera. It would make all the difference, change the gown from sweet and girlish to elegant and womanly. She would buy the silver slippers she had seen in the shop on Chartres Street, too. She hadn't spent any of the money that was her share of the profits yet; she'd been too busy for any indulgences other than the streetcar. And she'd take enough silver ribbon from the shop to do something with her hair that was more interesting than the neat coil at the back that she usually wore. Perhaps she could even find time to go to a hairdresser. Hannah could manage alone for a little while. If only she could have it done the way the woman who came to the Courtenay house had arranged it... that was the prettiest it had ever looked.

The shop door opened. Mary walked out from the protection of the screen behind which she did her sewing.

"May-ree! Is that you?"

Jeanne Courtenay rushed forward, threw her arms around Mary, embraced her with all her strength. Over Jeanne's shoulder Mary saw Berthe Courtenay. She looked thunderstruck.

Berthe didn't know, Mary thought. It was all Carlos. He threw me out, and no one knew about it. He must have told them some lie, that I had run away or something. She tried to concentrate on Jeanne's excited chattering. Something about a new gown and everyone talking about Rinck's and a masquerade ball and what did Mary think of going as Juliet and had Mary seen the opera last week and wasn't Bellini's music divinely romantic and wouldn't it be perfect to have a little cap made of pearls and her hair loose because her hair was truly a crowning glory but no one ever got to see it falling across her shoulders and on and on in typical Jeanne style.

Berthe's lips became a thin line. She seized Jeanne's arm. "Come, Jeanne, we'll go to Madame Alphande," she said. "This isn't a suitable place for a young girl to buy her gowns."

Mary knew, then, that Carlos Courtenay had not acted alone, and the old hurt came back. Why had they done it, what had she done wrong, why had she been driven out like a leper with no reason given, why, why, why was she treated so cruelly? The agonized questions strangled her. Mary reached out to Berthe, tried to speak. But Berthe was leaving, pulling Jeanne along with her.

"Maman," Jeanne protested, "I want to talk to May-ree."

Mary could hear Jeanne's voice becoming fainter as her mother hurried her away.

"Who was that, Mary?" Hannah came from the rear of the shop where she had been unpacking a new shipment of gloves.

"Some people I used to know," Mary said. "Nobody important." It was difficult to force the words past the tears in her throat. She had succeeded in putting the pain away, locked in the dark corner of her mind with all the other wounds that she would not think about. Now it had escaped the corner, and she felt it all again, more fiercely than on the morning when Carlos ejected her from what she thought of as her home. Then she had been numbed by shock. Now every fiber of her being was alive to the insult of the rejection, the injustice of it, the terrifying vulnerability and powerlessness and precariousness of her existence. She was alone and exposed to the buffeting, the capriciousness of an uncaring world.

"I'll be back in a few minutes," she said to Hannah. "I won't be long."

Mary snatched her shawl from its peg and ran out the door.

The rows of sycamores on the Place d'Armes had been cut down. The square was a bare, rutted area of dark earth with scattered tufts of uncut grass and weeds. The wind blew across it, cold under a low gray sky, tugging at the corners of Mary's shawl, sending icy fingers down the neck of her dress. It carried dirt from the square, flung it biting against her forehead and cheeks, stung her eyes.

She ran with the wind behind her, skirts billowing, face wet with tears, to the sanctuary of the cathedral at the end of the square.

Her fingers dipped into the font automatically, and she blessed herself hurriedly, urgent need speeding her into the house of God.

There she knelt and prayed, weeping softly. Blessed Mother, Heavenly Father, I'm frightened and alone. Comfort me. Be with me.

The hard floor beneath her knees was like the stone of the chapel in the convent school, the chill in the great spaces of the cathedral like the cold mountain air of Pennsylvania. The smell of candle wax and incense was homelike, and Mary's troubled heart was eased. The pain retreated to its corner and was locked away again.

She ran, against the wind, back to the shop and the silver lace for her gown. She was going to have fun with her friends. She did have friends, people who cared for her.

Hannah was more than happy to take care of things while Mary went to the hairdresser. "If the Creole ladies want to buy something, they can point at it. I don't need to speak French to see where a finger is aimed."

When Mary came back to the shop Hannah exclaimed loudly about the elegance of her massed ringlets and ribbon-woven crown of braids. She insisted that Mary take a silk scarf from the shop's inventory to protect her hair from the wind and that she go home early, in a horsecab, to get ready for the evening.

Louisa was home early, too. Mary heard her singing when she entered the house. An aria, not scales.

"Your voice sounds wonderful, Louisa," Mary said.

"Your hair looks beautiful."

They smiled together, happy to be festive. Louisa took Mary's hand, pulled her to the bed to sit side by side.

"Now, Mary, I've got to tell you some things quickly, before my brother gets here. His name is Michael; everybody calls him Mike. Mike Kelly. And he'll be calling me Katie. That's my real name, you see. Katherine Kelly. I changed it when I came to New Orleans. Who ever heard of an opera star named Katie Kelly? That's why I call myself Louisa Ferncliff. It's so much more glamorous sounding.

"Mike knows I go by Louisa now, but he forgets. I'd still be Katie to him if I was singing *Lucia di Lammermoor.*

"I guess I don't have to tell you that Mike doesn't have any idea that Mr. Bassington is interested in me. Let's keep it that way. I've put all the presents he gave me in your room. Mike wouldn't think of going in there, but he's more than likely to bust into my room the minute he comes through the door. Mrs. O'Neill let me invite him for supper... Are you going to dress up for supper or wait until after?"

The two of them were still trying to decide when Mike Kelly burst in as predicted. He was a big, florid man with a ginger mustache and muttonchop whiskers.

"Of course I remember Miss Mary," he roared when Louisa introduced them. "Didn't I see her pretty face every day on the *Cairo Queen?* It was a dark day for us all when you left the old *Queen* for fancier traveling, Miss Mary."

"Indeed it was," said Mary, remembering that Rose Jackson had arranged the change. She pushed the regrets aside and asked about Joshua.

"Same as ever," Mike laughed. "Uppity as Satan but nobody minds it, coming from him. He got off in Baton Rouge to be with his family for Christmas.

"And here I am to be with my baby sister. Then it's off to California and a fortune in gold, did Katie tell you?"

"Yes, she did. It's very exciting."

"And more exciting yet when I come back with a sackful of nuggets as big as my fist, in a year or two. Why, I heard a fellow talking on the boat, and he said that he heard..." Mike kept them fascinated until suppertime with stories of striking it rich.

During supper he told most of them again, fascinating Mrs. O'Neill and the Reillys. Paddy Devlin was more intrigued by Mary's curls than by gold nuggets. He couldn't keep his eyes off her.

"If you don't mind me saying so, you're looking very beautiful tonight," he said when Mary came out in her blue and silver ensemble to go to the ball.

"I don't mind at all," she answered gaily. She felt beautiful in her curls and silver slippers on the way to her first ball. She didn't know quite what to expect, but she was sure it would be wonderful.

The ballroom was not very large or very grand. The floor was rough in spite of a day's polishing, and the cold drafts around the window frames made the oil lamps sputter and smoke. But the walls were decorated with swags of bright green taffeta, and there were shining gilt ballroom chairs all around the edges of the room. Three fiddlers and an accordion player provided the music; it was fast and merry, and the people who weren't dancing clapped in accompaniment.

All ages were there. Old men and women sat carefully on the delicate chairs, children did jigs of their own in corners or ran among the dancers playing games of tag and squealing with excitement. It was very noisy.

"I don't know how to do that dance," Mary told Paddy when he gestured toward the dancing. The center of the floor was full of couples doing an energetic hop and skip and slide pattern that Mary had never seen before.

Paddy couldn't hear her. He bent his head, cupped his ear, raised his eyebrows.

Mary repeated herself, shouting the words.

"No squeamish holding back, Miss Mary," yelled Mike. He closed his big hands around Mary's waist, lifted her, and marched into the dancing with a deep, loud laugh.

Mary felt so silly, suspended like a rag doll, that she laughed helplessly with him. Mike set her down and began to dance. The steps were easy to learn, and Mary soon got the hang of the dance. She stamped and hopped and spun and slid without a thought for her fragile slippers. She was having too much fun to worry.

Paddy stood with Louisa, watching. Mary looked to him like a goddess among mortals. Her silver and blue gown was an aristocratic frivolity among the sensible dark silks of the older women and the gaudy cheap taffetas of the young ones. Her brightly colored cheeks made the rouge on other women look harsh and tawdry. And her small feet in their delicate silver coverings seemed barely to touch the floor, in contrast to the heavy dress boots of the other, more sensible dancers.

"Ah, but she's a beauty," he sighed.

Louisa patted his arm sympathetically. "She's not our class, Paddy. Give it up. You're running after the will o' the wisp."

His heavy jaw set mulishly. "Miss Mary is my lady," he said. "As soon as I get to be a screwman, I'll make her my wife. I'll take good care of her. She can have all the fairy shoes she wants, and she'll be able to stop spoiling her health by working."

"And what do you call it, Paddy Devlin, when a woman cleans and cooks all day, and her heavy with a baby on the way every year?" Louisa yelled.

Paddy didn't or wouldn't hear what she said.

When the dance ended, Mike brought Mary back to Paddy. "I've worked up a terrible thirst," he said. His face gleamed wetly, and a drop of sweat hung like a diamond on the tip of his nose.

Louisa flicked it off. "Mike dearest, please don't start the drinking so early. Dance with your sister, like the loving brother you are."

Mike grinned at her. "You sound more like Ma than like Katie, but I'll indulge you. Come on, then." He wrapped his arm around her waist and spun her into the dance that was just beginning.

Paddy took Mary's hand in his and led her into the dancers. "I'm having a wonderful time," Mary shouted. Then she was caught up in the music and the pounding feet and clapping hands.

Long tables at the far end of the room were covered with bowls and platters of food. After Mary and Paddy danced for almost two hours, they heaped plates and sat down to eat. Paddy jumped up after he had one bite of ham. "I'll get you some punch. It's specially for the women."

Mary smiled. She was thirsty, but she hadn't wanted to ask for anything to drink because the only thing she saw on the table were pitchers of beer. She had tasted beer at Mrs. O'Neill's and disliked it.

She watched Paddy walk to a corner behind the tables. He had to wait several minutes before he got a cup of punch. The corner was crowded four deep with men around the table with the punch bowl. Two kegs of whisky were under the table.

An hour later two full kegs were rolled in to replace them; no pretense of hiding the kegs was attempted this time. They were hoisted up onto the tables, now empty of food.

An hour after that the effects of the whisky began to make themselves evident. The dancing became wilder, people began to sing, some women started to cry, a big, red-faced man stumbled over his own dancing feet and fell crashing to the floor, taking his partner down with him.

The first fight broke out a half hour later. In less than a minute the room was filled with the sounds of fists meeting flesh, breaking glass, and exultant shouting.

Mary clung to Paddy. "I want to go home," she cried.

"You needn't fret, Miss Mary. I'll take care of you. There's hours of dancing yet."

"Please. Please. I want to go home."

Paddy nodded. "You can have anything you want, Miss Mary." He danced her to an open space near the door.

There were a half dozen women there, putting their shawls on before going outside. Another joined them, dragging two protesting children by the arms. Louisa ran up to Mary and Paddy.

"I'll go with you," she bellowed. With a tilt of her head she showed them where Mike was standing, laughing mightily, swinging the remains of a gilt chair at four men who were trying to get to him.

Mary was shaking when they left the building. Paddy took off his rented tailcoat and put it around her shoulders.

But she was reacting to the violence, not the cold. What frightened her most was that no one else seemed to be bothered by the destruction and the brutishness. They had all been laughing or smiling, the combatants. Like Mike Kelly. Even the women that were leaving seemed unaffected by the mayhem. And the musicians were still playing, as if bloody noses and broken heads were no different from dancing feet.

The corner of a jutting brick in the banquette hurt her foot; Mary cried for the broken evening, saying that she was weeping from the pain in her heel.

"You're bleeding," Paddy exclaimed when Mary turned her foot to examine it. He lifted her easily and carried her home through the cold in his shirtsleeved arms.

Mary couldn't stop her tears. She wasn't crying for her disappointment or for her throbbing heel. She wept because Paddy Devlin loved her and she couldn't love him.

Back at the boarding house Mary washed and bandaged the slight wound. She answered Mrs. O'Neill's questions by holding her ruined slippers high and smiling her best smile. "It was a wonderful ball," she said. "I've always heard of dancing your slippers through, and I did. They say that's the proof of an extra special good time."

Louisa's smile had twisted corners. "Tell my brother that one, Mary. He thinks the proof is a headache for three days. And skinned knuckles."

Mary had trouble falling asleep that night. She was trying to understand the people and the life of the Irish Channel. They made her feel pale and cowardly. Everything about them was so much bigger; their grief, their pleasures, their eating and drinking and joyful fighting were all so packed with emotion that she was dwarfed, overwhelmed.

I don't belong, and I never will.

She wondered if that was what Louisa meant when she said that Mary was from a different class. She knew that she couldn't change. And that she didn't want to. She wanted the life she had glimpsed at Montfleury, a life of order and beauty, of flower-scented galleries and green lawns, of tables lined with smiling, soft-voiced people holding glasses of shimmering crystal beneath the portraits of faces like their own.

She went for weeks now without thinking of the lost casket, the box that was her legacy. Sometimes she almost believed it was only a dream.

Then the moments like this one would come, when she felt so much a stranger in her life on Adele Street. She would remember the box, and be convinced that she belonged in a more refined, a more gentle and civilized world. I'll have the life I want, she promised herself. The shop is already successful. If I continue to work hard, I'll be able to have everything I want. I'm very good at my work.

And she would be ashamed of herself for her worldly pride, but at the same time that pride would comfort her.

When sleep finally came, Mary had her hands twined together, thumbs touching the abnormal length of the little fingers that had fit so exactly into the lace-cuffed glove in the casket.

A little more than a mile away, in the gracious old house on Royal Street, Celeste Sazerac locked the door to her room. Then she unlocked the door to an armoire and lifted out the scarred casket. Its wood gleamed from the nightly polishing she gave it. She opened it, placed its treasures before her on a table covered with a velvet drape, placed a silver candelabra in the center, lit the five candles. She turned out the gas lights then and sat on the bench in front of the table. She crooned wordless songs to the objects while she polished the box.

The old gloves held candlelight in their palms.

# 38

On the morning following the Quadroon Ball, Valmont Saint-Brévin had ridden out of the city at sunup. He rode without haste to his plantation, relying on his horse to pick his footing on the frost-rimed road. Val's attention was on the thoughts tumbling chaotically inside his head.

The girl Cécile was his for the taking, he knew it, no matter what Marie said. And he wanted her. More than he had wanted any woman since he left Paris.

The circumstances, however, were detestable. The girl was for sale, not for winning.

He could afford her easily. Buy her one of the houses near Rampart Street, some servants, a carriage, furnishings, clothes, and jewels. She could be the most lavishly indulged placée in the city without making a dent in his pocket.

He imagined the pleasure of indulging her, saw her opposite him at a small table, her shoulders bare, her throat in a collar of emeralds, an exquisite dinner with the finest wines...

All paid for. Like a race horse or a field hand. A superlatively beautiful creature and a slave, regardless of her papers attesting to her free status.

But she chose her life, Val argued with himself. With her beauty she could have married any one of a hundred men. She didn't have to offer herself as a white man's mistress; she didn't have to appear at the Salle d'Orléans.

And he knew he was lying to himself. Cécile was the daughter of a placée. She was by definition illegitimate. A luxurious illegitimacy, but a bar sinister known to all. Which made her ineligible for marriage to the wealthy free men of color who could maintain the kind of life she knew. The free people of color had their own society, with distinctions of class and lineage just as rigid as those in white society.

Valmont knew more about the world of this unique New Orleans population than probably any white man alive. Marie Laveau had written to him when she was growing up, when she was learning about her own place in that world, when she was puzzling about the written and unwritten laws that governed it.

He had been unable to answer her innocent questions about the particular problems of being black in a white man's country. Of being more white than black in fact but not in law. Of being free in law but subject in fact. Free men or women of color could own property and rent it to whites; they could operate a business that had customers who were white; they could file a lawsuit against whites and win. But they could not marry whites, or employ whites. Furthermore, the women had to wear the tignon whenever they went onto public streets, just like slave women. And any white woman could have a free woman of color arrested for being "unruly," if the white woman had two corroborating witnesses. The punishment was a public whipping by one of the jailers.

Free men of color were denied the most valued right a man could have: the right to defend his honor. He could not challenge a white man to a duel. Even though the best and best-known fencing master in New Orleans was Bastile Croquère, a free man of color who gave lessons to the sons of the foremost Creole families.

Free people of color had been part of New Orleans from its earliest days. When the French-owned island Santo Domingo was convulsed by a slave uprising, thousands of wealthy free people of color fled the island for safety in French-speaking New Orleans. Before the Americans came, they made up almost a half of the nonslave population of the city. They owned a third of the property, including plantations with hundreds of slaves; they had their boxes at the opera, a tier immediately above the boxes for Creole society; they had private schools for their children, with further education in France for the young men; they had poets and ne'er-do-wells, doctors and drunks, gamblers and philanthropists, rich and poor, saints and profligates—all the attributes that humankind has always had. Including the prejudice against the child not acknowledged by its father, the bastard.

Cécile Dulac could never marry a man who was her equal in education, cultivation, and refinement. She was destined from birth for plaçage.

Valmont knew all that, and he told himself that if it was Cécile's fate to be a white man's mistress, the white man might just as well be Valmont Saint-Brévin. He would treat her well, be more sensitive to the dilemma of her position than any other man was likely to be. She'd be lucky to have him. The alternative might be a loud boor like the cotton broker.

And yet... and yet... Val had never forced himself on a woman, had never made love to a woman who was not eager for his embrace.

For straightforward sexual gratification, he had always gone to the best whores. He never made love unless there was love on both sides. Not necessarily the kind of love celebrated by poets. He wasn't convinced that the love they wrote about existed outside their poetry.

He could love Cécile, by his definition of love. He could care about her feelings, her well-being, her happiness. He wanted someone to care about, to love.

But he wanted her to care about him, too. There was no reason to believe that Cécile did. Or ever would.

She would be a good mistress, Val was sure of that. She would be faithful to him, attentive to his needs and his desires, competent at managing the home he provided. He would have a pleasant place to go whenever he liked, with the food and drink he preferred, and a beautiful, agreeable companion. She would quickly learn, too, how to please him in bed. Although she was a virgin, she would have been taught by her mother how to delight a man.

He would have all the good that marriage could bring, without any of the constrictions. He would be a fool of the highest order if he didn't make an offer for the most beautiful, desirable woman he had ever seen.

But she didn't love him. Not even want him. She would submit. She might be so skillful that she could feign love and wanting.

He would know. There was no mistaking real surrender, the opening of the heart as well as the body.

And he would be disgusted. With himself. With the system of plaçage. With the buying and selling of the counterfeit of love.

Val's hands tightened on the reins. His horse was about to run away.

Then he recognized landmarks beside the road, and he loosened his grip with a laugh. Benison was only a mile or so farther. "Ready for the stables, are you?" he said. The horse's ears quivered. Val slapped its flank. "All right, then, let's head for home. A warm mash for you and a hot toddy for me."

There was so much to take care of at Benison that Val had no time to think about Cécile. It was already the twenty-first of December, and on the twenty-seventh he was scheduled to leave for Charleston, taking Snow Cloud and three more horses to race there. The Charleston races were the most famous in all America, with competitors coming from France and England and Ireland as well as from all parts of the United

States. Val had attended the races, but he had not entered horses of his own before.

"The Europeans bring their horses months in advance to acclimate them, but I don't want to be away from home at Christmas," Val told everyone. "So I'm planning to take Louisiana with me. My horses won't need to adjust to South Carolina. They'll hardly know they ever left home."

Everyone said he had more money than sense when they learned what Val meant. He bought an ocean-going steamship, custom-made to his design in Ireland. The ship had been moored in New Orleans for over four months. Practically every man in town had been over her, and they disapproved vehemently. When Val wasn't in earshot. The cabins were indecently large and luxurious, they said. There were separate accommodations for Val, the ship's captain, Val's jockey, his trainer, and even the grooms and exercise boys. The crew were in quarters with only four men to a cabin. The padded stalls for the horses were ridiculous. More absurd were the tremendous holds with room for Benison-grown feed and bedding straw and casks of water.

An elderly American who had studied Roman history muttered "Caligula" over and over again for hours. The Creoles shook their heads about the insult of the crew being imported from New England. No one could understand a word the captain said.

But everyone admitted that Saint-Brévin had style. And they arranged stupendous wagers on Val's horses. Win or lose, it would be a fine thing to show snobbish Charleston that New Orleans, too, was on the map.

The ship was named *Benison*, too. It would move slowly upriver to the other Benison on Christmas day, when there was no other traffic and every care could be exercised to find a channel for its deep hull.

Val spent Saturday and Sunday checking all the preparations for the horses. And for the unusual cargo. He had conferences with all the people who had worked on the arrangements, double-checked everything they had done.

In addition, he took time to go over the plans for the household again with his butler, Nehemiah. The Charleston trip would keep him away for more than a month. Then Val had to congratulate Agnes, his housekeeper, on the house decorations of ivy, holly, mistletoe, pine boughs, magnolia leaves, and massed red and white camellias. During his day in the city, the plantation house had been transformed to a festive bower. That led him to a long talk and tour with the head gardener; he was to be praised too. Despite the unusually cold weather, the gardens were full of blooms.

Val chose the finest flowers for cutting. He'd take them to the city when he went back. They would be good conversation starters with his many aunts and cousins when he made the obligatory calls on Christmas day. By the time each lady finished telling him what the gardeners were doing wrong, the required twenty minutes would be over, and he could move on to the next call with another selection of flowers.

Christmas was going to be hectic. He had to distribute the gifts to the slaves in the morning, attend mass in the plantation chapel, ride into the city to visit the relatives, then return in time to oversee the docking of the ship.

And it would all probably have to be done after no more than two hours of sleep. He had accepted Michaela de Pontalba's invitation for a Réveillon supper on Christmas Eve. The Réveillon was a Continental custom, not practiced in New Orleans, a leisurely meal of twelve courses for twelve diners that ended with champagne at twelve o'clock and a toast to salute the beginning of Christmas Day and the birth of the Christ Child.

He'd be lucky if he got back to Benison before five A.M.

Val was deeply fond of the Baroness and her sons. It was a blessing to have them in New Orleans. Even when there was no time to see them, he knew that a bit of Paris was nearby, and he missed France less.

But he cursed himself for agreeing to attend the Réveillon. There was so much to do before he left for Charleston. And behind his facade of carefree sportsman, he was perpetually worried about the voyage, the arrangements, and the odds against the success of his careful plans.

He was even more angry at himself and Michaela about the portrait she had tricked him into buying. He had to sit for Rinck on Monday, and again on Tuesday, Christmas Eve.

Mary saw Valmont arrive for his Monday morning appointment with Albert Rinck. It was no accident; Hannah had told her Val was coming.

"Albert is in such a state, Mary, you'd think it was President Fillmore himself he was painting."

Val looked tired, Mary thought, and grumpy. She moved away from the window before he could see her. She was tired, too, but she couldn't give in to it. There was sewing to be done.

• • •

"You look somewhat fatigued, Mr. Saint-Brévin," said Albert Rinck. "Tell me when you want to take some time to sit down."

Val was annoyed by Rinck's nervous, obsequious manner. He wanted the man to get on with his painting, get it over with. He started to say as much; then he noticed that the artist's hand was shaking, his brush spattering paint, his eyes suspiciously shiny. Dear heaven, was this the artistic temperament, American style? Was the wretched fellow going to break down and cry? The painting would never be finished at this rate.

Val adopted his most relaxed voice, the one he used with a spooked horse. "I have several friends in Paris who paint. None of them is very good, but I envy them all the same. It looks like magic to me when dabs of color turn into a tree or a face. People are the most difficult, I would think. Everyone has his own idea of what he looks like, but it's seldom the same as what other people see when they look at him."

That should do it, Val said to himself. Now he knows I don't expect the damned thing to look like me. He can paint a balloon with two dots for eyes, as far as I'm concerned.

Albert's hand was making swift, sure strokes.

Val smiled.

"Do you want to be smiling in the portrait, Mr. Saint-Brévin?"

Val wanted to tell Rinck to go to hell. Instead he simply said he thought it better if he did not smile.

Albert coughed, an announcement that he was about to speak. "I agree with you about portraits. They are the most difficult." He paused, then plunged into revelation. "I'm not very good, either, like your friends in Paris. I paint almost anything else better than I do faces. But no one wants to pay for a painting of a bowl of oranges. Lots of people want to glorify themselves... I don't mean that as an insult to you. I know the Baroness talked you into this portrait. It wasn't your idea. I sympathize with you. I know how it is. She started talking to me one day in Philadelphia, and the next thing I knew I was in New Orleans paying the highest rent I ever heard of in my life." Albert grinned. "She's a real pistol. If I don't starve to death, I'll never regret the experience of knowing her."

Val decided that Rinck was all right. He was worth getting to know.

"Is Philadelphia your home?"

"No. I'm from a wide spot in the road, not even wide enough to have a name. I was studying in Philadelphia. Hannah and I had saved enough for me to have a few months of lessons. I always wanted better than I could do. I see things with an artist's eyes, I really believe, but I can't paint what I see. I guess I'm too ambitious."

"Maybe too modest."

"No. Modesty has never been my problem. Plenty have told me so." Albert chuckled, mixed some paints on his palette.

"I've always considered it overrated as a virtue," said Val. He was beginning to enjoy himself.

Albert liked to talk. He particularly liked to talk about art and about himself. Val's encouragement opened the floodgates.

Val "sat" for two hours, standing with his elbow on the truncated fluted column that Albert had chosen as a suitably classical fixture. He learned a great deal about Albert's experiences and aspirations. He also learned why Albert would never be the famous artist he longed to be. It wasn't so much that he couldn't paint as well as he wished. That might improve with time. But Albert had no taste.

"Now you take the girl with Hannah in the shop, for example," Albert had said. "I guess I'm one of the few people that've ever really looked at her. Most people would say she's kind of plain. But what I see is deeper. This girl, Mary's her name, she has hair and eyes the color of sherry wine. Way down inside, there's golden lights in her eyes, and golden lights in her hair, too, when the light hits it. I'd like to paint her, paint what I see. I'd have her sitting next to a table, with the light coming from the side, making her hair shine with that gold deep inside. I'd have a decanter of sherry on the table, with that same gold in it. And her eyes looking straight out of the portrait at you, with the tiny bits of gold deep down . . . But I know I wouldn't get it right. It's too subtle, I guess."

"That's a wonderful idea," Val told Albert. You don't know how wonderful, he added silently. This sherry-eyed Mary, Rose Jackson's girl, was exactly what he needed to distract him from leaping into hot water and making Cécile Dulac his mistress. He had promised himself a week in his hotel with three good-humored whores. Rose's girl would be even better. She was clever. Her progress from brothel to respectability and independent prosperity proved it. It would be amusing to see how long she could maintain her act of "butter won't melt in my mouth."

And when she abandoned it, she'd have all the extraordinary talents that made Rose's girls the finest whores on the Mississippi.

# 39

"Good morning, Mrs. Rinck. Is Miss MacAlistair here?"

Mary was sewing behind the screen. She stabbed her finger with the needle when she heard Valmont's voice.

"Yes, she is," Hannah said. "She'll be right out."

Mary wiped her hand on her skirt, then hastily tried to rub out the blood stain. The needle was lost. Her head was spinning. She dropped the collar she was making on the floor when she stood up.

None of it mattered. He was asking for her.

"Good morning, Monsieur," she said when she walked from behind the screen.

The light was behind Valmont, silhouetting him the way the sunset had done the first time she ever saw him. His face was in shadow, but Mary had no need to see it. She knew it by heart.

Albert Rinck does have good vision, Val was thinking. There is a tiny candlelight of gold deep in the girl's eyes. Remarkable that I never noticed it. Probably because of the rouge she wears. Rose should have taught her a lighter hand with it.

He made a slight bow and smiled. Mary's heart turned over. "I'm going for a short walk to the levee to look over a ship there," Val said. "I'd like to have company, if you're free, Mademoiselle. We could take a coffee at the Market."

Mary didn't even look at Hannah. "I'll get my bonnet," she said.

"Take your shawl, Mary," Hannah fussed.

"It's too beautiful today for a wrap," Mary answered. It had turned warm again on Sunday. Mary sent a silent thank-you to all the saints. Because of the weather she had worn her best bonnet. She tied the striped bow under her chin with nervous, clumsy fingers.

"I'm ready, Monsieur Saint-Brévin."

Out in the sunlight Val could see that Mary's brightly colored cheeks were natural. It was the first surprise for him.

The second came when she spoke. She had switched to French, and her accent was perfect. "Are you going to look at the *Benison*, Monsieur? I heard about it from some ladies in the shop. I'd like very much to see it, if I may."

"To see her," Val corrected. "Ships are always women, Mademoiselle. They say it's because men love them so much even though they're so dangerous."

He waited for Mary to follow the lead he had given her, to flirt or to ask him how dangerous he liked women to be. Instead she sounded interested. "How odd, when women are supposed to be bad luck on a ship. Or isn't that true? I read it someplace."

Val was disconcerted. "I don't know," he said. He tried to see Mary's face, to learn if she was laughing at him, but the brim of her bonnet hid it from him. She was much smaller than he remembered.

If he had managed to see her, he would have been surprised again. She was biting her lower lip and wincing. Stop it, she told herself, stop talking so much. You'll bore him to death. And stop wondering about what's happening. It doesn't matter why you're here with him, you are. Don't waste a second. Notice everything so you can remember it later. Everything.

She looked up at Val's face. Her gaze was full of eager curiosity.

It was another surprise to him. She's as innocent as a five-year-old to look at her. I'm amazed that Rose didn't hold on to her. She must have been the best girl she had. Mary's expert innocence, as Val saw it, was such a superlative imitation of the real thing that it bordered on parody. He laughed.

Mary blinked. Then she laughed with him. Her laughter came from deep in her small body, with a robust, contagious merriment that made heads turn and lips smile.

She had abandoned herself to the happiness of the moment.

"Would you prefer coffee now or later?" said Val.

"Either or both," Mary replied. "It's always a good time for coffee. Which would you prefer?"

"Both sounds good. I missed mine this morning." He clasped Mary's upper arm. They had reached the tangled traffic of Levee Street. "Can you run?"

His warm hand seemed to burn through his glove and the sleeve of her dress. Mary wasn't sure her knees wouldn't give way at any moment. The weakness felt wonderful. "I can run," she promised. They plunged into the whirlwind of carts and animals and men.

Later Val had no clear memory of the half hour he and Mary spent together. The details were lost. He remembered only that all the vendors seemed to know her by name and that the coffee they drank was the best coffee ever brewed and that the gumbo they ate was the most flavorful he'd ever tasted and that the *Benison* was far and away the most beautiful ship in the river.

He had intended to arrange a time for her to come to his hotel apartments for an hour. Instead he invited her to go out to the plantation with him after his sitting the following morning to see Snow Cloud. That would give him more time with her, and he wanted more time.

She actually clapped her hands. Val thought that a touch too ingénue. Then she asked if she should arrange a chaperone. Of course, he told her, playing the same game.

He walked her back to the shop just as if she were the proper young lady she was acting so well. Then he hurried to the Saint Louis. On the way he thought of Philippe Courtenay's summary of Mary MacAlistair: She's not like a girl at all.

Poor Philippe. No wonder he'd been so smitten. Val considered Mary MacAlistair the most convincing actress he had ever seen. And her act was brilliant. Not flirtatious, not cold, neither too worldly nor too ignorant. No, she wasn't like a girl; she was such a good companion that it was easy to forget that she was what she was. Rose's girls always gave a man what he most wanted, even if he didn't know until it was given exactly what it was.

This one is the best I ever knew, Val thought. Tomorrow should be very interesting. He entered the hotel then, and put Mary out of his mind.

Mary sewed behind the screen, feeding her heart with her memories of every second of every minute she had spent with Val. She couldn't believe that it had really happened. From time to time she laid her finger on the crusted flower she had brought back to the shop in her pocket. It was proof. The gumbo man had given it to Val for lagniappe, and Val had given it to her.

When Val stepped through the doors of the Saint Louis Hotel, he entered the busiest spot in the French Quarter, with the possible exception of the Market. The hotel occupied a full half block. Or, as the Creoles called it, a half square. It had three entrances. One, on Royal Street, led to the hotel's two hundred guest rooms, four of them arranged as an apartment for Val's use year-round. Saint Louis Street had two entries, one to a staircase that climbed gracefully to the ballrooms, and a larger, more imposing, columned main entrance. Val used this last; he had business to attend to.

He walked through the big room known as the Exchange, nodding to men he knew, but indicating that he couldn't stop to talk by pointing at the opposite exit door. The Exchange was one of several in the city, a place where bankers, brokers, factors, and shipping firms dealt in sugar, cotton, and cargo of all kinds.

Val's destination was the Rotunda, the heart of the hotel, where the merchandise was more varied and everything was sold by auctions.

The Rotunda was deservedly famous, one of New Orleans's major attractions for visitors and local inhabitants. Its lofty dome was frescoed with allegorical scenes; gods, nymphs, mythical animals in fabulous settings frolicked high above the milling crowds on the marble floor. A winding cast-iron staircase led to an elaborate iron gallery that circled the Rotunda and allowed spectators a full view of the activity of the crowds and the auctioneers, as well as a closer look at the magnificent pagan antics in the frescoes.

On Sundays the Rotunda was closed. It was open for sight-seeing at all other times. And from exactly noon to precisely three o'clock it was jammed with men and women there to buy or sell or simply enjoy the excitement.

The variety of goods was breathtaking. A plantation of three thousand acres might be followed by a one-thirtieth interest in a suburban lot. A cask of wine by a pair of wineglasses. Furniture, nails, paintings, cooking kettles, bales of hay or cotton, hogsheads of rum or molasses, ladies' boots or men's suspenders, laces and perfume and tar and plows and crystal chandeliers and china and silks and bundles of bamboo poles . . . anything and everything that a person might need or want was knocked down after rapid, excited bidding, conducted simultaneously in French, English, and Spanish. The people of New Orleans loved competition and gambling. It was logical that they preferred auctions to almost every other commercial transaction. Even Creole ladies came when there was a new shipment of goods from France to be sold or when the furnishings of a fine home were auctioned to satisfy the debts of a bankrupted gambler.

The action was fast and furious. Three hours did not allow time for considering before bidding. There was too much merchandise to be moved. On exceptionally busy days two, three, or even four auctions were going on at the same time in different parts of the cavernous space.

Val saw at once that it was not a very busy day. One auctioneer was haranguing a cluster of twenty or twenty-five people. "You're going to let this magnificent mirror go for only forty-three dollars? Ladies and gentlemen, the mirrors in the palace of Versailles are no truer, no more beautiful..." The two men flanking him said the same thing, with the same intonation, one in French, one in Spanish.

Val walked past the small group to a second auction platform where a man was arranging the podium. "Hello, Jean-Pierre," he said. "I had a message that you have something for me."

The auctioneer nodded. "Exactly what you like, Monsieur Saint-Brévin. Come with me." He gestured to his translators; they took up the work he was leaving.

The auctioneer led Val to an area in the rear of the Rotunda where a low wooden barrier penned slaves slated for auction. There were three other men there already, examining the slaves, discussing their faults and merits.

Jean-Pierre was one of several New Orleans auctioneers who costumed slaves to be auctioned. On this day there were four men in ill-fitting green tail coats and red waistcoats above fawn trousers, plus six women in décolleté pink taffeta evening gowns. One of the women was very old, with arthritic hands and a narrow face webbed with wrinkles. Another was a girl of no more than ten years. All wore the required tignons. Theirs were cotton, a red and black pattern that contrasted ludicrously with the shiny pink of the gowns. All the slaves were smiling, pleased with their finery.

"They come from the Mardsden place, up past Natchez," said the auctioneer. "Mardsden finally died of meanness; probably wouldn't pay to get a doctor. This batch came in wearing rags. But they're in good condition. He took care of his property better than he took care of himself."

One of the other viewers suddenly asked the biggest male slave, "What is your name?" He was, naturally, speaking French.

The slave rolled his eyes. His smile faltered.

"Hell, they're all American-speaking," said the Creole. "I'm not going to start a school on my plantation." He stalked off, pausing briefly to take a plate of oysters from the tray offered him by a waiter.

"It looks like the competition is thinning out," said Val. He beckoned to the waiter.

"Send me a bottle of white wine," he said after he selected some oysters.

The management of the hotel provided free lunch for auction patrons so that they wouldn't have to miss an opportunity to bid. Waiters circled through the crowds with trays of hot and cold food and drink.

Jean-Pierre waited until Val finished eating a dozen oysters, drinking two glasses of wine, and wiping his hands on a towel provided by a grinning uniformed boy. Then he cleared his throat and suggested that he should begin the auction. "Even with so few, it will still take some time."

Valmont smiled. "Not too long, I hope. I'm counting on you, Jean-Pierre, to see my bid and be blind to the other gentlemen. Which are the family?"

Jean-Pierre sighed. "I regret that the old hag is part of it. Of course she will bring a small price, Monsieur, and she has been a cook, so she's not without usefulness.

"The others are the two strongest men, her sons both, and the woman standing next to the girl. The girl is her child; I was told that she's carrying a baby, but I don't believe it. One of the men is her husband."

Val's eyebrows raised. "So, of ten slaves, you expect me to buy half. No wonder you sent a message."

Jean-Pierre shrugged. "It's your preference, the family, Monsieur. I don't force you." Privately the auctioneer thought that Monsieur Saint-Brévin was foolish. It was possible, as he said, that buying a complete family prevented runaways and the costs of recapturing them. But it still seemed a waste of money to the auctioneer. He was grateful that Saint-Brévin wasted his money at the Rotunda auctions. In the last year alone, Jean-Pierre's commissions had risen nicely because of Valmont's extravagance.

As a sort of Christmas gift to a good customer, and because the bidding was so sluggish, Jean-Pierre sold the five slaves to Valmont for his opening bids.

When Val paid for his purchases, he added a hundred dollars to the total. "Please do me the kindness of spending half of this on sturdy clothing for the slaves, Jean-Pierre. I particularly want good boots for them, even the old woman. The shoemaker at Benison is overloaded now. The other half is for a gift that you believe your wife will enjoy. I'm obliged to her, I'm sure, for making you such an agreeable man to do business with.

"I'll send someone for the slaves tomorrow. That will give your people time to wash them well and dress them. I tolerate no lice in my slaves."

The auction had lasted only a half hour. Val strolled off, pleased with his bargain, to the hotel's huge, noisy barroom. The free lunch was even more varied and delicious there, and he was hungry. He decided he'd taste the gumbo, compare it to the one at the Market.

He lifted his tall hat and bowed to a lady he knew, but she was too preoccupied with the bidding on a plush settee to notice him.

A lady he didn't know watched him with unladylike obviousness. He was the handsomest man in the Rotunda, probably in the hotel; and he moved with a confident ease that proclaimed he knew it and didn't care.

Mary couldn't resist the temptation. She went up to Albert Rinck's studio on the pretext of not understanding a detail in the sketch of the gown she was working on.

While Albert explained it to her, she looked at Val's portrait, even though there was nothing to see except the outline of his brown coat and a few inches of his black necktie.

"Have you listened to a word I've said, Mary?"

"Oh, yes, Albert. Thank you very much." Mary took the sketch and hurried downstairs, humming to herself. She didn't need the portrait, even if it had been finished. She could see Val's every expression, every gesture in her mind.

And tomorrow she'd see him again. Hannah had already promised that she and Albert would go to Benison as chaperones. It would cause no problems. They had all agreed weeks ago that the shop would be closed Christmas Eve as well as Christmas Day.

# 40

Val rested his arm on the imitation marble column and let his mind wander while Albert Rinck painted and talked. He thought mostly about the trip to Charleston; would the ship handle well, would the weather be favorable, the seas calm, the provisions adequate? He scarcely registered what Albert was saying.

Until the painter said how much he and his wife were looking forward to seeing the Saint-Brévin plantation. Then Val paid attention. So that little minx Mary MacAlistair really had arranged for chaperones, had she? Val was angry, then amused, then pleased. He could see the game she was playing, he thought, and he liked games. He'd have to outwit her defenses to get her into bed, seduce her, just as if she were the innocent maiden she pretended to be. What a clever little creature she was. A challenge was what he liked most in life.

Suddenly he was looking forward to being with Mary MacAlistair very much.

The day was warm, even warmer than the day before, with a bright sun in a cloudless sky. Mary and Hannah carried parasols to shade their faces, gay, ruffled circles of rose silk that cast a flattering filtered glow on their skin. The men had no way of knowing that Mary had been awake all night sewing the silk onto old umbrella frames that she had found at a ragpicker's stall in the Market. Without a parasol she would have had to wear a veil, as most women did in New Orleans. Then she would not have been able to see everything. And she wanted to miss no detail of the day with Valmont.

She and Hannah sat opposite Val and Albert in the carriage. Because of the fine weather, Val hired an open landau. The two horses pulled it at a smart pace along the River Road; to their left they could see the river and the slow, upstream traffic on it. Two small sidewheelers were racing. The coachman whipped up the horses at Val's command, and for two miles the landau was part of the race.

Then the road became too rutted and they had to drop out. Hannah fanned herself with a fluttering handkerchief. "I'm not used to so much excitement," she said.

Mary's cheeks were scarlet; the golden lights in her eyes were more apparent than ever.

They drove for miles through and alongside a swamp after they turned off the River Road. There was no need for parasols then. Tall cypresses heavily fringed with Spanish moss screened them from the sun. It could be seen only in the wide pools of black swamp water. It turned them into bright mirrors that held a shimmering globe of warmth in their cold depths.

At the side of the narrow shadowed road, a log stirred, then moved with astonishing speed to splash into the waters of a black pool.

Hannah let out a small scream. Mary craned her neck, trying to see the alligator surface. Val watched, smiling slightly.

Then soon they were on a wide drive between tall spreading live oaks. A dozen shouting black children ran to meet them, then ran alongside the carriage, waving their arms and laughing. They had arrived at Benison.

The plantation was everything Mary had imagined it would be, and more. Its tall white columns supported a deep roof over a wide, tile-floored gallery on the ground floor and a white-painted cast-iron balcony that circled the second floor. The entry was floored in marble; a jewellike Persian rug was warm color on the cool stone.

A butler took hats, canes, parasols and asked Val where he wanted coffee to be served.

"The walled garden," Valmont said, "and then we'll go to the stables before lunch. Is that agreeable to you, ladies?"

Hannah and Mary said yes in unison. A maid asked them if they'd like to refresh themselves, led them to a cloakroom outfitted with everything they needed. Hannah goggled at the scented soap, the pitchers of hot and cold water, the heavy linen towels, the bottles of eau de cologne, the carved and painted *chaise percée.* "Lordy, Mary," she whispered. "This place is like a palace."

Mary smiled. Where else would a prince live, she said to herself. She was afraid she was in a dream. And every minute that passed became more dreamlike.

They had coffee, sandwiches, pastries at a table shaded by a magnolia tree. She sat beside Val on an iron settee, so near that his arm brushed her shoulder when he lifted his cup.

They walked through an allée of crimson blossom-covered camellias to the stables. Valmont cupped her elbow in his hand to steady her on the uncertain footing of the root-crossed path.

He was always near, so near that Mary's heart lost its steady rhythm and her breath caught in her throat.

When a groom brought the great white stallion into the stable yard Val left her side to examine Snow Cloud's legs and feet. His absence was a relief and a wrenching loss. She took long draughts of air into her lungs and feasted her heart on the sight of his beautiful dark head against the dazzling whiteness of the horse's flank.

Hannah and Albert were talking to one another, perhaps talking to her, but Mary didn't hear them. She heard only the wind off the river rustling the leaves of the trees overhead like music and the answering song of a bird serenading the beauty of the day, the beauty of life and love.

How can they eat? Mary marveled. Bite and chew and swallow and talk just as if this were any other food in any other place? She moved her fork on her plate, pushing the richly scented jambalaya from place to place. Her eyes moved from Val's face to the portraits that filled the dining room's walls, searching for similarities, envying these departed Saint-Brévins because they were part of his life.

"You've got some fine paintings here," Albert said. "It makes me nervous to be trying to do your portrait."

Val laughed. "Just don't make me look as unfriendly as they do, and I'll be satisfied, Mr. Rinck. Have you ever remarked that the more piratical the subject is, the more pious he looks in his portrait? The Saint-Brévins have a long and distinguished history of pillage and plunder, starting with the First Crusade. Adventurers, one and all."

Hannah asked, "Are you an adventurer, too, Mr. Saint-Brévin?"

Val's expression was sober for an instant. Then he smiled. "Some say so, Mrs. Rinck. They deplore the wagers I've made on Snow Cloud. I'll admit I like excitement, even a little danger. So far I've been lucky."

Albert was still worrying about Val's portrait. He said again that he was afraid his work wouldn't measure up to the paintings on the walls.

Val tried again to reassure him, but Albert continued to fret.

Finally Hannah interrupted him. "Be sensible, Albert. You may not like what you do as much as what the artists did in these paintings. But, sure as I'm sitting here, they felt the same way about their work. There aren't any Gainsboroughs on this wall, are there, Mr. Saint-Brévin? Albert says Gainsborough is the best there ever was."

"Nothing even close to Gainsborough, Mrs. Rinck." Val smiled at Albert. "How did you choose him; why not Romney?"

Albert looked uncomfortable. "I don't know anything about Romney. My teacher in Philadelphia had a copy of 'The Blue Boy' by Gainsborough. It's what he used to teach us about great art."

"That's the best way to learn, by looking at the masters," Val hastened to say. "And there's nothing wrong with using a copy when you don't have the original."

"It's kind of you to say so, but..." Albert would not be reassured.

Val tried again. "I have a portfolio of copies myself, Mr. Rinck. I had them done to help me remember the art I saw in Paris. I'll show it to you after lunch, if you like."

Albert's expression changed completely. "I'd like that very much. Thank you, sir."

Val waved off his thanks. "My pleasure," he said. He signaled for the next course. Albert was boring him. The sooner this visit was over, the better. He looked at Mary. If she's laughing, I'll wring her neck, he thought. The stakes in this game of hers are too high, if boredom is one of them.

Mary had been gazing at Valmont, her heart in her eyes. She looked away quickly when he looked at her.

Good, he thought, she's ashamed to meet my eyes. She knows she's gone too far... Look at that blush. I know women who'd give a fortune to learn how she does it.

After lunch Valmont took everyone into his library. It was a corner room with French doors open wide onto the gallery for air circulation. He untied the cords of a bulging leather portfolio and spread it open on the long table in the center of the room. "You'll find my collection heavily weighted in favor of Jacques Louis David, I'm afraid. I'm a classicist at heart."

Albert held his hands toward the portfolio as if he were warming them at a fire.

Val pulled a chair to the table for Hannah.

To Mary he said, "I'd like to show you something in the drawing room. Will you come with me?"

"Of course," Mary said. She was surprised to discover that she could talk normally.

She followed Val into a big room on the river side of the house. She could see the Mississippi beyond the lawn and the levee. Trees and house cast long transparent shadows on the green velvet of the lawn, just as they had done on that summer day when she had seen him on that levee, in front of this house. And now she was with him.

Val could see the pulse beating rapidly in her throat. He plucked a sprig of mistletoe from the garland of greens across the mantel. "Here you are," he said, "a holiday decoration." He tucked it into the braid above her ear. "Happy Christmas Eve." He was so near that Mary could feel the heat of his body. Her hands tingled, wanting to touch him. She looked up at him. His eyes were laughing. "You've been very silent, Mademoiselle. Have you found the day boring?"

Mary shook her head. She couldn't speak. She was mesmerized by his closeness.

Val touched the mistletoe. "I believe in old customs, don't you?" His finger traced down across her ear, her cheek, her throat. It stopped under her chin, tilted it upward, held it poised while his lips moved slowly toward hers.

Mary's "oh!" was a whispered breath. Then she lifted herself on tiptoe to meet his kiss. Her hands felt his arms, his shoulders, buried themselves in his crisp, twining hair. When his arms tightened around her waist, she leaned into his embrace, and her lips opened in response to the parting of his.

When Val relaxed his arms, she felt weightless, transformed into an essence of rapture, deaf and blind to everything that was not him.

"Damn," he muttered. "Rinck's calling me."

He kissed her eyes swiftly, then her nose and then her lips. "I'll return from Charleston at the end of February, Mary MacAlistair. Don't forget me while I'm away." He released her and strode toward the library.

Mary stood where he left her, eyes closed, lips softened and trembling, for a long time before her legs could carry her after him.

When she entered the library, she was amazed that no one noticed that she was a different Mary from the one who had been there before. Hannah smiled. So did Val, briefly, with mouth and eyes. Then he returned his attention to Albert.

Albert was stuttering with excitement about the paintings in the portfolio. He'd had no idea that such wonders existed in the world. He had to know from Val what it was like to see the originals. How had he felt? What was the light like? How big were they? Could he see brush strokes? The questions tumbled out, barely coherent.

At last, Valmont held up his hands in mock surrender. "My dear fellow," he said, "you're asking artists' questions, and I'm no more than a passionate viewer. I really can't tell you what you want to know.

"Also, I'm afraid the sun is setting. You'd better take the ladies back to the city while there's still daylight. The River Road isn't always safe after dark."

Albert tried to protest, but Hannah hushed him.

Val walked him toward the door, a firm arm around Albert's shoulders. "When I return," Val promised, "I'll talk to my banker for you. I've been told that his father had a fine collection that he brought from Paris after the Bastille fell. I'll ask if you can see them. The mother is a recluse, and no one ever goes to the house, but he's the eldest son. If anyone can get you in, he can."

"Is there a David?"

"I'm sure not, or I would have broken a window to get in. But there's something quite famous, a Delacroix, I believe. Or perhaps it's a Chasserian. Never mind. Whatever it is, I'll do my best for you."

Val nodded at the servants in the hall. A maid gave Mary and Hannah their bonnets and parasols. The butler held Albert's hat out to him. The landau pulled up to the steps.

Val left Albert, offered his arm to Mary. She put her hand on his wrist. He escorted her to the carriage, held her hand while she stepped up into it, then kissed her hand before he let it go. "Au 'voir, Mademoiselle."

"Au 'voir," Mary replied.

The same children who had run alongside the carriage to greet them ran out onto the road to wave goodbye when they left. Mary and Hannah waved until they were out of sight. Albert sat opposite, immersed in memories of the paintings.

Hannah sighed and settled herself more comfortably in the leather-covered seat. "I wonder what it's like to be that rich. Do you suppose a person like me or you could ever get used to it? I'd never lift a finger, I promise you that. How many slaves do you suppose he has? There must be one who does nothing but roll pastry. Did you try one of those éclairs? I wish I'd had on an apron; I would have put the rest of them in the pockets."

Mary had difficulty making appropriate little noises to feign attentiveness. She couldn't listen to Hannah; she was still feeling Val's arms, tasting his mouth. Her fingers tingled with the memory of his strong, springing hair; her palms felt the shape of his skull. The end of February. She could wait. She could wait forever.

When the carriage was gone, Val went back to the library, rang for coffee and a brandy. The day seemed long to him, and Michaela's Réveillon was still to come.

He looked through the paintings before he closed the portfolio. He hadn't taken time to study them for months; sugar making had kept him too busy. Sometimes he wished that he could hire an overseer, but he always rejected the idea. There was no one he would trust that much.

The paintings were copies of all his favorite works of art, reduced in size but skillful enough to bring back clear memories of the originals. They reminded him of Venice, Rome, Florence, London, Amsterdam, and Paris. Always Paris.

He pulled out David's portrait of Madame Récamier. What an exquisite creature. It was hard to believe that she was dead, even harder to think of her as being old enough to die. She should have remained forever twenty-two, as she was in the painting.

He started to put the painting away, then brought it back out. Cécile Dulac had the beauty of Juliette Récamier, and the youth. More, she was considerably younger, at least four years, more likely five or six. She would be even more beautiful in the diaphanous gauze gowns of Madame Récamier's era. Val imagined the lovely young quadroon reclining on an Empire couch, the curves of the furniture echoing the curves of her body.

Damn! He didn't want to think of Cécile Dulac. The MacAlistair woman was supposed to keep his mind off her... He thought that very likely she could. The ardent sweetness of her kiss had stirred him to a degree that surprised and pleased him. While she was in his arms she had almost made him believe that her kiss was an act of love, not simply an act.

"Louisa," Mary whispered, "I love him so much that I could burst."

"You'd better go ahead and burst, then, and be done with it. It'll come to no good, Mary. Love never does. A woman needs something more important than love or she ends up an old woman with ten kids before she's thirty. Stick to your shop. You'll make something of yourself by yourself. What's love got you? A dead flower and some dying mistletoe."

"And what happiness, Louisa. I've never known before how happy I could be."

"Well, Mary, I sure hope you don't ever have to learn how unhappy you could be. You always overdo things. Try to use your head for once. This Valmont person can't be as perfect as you make him out to be. Look for his flaws."

Mary woke in the middle of the night, her cheeks wet with tears. In her dreams she had seen the black children running with the carriage on the drive to Benison. But they were not laughing and waving; they were moaning and holding up heavy chains that strained their small arms.

Slaves. Of course Valmont's servants were slaves, the luxuries of his life provided by slaves. Mary had never come to terms with her confusion about slavery at the Courtenays'; now her mind was more torn than ever.

Could Valmont do wrong? She wouldn't believe it. But she heard the cool, clear voice of the Mother Superior: "One man cannot be the owner of another man. It is an abomination before God."

# 41

Michaela's Réveillon was a bit of Paris transported. She had invited the wittiest men and women in Creole society, all of them frequent travelers to France. Food, drink, and conversation rivaled anything in Europe. The dark river nearby might have been the Seine and not the Mississippi.

The Baroness had a surprise to announce as the cap to the dinner. After they had all saluted the first second of Christmas Day, she ordered the glasses refilled.

"I offer a secular toast now," Michaela said with a smile. "Ladies and gentlemen, I give you the Swedish Nightingale. She is coming to New Orleans in February, and she will be staying in the Pontalba buildings!"

"Michaela! How do you know . . . what do you mean . . . who told you . . . ?" Half the guests spoke at once.

The Baroness sipped her champagne, a small, pleased, wicked smile on her lips. Bit by bit she allowed them to extract the information from her.

P. T. Barnum had brought Jenny Lind to America after the young soprano became the most famous singer in Europe. Already she had dazzled New York, Boston, Philadelphia. In February she would be in opera-mad New Orleans for the longest stay in any city on her tour, more than a month. Michaela had been corresponding with Barnum since the previous July. She was largely responsible for convincing him that the opera lovers of New Orleans would pay premium prices to hear Jenny Lind. She had also offered the inducement that persuaded the Swedish Nightingale herself.

Jenny Lind was passionate about three things: music, food, and privacy. "She'll have to provide the music," said Michaela. "I've hired Boudro himself to cook for her. He's closing his restaurant during her stay, and I'm furnishing the center apartments in this building with the best that New Orleans has to offer. She'll stay there as my guest. In absolute privacy."

"Baroness, you are a generous woman," said one of her guests.

"Nonsense, chéri. She'll make these apartments famous, as they should be. And desirable, as they are."

Val stood, his glass held high. "I propose a toast to Michaela de Pontalba—for her charm, her brilliance, and her delightful want of hypocrisy."

"Michaela," they all said.

When Val said goodnight, the Baroness made him promise to return before Jenny Lind's tour was over. She would be in New Orleans from February seventh to March tenth.

"I give you my word. Barring unforseen emergencies. By the way, does the Swedish Nightingale speak French?"

"Who cares, my dear? I don't intend to talk to her. I despise temperamental women."

Valmont laughed all the way back to the Saint Louis. Michaela's rages were famous on two continents.

He changed quickly into riding clothes and left for the plantation. His spirits were high in spite of his fatigue. "Adventurers" he had called his ancestors. On the following day he would embark on an adventure none of them would have dared. He was eager for it to begin.

On plantations all over the South, slaves in their Sunday best grouped in front of the master's house on Christmas morning, to receive gifts of tobacco, candy, clothing, and sometimes whisky or wine. At Benison it had always been the same. But this year, the Christmas gift for many of the slaves was different. They were going to be given freedom. The ship that took Val and his horses to Charleston was going to smuggle them and the runaway slaves hidden on the plantation to Canada, the final stop on the Underground Railroad.

Val had begun his efforts against slavery immediately after his return from France, and the plantation had become a stop on the Underground Railroad as soon as he was confident that all the people who might tell the authorities had been removed from Benison.

Hiding places were built in lofts, stables, the attics of the house. Alarm signals were planned and practiced. Every adult on the plantation became a conspirator for freedom.

And every slave was given the opportunity to "travel on the Railroad."

Val could have freed them all at one time. But then the plantation would die, without men and women to work in the field and the workshops. And the freed blacks would have no place to go. There were few jobs in New Orleans. And outside the city, certificates of manumission were no protection against slave trappers who kidnapped former slaves and sold them to new owners in new cities.

Most important, Val's action in freeing his slaves would draw attention to him, label him an abolitionist, an enemy of the system, a renegade. Benison would be marked, watched, unsafe for runaways needing refuge.

So Val offered freedom to those who were willing to go Underground.

He was soon disappointed in the results. The Underground Railway was a desperate enterprise with terrible limitations. Intrepid escorts came South and took slaves by twos and threes from haven to haven, braving the rigors of travel in all weathers on foot, evading patrols, risking confrontation and capture by everyone they met.

The numbers were too small, the dangers too great. Val began to draw up the specifications for his ship. And he began to buy slaves.

No one must notice that Benison's black population abruptly dropped. The cabins had to be full, the fields planted and harvested. Everything must look normal at all times.

The ship was left in New Orleans's waters long enough so that everyone who might suspect anything could go over her thoroughly. Val made a fool of himself bragging in all the gaming houses and drinking houses about his scheme to win at the Charleston races. Until people began to believe he was a fool.

Everything was ready, except that he had no horse capable of winning. He had to have a winner, at least a near winner, or people would wonder why he went to the expense of the voyage to Charleston. There were three racetracks in New Orleans to provide the excitement of competition for most horses. He needed a champion before he could weigh anchor. Then Snow Cloud came up for sale and all the pieces were in place. When the ship *Benison* arrived at the plantation on Christmas afternoon, the paneled walls in the cabins would be opened to reveal narrow hiding spaces for forty women and children. The floors of the stalls would be lifted to allow room for fifty men. Shortly after dawn the spaces would be filled, the walls and floors closed, the cargo loaded. And at first light the ship would sail, with Val's jockey and grooms lolling in their cabins, Val's horses tied in rope cradles in the stalls, standing on the straw that covered false floors.

Once through the mouth of the river and into the Gulf of Mexico, the contraband passengers could come out, to use the extra cots and hammocks that fitted so easily into the excessively roomy hold and luxurious cabins, to eat the overabundant foodstuffs, to taste the air of freedom.

They would be hidden again for the entry into Charleston harbor and the unloading of the horses and their keepers. Then the captain would take the ship to sea for a "trading run up the coast" while Val enjoyed the festivities of Charleston's social season.

Using steam and sails, there would be just time enough to land the former slaves in Canada and return to Charleston before anyone began to wonder why Valmont Saint-Brévin was abusing the hospitality of the Charlestonians by prolonging his stay to excess.

Always assuming that nothing went wrong, that the ship wasn't boarded and searched by suspicious officials at any point in the thousand-mile voyage when the ex-slaves were out of their hiding places, that she was not driven off course and delayed by winter storms, that she hit no reefs in the treacherous waters off Florida, that no sickness broke out, or panic.

If the truth were discovered, the penalty for everyone on board could be anything from a fine and confiscation to prison or even, in some localities, death.

But if the ruse was successful, there were other races and other "trading runs" for Benison horses and the ship *Benison.* Hundreds of men, women, and children could be carried to freedom every year.

At five o'clock on the morning of Christmas Day, 1850, Valmont Saint-Brévin stood on the levee with his butler and ally Nehemiah. They wore dark cloaks for protection from the alternating cold rain and bright moonlight. Dark lanterns in their hands sent dim signals to the river. Neither of them spoke. Sound travels great distances over water.

Nehemiah was first to hear the splash of oars. He touched Val's arm. They dropped ropes over the bank of earth into the river. In a few minutes a small skiff emerged from the swirling moonlit mists that hovered above the water. The lone man in it caught one of the ropes and knotted it around a cleat in the bow of the skiff. Moving quickly and silently, he handed the oars up to the waiting men, then passed up a small black case. The second rope he fastened to a cleat in the stern, then used for a line to guide him as he climbed to join Val and Nehemiah. He shook hands with them, then stood to one side while they hauled the light skiff up and over the levee and out of sight from the river.

No one spoke until they had crossed the lawn and were in the house, in the library where curtains were drawn over the windows of the lamplit room.

"A joyous Christmas, Father," Val said then.

"Indeed it is," replied Father Hilaire. The priest was the most fervent and most skilled partner Val had in his enterprise.

He took off his cloak, washed his face and hands in the bowl waiting on the table, opened his case, removed the scarf folded on the top, and put it around his neck. When the case was closed again, he was ready.

Val escorted him to each of the concealed rooms where the runaway slaves were hidden. He waited and watched outside while Father Hilaire heard confessions and administered the sacrament to the slaves who were Catholic, prayed with the ones who were not. He gave each of them God's blessing and a small medal of Saint Christopher to carry on the voyage. The quest for freedom was nonsectarian.

The sun had risen by the time Father Hilaire visited the last of the hiding places, and the Benison slaves who had chosen to go to Canada were gathered outside the plantation's chapel. One by one they entered the chapel to make their confessions and be blessed. Then the rest of Benison's people joined them, and Father Hilaire performed a special joyful mass that combined the celebration of the birth of Christ with the celebration of the rebirth of the voyagers as free men and women.

After mass everyone walked, singing, into the yard in front of the chapel. Their faces were streaked with tears of happiness and exaltation. Val left them, then, to say all the things that wanted saying before parting. He wiped his eyes and went to the house where he bathed, shaved, pomaded his hair, and dressed in his finest, nearly foppish, lace-trimmed shirt and braid-trimmed jacket and trousers. There was just time for a coffee and eau-de-vie with Father Hilaire before he stepped into a barouche brimming with cut flowers for the trip to the city and the Christmas calls and dinner with his relatives. He intended to make the elegant, spendthrift, dandy Valmont Saint-Brévin visible in every main thoroughfare of New Orleans.

Cécile Dulac saw him as his carriage rolled along Rampart Street, and she smiled inwardly. The route was not the one usually taken by people coming from upriver plantations. She was confident. He wouldn't be able to stay away from her much longer.

On Esplanade Avenue Jeanne Courtenay looked from the window

of her bedroom and burst into tears at the sight of him. Berthe took her only child in her arms and wept with her. The American, Will Graham, was coming to the house for dinner with the family. Carlos would announce the betrothal and introduce him to all the aunts and uncles and cousins.

On Royal Street Val touched his gold-headed cane to the brim of his tall beaver hat, saluting his friend and banker, Julien Sazerac. Julien bowed, forced a smile. He was dreading the family dinner at his mother's house. She would be vague and morose, as always. And, as always, his brothers would demand that Julien, the eldest, do something about the deterioration of the house that became more visible every year. Later Julien's wife would complain on behalf of their children and the wives and children of his brothers. He had to change the Christmas tradition, she would say. He had to insist that dinner be at their house. It was too depressing, going to his mother's. And too scary. His sister Celeste was growing crazier every day.

Val left flowers for the Baroness de Pontalba; the ribbon tying them was marked with the curving AP monogram of her balconies. The bouquet left on the sagging gate of Marie Laveau's cottage had a letter tucked in its center. The bouquets he gave to aunts and cousins on Condé, Toulouse, Bourbon, Orleans, Conti, Dumaine, Ursulines, and Hospital streets contained miniature vermeil mangers with an enameled infant Jesus. He directed his driver to cover the length of Canal Street and make a circle through the fashionable part of the American Sector. Then there would be just enough time left to race back to the French Quarter and the old house on the corner of Chartres and Saint Philip where his maternal grandmother ruled her family from a brocade-upholstered wheeled chair. The largest and most beautiful bouquet was for her. It held a big tin box of her favorite snuff.

Carriages with elegantly garbed gentlemen in them never made their way to the Irish Channel. But Mary MacAlistair saw Valmont surrounded by the flowers of the camellia allée at Benison. She sat at Mrs. O'Neill's heavily laden table and smiled and agreed with everyone that the roast pheasants were the most delicious holiday food she had ever eaten. While her mind turned through her memories like the pages of a scrapbook. And the leaves of a sprig of mistletoe tucked inside her dress scratched the tender flesh over her heart.

# 42

The next morning Mary left the Widow O'Neill's at first light and picked her way through the mud and refuse of Adele Street to the levee. The long airy branches of the willow trees were stirring gently in the mist rising from the river. She stood leaning on the trunk of one of the trees and watched for Valmont's ship to pass by. From time to time a new-leafed branch swayed, brushed against her cheek in a whispering caress. She was perfectly happy.

She had given her heart to Valmont. And she believed he had given his to her. Mary was ignorant of the ways of men with women. To her, Val's kiss could mean nothing less than a declaration of love.

When *Benison* went by, she waved her handkerchief, even though she didn't expect Val to see it. She strained her eyes looking for him, but the ship was in a channel on the far side of the broad Mississippi, and the figures on deck were too small to distinguish. No matter, she thought, and she walked down the levee to the Place d'Armes and the shop.

The weeks that followed were frantically busy. Epiphany, the day of the Three Kings, was the day for gift giving in New Orleans. Immediately after Christmas the shops were suddenly under siege by people searching for presents. Hannah's inability to speak French was no handicap. Customers picked up fans, scarves, gloves, ribbons and thrust them at her or at Mary with one hand, holding the other hand out with money ready to pay.

There were also so many women wanting to order ball gowns that they had to turn away three for every two they accepted, in spite of the additional seamstress they hired. Mary stayed late every night to sew.

In addition, Michaela de Pontalba picked this time to carry out her intention of getting to know Mary. She invited Mary to visit for a coffee when her day's work was done. The invitation, it was clear, did not admit any possibility of refusal.

When the Pontalba footman delivered the note to the shop, Mary glanced at it and put it aside. She was too busy to think about it. Later, when there was a brief lull, she speculated to Hannah about what the Baroness might have in mind. "If she wants me to hurry up with her pelisse, I'll have to say no," Mary declared. "It'll be ready when it was promised, and that will have to do."

Hannah begged her to change her mind. The Baroness was their landlady, she reminded Mary, and Albert's patroness. Without her help, they could be ruined. "Give her anything she wants, Mary. Please."

At the end of the day when she rang the bell for the Pontalba apartment she was tired and more than a little belligerent. The one thing she hated about shopkeeping was her helplessness in dealing with the rich and powerful. Her solace when customers were rude and demanding was to think of the growing sums in the little book that recorded her deposits in the Louisiana State Bank.

Michaela de Pontalba's welcome was not designed to put visitors at ease. "What are you standing there for?" she demanded when Mary was shown into the sitting room. "Come into the light where I can see you . . . Stand under the chandelier . . . Now come sit in this chair."

Mary's control snapped. "In the untitled world where I come from, it's customary to say 'how do you do?' or 'good evening,'" she said coldly.

Michaela threw her head back and laughed. "Very good, Mademoiselle, very good. Good evening. Won't you sit down and take coffee? I believe I'm going to like you, and I like very few people."

Thus was an unusual friendship born. The coffee after work became a daily ceremony.

The Baroness admired Mary's spirit and determination and capacity for hard work. Most of all she liked the fact that Mary never complained and never made excuses for herself. These were all traits that were parts of Michaela's own nature. To some degree she saw herself in Mary, and therefore she liked what she saw.

Mary also recognized some of the similarities between them. She respected them more in Michaela than in herself. She had no alternative to hard work, she believed, because she was poor, while the Baroness was rich and had no need to supervise the builders by climbing their own ladders or to hammer in the stakes herself for the gardens she had designed for the Place d'Armes.

She admired Michaela mostly for the older woman's knowledge of the world. She often felt appallingly ignorant because she understood none of Michaela's references to writers, artists, and government figures who were part of her circle in Paris.

When she said she felt ignorant, the Baroness was unsympathetic. "Of course you're ignorant, but you're not stupid. Ignorance can be cured;

stupidity is fatal." She gave Mary the Paris newspapers when she finished reading them, and lent her books.

She was impatient when Mary did not read them immediately. "You'd do much better to invest in your mind and let your bank account wait. Hire someone to do some of that tedious hand finishing that you've monopolized. What are you, Mary? Not yet seventeen? Young people have the delusion that there is all the time in the world stretching out ahead of them. But there is not. You must use it now for learning and for life. The way you're going, you'll discover yourself at twenty-five a boring, ignorant, half-blind, juiceless woman with horizons no wider than the walls of that shop."

She sent the coffee tray away and ordered champagne when Mary reported that she had lured Marie Deux, the embroidery expert, away from Madame Alphande. "It was easy," Mary said. "Just a question of more money. Money can do anything."

"Now you're being stupid," said Michaela. "Even money has its limitations, but you will learn that on your own. In the meantime we will drink to your success and to revenge. The Alphande woman must be hysterical."

Mary said she hoped so. She drank the champagne with a private toast to herself. It was January fourth, exactly six months since her arrival in New Orleans. She had survived misfortune and treachery, penury and drudgery. Now she was part owner of a thriving business, drinking the finest wine with a Baroness.

And in love with the most wonderful man in the world.

Mary made arrangements with Mrs. O'Neill to have her supper plate kept warm on the back of the stove. She never knew how late she might be, especially now that she was visiting the Baroness. The widow grumbled, but not very much. She was proud of Mary's success in business.

Mary didn't mention her new friend to Mrs. O'Neill. She was more aware now of the realities of class distinctions, and of the sensitivity of the people on the lower rungs. She wished she could find a way to let Paddy Devlin know that his dogged quasi-courtship was hopeless. He worried constantly about her long hours and late homecomings. He even wanted to go to the shop and escort her through the darkness, but Mary wouldn't allow it. Without knowing it, Mary was leading Paddy deeper and deeper into his illusory belief that she cared for him. She was kinder now, more concerned not to wound his feelings. Blissful in her love for

Valmont, she loved the whole world. She wanted everyone to be as happy as she was.

Even the sour-spirited, whining young woman who lived in Louisa's old room. She was Mrs. O'Neill's niece, come to live with her aunt, to help her with the house, and to find a husband.

Mary missed Louisa, even her scales. She was living all the way out in Carrollton now, at the end of the streetcar line. She had waved goodbye to Mike and watched his ship leave its dock for the long voyage to California. Then she had packed, kissed Mrs. O'Neill, Mary, Paddy, and both Reillys, and left without telling anyone except Mary where she was going. Mary had promised to visit her as soon as she could.

But she was very busy.

January sixth was Epiphany, the day for gift giving. Mary had supper with Hannah and Albert, exclaimed joyfully over the perfume they gave her, giggled when Hannah opened her gift and found the same perfume. It had not been as popular as they had hoped, and the shop had a too large stock of it.

Then she went to Michaela's bearing a brightly wrapped flacon of the same perfume. Michaela gave her a copy of the collected plays of Molière.

Lastly she went home. With a vial of perfume for Mrs. O'Neill. She was just in time for the cutting of the cake, a special treat for Twelfth Night.

There was a package on the table at the place where she always sat. A gift from Paddy. Mary thanked him with convincing enthusiasm. He had chosen a bottle of blue and red swirled glass, containing an overpowering oily perfume. Late that night Mary poured it into an empty milk bottle, washed the blue and red bottle and poured her good perfume into it. She dropped the milk bottle into the river before she went to the shop the next morning.

January eighth was a gala day for the whole city. It was the anniversary of the Battle of New Orleans, when General Andrew Jackson routed the pride of the British army with a ragtag assortment of white militia, free men of color, Choctaw Indians, and Jean Lafitte's pirates. Two thousand uniformed British died. Jackson lost seven men. And the War of 1812 was over.

Mary and Hannah decorated the shop with bunting just as all the other shopkeepers did. The Baroness hung streamers of red, white, and blue silk from the ironwork galleries of her buildings on both sides of the Place d'Armes. There was a parade through the city, ending at the Place. Then speeches. Michaela made the last speech, just as dusk was falling. She announced that she was donating the gardens that would soon fill the square. Plus an iron fence to surround it.

Plus a bronze equestrian statue of General Jackson for the center of the gardens.

And she declared that the Place d'Armes would, with the enthusiastic accord of the Municipal Council, be forever after known as Jackson Square.

With her strong voice still ringing in the air, the fireworks began, and lasted far into the night while the marching band played and people danced in the newly named square.

Mary shivered when she saw their faces lit by the colored skyrockets. She was reminded of her nightmare arrival in New Orleans. Then she remembered Valmont's rescuing her; she linked hands with Hannah and Albert and pulled them with her to join the dancers. She was spilling over with joy. In love with Val. In love with the city. In love with life.

After Epiphany, the pace of the Season had accelerated. Easter, and therefore Lent, was extremely late that year and the Season was weeks longer than usual. Nonetheless there were parties and balls every day and night of the week. Even on Sundays the Creoles gave small dances in their homes.

The shop was deluged with orders. At first Mary thought they'd ruin the reputation they had worked so hard to build. It seemed as if they'd have to refuse many more orders than they accepted.

Then she realized that more and more of the most important social events were masked balls. Women were clamoring for costumes, not elaborate ball gowns. Fine detail wasn't necessary if the costumes were sufficiently striking. Imagination was all-important. She ran to Albert with her discovery, fired him with her excitement. After an hour the floor of the studio was littered with bold sketches.

After a week, all the talk among fashionable women was about the delectable lagniappe being given by Rinck's. The window was full of masks. From the simplest shaped silk covers for the eyes to full faces held on gilded sticks, masks were the shop's new theme, and every purchase was wrapped with a mask included.

Hannah was ecstatic. At last there was something she could do. She glued false jewels, sequins, laces, bows, feathers and fringes to the plain mask shapes that Mary had found at a wholesale warehouse. Albert painted or gilded papier-mâché face forms. The Baroness claimed that the smell of glue seeped through the brick walls into her apartment, but she congratulated Mary on her cleverness.

"Let us make you one, Baroness. Something fantastic, something extraordinary. We'll do a costume, too. Albert will surpass himself if he knows it's for you."

"Thank you, Mary, but no. I have refused all invitations for masked balls. They alarm me."

"But why? They're more original, surely, more amusing."

"No. They're frightening. Something happens to people when they're masked. They become too free, uncivilized. They may do anything. Especially here in New Orleans."

Mary was puzzled. Why especially in New Orleans?

Michaela explained. She spoke more slowly than she usually did, without the dogmatic forcefulness that was her habit, as if she were still uncertain of what she was saying.

"This city, this place, these people are unlike any others. They live every day in defiance of death and under the shadow of death. Look around you, Mary. A pile of earth is the only thing that holds out the torrents of the mightiest river in the world. The city is like a bowl begging to be filled. And the river is always there. Pressing, pressing, sending silent eddies to eat the underpinnings of that thin earthen wall.

"In summer the storms come with bolts of lightning and sheets of rain. Sometimes terrifying cyclones attack without warning, forcing waters from the lake at our backs up onto the land, sending trees and animals and houses flying in its measureless winds. Always the fevers strike, capricious and swift, and hundreds die, thousands.

"The fevers frighten me most. But what do the Creoles do? They make jokes, call yellow fever 'Bronze John,' pretend that the dead are not there, that the funerals are nothing out of the ordinary.

"They laugh at death, because they know that it is always there and may take any one of them at any minute. It is at one's elbow, as the swamp is at the elbow of the city, only a few squares away, dark and silent, filled with poisonous snakes masquerading as vines and hungry crocodiles masquerading as logs.

"They laugh because if they do not they may scream in fear. They fill their hours with pleasure because each hour may be the last.

"And they turn death into a dancing partner. At masquerades there are always men costumed as death. My blood chills when I see them, but young girls step laughing into their arms.

"I had been away from New Orleans ever since I was your age; I remembered only the gaiety, the joie de vivre. But my eyes are older now and I see shadows everywhere.

"I have come near to death, and I know what happens. A desperate need for life takes possession of you when you believe that you are in death's hands. You do not care about the things you were taught to care about. There is no right and wrong, good and bad, only life and death, and you will do anything for one more hour, one more minute of life.

"Do you understand, Mary? You will do anything to live and to prove to yourself that you are alive. That is why masked balls alarm me. In this place where life is so uncertain there is a gluttony for life and for the sensations of being alive. They are controlled by the taboos of society and religion. But when you are masked, when you cannot be recognized, you cannot be held to account. Then those taboos have no power over you, and you are free to satisfy that gluttony, whatever form it may take."

Michaela pulled her shawl closer around her body. She was shaking.

Mary searched for words to say, found none. She poured hot coffee from the silver pot between them and offered the cup to the Baroness.

Michaela shook her shoulders as if she were throwing something off them. Then she took the coffee from Mary's hand. "I have too much time to think on these long winter nights," she said. "I conjure goblins. I will be glad to get back to Paris where my thoughts run to literature and politics and not to humanity."

Mary asked how the apartments for Jenny Lind were progressing. The Baroness set her cup down with a crash and began to rage about the incompetence of the upholsterers she had hired. Mary hid her smile in her coffee cup. Michaela's temper could always be depended on. The gloominess was gone.

On her way home she thought about the strange speech the Baroness had made. She decided that it was nonsense. As Michaela had said, long dark nights and too much thinking could conjure goblins. It made more sense to dance the nights away. And a masquerade ball sounded like great fun.

# 43

Sunday was traditionally the busiest shopping day of the week in the French Quarter. The custom was deplored by the Protestant Americans. They said it was sacrilege, Papist depravity. But they came down from their neighborhoods uptown to take advantage of it, and added to the busyness.

Mary and Hannah's shop was ideally located for Sunday trade. People leaving the Cathedral after mass often bought a coffee from the black vendor near the door, then strolled through Jackson Square to see what had been done on the planting of the gardens, then stopped to look at the latest mask designs in the window. The women usually gave in to temptation and entered the shop to buy while their husbands smoked a cigar outside.

Mary changed the window display every Sunday morning while the shoppers were at mass. There was an earlier mass; Mary came downtown before dawn to attend it, because it gave her the rest of the day to work in the shop. She had left Saint Patrick's and Paddy Devlin behind when she left Madame Alphande's for the partnership at Rinck's. Once in a while she sighed for the luxury of having Sunday free. Or any other day. But she and Hannah had agreed that they had to make the most of the Season. Both of them worked in the shop seven days a week.

Mary told Albert it was impossible when he asked her to leave the shop one Sunday afternoon in mid-January. "You know how busy we are, Albert. And we have to make up for yesterday. Hardly a soul came in. Everybody was watching the fire."

She knew she was being mean. Albert, too, had raced uptown to watch the fire. The Saint Charles Hotel, the pride of the American Sector, had burned to the ground in a spectacular conflagration that spread to consume four blocks of buildings around it. The balconies and roofs of the French Quarter had been crowded with spectators watching the famous cupola of the great hotel as it crumbled. The flames could be seen from every part of the city.

Albert did not react to Mary's meanness. He didn't even notice it. "But you must come with me, Mary. To think that in all these months I've been here, I didn't know. A man I met at the fire told me. Every Sunday afternoon there is voodoo dancing at Congo Square. Just imagine the colors and the patterns of the voodoo robes. I have to sketch it. And I'm sure there will be inspiration for masquerade costumes. That's why I need you along. You must tell me what adaptations to make so that white women will dress like voodoo dancers. It will be a sensation."

"Well... it's an idea... you may have something, Albert... but, the customers..."

Hannah decided for her. "You go, Mary. I don't want to. I'm scared of voodoo. You go, to take care of Albert for me. I'll be worried sick if he goes alone."

The real name of Congo Square was Circus Place, but only the mapmakers used it. It was six blocks from the shop, on the far side of Rampart Street between Saint Peter and Saint Anne. Albert and Mary walked there in less than ten minutes.

They heard the drums from two blocks away.

With one block to go, they heard clapping and shouting, a chorus of voices crying "Badoum ...badoum ..." Mary imagined that her pulse was beating in time with the drums. It was exciting.

The square was divided by a picket fence that enclosed two thirds of it. The fence had gates in all four sides with a patrolman guarding each gate. "What are the policemen there for?" Mary asked Albert. "Are they keeping them in or us out?" Spectators, most of them white, were lined up along all sides of the fence watching the dancing. In the unfenced third of the square people gathered around umbrella-shaded tables where black vendors were selling pralines, coffee, calas, gumbo, beer.

A thin, goateed white man near Mary and Albert cleared his throat and lifted his broad-brimmed gray hat. "Pardon me," he said. "I couldn't help overhearing your question, Miss. If you will allow me, I'd be happy to tell you about this interesting spectacle. I've made quite a study of it. I'm writing a book on African ceremonial customs as they survive in other countries. My name is Professor Hezekiah Abernathy."

Mary smiled at the professor, started to introduce herself and Albert. But Albert cut her off. "There's nothing for us here," he said. "The dancers are wearing cast-off white man's clothes. Let's go."

Mary put her hand on his arm. "Let's stay a little while. I'd like to watch." Her foot was tapping to the drumbeat.

The professor was droning on close to her. "The dancers and musicians are all slaves. Hence the guards. It is a city ordinance that slaves be allowed to congregate here on Sunday afternoons from three fifteen until six or until sunset, whichever comes earlier. That is governed, of course, by the time of year. The musical instruments are an interesting mutation of instruments native to regions..."

Mary edged away.

The spectacle was fascinating. Exotic. Barbaric. Mary shivered when she looked at the men beating the drums. They were concentrated, withdrawn, almost in a trance. They beat the insistent rhythm on taut-drawn skins stretched on what looked like hollowed-out tree trunks. They beat with long, knobbed, glistening white bones. The drums were the only musical instruments. The tune was made by a strange, droning half-chanting, half-singing.

All the dancers sang as they danced. They were all singing the same song, but it was as if each of them was singing only to himself. Their voices were low, private, sometimes only a hum, and the pitch was high, nasal, a minor-key vibrating. The air itself seemed to be resonating.

The dancing, too, was individual, private, as if each man and each woman was dancing for himself alone.

Men and women danced in very different styles. The men spun around in narrow circles, leapt into the air, stamped their feet, made colorful flashes all over the square. The women scarcely moved their feet at all. They kept them side by side, touching, planted firmly on the packed earth. While their bodies shook or undulated, twisting and swaying from their bright tignons to their ankles.

Mary could understand an occasional word of the song they were singing. "Dance, Calinda, badoum, badoum," was the refrain. But the verses were in a patois that was foreign to her. She was tempted to ask the professor what the song was saying. Then she decided she didn't need to know. And probably she wouldn't understand what it meant even if she knew what it said.

She felt suddenly guilty to be watching all these people who were singing and dancing in a public square in such a private way. There was something inexpressibly sad about the slaves' hand-me-down finery and about the amused white spectators' reaction to their intensely personal expression of whatever they were saying with their bodies and voices. She turned away, looking for Albert.

A few yards away she saw Jeanne Courtenay with her father and Philippe. Jeanne saw Mary at the same instant. She smiled, started forward. But Carlos Courtenay took her arm and turned her away. Philippe made a half gesture toward touching his hat brim; then he hurried after his father.

Mary felt her face grow hot at the deliberate cut. But then she smiled to herself. Carlos Courtenay couldn't hurt her any more. The loss of Jeanne's and Philippe's friendship was inconsequential. She was too happy to care about such trivial things. In only five or six weeks Val would be coming home.

There was a stirring and shifting in the crowds along the fence. Inside the square the drumming and dancing stopped. Mary squeezed back into the place she had vacated, curious to see what was causing the change.

A woman was walking to the center of the square. The slaves moved to make a path for her as if she were royalty. Her bearing and her slow steps were regally ceremonial. Her clothing was obviously not the discarded dress of a white owner. The rustle of her blue silk skirts could be heard throughout Congo Square. The dress fit her proudly voluptuous body as if the finest house in Paris had made it for her. And she was wearing a queen's ransom in diamond and ruby bracelets, earrings, rings on every finger.

"That's Marie Laveau, the Voodoo Queen," Mary overheard. She touched her simple coiled chignon. She could hardly imagine that her ordinary brown hair had ever been washed and brushed by such a fabulous woman.

"Mary, are you coming or not?" Albert was directly behind her.

"I'm coming." She turned from the fence just as the drumming and dancing began again with a new intensity.

The next morning Jeanne rushed into the shop just as Hannah was opening the door. Mary was taking the muslin covers off the counter displays. "May-ree," Jeanne cried, "I wanted to talk to you yesterday, but Papa wouldn't let me. I made Miranda come with me today. I'm supposed to be at that horrid Madame Alphande's right this minute for a fitting on my wedding gown, but she'll just have to wait.

"Oh, May-ree, you should see it. Never has there been a bride as beautiful as I shall be. The veil is lace, naturally, and so long that the Cathedral may not be big enough to contain it..."

Jeanne never changes, Mary thought. She's still a champion chatterbox.

Jeanne showed Mary her engagement ring, a sapphire that reached to her knuckle with a cluster of diamonds on each side, described the diamond and sapphire parure that was to be her wedding gift from Mr. Graham.

He was hideously old, she said cheerfully, but he'd do anything she wanted, she could tell already. He had promised her that she need never set foot above Canal Street if she didn't want to, had bought a house on Esplanade Avenue only a block from the Courtenays'. Berthe was decorating and furnishing it for him. And training the slaves. Miranda would be one of Jeanne's gifts from her family, if Jeanne decided to keep her. She thought perhaps she'd rather have a new maid, one who wouldn't scold her like a child after she was a married woman with a house of her own. And a carriage. And a cottage at the lake. And a box at the Opera.

Miranda tapped on the window. Jeanne grabbed Mary's arm and told her why she had come to see her.

"May-ree, everyone says that the artist upstairs is painting a portrait of Valmont. It's true, isn't it? Oh, May-ree, take me to see it, I beg you. I will die if I cannot see him at least once more before I am married, and he has gone away." Jeanne's beautiful, tear-filled eyes were beseeching. Mary took her to the studio.

Albert wasn't there, and Mary was glad. "It doesn't look like Valmont at all," were Jeanne's first words. Then she said, "But I'll pretend it does. I must have something." She traced the painted mouth with her finger, put her palms on the place where the heart should be.

"May-ree," she said softly, "Maman and Papa are giving the wedding bed. It has come already, and been set up in the big guest room. Do you know our marriage customs, May-ree? After the wedding, we will go home to Papa's house for a so-beautiful party, a dinner of every delicacy, a cake so tall it almost touches the chandelier, musicians from the opera house to play for dancing. But there'll be no dancing for me. Maman will take me up to that room and undress me and help me into the nightdress that she ordered from Paris. She'll steady the steps for me to climb into the fine bed from Maillard. Then she'll leave me there to wait for Mr. Graham.

"A week, May-ree, a whole week we'll spend in that room. Servants will leave trays of food and drink outside the door. But I'll see no one except my husband. And he'll see no one except me. I don't know how I will stand it. I used to dream of that week with Valmont. How he'd hold me and caress me and show me the way to love him. A week was too little, I thought then. Now it will be an eternity."

Jeanne looked at Mary. "Why did he not love me?" she said in a small wounded voice.

Mary, sure that Val loved her, felt her heart break for Jeanne. There could be no pain greater than the pain of lacking Valmont's love. She held out her arms, and Jeanne stumbled into her embrace. They wept together for Jeanne's sorrow.

Miranda found them, pulled Jeanne roughly from Mary's arms, wiped her face, marched her out of the studio and down the stairs.

Mary dried her eyes on the hem of her skirt. Her breath was still coming in shuddering sobs. She looked at the bad portrait of Val until she was calmer. Before she returned to the shop she pressed a kiss onto her fingers and touched them to the lips of the painting. "How lucky I am," she whispered to Val, "and how much I love you."

Jeanne was married the following Monday. Mary joined the crowd that gathered in Jackson Square to watch the guests and wedding party arrive. Jeanne was indeed the most beautiful bride imaginable. And Mary was able to see, before the Cathedral doors closed, that her lace veil stretched almost the entire length of the aisle.

She was surprised when she glimpsed Cécile Dulac in the crowd. She would have expected the angry quadroon to avoid anything that involved Carlos Courtenay. Or, worse, perhaps to make a scene. Instead Cécile was dressed in a drab, shapeless frock and dull, colorless tignon that hid her beauty. And she was smiling.

Peculiar. But then Cécile had been behaving oddly ever since Christmas. She had returned the reports Hannah sent her about the shop's profits with a short note saying that she was too busy to bother with the business anymore. She had also stopped ordering gowns.

Mary shrugged, then laughed at herself for being so Gallic. She went back to work with her head full of visions of weddings, particularly hers. She marveled that Val had singled her out for attention when there were so many women in the world more beautiful than she, wittier, more seductive, more clever, wealthier, with families that were known and respected. She couldn't imagine why Val would choose her, but she was ecstatically happy that he had.

She decided to tell him all about herself, even though she feared he would realize that she was extremely ordinary. She'd tell him about her legacy, too, the lost casket. She had never told anyone, after the Widow O'Neill's reaction. She didn't want to give people the impression that she thought she was special or that she was asking for pity.

It was easy enough to keep her past history to herself. People rarely asked, and if they did, she replied that she was alone in the world and making a life for herself. That, and the way she said it, always satisfied questions.

But Val had a right to know all there was to know. Also, it pleased her to think that he'd be happy that she was half New Orleans, and that half a descendant from one of the casket girls. The story of her legacy would be a gift from her to him.

She would give him other things, too. She had almost all her profits from the shop in the bank. Before the season was over, she'd have a lot more. She'd be able to afford a special gift, something as fine as he deserved. Or better yet, she'd have Albert act as her guardian and give Val the money as her dowry.

She never doubted that they would be married. Val had kissed her. For Mary that was a solemn pledge.

She made a little calendar, crossed off each day when it was over, counted the days remaining before the end of February when he would come back to her. And she held her happiness close to her like a precious treasure.

The Baroness accused her of inattentiveness one evening over coffee.

Mary started, then admitted her guilt. "I'm sorry. I was wondering when spring would be here. This is my first year in New Orleans, and I don't know what to expect. It always feels warm to me. There's no winter. Does that mean there won't be any spring?"

"Foolish girl. Of course there's a spring. What difference does it make? It will come when it's time for it to come."

Mary confided that she was in love, and she'd always associated love with spring.

Michaela's laughter was the last thing Mary expected. She grew offended when it was so prolonged. Finally Michaela stopped.

"Forgive me," she said. "I forgot how young you are. Listen to me, Mary MacAlistair. You're an intelligent young woman. You have character. You can make something of your life. Love will only slow you down. I suppose you have to go through it once, as a vaccination. But try not to do anything too foolish. I tried love several times, and I found it vastly overrated.

"I can tell you where the real excitement lies. In power. Power is the most exciting thing in the world. Obtaining it. Exercising it. Knowing that you have it. Forcing people to do your bidding. Punishing enemies. Seeing fear in people's eyes. It is thrilling in a way that no mere man can ever equal."

Mary had never heard the Baroness speak with genuine passion until now. Even when she was at her stormiest, Michaela was always in control of herself. She measured out her rage for effect. But now she had lost her icy center. Her eyes were gleaming, her voice hoarse with burning emotion. It was almost frightening. It was indelibly impressive.

# 44

February brought rain, and the rain brought spring. Seemingly overnight the air was filled with the pervasive perfume of jasmine and orange blossoms, and roses spilled over the walls that protected courtyards from the eyes of passers-by.

Mary's patience evaporated like the drops of the brief soft showers. She missed Val, wanted him to come home, hated his horses and everyone in Charleston because he was with them and not with her. She slept badly, woke half-dreaming in the night when her hands stroked her breasts and her body and the pulsating moistness between her legs.

The Season's celebrations became almost continuous, a profligacy of gaiety. On her way to work Mary often shared the banquette with costumed kings and queens of France or Roman senators going home after dancing through the night. Bits of confetti floated in the rain-filled gutters, dots of color that stuck to soggy discarded dance cards and theater programs in the pools that formed at street corners. Mud weighted skirt hems and boots, soiled errant white curls that had dropped from fancy-dress wigs, and ruined masks that had been thrown away after a night of revelry.

The Baroness de Pontalba ignored rain, mud, the seductions of spring, and the festivities of the Season. She harangued and threatened and supervised and shouted at the workmen who were finishing the second row of monogrammed buildings. And at the men who were putting in the paths and flower beds of the gardens in Jackson Square. And at the crews of slaves she had hired to keep the square clean of all the frivolous trash that colored and littered the rest of the Quarter. Everything must be perfect for the arrival of Jenny Lind.

Posters on all the lampposts heralded the approaching concerts and overshadowed the smaller announcements of deaths and funerals. Reporters from the city's newspapers kept vigil on the levee near the Market lest the ship carrying her arrive before schedule. The Saint Louis Hotel filled its rooms with music lovers from the length of the Mississippi, and tickets for the first concert were auctioned in the Rotunda for prices as high as two hundred and forty dollars. Her apartment was ready, with four parlors, ten sleeping rooms, and a silver door plate engraved *Miss Jenny Lind.*

On Friday, February seventh, exactly as promised, the steamer *Falcon* approached the wharf opposite Jackson Square. Thousands of people stood on the wharf and the levee cheering and waving flags. On the deck of the ship a small woman in a dark dress and bonnet raised her hand in response. The jovial man at her side raised both his arms in a triumphant gesture of success. His name was Phineas Taylor Barnum, and he was, at forty, already the greatest showman on earth.

Mary didn't join the crowds on the wharf and levee. She had too much to do. But she and Hannah and Albert were among the throngs in Jackson Square who applauded when Jenny came out onto the balcony of her apartment with the Baroness de Pontalba. The cheering went on until Jenny appeared again. Then again. And yet again, more than thirty times.

Michaela went onto the balcony only once. She considered that sufficient. Her point was made. The Pontalba buildings would be seen by every man and woman in New Orleans before the Swedish Nightingale flew away.

Mary had gotten two tickets to Jenny Lind's sixth concert through Michaela. On the evening of the singer's arrival she took them with her after the shop closed and rode the streetcar to the end of the line in Carrollton. One of the tickets was for Louisa Ferncliff, née Katie Kelly.

Reportedly the tracks ran between pastures and farmland for the last half of the almost five-mile trip, but it was dark and Mary couldn't see them. She could feel the change, though, when the last city squares were left behind. The breeze was stronger, and the smell of flowers was replaced by the crisp, green sweetness of newly sprouted fields. There was a sensation of room, of openness that made Mary realize for the first time how confined the crowded spaces of the city really were. She had the awninged roof level of the street car all to herself after Jackson Avenue. It made her feel like an empress to be seated so high. The empty darkness to each side was a mysterious invisible kingdom. The chuffing, spark-spitting locomotive was a dragon harnessed to her service.

She was a little sad when the lights of Carrollton could be seen ahead.

Louisa was delighted to see her, overjoyed by the ticket. "I was so afraid I wouldn't get to hear Jenny Lind," she said. "Now that I don't have a job, I don't have a salary, and old Bassington turned out to be a real tightwad. He says that paying for this house and my lessons is about to bankrupt him, but I'll bet you anything his wife and his revolting children are all going to one of the concerts. I hope it's not the same one. I don't want to see any more of him than I have to."

She kept up a chorus of complaints about Mr. Bassington the whole time she was showing Mary through her house. It was a curiously arranged structure, four rooms in a row from front to back. Louisa giggled when she showed Mary how it got its name. She positioned Mary outside the open back door, walked through the bedroom, the room furnished with only a piano, the kitchen, and the parlor, leaving all doors open. Then she stepped out onto the shallow front porch and turned to face Mary. They had a direct view of one another.

"See," Louisa yelled. "This is why it's called a 'shotgun house.' You could fire a shotgun in the front door, and the pellets would go out the back door without hitting a single thing. Isn't that funny?"

All of a sudden Louisa's face crumpled. She ran inside, slamming the front door behind her and sat on the floor with her back against the wall. "Oh, God help me," she cried. "Mary, I'm going to have a baby."

Mary offered what comfort she could. Even while she talked, she knew she was doing no good. She had nothing to offer. By all the rules of the world she knew, Louisa was ruined, and no decent person would ever have anything to do with her.

But Louisa was her friend. She had committed a terrible sin, broken one of the commandments not once but many times. And yet Mary still valued her, liked her, wanted her friendship. Although she believed that she should not, and worried that perhaps liking a sinner like Louisa was a sin in itself.

Her dilemma was so obvious that in the end Louisa had to comfort her.

"Look, Mary, you go on home. You have to work tomorrow. I really do thank you for the ticket. I'll be at the theater with bells on. And if you decide not to come, I'll understand. But don't be a complete goony. Sell your ticket if you're not going to use it. You can get four times what you paid for it."

Her friend's unselfish concern for her made up Mary's mind. "I'll be there, if I have to swim," she said in a firm voice.

Louisa hugged her. She walked with Mary to the streetcar terminal. It was in front of the Carrollton Hotel, a broad-galleried summer resort surrounded by gardens that were in full spring flower. Some of the hotel's windows were lighted; inside, black men with rolled-up shirtsleeves were waxing floors, singing as they pushed flannel-wrapped stone weights across the pine boards.

The two young women listened, their arms circling one another's waist, while a warm sprinkling rain fell on their heads and shoulders. Mary was thankful for it. Louisa wouldn't be able to tell that the drops of water on her cheeks were tears when the locomotive's headlight struck them.

Louisa kissed her goodbye when the streetcar came. "I'll see you on the sixteenth," she said. She laughed and lowered her voice. "I guess I should have worried when he told me he'd bought a shotgun house to put me in. Not that a shotgun would do me much good. He's already married."

Mary was distressed by the harshness of Louisa's laughter and the bitterness in her voice. There must be something I could do to help Louisa, she thought on the way home. Maybe if I talked to a priest. Or if we could find something for her to do in the shop. She's so alone up there in Carrollton.

She made up her mind to ask Hannah.

Then the shop was so busy she forgot. With Jenny Lind living in the building, there were crowds in Jackson Square both day and night, hoping to catch a glimpse of her.

Sooner or later every woman in the crowds came into the shop to ask if Mary or Hannah knew when Jenny would be leaving or would be coming back or would be practicing her singing near the windows that were open onto the galleries.

When they locked up for the night, Hannah and Mary were exhausted and angry.

"They didn't even intend to buy anything... they kept out the regular customers... they messed up all the things on the counters... there are dirty finger marks on this scarf... half the masks are missing from the window..."

"We've got to do something about this," Mary said. She stamped her foot for emphasis.

"What?" said Hannah.

Mary had no idea.

She stamped up the stairs to Michaela de Pontalba's apartments to complain. To her surprise the Baroness was expecting her to come for coffee as usual.

They talked and then they laughed.

And the next day the shop was rearranged. The window held a framed sketch of Jenny Lind that Albert had done during the night. The counter was piled with scarves and gloves and ribbons around a card on a gilt easel. The card read, *As Worn by Jenny Lind.*

"She'll never know the difference," Michaela had said, with a flip of her hand and a rasping laugh.

When Mary confessed the deception, she was almost sure that she heard a laugh from the priest's side of the grate in the confessional. And she was not told that she must stop.

She wondered if the Jenny Lind seekers had also been a problem in the Cathedral.

But the thought was fleeting. With every day that went by, she became increasingly preoccupied with her little calendar and the question of when Val would come home.

She went more often than necessary to the warehouse near the levee that supplied the scarves and gloves for the shop. She stood at the door while the package was being readied, scanning the shapes and trims and names of the ships on the river, searching for the *Benison.*

On February sixteenth Mary met Louisa at the Saint Charles Theater for the concert, and she learned why Jenny Lind was called "the Swedish Nightingale." The small, thin, rather plain young woman stood on the tremendous stage with her hands loosely clasped at her waist. As the first notes sounded on the piano behind her, she lifted her chin. Then she opened her lips and a cascade of shining pure melody filled the great spaces of the auditorium. The audience grew still at once, enchanted into immobility.

When the curtains closed for the sixteenth time and did not open again despite the demanding applause, Louisa kissed Mary's cheek. "I can't find words to thank you," she said. Her voice was quavering.

Mary returned her friend's kiss. "I know," she said. "I felt it, too. I had almost forgotten what music can do to a person."

Louisa's smile was heartbreakingly sad. "I never knew what the human throat could do. I'm going to stop taking lessons now that I know. I don't want to hear the sounds I make ever again."

Mary took her arm. "Don't be silly, Louisa. There's only one Jenny Lind. No one can sing like her. You can still be an opera singer."

"Don't be upset. I shouldn't have said anything. I'm sorry."

"Louisa!"

"It's all right, Mary. I was being silly. I didn't mean it."

But Mary was afraid she did.

She got up early the next day and rode out to Carrollton to make sure that Louisa wasn't lonely and sad.

A man opened the door when she tapped on it. "What do you want?" he growled. "It's still pitch dark."

"Excuse me, I have the wrong house," Mary stammered. She ran away, tripped and fell, scrambled to her feet and hurried to the streetcar.

The crosshatches on Mary's calendar were carefully aligned so that the unmarked days to come stood out in their bareness. When she made the calendar the bare area was dauntingly large. It pleased her to take a neat bite out of it each evening. When there were only four bare days left, she began to worry. Then the last day was gone.

Mary sat alone in the locked shop and shook uncontrollably. There were so many things to fear, storms and sinkings and exploding boilers and hulls holed by hidden reefs.

What had happened to Valmont and his ship?

The Cathedral bells rang the hour. Usually the nearby bells were a pleasure. Now they sounded as if they were only cold metal.

# 45

The band's brass horns looked like gold in the sunlight, and the strains of "The World Turned Upside Down" were merry in the sweet-scented air. One by one the brigades of volunteer firemen marched along Chartres Street and turned into Jackson Square. Their engines gleamed from hours of polishing; the coats of the horses that pulled them shone from long grooming; red pompoms decorated the horses' braided manes and tails.

Each brigade had its own insignia painted on its own pennon. Uniformed boys carried them, their poles supported by holsters on the front of sparkling white webbed belts. As the parade passed in front of Jenny Lind's iron balcony, each flag boy dipped his pennon in salute.

"Isn't this wonderful, Mary?" Hannah Rinck exclaimed. "We would never have been able to see the parade if the firemen hadn't changed the route because of Miss Lind."

"Yes, wonderful," said Mary. She was doing her best to hide her desperate anxiety about Val. It was now the fourth of March. She stared down at the parade without seeing it, and her hands were white-knuckled, holding tightly to the iron railing of the gallery in front of the Rinck's apartment.

"Damn decent of the city to put on this welcome home for me."

She thought the voice was a hallucination. She turned her head slowly, afraid that her eyes would see nothing.

Val was standing in the open window of Michaela's sitting room, smoking a thin cheroot, laughing with Alfred de Pontalba.

Mary closed her eyes, rested her head against the cool iron upright at her left.

Safe. He was safe. And back home.

The music ran through her body like bubbling wine. She opened her eyes, and the gaudy, festive scene below was the most brilliant she had ever seen. "Wonderful," she murmured; "wonderful," she shouted.

The days that followed were touched with magic. Val had a sitting for his portrait every morning; he came to the shop after the sitting and took Mary with him to the Market for a coffee.

The first day they went for a walk after coffee. Standing so long in one place made his legs need stretching, Val said, and he didn't know why it was called a "sitting."

Mary was of the opinion that it was because the artist got to sit. Also because it had to be called something. If what Val did were to be called a "standing," then what would one call a portrait of one person standing behind another person sitting? She suggested "stitting."

Val amended it to "sitanding."

Mary said that sounded like an Asian country.

Val said she was changing the subject before he had finished with it. He named the portrait session for a child a "wiggling," for an old man a "dozing."

Mary added a "wetting" for an infant, then blushed.

She asked him about Snow Cloud and the races in Charleston.

Snow Cloud had come in a close, respectable second, Val said. But he wasn't discouraged. He'd bought the horse that defeated the big white stallion.

Mary held her breath, hoping he'd invite her out to Benison to see it, but Val changed the subject. He was going to hear Jenny Lind sing. What did Mary think of her?

She refused to say more than that he'd be surprised.

She wanted him to have the same enthralling experience she had had, and she was sure that it would be less exciting if one expected it.

Gradually, as they walked, their forced conversation became less considered and more comfortable. It was relaxing for Val to be able to put aside his role of social dandy for a while, and with Mary he could. She'd never be in the position to compare notes with anyone he knew. Or so he thought. Mary didn't mention her friendship with the Baroness.

She did tell him about the fraud she and Hannah had staged for the hoards looking for Jenny Lind. "We call them the birdwatchers," she said.

Val's laughter made her laugh, too, and she forgot to worry about the impression she was making. She was ecstatically happy from that moment on. And, as before, Val found her happiness contagious. The sun seemed brighter, the river wider, the spring blossoms sweeter.

So that he began to look forward to the coffee after his sittings.

And the brief outing began to last longer every day.

Hannah assured Mary that one person in the shop was adequate for selling souvenirs to the birdwatchers; she urged Mary to go out for as long as she liked.

Mary thanked her. She didn't feel the need to tell Hannah that the shop, the Swedish Nightingale, and all the birdwatchers could float away down the river for all she cared. A minute with Val was worth more to her than all of them.

She did, however, work late every night on the costumes she had promised customers. When she wasn't with Val, her sense of responsibility returned. She gave up her coffees with Michaela, pleading the urgency of her work on the costumes. Which was partially true. The Season was almost over. But mostly she didn't want to expose her happiness to the Baroness's cynical view of love.

Or risk having Michaela ask her the questions she would not ask herself. Why did Val never say he loved her? Why didn't he kiss her again? Why did he talk so freely and amusingly about the parties and balls he attended every night, but never invited her to go to any of them?

The nightly balls were, had Mary but known it, an important influence on Val's feelings for her. He played the dandy with single-minded concentration at them, as if dancing and flirting and drinking and gambling and horse racing were the only reasons for living.

At masquerade balls he always wore the costume of a courtier at Versailles, with powdered ringlets, beauty patches, and jeweled buckles on high-heeled court pumps. His brocaded silk coats and knee breeches were the envy of both men and women because they were unmistakably Paris-made. The wide lace ruffles on his silk shirts belonged in a museum. And the ribbon rosettes on his knees and wrought gold scabbard were the ultimate in foppishness.

He felt like a fool.

And hoped he was taken for one. The voyage to Charleston had been an unqualified success. The slaves reached Canada without mishap, and the *Benison*'s performance was flawless. Now he was readying her for another, more ambitious, journey. Without the horses this time. The entire area below decks would be filled with slaves. There was room for two hundred or more.

The excuse for the trip was an affair of the heart, as well as an augmentation of the purse. Two reasons that any Creole could understand. He had met an heiress in Charleston, the daughter of the man who had owned the winning horse. She would be spending the summer with her family in the exclusive little community of houses owned by

Charlestonians in Newport, Rhode Island, an enclave known as "the Charleston of the North."

There was enough truth to the story for it to withstand investigation. He had paid court to the daughter of the winning horse's owner. And she was a great heiress. She was also a young woman of extraordinary intelligence and learning; she had been repulsed by the mindless dandy that Val pretended to be. It was perfectly safe to pursue her to Newport. He'd be equally repellent there.

And Rhode Island was distant enough that no one would know that the *Benison* had gone to Canada first.

If all went well. If everyone believed that Valmont Saint-Brévin was capable of fortune hunting and mooning after a capricious Charleston belle. If he were convincing enough in the role of fool.

Therefore, Val danced until dawn and urged his fellows to go on to a gaming club and gamble until the sun was well up. Then he went back to his rooms at the Saint Louis and released his disgust by cursing in four languages at the fool he saw in the mirror.

After that it was an antidote to go walking with Mary MacAlistair, who need not believe that he was a fool and a wastrel. He could talk without caution, shed his feigned blasé view of the world, enjoy the sky and the river, and share her enthusiasm for life.

She was so different from the women he danced and flirted with every night that it was refreshing to be with her. Her bright coloring was the antithesis of the fashionable pallor of Creole beauties. Also her boyish shape and brisk movements. Mary could never be a languid voluptuous beauty.

She could never be a beauty of any kind. And yet, the submerged golden flecks in her eyes were fascinating. And the way her hair changed color in sun and shade was always a surprise.

The best thing about being in her company was her curiosity. The most ordinary, inconsequential things were surpassingly interesting to her. She wanted to know the name of every tree and flower, the reason that keelboats could go upriver but flatboats could not, the origin of customs like giving lagniappe and eating red beans and rice on Mondays and selling food on street corners. It amused and delighted Val to watch her eat. She relished every mouthful, and she'd try anything that was offered any time he suggested it.

He took her on the barge trip along the canal from the city to the lake to see her fascinated reaction to the boats and ships and their cargoes.

She surprised him when they reached the end of the short ride by staring at the lake as if she'd never seen water before. And he saw, for the first time, that the lake was immense, that its far shore was too distant to see, that it was to all appearances as big as the Gulf or the ocean. He had always known it was only a lake. He'd never really looked at it.

Or at much of the city that was his home. Mary looked at gates and roofs and walls and windows and chimney pots with a particularity that made Val see that each was unique.

And she loved New Orleans and Louisiana with a fervor that made him ashamed that he took its beauty and grace for granted.

For five days Val and Mary explored and enjoyed the byways and the simple pleasures of New Orleans in the spring. Then the idyll came to a jarring end for Val.

He was being his most foppish. And also dutiful. He was dancing the minuet with one of the season's wallflowers.

"Are you going to accept the *soirée dansante* at the Will Grahams?" asked his cousin Jeuditte. She laughed maliciously. "None of us are going, and I don't think you'd enjoy it. Jeanne Courtenay married an American and now she's trying to get back into Creole society. I say she should find her friends above the Neutral Ground. We don't want Americans down here."

You don't want Jeanne Courtenay down here, thought Val, because when she's around you're a flower on the wall.

Then the mention of Jeanne made him remember her introduction to society, the box at the opera, Mary MacAlistair. He had warned Carlos Courtenay that the fresh-faced, innocent-looking Mary was one of Rose Jackson's whores. But he had forgotten it himself these last days. He cursed himself for a fool, cursed Mary ten times over for her skilled deception.

"What's the matter, Valmont?" said Jeuditte. "You look as angry as a storm."

Val forced a laugh. "You trod on my foot."

"I certainly did not."

"Then I did. In any case I have to go see to my injury."

Val went directly from the Saint Louis ballroom to the bar. His anger was so evident that not even the drunkest man there made the mistake of laughing at his wig and rouged face.

The bartender poured a saucer of champagne, but Val pushed it aside. "Tafia," he said curtly.

The bartender blinked in astonishment. Why would the elegant Monsieur Saint-Brévin want to drink the cheap locally made rum? And why order it in the fashionable Saint Louis Hotel bar? Tafia was the drink in the stewpots of Gallatin Street where sailors did their drinking.

"The Saint Louis doesn't sell tafia, Monsieur. A Barbados rum, perhaps?"

"No. Brandy."

Val swallowed the fine cognac in one gulp. He wanted the fire in his throat and belly, not the taste. He was pale and cold with fury.

Mary MacAlistair was playing him for a fool, he was sure of it. And doing it damnably well. It was one thing to choose the role of fool in society, although God knew that was disagreeable enough. It was another thing altogether to be tricked into actually being a fool, by a clever deceiving harlot.

And he had believed her. That was the shame, the unforgivable insult. Her masquerade of innocence made his act of dandy look like rank amateurishness.

He couldn't even remember how she had done it. First, Albert Rinck told him that Mary had been worried about him, so he took her along for a cup of coffee. He must have been aware then of what she was. Yes, he was sure of it. There had been the day at the plantation when she played that trick with the chaperones. He hadn't forgot that.

But somewhere, sometime, he had forgotten. She had become a companion, a friend even. He had almost forgotten she was a woman, because she was so easy to talk to, and she had none of the tedious coquettish ways that all women had. He had altogether forgotten that she was a whore.

God! How she must have laughed at him.

"Brandy," said Val, pushing his empty glass forward on the bar.

He downed the cognac. Then he went back to the ballroom to continue the charade of Saint-Brévin, empty-headed bon vivant.

He hoped some hothead would find an excuse to challenge him. The clash of swords would suit his temper tonight. He was sick of mincing and simpering. He hated being a fool.

But there was no respite from the role. He acted his part until five A.M., then he tore off the detestable costume and fell across his bed. He had never been so exhausted in his entire life.

So exhausted that he couldn't sleep. His mind would not stop thinking about his humiliation by Mary. He had to find some way to pay her back.

What did she want? Women like that never spent time with a man without payment, but she had asked for nothing. On the contrary she had acted thrilled when he bought her a praline or a bowl of gumbo. She must be playing a deeper game than he could understand.

To hell with it. He understood one thing, the function of a whore. Tomorrow was his final sitting for the artist. After that he'd never go near that cursed shop again, not even to visit Michaela de Pontalba. He'd be through with Mary MacAlistair and her tricks.

But first he'd get payment for his gullibility. He'd find out if Rose Jackson's girl was as skillful on her back with her legs spread as she was walking and talking and laughing at him.

# 46

On Monday morning Mary could hardly stand still. Today had to be the day Val would say what she was hoping to hear, that he loved her as much as she loved him and that they'd be married soon.

She had told herself not to worry that he hadn't said something as soon as he got back from Charleston. We had to get to know each other again, she reasoned. He was away for more than two months.

But she did worry.

When he said nothing about taking her to any parties, she worried more.

When he made no mention of introducing her to his family, she worried most of all.

All the worrying was done in the evening, however. When she was with him the next day she was too happy to remember it.

Then Albert mentioned that the sitting on Monday would be the last. Mary's worries blossomed into panic. Suppose she never saw him again?

She didn't really believe that could happen. But just suppose. When he's with me I'm sure that he loves me. But he hasn't said anything. And he hasn't kissed me again. If we were truly engaged, surely he'd kiss me. I want him to with all my heart.

She remembered Louisa's lectures on class differences, and decided that she'd found the answer. He doesn't know that I come from the same world he comes from, that I'm half Creole. He loves me but he's afraid that I wouldn't fit in. He's afraid that I'd be unhappy.

Be honest, Mary, she scolded herself. Val's not a saint. He's afraid that he'd be unhappy, that I'd be an embarrassment to him, a nobody American who sews in a dress shop. You can't blame him for that. You wouldn't think of marrying Paddy Devlin.

She sighed with relief. She should have figured it out sooner, saved herself all that worry. All she had to do was tell him about her legacy. She was a descendant of a casket girl. One couldn't be more Creole than that.

She'd tell him Monday. She could hardly wait.

"Good morning, ladies." Val's voice had a strange ring to it. He didn't sound like himself. Mary smiled a secret smile. He sounded excited and edgy. That was all right. When she told him about the casket, he'd be able to relax.

"What's all the commotion in the square?" he asked Hannah.

"Jenny Lind is leaving today. And thank goodness, I say. All those people are waiting to mob her on her way to the steamboat. Then they'll go home and stay there, I hope. I'm sick to death of selling the same old scarves and gloves."

Val looked at Mary. "I hope you don't want to see Jenny leave," he said. "I had the hotel pack a picnic lunch. I thought we'd go to the lake again."

"I'd love it." Mary grabbed her bonnet and parasol.

"Let's take the railroad," Val said.

Mary said truthfully that she'd like that. She'd never been on a railroad.

What she didn't say was that she'd also like the railroad because it would be faster. Val had an air of determination about him that was exciting and unnerving. He was going to propose, she was almost sure. But he didn't look very loving. He must be nervous. Why not? She was.

Occupied with their private thoughts, Val and Mary spoke very little. The five-mile trip along the road called Elysian Fields took twenty-five minutes. The noise of the engine and the iron wheels made it difficult to hear, and they abandoned the effort to talk.

At the lake end of the line the tiny resort community of Milneburg was asleep. Windows were shuttered and no one was in sight at the cottages. The only activity was at the commercial dock for lake ship traffic. Val took Mary's arm and steered her in the direction away from the dock.

He stopped at a clump of willows a few minutes later, set the woven hamper on the ground, unbuckled the straps that held a rolled lap rug, and handed the roll to Mary. "Spread this out. The ground may be damp."

Mary glanced nervously at the clouds piled on the horizon above the broad waters. If it wasn't damp now, it soon would be. She hoped the most romantic moment of her life wouldn't be spoiled by a deluge.

"Val, I have something important to tell you," she said while she unrolled the rug. "Even before we unpack the lunch."

"Do you? I'm eager to hear it," he said. Now it comes, he was thinking. What will it be? A sick grandmother who needs an operation that costs a great deal of money? Or perhaps the offer of pleasures I've never known if I'll set her up in a cozy little cottage and get her out of the hard work at Rinck's shop. Whatever it is, it's sure to be interesting.

He stretched out on his side, propped on an elbow. Mary sat facing him. Her face was shadowed by the trees. Her voice emerged from the green darkness.

"On my sixteenth birthday, when I was just about to graduate from school, I received a present from my mother. My real mother, who was dead but I didn't know that until later... Oh, I'm telling this all wrong."

"Not at all. I'm fascinated. Do continue."

Mary was too flustered to hear the sarcastic edge to his voice. "The main thing is about the present," she said. "It was a box, a very old dirty box." She was talking too fast, racing the clouds. "I found out later what it was. It was a casquette, Val, from those early days when the King of France gave dowries to girls who came to New Orleans. And my real mother had left it to me. Don't you see what that means? New Orleans is really where I belong. I'm half Creole by blood. Is it any wonder I love the place so much?"

"Not at all. It makes perfect sense."

"I knew you'd understand."

Val lifted his arm, pulled Mary down to lie beside him. Before she could exclaim he covered her mouth with his.

Mary clasped her arms across his back and returned his kiss with all the stored-up passionate longing of the months without him. He lifted his head, but she moved her hands to pull it down again, to cradle it in her palms, to hold his lips on hers. She wanted to kiss him for the rest of her life, to hold him forever.

She heard the raindrops strike the canopy of leaves, but she didn't care. She kissed each corner of his mouth, his chin, his nose, his mouth again.

A shock of warmth, a tingling, lightning-bolt sensation, ran through her body and made her cry out in ecstatic surprise. She felt her back arch, then she realized that her bodice was unfastened, that Val's hands were on her breasts, stroking and squeezing and making her feel weak and wanting his hands to touch her everywhere and never to stop... stop... She must make him stop. It was too soon. This was wrong until they were married.

Mary pressed her hands to his chest, turned her face away from his kisses. "No, Val, no. Stop. Please, please stop." She fought his hands with hers, tried to pull the edges of her bodice together, crying "no" and "stop" and "please" again and again.

Val sat up abruptly. His face was furious. "What do you mean 'stop'? What kind of tease is this?"

Mary held her dress together. Rain was pouring on her head and shoulders and on the skin exposed at her throat. "I love you," she said, "you know that I do. But this is wrong until after we're married. You know that, too, Val."

He sat back on his heels. Married. So that was her game. The rain pelted his shoulders; water seeped inside his collar. He felt like slapping her, hitting her. Did she really think he was that big a fool? Marriage!

You've overplayed your hand, Mademoiselle, he thought. You've tricked me too often; you believe this trick is your triumph. You think you've won. But I am going to trump your trick this time.

"You're right, of course," he said. His voice was tender. "I lost my head because I want you so much. I can't bear waiting, Mary. We'll be married tomorrow. Mardi Gras. The whole city will celebrate our wedding." Val put his arms around her and held her close tucking her wet head inside the shelter of his jacket. She couldn't see the cruel, vengeful smile on his face.

They left the sodden rug and hamper behind and ran for the train, but it was gone. Val found the manager of the freight depot and paid him for the use of his horse and buggy. He couldn't wait for the next train. He had to get rid of Mary before he lost his temper and hit her, maybe killed her.

She looked like a drowned rat.

She felt like the most beautiful, desirable, ecstatic woman on earth.

"You need dry clothes," Val said, when they careened into the city. "Where do you live?" He whipped the horse again.

"I'll go back to the shop. I have things there." She didn't have regular clothes; she'd borrow something from Hannah. And then begin at once to work on her costume. Everyone was in fancy dress for Mardi Gras, Val had said. He had told her what to do. Meet him at the Saint Louis at six. By then he'd have made all the arrangements. Be costumed and masked. There was a Mardi Gras ball for their wedding reception.

# 47

Shrove Tuesday, the final day of worldly indulgences before the forty days of fasting and self-denial during Lent.

The Creoles called it Fat Tuesday.

Mardi Gras.

The entire city was on holiday. No business was done in busy New Orleans on Mardi Gras. No seriousness was permitted, no sadness allowed. Even the skies were forbidden to frown; it was one of the city's legends that it has never rained on Mardi Gras.

Mary MacAlistair woke smiling. Already, as the sun was rising, there were sounds of celebration from the street outside. Firecrackers snapped and banged; boys yippeed and shouted. It seemed appropriate to her. Everyone should be celebrating. It was her wedding day.

Her wedding gown hung on the back of the door. "Costume," Val had ordered. "Costume" she had called it when she showed it to Mrs. O'Neill. She'd tell everyone at the boarding house about her marriage tomorrow, after the wedding, when she came to get her things. She didn't want to ruin Mardi Gras for Paddy Devlin. And she didn't want the memory of his sadness or anger to ruin her wedding.

Hannah and Albert knew. She had run into the shop incoherent with happiness when Val left her at the door the day before. It was Hannah who had helped her put together her "costume." And Albert was going to give her away. They'd be waiting at their house this evening for Mary and Val."Surely we'll be married in the Cathedral," Mary told them, "so we'll call for you on our way."

Mary stepped out of bed and lifted her wedding clothes down from their pegs. They were just as beautiful as she remembered. She spread them out on the counterpane. The white silk stockings, the blue ruffled garters, the three lace-trimmed crinolines. All were the finest the shop had. The gown was white silk, a hybrid made from Hannah's best high-necked, long-sleeved shirtwaist and a voluminous skirt that Mary had sewed from fabric in the workroom. Hannah lent her a tiny gold bar pin with a cameo in the center to wear at her throat.

"Something old," Mary said, arranging the sleeves of the gown. "Something new." She smoothed the shining folds of the skirt. "Something borrowed." The cameo was already pinned to the collar. "And something blue." She giggled when she stretched the garters.

She unfolded the tissue-wrapped parcel on the washstand and touched its contents with loving fingers. A mantilla of cobweb-fine white lace for her veil and fan of stronger white lace attached to carved ivory sticks. For Mary the fan was a stand-in for the "something old" she wished she could carry. If her box had not been stolen, she would have held the lace fan that had belonged to the grandmother or great-grandmother she never knew.

Her carnival mask lay under the fan. It, too, was made of lace. Hannah had wielded reckless scissors, cutting into a lace shawl for the medallions she glued onto an eye-mask of white satin.

Mary would be costumed as a Spanish lady. She would also be dressed as a bride.

She wanted to put on her gown at once, be married immediately. Six o'clock was an eternity away. But Val had said six, and she intended to be an obedient wife as well as a loving one. She'd have to wait.

She put on her brown dress and went to the dining room for breakfast.

When she entered the door the younger Reilly threw a fistful of flour at her. Mary screeched, flapped her hands at the choking cloud of white dust.

"And didn't I tell you not to throw flour inside the house?" Mrs. O'Neill shouted. But she was laughing, too. There was flour in her hair, on the floor, on Paddy Devlin's face, in the elder Reilly's ears and eyebrows.

The widow helped Mary brush the white streaks from her skirt. "If I had one tenth of the flour wasted on Mardi Gras, I could do my baking for the year," she grumbled. "It's a terrible custom and no fun in it at all to my way of thinking."

Mary agreed with her. But then, after breakfast, she went out with Paddy and the Reillys, and she had to change her mind. The streets were full of people, all the streets from the meanest to the most fashionable, and all sorts of people from the poorest to the wealthiest. Men, women, children, white and black, some costumed, some masked, all in a carnival mood, all marked somewhere with flour, most of them carrying little bags of flour and tossing pinches or handfuls. Running, laughing, squealing, shouting, everyone she saw was like a child at play, with all the spirit and energy and un-self-consciousness of childhood.

Soon Mary was tossing flour, too, at figures dressed as animals, as devils, as angels, as witches, Indians, trappers, clowns, kings, generals, heroes, monsters, pirates. Her brown dress was mostly white, and she could see white on the ends of her eyelashes. She got separated from the others in the crowds, but it made no difference. On Mardi Gras, everyone in New Orleans was the friend of everyone else. A man dressed in women's clothes bought calas from a street vendor for everyone nearby. A masked woman in doublet and hose kissed everyone. A man on stilts threw flour from above and the roses on a wall became snow-covered. There was music from open doors and windows, music from costumed fiddlers on one street corner, music from a bugle played by an earringed pirate on another. There was merriment everywhere.

Impromptu parades of revelers marched to their own singing for a few blocks then dispersed. People blew horns, rang bells, played penny whistles, drums, and combs wrapped with tissue paper.

It was noise and color and giddiness and joy. Mardi Gras.

Mary made her way back to the boarding house shortly after two. She was exhilarated and disheveled. There was going to be a real parade, people had said. With a float perhaps. One year there was a huge wooden rooster with a bobbing head. The marchers always threw sweets to the crowds. It was exciting.

But Mary didn't mind missing it. She was going to bathe, wash and dry her hair, make herself ready to be married.

Mary used the cotton counterpane from her bed as a wrap over her head and shoulders and gown to protect her clothes from flour. She wanted to be fresh and clean and unspotted for Val. Her resoled silver slippers were white from walking through flour on the streets, but that was all right.

Inside the entrance to the hotel she pulled the counterpane off and handed it to an astonished servant in hotel uniform. He was a guest in costume.

"Monsieur Saint-Brévin is expecting me," she said to one of the men behind the high mahogany counter. "Will you send word, please, that I am here."

Valmont had, as promised, made all the arrangements for the evening. The hotel clerk summoned a bellman. "This man will take you to Monsieur Saint-Brévin, Mademoiselle."

Mary followed the bellman without thinking twice.

"Cool customer that one," said the clerk. "Imagine a tart dressing all in white like a virgin. No tits, either. I wouldn't pay for her."

"That Saint-Brévin is a strange one, anyway," said the second clerk, "with his fancy clothes and nancy ways. If I hadn't seen him fence I'd wonder if he was a man or not."

Val opened the door when the bellman tapped on it. He smiled at Mary in her white gown and veil. "Come in, my dear, and meet my friends." He bowed with a flourish, then took Mary's hand and ushered her into a sitting room.

There were three men in the room. One was a Pierrot, the second Napoleon Bonaparte, the third a priest. An altar was set up in a corner of the room, a table with a lace cloth and two silver candlesticks on it. Two cushions were on the floor near it.

"Val," Mary said, "I don't understand."

"Hush, my dove, you haven't been introduced. Gentlemen, meet my fiancée, Mademoiselle MacAlistair."

The men bowed. Mary smiled, curtseyed. "Val," she said, pulling on his sleeve, "I thought . . . the Cathedral . . . Hannah and Albert are expecting . . ."

Val put a finger across her lips. "You're mistaken, my bride. You don't understand how we Creoles manage these things. A wedding on Mardi Gras is different. Less formal. Because there can be no weddings during Lent, Mardi Gras is always very busy . . . Isn't that correct, Father?"

The priest nodded, mumbled something Mary couldn't understand.

She couldn't understand anything that was happening. Val was like a stranger, dressed in a satin coat and knee breeches of daffodil yellow with revers and cuffs made of blue velvet embroidered with gold thread and topaz beads. His gestures and his voice were strange, too, over-decorated like his clothing. And he treated her as if they were playing a game, not as if they were about to become man and wife.

There must be something about those two friends of his, she decided, something he'll explain later. He is Val, and I love him, and I'll trust him.

She allowed him to take off her mask, lead her to the corner; she knelt with him at his command; she repeated the words the priest told her to repeat; she held out her hand for him to slip a wide gold band on her finger.

And they were married, he said. New Orleans Mardi Gras style.

Mary held back her tears. There had been no communion, no

nuptial mass, no altar boys, no incense, no sermon, no blessing. It was not the wedding of her dreams.

Val held her face in his hands and kissed her, and the hurried little ceremony became the most beautiful sacrament to her. She was the wife of the man she loved.

They rose to their feet in unison, hands linked. Mary smiled, began to speak to the priest.

But before the first word left her mouth, Val dropped her hand then swept her up into his arms. "We leave you now, my friends," he said, and he carried Mary through a door near the altar, then kicked it shut behind him.

They were in a huge bedroom, Mary saw. Its two tall windows were open. Outside the sky was red, with violet clouds across it in thick uneven bars. The sunset light stained the air in the room a dark rose and made the blue hangings look purple on the tremendous canopied bed.

Val set her on her feet. He took the mantilla from her head and dropped it on the floor. Then he deftly unbuttoned her bodice and began to fondle her breasts.

Mary wanted to ask him to wait, to give her time to accustom herself to this place, to what had happened, to him.

But she couldn't speak. His hands on her body made her heart pound and her knees turn to water. She could only gasp his name.

"Isn't that what you said, my bride? That I mustn't make love to you until we were married? Isn't this what you want?" His mouth was against her throat, her neck, her ear. His hands were sliding the gown from her shoulders.

"Damn. These sleeves are too tight. Take your clothes off, Mary, and loosen your hair." Val's hands left her, and she felt cold. She did as he had told her, her movements mechanical. She looked at his face, at his eyes and his mouth, searching for tenderness.

But he didn't meet her gaze. He was stripping off the complex layers of his costume. Mary watched his quick, efficient motions, so unlike a woman's, and she thrilled to the maleness of him. When he pulled the shirt over his head she saw his flat belly and the sculpted muscles of his broad chest and the mat of black curling hair on it, and she wanted to feel the crispness of the hair against her palms and her cheeks, stroke the smooth skin on his stomach. She ran to him then, her hair her only clothing, and she felt no shame, no shyness. Only a consuming desire to be warmed by his arms and set on fire by his touch.

Val laughed at her eagerness, and his laughter was ragged with reflected passion. "Wait for me," he said. He lifted her onto the bed, and his tongue explored her mouth while he removed his breeches and his hose.

Then his weight was on her body, pressing it down into the bed, warming her skin and her heart, and Mary closed her arms around his neck, holding on to him for safety while she drowned in waves of love for him that compressed her heart with joy.

She felt his hands on her, and each touch sent tingling warmth flooding through every inch of her body. Her hands felt his hair, his skin, the neat geometry of his spine, the ridges of elastic muscle that criss-crossed his back. She discovered his strength with her hands, worshiping it because it was his. And her strong young body strained to be closer to him. She wanted to be inside his skin with him, to be part of him, to merge her heart with his and her blood and her breath, her life and her love.

"Je suis la tienne," she cried out.

And then she cried out again because a pushing and a pain were tearing her apart, and she was in agony.

Until she understood that Val was part of her, that the fullness inside the pain was Val, that all the emptiness and unhappiness she had ever known was over at last now that she and Val were one being.

She heard sobs and knew that she was weeping. From pain, from happiness, from the ecstasy of giving the love that she had been storing all her life, longing to have someone want it.

Then Val rose to his knees, pulling her up, pressing her close against his chest. "Hold me," he said; Mary's arms held herself to him, him to her. His hands slid down her back; his fingers spread to cup her buttocks; they dug into her flesh, pulled her closer, closer, while he thrust into her, deeper, deeper until she screamed from the pain and the possession and the terrifying ecstasy of becoming his, feeling him become hers when his cry of elation mingled with her screams.

She continued to hold him close until Val took her arms and pulled them away. He lowered her head and shoulders to the bed and then he left her. Mary was limp, boneless, weak with love spent and love welling in her heart. She wanted to speak, to tell him what she felt, but she knew no words grand enough to express her feelings. She loved him with her eyes instead.

Val walked past the bed, out of sight. Mary heard splashing water and imagined him washing. She wanted to go to him, to take the cloth from him, to wash his beautiful, strong, beloved body. But she was hurting too much to move. Later, she promised herself. We have the rest of our lives. Perhaps she'd learn to shave him, too, and every morning she'd bend over his wonderful face, give him a beard of lather, then slowly clear it away, stroke by stroke, with soapy kisses after each swipe of the blade. Her tongue ran across her lips, imagining the taste.

Then Val was standing beside her. Mary held up her arms to him. He moved away.

She saw that he was already dressed, not in his satin court costume but in a domino, a hooded cape with an attached mask that covered the top half of his face. Val's domino was black; beneath it he was wearing a white shirt and black trousers. He looked mysterious, almost threatening in the near-dark of the room. Mary smiled. "You look dangerous, Val. Like a highwayman or a pirate. One with a good tailor of course."

He didn't laugh at her little joke. Instead he fastened a plain, deadly-looking swordbelt and sword around his waist.

Then he walked slowly to the side of the bed. And now he laughed. "My compliments, Mademoiselle. You're even more accomplished than I expected. I intended to pay you two dollars, the going price for a good clean whore. But I've decided you're worth more." A gleaming gold coin fell on Mary's bare breasts. The metal was cold.

She struggled, sat up. "I don't think that's funny, Val. That's a nasty joke."

He laughed again. "And the joke's on you, instead of me. A turn of the tables. How do you like masquerades now, Mademoiselle? The priest was exceptionally good, don't you agree?"

Mary shook her head, denying his words. It couldn't be true. He couldn't do such a thing. She tried to see his face, to find reassurance. But the domino hid everything except his mouth and chin. His mouth looked unfamiliar, thin-lipped and cruel.

It smiled, then laughed. Then he went away. She could hear his voice from the sitting room. "I hope I haven't kept you gentlemen waiting too long. I'm grateful for your help in this amusing little charade. I trust you'll allow me to stand you to dinner before the ball."

"Dinner plus the drinks all night, Val. You said we'd only have to wait five minutes, and it's been nearer fifteen."

Val's laughter was as carefree as a child's. "She was more entertaining than I expected. I'd recommend her to all of you, but now I don't want to wait. I'm deuced hungry."

Mary was holding her hands over her ears.

But she heard him anyhow.

# 48

The streets were more crowded, more boisterous than before. Masked faces were doubly masked by shadows. Night had fallen. The widely spaced street lights illuminated costumes when cavorting figures passed beneath them. Open coffee house doors cast a glow on the revelers closest to them. Between them the darkness was a sensed but not seen mass of moving disguised humanity.

Mary stumbled along Royal Street, caught in the tide of motion. Her arms cradled her aching body, trying to protect it from further harm. She collided with merrymakers at every step, winced from the painful jostling, forced herself onward. Her head and face were covered by the white lace mantilla, and she kept away from the light as much as she could. She was trying to hide her shame.

There were dozens of dominos. Mary cringed each time she saw one; her tiny whimper was unheard in the din of celebration all around her. Horns and whistles blew near her ears, a jester rattled his bells in her face, pirates and transvestites grabbed her and kissed her through her veil. She was numb to all of it.

She reached the gardens behind the Cathedral and rested against the iron fence, holding on to its palings to keep from being carried onward by the buffetings of the roistering, capering crowds.

A trio of Renaissance pages passed by, carrying flickering torches. They lit Mary's hunched white shape and the gardens near her with a brief uneven glare. Mary turned her face away from them. On the other side of the fence she saw two masked figures copulating amid the discarded silks of their costumes.

She bent her head and ran, oblivious to pain and obstacles, until she was at the door of the Cathedral.

Inside, there was quiet. The riotous gaiety in the streets was only a distant murmur.

There was light. Candles burned clear and serene.

There was space. Mary was alone.

She fell to her knees before the altar. Then fell forward, arms extended, abasing herself. Her lips moved against the stone floor, uttering broken prayers, for forgiveness and for comfort to her ravaged spirit.

At the end of three hours she was shuddering uncontrollably. Her body was chilled to the marrow. Her soul was heavy with despair, its cries unanswered.

The candles on the altar guttered and died.

Mary pulled herself, shaking, to her feet. "Alone," she sobbed. The sound of her voice was lost in the great dark spaces of the old building.

A tremor of warmth began in her heart, ran through her body like unchecked fire. Hatred and rage consumed her youth and her innocent trust in the world of man and of God.

Her spine straightened and her thin shoulders drew back. She lifted her chin in defiance of fate, injustice, despair. "So be it," she shouted.

This time her words echoed around her, reverberating into every corner.

# 49

Hannah Rinck clattered her spoon in her saucer to get her husband's attention. Albert looked up from his book.

"Did you say something, Hannah?"

"I said I was worried about Mary. She wasn't like herself today. So quiet. And she didn't go to church. On Ash Wednesday. Everyone who came into the shop looked at her funny because she didn't have a smudge on her forehead."

"For goodness sake, what do you expect, Hannah? She thought she was getting married, and it fell through. She's bound to be upset. So am I, if it makes any difference to you. We missed most of Mardi Gras sitting here waiting for her. I was counting on getting some ideas for a painting. Maybe even a series."

"I think Valmont Saint-Brévin is a swine."

"He's no such thing. Mary misunderstood; she said so herself. Saint-Brévin is the best friend we have. Didn't two more men commission portraits because of him? Didn't he promise to get me in to see the Sazerac paintings?"

"He hasn't done anything about it that I can see."

"He will. Carnival wasn't the right time, that's all. Everybody was too busy."

"They're not too busy now. The city's like a tomb. There weren't more than five customers all day."

"No wonder you're gloomy."

"I'm not gloomy. I'm worried about Mary."

"For goodness sake." Albert ostentatiously returned his attention to his book. Hannah stared at him.

After a minute he looked up again. "Leave it be, Hannah," he begged. "Mary will be all right. She's not sitting around moping, is she? She's got plenty to occupy her mind. Isn't she with the Baroness right this minute?"

"Yes. Working. She needs pleasure, Albert, not work."

"Well, I don't know what you expect me to do about it, Hannah. If I knew what to do, I'd do it."

"So would I."

• • •

Hannah Rinck was wrong about Mary. Work was exactly what she needed. She could concentrate on it and interrupt, for a moment, the endless circle of guilt and anger and self-recrimination that tortured and dulled her mind.

"Four pairs of cut crystal lustres, have you got that?" said Michaela.

"I've got that. And four more pairs in the other parlor. Are you selling them as a lot?"

"Certainly not. One pair at a time. They'll bring twice as much that way... Now. One oil painting of Louisiana landscape in ornate gilt frame... One large mirror, gilt, with mosaic enamel insets... Two bell pulls, embroidered and tasseled, one with blue background and gold tassel, one with..."

Mary added each item to the list as Michaela dictated. They were making an inventory of everything in the apartment that Jenny Lind had occupied. The Baroness was selling it all by auction the following day, before the Swedish Nightingale had time to fade.

She expected to realize at least three times the money she had paid for the things. She had bought them at special discounts, because they would be used by Jenny Lind.

Like Hannah, the Baroness noticed that Mary was very subdued, but she didn't worry about it. The work would go faster without conversation.

In fact they were finished before nine o'clock. "We'll go to my house and eat dinner," said Michaela. "Before we go, I want you to select something for yourself, Mary. You've been invaluable."

Mary started to protest that she hadn't done anything at all remarkable, that she didn't deserve any reward. Then she stopped in midsentence. "I'll take the green settee in the dressing room," she said.

"You have good taste. It's a beautiful little piece."

"It was what Jenny Lind used for her siestas before the concerts. It will bring more than anything else, other than her bed."

Michaela smiled. "Good girl. I loathe sentimentalists."

Mary walked slowly from the streetcar stop toward Adele Street. She dreaded going home, feared a repetition of the dreams that had ruined the little sleep she had the night before.

Then she saw Paddy Devlin ahead, waiting on the corner, and her steps slowed even more. She didn't want to talk to anyone.

But Paddy had seen her, too. He ran to meet her. "Perhaps you won't be wanting to go home, Miss Mary. There's two policemen there waiting for you. You don't have to tell me what you've done. I'll take you someplace, to another boarding house or a hotel maybe. I've got some money."

"Don't be ridiculous. I haven't broken any laws. I don't have anything to worry about. I'll go talk to the police." Mary's voice was firm and without emotion. But her heart was pounding. Was Valmont going to persecute her? How? He could say or do anything he wanted, and she'd be powerless to stop him.

"Is your name Mary MacAlistair?"

"Yes, officer. Why do you want me?"

"Are you acquainted with a woman by the name of Katherine Kelly?"

Mary almost fainted from relief. "Yes, I am," she said.

"Then we'll ask you to come with us, Miss, to identify the remains. She's killed herself."

Mary fainted.

Louisa Ferncliff had left a note for Mary. She had signed it with her real name and placed it carefully on the pillow of her bed. Then she had arranged herself carefully on top of the freshly washed bedlinen before she committed suicide during Mardi Gras.

She tried not to make a mess. She put a bowl under her left arm before she slashed it from elbow to hand with the knife she had sharpened.

But the severed artery pumped too much blood for the bowl to contain. When Mary was led into the room, the smell of the blood-soaked mattress made her gag.

"Feel faint again, Miss?"

Mary swallowed. "I'm all right," she lied.

The policeman held his lantern over the bed. The blood was only a dark splotch. Not red at all, Mary thought wildly. I always thought blood was red. She couldn't look at Louisa.

"Is this Katherine Kelly?" insisted the policeman.

Mary forced her eyes to move, to look.

She wanted to cry out. "No, that's not my friend. My friend was full of life. That's only a replica, a wax figure, a mockery." The dead body was so empty of Louisa, it seemed to have nothing to do with her. But yes, Mary could identify her.

"Is this Katherine Kelly?"

Mary smoothed a straggling lock of hair back from the cold forehead. "She asked me to call her Louisa," she said. "Her name was Louisa Ferncliff and she practiced her scales for two hours every day."

"You mean this isn't Katherine Kelly?"

"No, officer. That's not what I mean. I identify her as Katherine Kelly."

The policeman escorted Mary into the sitting room. "There's a paper for you to sign," he said. "Then I'll give you the letter she left for you. That's where we got your name."

Mary scribbled a hasty signature.

She held Louisa's letter in her hand for a minute, afraid to open it. What if it said that she was to blame, that if she'd bothered to help Louisa, this never would have happened?

What if it does, she decided. It's done. I don't feel anything any more except anger. Not even sorrow for Louisa. So I won't feel sorrow for my guilt. She ripped the thin envelope.

Dear Mary,

When I told Mr. Bassington about the baby he gave me the deed to the house and a hundred dollars to get rid of me.

Please use the money to send me home. Mrs. O'Neill has the address. I'm giving the house to you. You were the best friend I ever had. I tried to leave things tidy for you. I'm sorry to be so much trouble. I'm not sorry to be dead.

Love from<br>Your Friend<br>Katie Kelly

P.S. The money is in the box of rat poison. Nobody would look there to steal it before you get it. It's a gold piece. Don't bite it to see if it's real. Ha. Ha. The deed is there too.

Mary folded the letter. "I need to find out how to send her home. Will you help me?"

"I'll tell you the name of an undertaker who can."

"Thank you. I'd like to go talk to him now if it isn't too late."

Mary covered Louisa's face with a handkerchief. Then she left with the policeman. She carried the box of rat poison with her.

The next morning she told the auctioneer that Jenny Lind's green settee wasn't for sale.

The day after that was Friday. She waited until Paddy and the Reillys went to work, then she told Mrs. O'Neill that she was leaving. She didn't want any difficult goodbye scenes.

"But where are you going to be, Mary?" the widow asked. "There's some will want to know."

"Tell Mr. Devlin not to look for me. Not to come to my shop or speak if he sees me on the street. Tell him . . . tell him I'm getting married."

The widow looked at Mary's rigid expression and asked no more questions.

Mary didn't care what Mrs. O'Neill was thinking. And she didn't care what Paddy Devlin was going to feel. Let him hurt. He was a man. He could pay for what Valmont Saint-Brévin had done to her, what Mr. Bassington had done to Louisa.

She wished she had the power to make the whole world pay.

Book Four

# 50

The Baroness was pleased with the results of the Jenny Lind auction. As she expected, the proceeds were far greater than the original cost of the furnishings.

Mary was pleased with the settee she didn't sell. On Friday she had it carted up to Carrollton and put in the sitting room of the shotgun house; instantly the little room took on an air of delicate elegance. Mary's imagination began to create pictures of the room with other furniture, rugs, draperies. The stirring of interest was like the beginning of a thaw. The icy, silent numbness that gripped and deadened her was eased a very little bit.

Most of the people who attended the auction were pleased. Even if they paid a premium price, they came away with something they wanted, either because of the association with the Swedish Nightingale or because of the quality and beauty of the piece. The Baroness had bought only the best for her famous guest.

Marie Laveau was pleased because the girandole she bought was the final thing she needed to complete the work she had undertaken at Valmont's request. She sent a message to him at his hotel. "My house. Four o'clock. Marie."

"You've behaved badly, Val," was her greeting to him.

"What do you mean?" he said quickly.

Even Marie's network of information couldn't have known the farce he'd staged to trick the MacAlistair woman. Or that he was feeling uncomfortable about it. She deserved it, considering the way she had tried to trick him, but he shouldn't have paid her back quite that way. A bogus priest and bogus altar were blasphemous.

"You've taken advantage," said Marie. "Of me and of our friendship. You left me a letter of instructions just as if I were your servant. Then, after more than two months, you came back and did not even bother to come see me. I had to send word to you."

Val bowed low, hands on knees, presenting his back as a target. "Beat me," he said with a laugh. "Flay me with a cat-o'-nine-tails. You're right, and I'm sorry."

Marie put her foot on his buttocks and kicked him across the room.

He fell sprawling against the hearth, cracking his head on a black andiron. The edge of his coat caught fire from the coals in the fireplace. Marie watched impassively while he beat the flames out.

Val looked at her with a rueful smile. "I believe you've made your point," he said.

Then Marie returned his smile. "Now we'll have coffee, and I'll tell you what I've done for you."

She opened the tin box on the table after she poured coffee for the two of them. "This is your contract of plaçage with Cécile Dulac," she said, spreading the document open. "It's more generous than most, less extravagant than you offered. You have still to sign and have it notarized; Cécile accepted my guarantee that you would do so."

One by one, she unfolded papers and put them in front of him. "This is the deed to the house on Saint Peter Street near Rampart. It's already in her name, as you wanted . . . This is the receipt for the slaves . . . for the carriage . . . for the horses . . . for the year's rent at the livery stables . . . This is the account of moneys spent for the furniture and decorations . . . These are letters from the dealer in Paris and copies of my letters to him . . . This is the paid bill of lading and cartage . . . This is the record of amounts drawn from your bank . . . And this is the authorization to the bank to release funds that you left with me.

"Take them. I'm tired of the whole enterprise. The box is a gift from me." Marie folded the documents in one batch and crammed them into the box.

Val caught her hand and kissed it. "A thousand thanks, my Queen. You overlooked only one thing. I asked you to select a suitable bagatelle for yourself." His eyes were laughing. "Don't I even get to see it?"

Marie loosened the collar of her red calico dress. She was wearing a necklace of diamonds and emeralds. "The Paris dealer was most obliging," she said. "You should beware of giving carte blanche, Val, even to an old friend.

"I kept the receipt myself, naturally. It confirms ownership." Marie kissed his cheek. "A million thanks," she said. "That's about what it cost in francs."

Val cleared his throat. "Under the circumstances I believe it's permissable for me to ask for another cup of coffee."

While he drank it, Marie left the kitchen, returned with a large paper-wrapped package. "Your boy from the plantation brought this just before you arrived. He said you'd sent for it."

"Good." Val drained his cup, set it to one side, took the package and tore off the wrappings. "These are drawings I brought back from Paris," he said. "Ingres, Prudhon, David. Especially David." He put the copy of David's portrait of Madame Récamier on top of the others. "This is how I want Cécile to look," he said. "She'll have to find a good dressmaker."

Marie pushed away from the table. She was frowning; her mouth drooped with worry.

"This is going too far; I don't like it. What's the meaning of these dress-up games of yours, Val?"

"It's easy enough to understand, Marie. I detest corsets and crinolines. They turn women into artificial objects. Look at these drawings. Only fifty years ago—thirty even—women were the loveliest they've ever been. Look how simple and graceful this style is. They call it Empire or Directoire now. That's the style of the furniture I had you order. That's the style that Cécile should wear in those rooms."

Marie nodded. She was still frowning. "Very well, Val. It's the role of a placée to please her patron. Cécile will play Josephine to your Napoleon if that's what you want. But you haven't really answered my question. Not the most important part of it. What about you? I hear things. What role are you playing? More and more lace on the cuffs, more wagers on nonsensical contests, more drinking and masking and squandering. You're not that kind of person. I know it. Why are you deliberately making yourself ridiculous? What deep game are you in?"

Val was pale. Deep lines were suddenly clear on his face from his nostrils to the corners of his mouth, and between his eyebrows. "Have you talked to anyone about this, Marie?"

"Am I not your friend? I've said nothing."

He held her shoulders, looked down into her eyes. "I swear to you that I would explain if I could," he said. "But I can't. There is one part of my life I cannot open to you. I can only ask you to trust me and to guard my secret. It's necessary that I be regarded as the most inane fool in Louisiana. I can't tell you why. I can only beg you not to defend my reputation and to forgive me for cheapening it."

Marie looked deep into Val's eyes and at his face. She saw the man he had never revealed to anyone, resolute and dedicated to a cause he believed in with all his strength. This is a man, she thought, and she was sorry they could never become lovers. She smoothed the lines on his brow with a strong finger. "We can trust each other," she said. It was a vow.

"May-ree, I must talk to you right away." Jeanne Courtenay, now Jeanne Graham, was the first customer in the shop Saturday morning. Mary was there alone.

If she says one word about Valmont or his portrait, I'll scream, Mary thought. I won't be able to hold it in. I'll scream and keep on screaming. Only three days had gone by since the disgraceful mock marriage.

"Good morning, Jeanne. You're looking very beautiful," she said.

"Yes, yes, I know. May-ree, you must tell me. It's true, is it not? You've bought a house in Carrollton."

Mary shrank inside herself. The house was already her refuge, after only one night in it. She didn't want to share it, not even the knowledge that it existed. Only Hannah knew.

"Where did you get such an idea, Jeanne?"

Jeanne giggled. "You're such a slyboots, May-ree. Is it a secret? I won't tell."

"How did you hear? Who told you?"

"Nobody told me. I can be a slyboots, too. I wanted that darling little Jenny Lind settee, but the auctioneer told me it wasn't for sale. Then I saw a cart trundling off with it, so I sent a servant to follow. I was going to buy it from whoever had it as soon as I learned who it was and where she lived. Imagine my surprise, May-ree, when it was you. And in Carrollton. Tell me all about your house. How big is it? How long have you had it? Who lives there with you?"

Mary tried to deflect Jeanne. "It's very small and plain, and I've only been there one day," she said rapidly. "Have you heard about the new rage in Paris, Jeanne? Blue gloves, a lovely pale blue. Let me show you the color."

Jeanne wouldn't be put off. "I want to see your house, May-ree. Won't you let me see it?"

"Naturally, when it's finished I'd love to show it to you . . . oh, here's Hannah. You remember Mrs. Rinck, don't you, Jeanne?" She threw a meaningful look at Hannah. "Do you need me for something?" she asked in English, spoken slowly so that Jeanne could understand.

Unfortunately Hannah missed the cue. "No, not really," she said cheerfully.

"Good," Jeanne said. "I need May-ree, Mrs. Rinck. You will allow her to go with me, isn't it?" She beamed at Mary. "Look you how fine is my American now that I practice with Mr. Graham, May-ree."

"Fine," Mary said.

"We go now. I have my brougham outside."

Mary yielded. She knew how tenacious Jeanne could be. Better to get the visit over with. "I'll be back within the hour, Hannah."

The carriage in front of the shop was dark green, with gold trim. A coachman in gold-trimmed dark green livery sat on the high front seat, using his whip to flick away flies from the backs of the matched pair of gray horses. When Jeanne and Mary stepped from shop to banquette, a liveried light-skinned young footman jumped from his perch on the back of the carriage to open the door for them.

Jeanne put her head inside the carriage. "You, Milly, go hide yourself someplace until I come back here for you," she ordered. A young maid scampered out and away, toward the Market.

Jeanne smiled at Mary. "I gave Miranda back to Maman. This one's name is also Miranda, but I refuse to call her that. She's much more satisfactory. I scare her half to death." With a pleased giggle, Jeanne climbed into the brougham. Mary followed.

"To Carrollton," Jeanne said. She closed the window, shutting out the coachman. "Isn't it chic, May-ree, my equipage? I'm partial to green right now. You observed, did you not, that the trimming on my dress is green, too, and my boots. It's such a pity that there's hardly ever any reason to use the carriage. Everyone always walks everywhere."

Mary settled back in the seat, ready for a typical Jeanne stream of chatter about fashion and frivolity.

She was stunned when Jeanne clutched her arm with a grip of desperate urgency. "May-ree, I am so miserable. You must help me."

Her marriage was a disaster, Jeanne said. Will Graham did not love her. "I knew I'd never love him, but I never asked did he love me. I had so many beaux who all loved me. I thought he was another one. But he doesn't, May-ree, not at all."

Mary tried to stop her, but to no avail. Jeanne insisted on telling her the most intimate details of her married life. The honeymoon week was very exciting. They were locked in, and there was nothing to do but make love. Graham delighted in her, in stroking her skin, playing with her breasts, brushing her long hair. But he wouldn't brush her other hair, her private hair, even though Jeanne told him to. He wouldn't do anything she requested, only what he wanted. And that was all right at first, because he roused easily and mounted her with ardent vigor. Six or more times a day. As long as they were locked in.

But after that week he changed. He was more interested in his business than he was in her. He didn't want her to sit on his lap or unfasten his clothes or rub herself against him in invitation. He came to her bedroom three times a week, always the same time and always on Tuesday, Thursday and Saturday. And he didn't even remove his nightshirt.

"He makes duty, not love, May-ree! He wants me to give him a son, not give him myself. Hello, Jeanne, pam, pam, pam twenty times and then it's over. No kisses, no fondling, no little playfulnesses. Nothing for me. I cannot bear it. And he'll get no son from me. Marie Laveau still dresses my hair. She sells me powders that prevent babies. But her gris-gris don't change my husband.

"May-ree, you know what I am, what I was. I longed for the day when I would learn about men and women, when I would be able to have a man's hands on me instead of my own, when I would learn about love and have it all the time.

"Now I know a little. I know that I was right, that I needed love, needed a man's body next to mine and in mine. Now that I know, it's even worse not having it. I need it, May-ree. I need to be loved."

Mary held Jeanne's hands in hers. It was the only thing she could do. Jeanne's confidences embarrassed her and made her uncomfortable. She had to exert all her willpower to prevent them from triggering memories that she wasn't strong enough to face.

She looked through the window and saw the Carrollton Hotel ahead. Thank heaven. "Jeanne, you must hush now. We're almost there. I'll have to open the window and tell the coachman where to turn. You don't want him to hear you." She slid the panel back before Jeanne could argue.

"Driver! Driver, turn right at the corner just before the hotel. Then go one block, and I'll tell you when to stop."

She squeezed Jeanne's hand. "You'll see how near the house is to the hotel," she said. Her voice was too bright, like a woman talking baby talk to an infant.

"But it's perfect, May-ree," Jeanne squealed when she saw the interior of the house. She dashed from room to room.

Mary was pleased in spite of herself. "It's going to be, I do think so. I have to get some more furniture, replace many of the things that are already here. Those curtains first. I want something more colorful. I thought perhaps..."

Jeanne cut her off. "But that doesn't matter. You have the charming Jenny Lind settee and you have a handsome big bed. With a brand new mattress, isn't it?" She sat on the bed, bouncing.

Mary had to look away. She still saw the old mattress in her mind, with the horrible dark stain that covered too much of it.

Jeanne came to her side, put her arm around Mary's waist, kissed her cheek twice, three times, four. "May-ree, you are my friend, my good, my best friend. Isn't that true? It doesn't matter to me that you left our house, I still love you. You love me, too, don't you, May-ree? You don't want me to be unhappy. Say you don't." Her voice was child-like, wheedling.

"Of course I don't, Jeanne. I'm truly sorry you're not happy."

A dozen kisses. "I knew you'd help me," Jeanne exclaimed, no longer a child. "It won't be any bother to you at all, because you're away all day. There's a man, May-ree, so handsome and so strong, and he whispers wonderful things in my ear when we dance. I promised him I'd find a place to meet, someplace where no one knows us."

"No!" Mary pushed Jeanne away. "No, you can't come to my house."

"But May-ree, where can I go? I can't be away too long. The servants will tell Mr. Graham. And he has all my money, May-ree. I can't buy a cunning little house the way you did.

"You've got to help me, you've got to. May-ree, I'll go crazy if I don't have a man to love me. Someone tall and strong and beautiful to look at, to feel with my fingers and my mouth and my body, to touch me and hold me in his arms and..."

"Stop, Jeanne, stop it. I said no, and I mean no."

"But you're my friend. You love me."

"Not that much. I won't have my house spoiled, my bed smelling like a man."

Jeanne hissed. "I see," she said. "You want everyone to be cold like you. No wonder your bed doesn't have a man's smell to it. No man would have you. You're nothing but a stick, dry and hard. You're not even shaped like a woman. Who'd want you in his arms?"

Valmont Saint-Brévin, Mary almost shouted. The man you wanted and couldn't get. But the words died in her throat. Because Jeanne was right. He hadn't wanted Mary in his arms. He'd only wanted to hurt her.

"You'd better leave now, Jeanne. I'll take the streetcar back to the city. There's nothing left for us to say to one another."

"You could change your mind."

"Never. I swear it. Go. I'm not going to let you have my house."

"You're cruel and cold, May-ree. I don't know why I thought we were friends . . . Cruel and cold." Jeanne slammed the door as she left.

Mary crawled up on the bed and covered her head with crossed arms. She didn't want to think.

But the thoughts came, with bitter honesty.

How could she judge Jeanne? She had the same hunger for love, the same desires. She had wanted Val to handle and possess her.

She called it love, told herself she loved him. But she had fallen in love with a broad-shouldered silhouette in front of a romantic columned plantation house. What kind of emotion was that? It didn't deserve to be called love.

And later, when she was with him, when she felt light-headed with happiness and love, wasn't that because already she was imagining the taste of his lips when she watched them move as he talked? Wasn't she longing for exactly the kind of love Jeanne was talking about? A matter of bare skin against bare skin, and touching and burning to be touched. Passion. Lust. Animal drives.

Not love.

He must have recognized the demon that I dressed up in the disguise of love, Mary thought. He gave me what I was asking for, a brief, frantic coupling, the mating of a male with a female in heat. Like the goats in the Irish Channel. I always pretended I didn't see them. It offended me. How proper and ladylike. When all the time I was no different inside.

She writhed under her self-flagellation.

Then she shouted "No" and sat up.

It wasn't all her fault. She hadn't given in to her body's clamoring. She'd wanted to, yes. At the lake, in the rain, she'd wanted to. But she hadn't. He had betrayed her, lied to her, pretended to marry her.

She'd been wrong to tell herself that she loved him. Dishonest with herself, even. But not knowingly.

He'd been a villain to manipulate her emotions, no matter how base they were. He'd deceived her deliberately, used her ignorance against her. And then laughed at her. He was despicable.

She deserved to be ashamed for what she had felt, but not for what she had done. That shame was his. That dishonor.

Mary fell back on the bed. Her head was cradled by Louisa's pillow.

"And what if I'm going to have a baby?" she said aloud, voicing her greatest fear. "What will I do then, Louisa? Should I leave your house to Jeanne?"

She buried her face in the pillow. "Oh, Louisa, I'm afraid I might not have as much courage as you did. I want so much to live."

Hannah Rinck was more agitated than Mary had ever seen her.

"I'm so glad you're back. I've been watching for you. You'll never guess who was here, Mary, not in a million years. Cécile Dulac. She came in not ten minutes after you left.

"Mary! Have you ever noticed how much she looks like your friend Jeanne Courtenay? Do you suppose?"

Mary nodded. "I know for a fact. Cécile's mother was Carlos Courtenay's mistress."

"Well! I guess I'd better not tell Albert. You know how he is. It makes me feel very sophisticated, though."

"Did Cécile want her money from the profits?"

"No. Just the opposite. She ordered twenty outfits. Not just gowns, but all kinds of mantles and jackets and shawls and other things to go with them. She doesn't care what they cost, either. Some man is giving her the money. A house, too. She's going to be kept. Just like her mother, I suppose.

"Do you realize what this means for us, Mary? We'll be busy even though the Season's over. We won't have to close the workroom and fire our seamstresses. Twenty complete outfits. We'll be rolling in money."

"Good. I want to buy some furniture."

"They're different from usual, though. We don't have any patterns, only these pictures."

Mary recognized Valmont's portfolio instantly. She put a fist against her throat to stop its unruly racing.

After all, it was no business of hers. Cécile knew what she was doing. Cécile knew better than to tell herself she was in love.

# 51

"Bonsoir, Michie," said Cécile.

Val stood in the doorway and stared.

Cécile was arranged on a Directoire couch. Her left elbow rested on two small velvet bolsters. Her right arm followed the curve of her semireclining body, lying along her side and on top of her slightly elevated right leg. Her feet were bare.

She wore a gown made of white silk gauze, with a low square neck and a waistband under her breasts. They were emphasized and barely covered by the cut and fabric; her dark pink nipples showed clearly through the gauze. The gown had short, slightly puffed sleeves and a separate train attached to the high waistband in the back. The train draped across her side and her knee and fell in graceful folds to the floor.

At one side of the couch a tall bronze tripod based stand held an Aladdin's lamp of burning perfumed oil.

The scene was a re-creation of David's portrait of Madame Récamier.

Except that Cécile was much more beautiful, and her hair fell in heavy gleaming black waves over her shoulders and down her back to the velvet cushion of the couch.

"Bonsoir, Cécile," Val said. "You can relax now. How long have you been posed like that?"

Cécile stretched her arms and legs slowly, sighing with pleasure. She was like a cat. "Too long," she said. "I'm glad you're here."

"So am I." He looked around the small, beautiful gold and white and red room with appreciation for Marie Laveau's careful, tasteful efforts. It might have been one of the rooms of the Empress Josephine at Malmaison. Even the roses in bowls on all the tables looked like varieties from her gardens there.

Val removed his coat and dropped it on a stool. He sank into a deep cushioned chair. "I'd like an absinthe mixed with cool water," he said.

Cécile stood. She looped her train over her arm and walked toward a door in the rear of the room.

"Why are you going? Ring for a servant. Surely Marie remembered to get servants."

"I told them to leave us alone this first night. I'd rather give you everything you want myself."

Val smiled. "As you like. Bring the bottle and a pitcher of water, then. I shall probably drink a great deal."

Cécile went to do his bidding. Her walk was like a work of art.

She returned bearing a tray holding a teardrop decanter of green liquid and a silver pitcher of water. Also a crystal goblet and a large bowl of steaming red beans and rice.

"It's Monday," she said. She smiled, placed the tray on a low table near Val's right hand, then sank to her knees with a fluid movement. Her hands moved in graceful arcs when she mixed Val's *pastisse.* She held the goblet out to him cupped in her two hands. The gesture cradled and lifted her full breasts half out of her gown.

"Very nice," said Val. He took the drink from her. "I'm going to tell you what I want from you, Cécile. Take a comfortable seat and listen. What I want may surprise you."

"I think not, Michie. I've been well taught in the ways of men." Cécile looked directly at him when she spoke. There was no coquettishness in her gaze.

Val grimaced. "I haven't been well taught in the ways of plaçage. And I don't propose to learn. What I want, Cécile, is a hidey-hole, a place where I don't have to think or plan or talk. Order and beauty and tranquillity are in short supply in my life, in anyone's life. I'm trying to buy some here in this house."

"I understand, Michie."

"For the love of God, will you stop calling me that? My name is Valmont. Val, if you prefer."

Cécile was surprised.

She was surprised again when he picked up his fork and asked where her supper was. "I've already eaten," she said.

"Do you like eating?" Val wanted to know.

"Not particularly." She wondered why he was interested.

"That's a pity. It's a great pleasure if you like it." He obviously did. The beans and rice were gone very fast.

"Would you like some more, Mich . . . Valmont?"

"Maybe later, not now. They were very good. Did Marie cook them?"

"Yes. I don't cook."

Val grinned. "Somehow I didn't think you did. What do you do, Cécile? What interests you?"

"Why do you want to know?"

"We're going to be spending considerable time together. I want to know what you're like."

"I'm a placée, Monsieur. I'm a beautiful ornament in your Directoire tranquillity. I do whatever will please you. I light your cigars, serve your drinks, pose on your couch, participate in whatever kind of sex you fancy.

"I don't spread out my thoughts or my emotions for your amusement. 'What I'm like' as far as you're concerned is an expensive, exquisite toy."

Val was taken aback by Cécile's calmness and offended by her rejection of his interest in her. From the beginning her haughtiness had intrigued and enticed him. But he hadn't expected it to continue after the contracts were signed.

He scratched his chin, thinking. What, in fact, had he expected? An oasis? A simulated home without the responsibilities of marriage? A beautiful, exciting woman who would adore him without demanding love in return? He realized that he didn't know. He hadn't thought past the decision to place Cécile in a setting that satisfied his esthetic inclinations. The liaison would reinforce his chosen role of bon vivant; the house on Saint Peter Street would give him a place where he needn't act the role.

He looked at his self-possessed mistress. "Do you speak English, Cécile?"

"Enough."

"Then I'll use an English phrase. It looks as if we'll just have to muddle through."

"Muddle" was too ungainly a word for the pattern that quickly established itself in the jewel-box little house on Saint Peter Street. It was, for the most part, Cécile's pattern. Val spent few nights there. He was often not in the city now that the Season was over. The plantation demanded his attention. There was the cane crop to watch and the summer Underground Railroad trip to plan for. He bought slaves every week or ten days and sent them out to Benison.

After the auction he always spent a few hours fencing with Pepe Lulla, the Spanish *maître d'armes,* at his academy on Exchange Alley. Fencing was fashionable; it befitted Val's role as a fop to be passionate about the art of the sword. It also kept his skills at a fine pitch, and he had no desire to be wounded in a duel for want of practice.

Later he would manage to be seen at a cockfight or gambling house or theater or the Exchange. Seen in the full peacock glory of his Paris fashions.

By midnight he generally felt that his day's work was done. Then he would go to Cécile's. And he made no secret of where he was bound. He pretended to enjoy the ribald envy of the men around him.

When he arrived at Cécile's, she had brandy ready, warmed. He took the first glass like medicine, to wash the taste of the evening out of his mouth.

Then he had coffee, followed by a brandy that he sipped slowly while the peaceful beauty of the room seeped into his tight-strung nerves. Sometimes he spoke. Often he was silent for an hour or more after he said hello and inquired about Cécile's well-being.

When he wanted quiet, Cécile sat without moving. Always perfectly groomed, beautifully dressed, excitingly scented, and near a many-branched silver candelebrum so that Val could enjoy looking at her.

She didn't mind the silence or the many days and nights without him. She had her own thoughts, her own activities, her special satisfactions. She was tormenting the Courtenays, Jeanne Courtenay Graham in particular. Jeanne knew about Cécile and Val before he had been to Cécile's house the second time. Marie Laveau told her. Every time Marie came to arrange her hair, Jeanne pressed her for details; Marie "reluctantly" divulged information about Cécile's pampered life, provided by Val. And she repeated gossip, largely fictional, about the torrid sexual liaison.

Afterward she fed Cécile's craving for revenge by reporting Jeanne's furious, heartbroken reactions. Cécile had a banquet of food for thought.

Occasionally she thought about Valmont. He interested her because he was as self-contained as she was, as much a mystery to her as she was to him.

He was unfailingly considerate, a surprise to Cécile. She received notice of his visits at least twelve hours in advance. Unlike most placées, she didn't have to be constantly available.

He also sent gifts of game or flowers or sweets from time to time to Cécile's mother. Such thoughtfulness was beyond Cécile's experience or comprehension. She only knew that her mother's depression lifted for a day or two or three after the present was delivered. There could be no richer gift for Cécile. She loved her mother above all else.

Val invariably asked Cécile if she would go to bed with him. Even though both of them knew that it was permissible for her to deny him only if she was having her menses. Cécile used lovemaking as her way of showing appreciation for his generosity. To her and especially to her mother. She had been trained from childhood in the ways to please a man sexually. Her body was as supple as a dancer's, and as strong. Her fingers knew every sensitive spot on a man's body; they discovered the individual sensitivities of Val's. She knew how to relax him and how to stimulate him and how to prolong or accelerate his pleasure. She could tease or satisfy. Or alternate the two until he reached a peak of excitement he had never known before. When he told her what he wanted, she gave it to him. When he disliked certain refinements of sensuality, she ceased immediately and never repeated them. She oiled or perfumed or decorated her body and displayed it for him, knowing that her beauty was ravishing to both his body and his mind. She whispered sometimes, cried out loudly sometimes, used words that were tender or gutter coarse, or a combination of the two in ever-different variations. She was never predictable. She was always more thrilling than she had ever been before.

She was sensuality personified, every man's wild fantasy of sex.

And yet...

When Cécile ignited his passions with kisses, caresses, mouth, tongue, hands, teeth, nails, nipples, Val knew that his rapture was his alone, that Cécile's was a magnificent sham. And when he climaxed in a spiral of blind ecstasy, in the midst of the overwhelming pleasure, there was a piercing cold dagger of loneliness in his heart.

He told himself that he had no right to ask for more from Cécile. He was receiving exactly what he had wanted, a refuge and a satisfying bed partner. He didn't want love. There was only tragedy in love between white and colored in America.

After weeks of vague, unnamed disappointment, he realized that what he missed was comfort. The perfectly furnished house was lifeless, a museum of style. There was no comfort there, no human warmth. Not even in the heat of Cécile's bed.

Val wanted shared peacefulness; there were separate silences. He wanted laughter, argument, conversation, discovery, confusion, understanding. Human companionship. Perfection was cold and bleak.

Cécile served gumbo one night, and Val thought of the gumbo in the Market. It tasted better than any other gumbo in New Orleans. It was then that he became aware that he missed the untidy, unorganized, unplanned good times he had known with Mary MacAlistair.

He laughed at himself. After all his complicated arrangements to outtrick her, she had won the game after all. He would give anything to exchange the exquisite Cécile, seductively curled on the polished Directoire couch, for plain, curious Mary, stepping in a patch of mud because she was looking up at the color of the sky.

What a joke on the well-traveled, well-educated, fastidious Valmont Saint-Brévin.

Val's sense of the ridiculousness of life had been submerged for too long. He laughed at himself, and it healed him. He saw his playacting the fop as comic, not disgraceful. The pursuit of the Charleston heiress was a delightful farce, not a disgusting portrayal of a fortune hunter. He could have fun with his deceptions and still accomplish their purpose. His work for the Underground Railroad was serious. But it needn't drain the humor from his life.

He laughed at himself, and continued to laugh. Because it felt good.

# 52

At the same time that Val was gradually discovering the aridity of the Directoire house on Saint Peter Street, Mary's house in Carrollton was developing into a true refuge for her.

She had never had a home of her own, not even a room where she had any choice of what went in it. The house, which had come to her in sorrow, soon began to give her joy. It started when the Jenny Lind settee was delivered. It made the rest of the furnishings in the sitting room look heavy and drab, and it triggered Mary's interest in changing the rest of the things in the room.

Interest became determination, then passionate dedication. It widened the constricted limits of her life. She talked to furniture makers and antiquarians, upholsterers and gilders, importers and auctioneers, always asking questions, always learning, often making new friends.

She ran across old friends, too. Every day she scoured the miscellany of broken, discarded, and stolen objects for sale in the ramshackle stalls on the edge of the Market. She was bargaining for an almost intact brass lamp one day when she saw heard warm chuckle, and a familiar voice say, "Tell him you'll pitch it at him if he don't sell it to you cheap."

It was Joshua, the big black cargo boss who had steered her to the Widow O'Neill when she had no place to go.

Mary almost hugged him. "I'm so glad to see you, Joshua. How have you been? Let's have a coffee and talk."

"Now, Missie, you know better than that. You and me can't sit down at the same table. You go up on the levee, and I'll bring you some coffee like I was waiting on you."

"Bring some for you, too."

"Don't worry. I'll have something better than coffee for Joshua."

They talked for almost an hour. Mary did most of it. A lot had happened to her since Joshua turned her over to the policeman on Canal Street. She told him about the Irish Channel and Madame Alphande, about the shop, Hannah, Albert, the Baroness. She didn't mention Valmont.

She told him about the house last. And about Louisa.

Her tears came when she was in the middle of a word. Mary let them come, made no effort to stop them.

"Missie..." Joshua was alarmed.

"No," Mary sobbed, "no, don't be upset. I'm so glad. I haven't been able to cry until now. I wanted to, but I couldn't."

Bit by bit the shotgun house took on color and brightness and enchantment. The money that Mary had accumulated was spent on furniture, rugs, fabrics. She thought less and less about the time when she had designated it her dowry, to be given to Val. The searing rage against him and all the others who had injured her was sidetracked by the preoccupation with her house. She even became more like the old Mary, cheerful and enthusiastic. Outwardly.

Inside, she was careful, guarded. She'd never let anyone get close enough to hurt her, never again. It was her promise to herself. She was alone, and she preferred it that way. Her house and her work were all that she needed.

The Baroness returned to France in April when the gardens in Jackson Square were completed. She gave Mary the forty books that she had kept in her New Orleans apartment. She sold her the rosewood bookcase where she kept them.

Mary wasn't sad to see her go. The hours that had been spent over coffee at the end of the day now could be devoted to the house.

And the tiny garden behind it. The days were growing longer and there was light to work by when she got home. She snapped off the ends of vines and the twigs of trees that hung over garden walls and rooted them, beginning the transformation of the square of earth outside her door.

There weren't enough minutes in the day to do all she wanted to do. Even though the Season was over, the shop was still busy enough to consume most of her time. She felt that she was stealing the hour in the middle of the day when she looked for furniture and fittings. She had Wednesday afternoon off; it was always crammed with places to go, people to talk to, things to look at. It was her favorite of all the days of the week. She liked being busy every second. Then she was tired enough to fall asleep at once when she went to bed.

April twentieth was Easter. Mary worked in her garden in the morning, at the shop in the afternoon. The churchbells' ringing stirred memories of the convent school, but she squashed them. There was no longer room in her life for the duties of religious practice. When she had most needed God, He hadn't been there. She didn't need Him any more.

She didn't need anybody.

• • •

Valmont asked about Mary when he finally came to pick up his portrait. Albert had sent six messages reminding him about it.

Mary wasn't there, Albert said. She was off Wednesday afternoons. Val was both disappointed and relieved. He didn't know what he'd say to Mary if he saw her. But he'd like to see her.

Albert supervised the loading of the portrait into the cart that would take it to Benison. While he and Val were standing side by side near the cart, he asked if Val had spoken to his banker about letting Albert see the Sazerac paintings.

"My God, I forgot, Mr. Rinck. I'll do it right this minute before it slips my mind again. My men know where to take the picture." He bolted off along the banquette. There were too many memories at Rinck's. Val was glad to get away.

Julien Sazerac was delighted to see Val. He had another horse to sell him. "A mare, Valmont, with champion bloodlines. You shouldn't waste a stallion like Snow Cloud. Start breeding your winners instead of buying them."

Val pored over the mare's genealogy with Julien, dickered about the price, bought her sight unseen. He didn't like Julien, but he trusted him. He forgot all about Albert Rinck until Julien poured drinks to seal the bargain and offered a toast. "To the Benison colors and family."

That reminded Val, and he told Julien about Albert.

He was in luck, Julien replied. This was the perfect time for Albert to go to his family's house. His mother and sister were both away, visiting Julien's brother at his plantation. He scrawled a note for the butler. "Give this to your painter fellow, Val. It will get him in."

"Be a friend and send it down by one of your messengers, Julien. I've promised to give Pepe Lulla's prize pupil a lesson in humility."

Julien rang for his secretary, gave him instructions about the note. Then he walked across to Exchange Alley with Val to watch the fencing match. He considered Saint-Brévin a tiresome, affected jackass. But the man could fence like an angel.

Julien was wrong. Celeste Sazerac was at their brother's, but Anne-Marie Sazerac had decided at the last minute not to go. Even a visit to see her son wasn't a strong enough incentive to overcome her habitual solitary depression. And her need for the peaceful half-alive daze that increasing doses of laudanum gave her.

She didn't understand what Albert Rinck was doing in her house. When he explained that he had come to see her husband's paintings, she told him that her husband was dead, and been dead for years.

Albert was patient with her, although he was frantic to see what the shadowed rectangles on the walls were. His fingers itched to pull the draw cords on the draperies, to let in some light.

He explained again who he was, why her son had written the note for him, what he wanted.

Anne-Marie Sazerac concentrated hard. Finally she understood. "Ah," she said, "you'd like to see the Fragonards."

Albert nearly babbled with excitement. He hadn't expected one of the great painters. He could barely remember his limited French vocabulary. He nodded vehemently.

Madame Sazerac gestured toward the alcove near the fireplace. "That's one of them."

Albert reached for the drapery cord.

"No!" said Anne-Marie. "Sunlight hurts my eyes."

Albert gathered all his resources of patience and persuasion. He went down on his knees and begged. At last he got his way.

It was late in the afternoon by then, and the light was muted. Madame Sazerac blinked, squinted, but did not have to cover her eyes.

Albert took a deep breath to steady himself. Then he turned from the window and looked at the riches of the room.

The furniture was old. Its gilded and painted wood was faded, gentled by age. The velvets and brocades that covered chairs and settees were faded also. They looked more beautiful because of it; they held color deep inside, beneath the surface. Crystal prisms glittered as if rejoicing in the light that gave them life, and the flowers on the Aubusson carpet bloomed. Albert saw none of it. He was transfixed, gaping at the most magnificent work of art he had ever seen or was ever likely to see.

"I thought you said you wanted to see the Fragonards, Monsieur. That's a Goya you're looking at. It didn't belong to my husband at all."

"Please, Madame, please. Let me look." There were tears of awe-struck feeling in Albert's voice.

"You said the Fragonards. You haven't looked at them at all." She tugged at Albert's sleeve. "They're over here. Come look and then go away and leave me alone."

Albert couldn't bear to be pulled away. He wanted to look his fill, then look again and again, studying every inch, every shading, every detail, every brushstroke. He seized on something to say that might deflect Madame Sazerac from her insistence on the Fragonards.

"Look, Madame, at the figure's hands. The fingers. The artist almost insists that the observer see them. They are unusual, almost impossible, one would say. But I know that such fingers do happen in nature. The girl in my wife's shop, her partner in fact, she has the same too-long little finger."

The pulling on his sleeve stopped. Albert was pleased with his success. Until he felt the small weight of Madame Sazerac collapse against his arm and slide down his side to the floor. She was in a dead faint.

"Monster! What have you done to Madame?" The butler rushed from his watchful stance in the doorway. "Michelle!" he shouted, "René! Valentine! Come quickly."

Albert ran away.

Mary was polishing the silver bowl she had bought that day when the knock came on her door. She was expecting delivery of her other purchase, an armoire for the bedroom, so she threw open the door without asking who was there.

A well-dressed man, a total stranger, was standing on the tiny porch. Mary tried to slam the door, but he was too quick for her. His hand stopped it. "Please, Mademoiselle, I mean you no harm. I only want to talk to you for a moment. I won't even come inside."

It was after eight o'clock, and dark. Not a time when a young woman alone in the house talks to strange men, regardless of their attire. Mary pushed her hardest against the door.

"Mademoiselle, I beg of you. I know this is irregular, but I can explain..."

He had no opportunity. A small woman in black appeared suddenly from the blackness behind him. "Let me see," she cried. She ducked under his outstretched arm, threw herself against Mary, tiny hands plucking at her sleeve, her wrist, touching one of the hands she was holding against the door. The woman's fingers were like insects scrabbling across Mary's hand, Mary's fingers.

"It is," she cried, "I knew it. My darling little Marie." She tried to embrace Mary, clutching at her arms, her shoulders, her neck.

She was terrible and terrifying, a bony specter in black with black staring eyes in a chalk-white face.

Mary backed away from her. The door swung open.

"Maman, Maman, stop, Maman." The man caught the reaching woman around the waist. "Quick, Mademoiselle, I implore you. Tell my mother that she is mistaken."

"You're mistaken, Madame," Mary said hurriedly. "Please believe me. You've come to the wrong house. I don't know you, or your son."

"The name," the woman howled. "The name is correct."

"It's a common name, Maman. Listen. Can you listen? Concentrate, Maman, please. I'll ask the girl. Now listen to what she says."

Mary saw that the man had tears in his eyes. "What is your name, Mademoiselle? Is it MacAlistair?"

"It is. Why do you want to know?"

"Forgive me. It's for my mother. She thinks you're someone else. Will you tell her, please, that your mother is still living."

Mary felt a shiver at the nape of her neck. "My mother is dead, Monsieur. I never knew her. She died when I was born."

"Marie," moaned the woman trapped in her son's arms. She held out her hands to Mary.

The man tightened his hold on her. "Mademoiselle, please, one more question. Your mother's maiden name."

"I do not know it. This is awful, Monsieur." Mary felt weak. She spoke in a rush. "I may be able to help you. You want to know who I am. I want to know, too. I had a legacy from my mother, a wooden box. Inside it there was the name Marie Duclos and the address Couvent des Ursulines, Nouvelle Orleans."

"Dear God," the man breathed. "It is true." He stared open-mouthed at Mary.

His mother no longer struggled in his arms. "I told you, Julien, I told you. And now look what your stubborness has done. You've frightened Marie."

She smiled at Mary, and her haggard, maenad's face was suddenly beautiful. "My dearest child," she said gently, "I am your grandmother. I've been looking for you for many years."

"Won't you come in?" said Mary. She didn't know what else to say.

# 53

"I can offer you coffee," Mary said after her grandmother was seated on Jenny Lind's settee, Julien by her side, watchful.

"No, thank you, dear. Do you see what lovely manners Marie has, Julien? And how perfectly she speaks French? You have lovely manners, Marie. I would like a glass of water."

Mary looked at Julien. "Monsieur?"

"What? Oh . . . yes, thank you, thank you, a glass of water." Mary went to her small kitchen and washed the streaks of silver polish off her hands. Then she poured water for her guests. Her first guests in her house.

When she returned to the sitting room, she put the glass of water on a table near her grandmother.

She put a cup near Julien. "I have only one glass," she said. "I live alone."

"Only one glass," her grandmother echoed. "My poor lamb."

Mary's back stiffened. She felt no need to apologize for the limitations of her house. She hadn't invited these people. She felt no affection for them. They had come too late.

"I suppose we'd better begin at the beginning," Julien said. "I haven't even introduced myself. My name is Julien Sazerac, Marie. Your Uncle Julien."

Sazerac. Mary started to speak, bit back the words, spoke different ones. "My name is Mary, Monsieur, not Marie."

"Oh, no," said Anne-Marie Sazerac. "Marie. The first daughter is always called Marie. Your mother was Marie-Christine. You'll have her room. Marie's room. The house will be happy again, as it was before. Come, Marie, let us go home." She held out her hand to Mary.

Mary remained standing, out of reach. "May I ask a question, Madame?"

"But of course, Marie."

"Have you a relation, Madame, a woman of middle age named Celeste Sazerac?"

"But of course. She is your aunt, my daughter. How do you know of her?"

Mary had suspected Celeste the moment Julien Sazerac told her his name. Even so, it was a shock to have her suspicion confirmed. She had trouble believing that she'd been betrayed by the sister of her mother. Celeste's treachery was worse than the cruelty of anyone else.

Mary's hands balled into fists. Fury made her voice thin.

"Let me tell you how I know your daughter, Madame. It's a long, ugly story. When I'm done, you'll realize why I can never live in your house."

She began at the beginning, when the casket was delivered to her at the convent school. Without emotion she told about her father's death, her discovery that her supposed mother was really her stepmother, her faith that the casket would lead her to her family in New Orleans.

She was naive, she said, to trust Rose Jackson, and she paid for her folly. "I won't tell you how frightened I was, how sickened. It's enough to say that I was able to get away from that horrible place."

Mary described the kindness of the nuns, the seeming kindness of a woman at the convent. "She offered to help me, to retrieve my legacy and my money. I was very grateful. Even when she said that she had been unable to get my possessions, I was still grateful, because she promised to help identify my family and to unite me with them.

"The woman's name was Celeste Sazerac."

Julien leapt to his feet. The cup and saucer fell to the floor and broke.

Anne-Marie Sazerac shook her head. "I don't understand," she said. "Celeste couldn't have been the woman. She would have known at once who you are, Marie. She used to love to see me open the casket and tell the stories of the Maries who had owned it."

Julien looked at Mary, asking her without words to be compassionate and patient with his mother, her grandmother.

"There's no question, Maman," he said slowly. "Celeste did know. You must concentrate, and understand. Celeste did know. She kept Marie from us deliberately."

He looked again at Mary. "The injury is too great for forgiveness, Mademoiselle. Will you permit me to make whatever amends are possible? I'll do everything a man can do, anything you ask." Julien was beseeching her, and begging was so clearly foreign to him that Mary felt a quiver of pleasure. Let him be humbled. Celeste's brother deserved to be punished, because he was her brother.

"I plead with you, Mademoiselle MacAlistair. You see how my mother is. Believe me, she was once a happy, active, loving woman. A wonderful mother. The last ten years since she was widowed have been a nightmare. Watching her slowly become what she is today. For ten years she has been sinking ever deeper into a darkness that the best doctors cannot penetrate. The only thing she cared about was finding you. She hasn't willingly left her house in years. Not until tonight. Then she walked, alone, to find me because I could lead her to you, by asking the painter.

"You can help her back to the light, Mademoiselle. You can restore life to her. I implore you to come with us, live in the home that is yours, join your family. If you can't love your grandmother, at least can't you pity her?"

Anne-Marie was still shaking her head. "I don't understand," she said over and over.

Mary looked at the woman who was her grandmother. She felt no love, not even pity. Too late, her mind said. I could have pitied her, even loved her. In the beginning. If Celeste had taken me to her then. But too much has happened. I've changed too much. I don't want to give up what I've earned. My house, the shop, my privacy. It's not up to me to make Madame Sazerac happy. I have my own happiness to think of.

"I give you my word," said Julien Sazerac, "Celeste will pay for what she has done."

The same quiver of joy touched Mary.

"I'll come with you now, Monsieur. But I don't promise that I'll stay."

"Thank you, Mademoiselle... Maman, Maman, are you ready to go home? Marie is coming with us."

Madame Sazerac smiled. She held out her hand again. This time Mary took it.

Anne-Marie Sazerac fell asleep in the carriage, her hand in Mary's; her head slid over onto Mary's shoulder, and she snored in gentle puffs of breath. She was smiling.

Julien carried his mother into the house. "Jacques," he said to the butler, "tell the maids to prepare Mademoiselle Marie's room. She has come home. And light all the candles. There will be no more darkness in this house."

He looked solemnly at Mary. "Thank you," he said. "I'm going to take Maman to her room. If you'll come with me, we'll go together after she's settled, and we'll find your inheritance."

The door to Celeste's bedroom was locked. Julien muttered a curse. Then he stepped back and burst it open with a powerful kick. Mary drew in a long, satisfying breath. The crashing and destruction was the perfect expression of her rage.

The room was like a portrait of Celeste's diseased mind. Every drawer, every cupboard, every wardrobe was locked. Julien took the poker from its hook on the mantlepiece and pried open a cupboard. The wood splintered with a cracking noise. "Look inside while I open the next one," Julien said. He was breathing heavily, and his face was red.

"Give me the poker," Mary ordered. "I'll open the next one. I want to do it." She attacked a carved rosewood armoire. Her arm faltered. It was a magnificent piece of furniture. But her urge to damage Celeste won. She laughed when it flew open.

Julien held a lamp above her shoulder. The casket was there. She was elated. But disappointed that the violent wrecking was over. She held the box in her arms, remembering the feel of it.

For a moment she was that earlier Mary again, longing for a place where she'd belong, for a family, for love.

Then the moment was past. She was alone, self-sufficient, and better off that way. No one could hurt her.

"Would you like to open it?" Julien asked. "I'll turn my back."

"I don't think that's necessary, Monsieur. There's nothing you can't see." Mary put the box on top of a bureau, lifted its lid. "Everything is here," she said. Julien, she saw, had his back turned.

He asked her if she'd mind going downstairs for a talk. Mary agreed at once. There was a lot to talk about.

After four hours and three pots of coffee, they said goodnight. Mary had a list of her closest relatives: uncles, aunts, and first cousins. Also a list of the servants: butler, cook, gardener, coachman, footmen, maids. There would be a small family dinner the following night.

It was agreed that she would address her aunts and uncles by their Christian names, and that she would be called Marie.

She had learned from Julien that her grandmother was dependent on the opium solution called laudanum, and had promised to do what she could to wean her from it. She had also promised to call her "Mémère," the Creole diminutive for Grandmother.

She had not promised to make the Sazerac house her permanent home; she'd see how things developed.

Julien escorted Mary to her room. "Bolt your door," he said. "Celeste is not expected until tomorrow, but with her, one never knows. I will stay in this house until she returns. Then I'll deal with her. You don't even have to be present."

But she wanted to be, Mary said. She closed and bolted the door.

Dozens of candles made the room almost as bright as day. It was a room of flowers and ribbons and ruffles, a room for a young girl.

My mother's room, Mary thought, and for the first time she believed in what had happened. She was in a family, her family. She put the casket on an armchair and opened it. One by one she laid the keepsakes on the bed. The fan, the locket, the arrowhead in its worn leather pouch, the lace-wrapped Spanish moss, the gloves.

She picked up the gloves again, put her hands into them. Her family.

Which of the treasures had her mother put in the casket, she wondered. What had she been like?

Mémère could tell her.

Suddenly Mary was eager for morning to come.

# 54

"Bonjour, Mémère, I've brought your coffee." Mary carried the tray carefully. She could see only dark outlines in the curtained bedroom. She wondered if the cook had been right about her grandmother's bell ringing.

A voice from the darkness reassured her. "Marie? Marie, is it really you? I thought perhaps you were a dream." Anne-Marie Sazerac's voice was much less slurred than it had been the night before. "Come to Mémère, my love. Let me kiss you."

"I'm coming. I can't see very well." Mary's knee hit a table leg. She set the tray down on the table. "I'll open the curtains, Mémère. Then I'll be able to find you," she said.

"No! I can't stand the light... Yes, open them just halfway. I want to look at you."

Mary groped her way to the window. The pull cords were stiff from disuse. She yanked, and the curtains opened to their full width. The cord broke off in her hand.

"I'm sorry..." she began, but her grandmother interrupted her.

"No matter. No matter, my child. Come here." She was sitting up against a half dozen pillows. She looked small and fragile in her lace-edged cap and wide-collared nightdress. Her arms were extended. The full sleeves of her dress were like wings.

Mary walked to her, bent to be embraced. Her grandmother's eyes were clear and focused this morning, she noticed. Perhaps this would be a good time to ask.

"Dear Marie, you're very thin. Do you get enough to eat? Your mother never seemed to eat enough, no matter how much I fussed. Where's the tray? Is there bread and butter? I want you to eat every bite, and all the jam, too. Put lots of sugar in the coffee."

"But this is your tray, Mémère. I've already had breakfast."

"No matter. You'll have another, and I'll ring for another tray. Eat, my lamb. It will make me very happy."

Mary didn't mind. She had been up for hours. And the brioche was delicious.

Also, she wanted to ask about her mother. She had looked closely at everything in her bedroom, but there were no clues, no small personal things, not even books.

"Was my mother thin like me? Will you tell me about her, Mémère?"

Her grandmother's eyes filled with tears. "I have missed her so," she said in a whisper. "I loved her best of all of them. Marie-Christine." She looked up at the flowered silk canopy over her head. "She was the most beautiful baby in the world. Oh, I was so happy when she was born. I wouldn't have cared if she was hideous. There were five boys, you know. Five children, and all of them boys. My husband was glad. Sons were a man's strength, he said. But I prayed for a girl. Even when two of the boys died, I prayed that the next child would be a girl.

"And my prayers were answered at last. By my beautiful Marie-Christine.

"She wasn't red and bald and crumpled like my other babies. Her skin was like whipped cream, and she had a full head of hair. Black as night, curling on her sweet little forehead. Her eyes were blue, of course, like all babies at first. They were the deep velvet blue of a pansy. They didn't turn brown until very late. I had begun to think they would stay like pansies. But then one day after that they changed very quickly. They were beautiful, too, her brown eyes. Wide and bright and full of mischief. She was an imp, an adorable imp."

Madame Sazerac's voice faded away. She seemed lost in her memories. "What was she like?" Mary asked, bringing her back.

Her grandmother chuckled. "She was very naughty. Headstrong. Afraid of nothing. She did everything her brothers did. How cross the boys used to get. No one could stay cross with Marie-Christine, though. She was always laughing, always so happy, and so loving. All she had to do was beg forgiveness, and the hardest heart would melt.

"Until . . . until . . ." The tears began to drop slowly down Mémère's cheeks. They looked like transparent pearls. Her hand fumbled among the clutter on the table by the bed. "It's time for my medicine. Ring for Valentine, Marie. She always fixes my medicine."

Mary caught hold of her hand. "Valentine will come in a minute, Mémère. Tell me about my mother until she comes. Was she beautiful when she grew up? How did she meet my father? Were they very much in love?"

Anne-Marie Sazerac's head turned away. Her shoulders were shaking with her sobs. "I can't, I can't talk anymore. It's too bright, my eyes hurt.

"Valentine! Close the curtains. My head hurts, Valentine. Give me my medicine."

Mary dropped her grandmother's hand beside her on the bed. Then she jerked sharply on the bell pull and left the room.

She found Julien in the library where they had talked the night before.

"I can't stay here," she announced. "It won't work. I did as you asked, Monsieur. I took her tray, I called her Mémère, I even let her kiss me. Now she's up there calling for her laudanum. I won't be nurse-maid to an opium fiend. I'm going to work, just as I always do, and after work I'm going home to my own house."

Julien begged her to sit down, to reflect, to calm herself. "She can't be cured in a day, Marie. Tell me, did she know who you were?"

"Yes, and she was happy to see me; I believe that. She told me I must eat her breakfast because I'm so thin. My mother never ate enough, she said. Then I asked her about my mother; she talked for a minute, and then all of a sudden she was looking for her medicine and shouting 'close the curtains, my eyes hurt,' and mistaking me for her maid."

Julien touched Mary's arm. "Do you mean her curtains were opened?"

"Yes, I opened them."

"And she allowed it?"

"Of course. It was black as pitch in the room."

Julien Sazerac clasped his hands together against his chest. "My dear girl, it's a miracle. Those curtains have been drawn for six years. You don't realize. You can't imagine what this means."

Mary sighed. "You're trying to ensnare me, that's what it means. Look, Monsieur, I'm not heartless; I'm glad she let me open the miserable curtains. But I have myself to think of first. I'll be happier the way I was."

"Please listen, Marie... Mary. I won't argue with you. Just let me tell you about your mother. You want to know about her, don't you?"

"Of course I do."

"Well, then, I'll tell you. Marie-Christine was the most enchanting and the most infuriating creature ever to set foot on this earth. She wasn't beautiful, though everyone will tell you she was. She looked like many other Creole girls, with fair skin and dark hair and eyes. What set her apart was her spirit. She was as curious as a cat; everything was fascinating to her. She wanted to know everything, try everything, do everything. And she loved the doing. She was always happy. She'd climb a tree and fall. Scare us all to death. Then laugh at our terrified faces.

"She'd never take no for an answer. Even when she was warned that there was a terrible punishment for something, like not doing her homework, for instance. She'd play with her toys instead of doing her homework. Then she'd be punished. And she'd say that she thought it was a fair exchange, hug or kiss whoever had punished her, and go on her way. She was incorrigible, and irresistible.

"Maman spoiled her outrageously. Anything Marie-Christine wanted, Maman insisted she must have. Even Papa gave in when Marie-Christine kept after him long enough, although he was a martinet with the rest of us.

"Come with me, Mary. I want to show you what my father was like. Please. This will only take a minute."

Julien led the way to the drawing room. He opened the curtains, revealed the gilt and crystal and rich brocades. Mary gasped.

"This was my father's world: France before the Revolution. He managed to bring these things with him when he fled the mobs. He was the only one who got away; the rest of his family went to the guillotine.

"He came to New Orleans because it was a French city. Inside this room it was Versailles, and he ruled as if he were Louis Quinze, the Sun King. His word was law, and there was no appeal. That is unless the lawbreaker was Marie-Christine.

"I can see her now. She'd tiptoe in from that door over there. Papa always sat in that big chair, so she'd be behind him. Then she'd put her hands over his eyes and demand that he guess who she was pretending to be.

"Papa was an extremely dignified old man. He never gave up knee breeches and long coats, and his hair was as white as if he had powdered it. He was over sixty when Marie-Christine was born. But she played games with him. 'I'm Madame de Pompadour,' she'd giggle, 'and you love me better than anyone in all of France.'

"He probably loved her more than anyone else in the world. I believe that's why he was so cruel after she broke his heart.

"He had arranged a brilliant match for her, a Frenchman like himself, but young and handsome. His name was Giles d'Olivet. In France he would have been the Vicomte d'Olivet. His parents had fled the Revolution, too, but they were less provident than Papa. They were penniless. It was Giles who made a fortune. By the time he was twenty, he owned a plantation of a thousand acres. At thirty he had increased it to ten thousand. That's when my father betrothed Marie-Christine to him. With a dowry fit for a queen.

"On the eve of her wedding, Mary, your mother ran away with a man she had met for the first time that afternoon. He was your father.

"Papa was like a madman. He cut her name from the tapestry that shows the Sazerac family tree since the tenth century, and he burned all the clothes and books and trinkets in her room. Her name could not be spoken in the house.

"She wrote letters. He sent them back to her. He wouldn't answer them, and he wouldn't allow anyone else to write to her.

"When the letter came from your father, he sent that back, too. I remember that day with horror. Marie-Christine was dead, and we were not allowed to mourn her. Maman kissed his boots, begging him to let Marie-Christine come home to rest in the family tomb, but he refused.

"Do you understand, Mary, why Maman can't talk about your mother without so much pain that she calls for opium?"

Mary had listened wide-eyed. "What a terrible story," she said. "Your poor mother. At least she wasn't the one who was cruel, it was your father."

Julien's shoulders sagged. "Maman helped Marie-Christine run away. She always gave her everything she wanted."

He straightened, cleared his throat. "Let's be more cheerful. There's one thing in this room that didn't come from France with Papa. Look to your left, beyond the window. That's a portrait of Marie-Hélène Vejerano, your grandmother's grandmother. She's the one who helped us find you. Look at her hands."

Mary looked at the painting, and her breath stopped for a long half-minute. The hands were her hands. They were holding the fan that was in her legacy.

"Will you stay, Marie?" Julien asked.

"Yes."

Mary went to the shop to talk to Hannah and Albert. They rejoiced in her good fortune.

"I'm not sure yet whether it's good or bad," Mary said, "but I've promised to stay for a year. But I told my uncle . . . that sounds so strange to me . . . I told him I'd keep working while I train someone to take my place. I'm sure we can find a good clerk at one of the other shops, and her salary will be much less than my share of the profits. I won't need any money; Julien is signing over some shares of something to me, and I'll have more than I could ever spend."

Hannah and Albert exchanged guilty looks. "We have something to tell you, too, Mary," said Hannah. "We've decided to go abroad. After Albert saw the Goya in your grandmother's house, he felt that he needed to study in Europe."

"It's technique," Albert said, "all technique, I'm sure of it. All I need is a really first-rate instructor who knows the old masters. I can figure out how they did it when the originals are right before my eyes. Then I only have to learn the technique they used. My problem is that my teacher in Philadelphia only had a copy to work from."

"We've saved enough from my profits to live in Spain for a year at least," Hannah said. "Or London," she said in a whisper. "We'd never learn to speak Spanish."

"When do you plan to leave?" Mary asked.

As soon as possible, Hannah told her. The rent for both shop and apartment was paid through the end of May. That was almost three weeks off. Plenty of time to arrange things. Including selling the shop's inventory to another dressmaker and settling accounts with Cécile. Hannah would take care of everything. Mary needn't go see their partner in her new house on Saint Peter Street.

Mary was more grateful than she could say.

Julien Sazerac was pacing the length of the long hallway when Mary returned to the house on Royal Street. "Did all go well?" he asked. "Will you be able to finish your duties at the shop soon?"

"Sooner than expected," Mary replied. "It's over. I'm through." She was downhearted. The shop meant a great deal to her.

"That's extremely good news." Julien all but clapped his hands. "I have good news, also. Celeste came back while you were gone. Luckily Maman was dozing and didn't hear the appalling scene.

"Celeste won't come here again, Marie. I've had her taken away. There's a place near Natchez for her kind of sickness."

Mary tried not to imagine what Julien called a "scene." There were still glittering shards of mirror on the floor, and the wall showed a great square of darker wallpaper where the mirror had been. All the furniture that had been in the hall was gone, and the rugs. Julien had changed his clothes. One sleeve of his coat bulged as if a thick bandage might be covering his forearm.

"The Rincks going, Celeste gone. How very neat my life is becoming," said Mary. "Thank you, Julien." She made no effort to disguise the sarcasm in the word "neat."

# 55

Julien took his leave then, with a reminder to Mary that the family would be coming for dinner that evening. The servants had everything under control, he assured her. There was nothing for her to worry about.

The house was very quiet.

"Nothing to worry about." Mary's thoughts echoed Julien's words. Nothing to do would be more accurate. She couldn't remember a time when she had had nothing to do. She went up to her room to choose a dress for the evening. She'd have to iron it; her packing had been hasty.

But all four of her dresses were already washed and ironed. They looked very small in the tremendous armoire.

She decided to wash her hair. If she rinsed it an extra time or two, that would consume another ten minutes.

She started to go in search of the kitchen to heat some water. She halted after three steps. She wasn't in the Irish Channel or Carrollton now.

She rang for a maid.

"I'll never get used to this," she grumbled aloud. She wished she was in Carrollton. Her garden needed weeding.

Julien's wife told people, his brothers told people, people told people. While Mary MacAlistair was washing her hair all of Creole New Orleans was talking about the dramatic discovery of the Sazerac granddaughter in a shotgun house in Carrollton.

"Clerking in a shop, imagine it! I remember her very well. I thought at the time that she was too aristocratic-looking to be a clerk in a shop."

"Marie-Christine's daughter, think of it. Do you suppose she's as beautiful as her mother? As wild?"

"They say Celeste Sazerac has gone into a convent in gratitude for the answer to her prayers."

"They say that the curtains of Anne-Marie Sazerac's room are open."

"They say that Julien Sazerac has given her a million dollars."

"They say that she'll be Anne-Marie's heir."

Carlos Courtenay sent orders to Philippe to come to town at once. He was sure that his adopted son would be the favored suitor. After all,

Philippe had been kind to the girl when she was nobody.

Jeanne Courtenay Graham got a cramp in her wrist writing invitations to a soirée dansante on Sunday next. May-ree was her friend. Everyone would die of envy when Jeanne was the first to entertain for her.

Valmont Saint-Brévin's friend the mock priest bought a ticket for the next ship sailing to Europe.

Valmont bolted the doors of his rooms at the Saint Louis and sprawled in a chair, staring at a wall, despising himself. She had tried to tell him, and he thought she was lying. He believed his own lies about her instead. He had raped her because of those lies. There was nothing he could do to make up for the injustices, the crimes he had committed against her. She'd never believe him if he tried to explain. Why should she? He hadn't believed her.

The Widow O'Neill didn't say anything about Mary. Nor did Paddy Devlin or the Reillys. Creole society gossip never reached the Irish Channel, and they had no reason to talk about her. A second niece of the widow's was living in Mary's old room now. She was a good-natured buxom girl with flaming red hair and green eyes that Paddy thought were more beautiful than the hills of Ireland itself.

Mary dried her hair in the center of the courtyard, where the sun fell directly on her head. After a half hour, she was called inside by her grandmother. Madame Sazerac was dressed in black as usual, but with a fichu of white lace over her shoulders and breast. She was alert and happy.

"Darling Marie, you'll ruin your skin in the sun like that. Come sit at my feet and I'll brush your hair dry. While I do we can chat and get to know one another and make plans."

Mary realized before her hair was half dry that she wasn't going to have to worry about having time on her hands. There was going to be plenty to do. Anne-Marie was talking about the opera, the theater, calls to pay and calls to receive, parties to give and attend, new wardrobes for both of them, shopping and fittings and hairdressers and bootmakers, cousins and second and third cousins that Mary had to meet, in town and on their plantations. And all of this at once. Before everyone started to leave the city for the summer. "Mémère's so happy and so proud of her dearest Marie that she wants to introduce her to everyone," she cooed. Between strokes of the brush she kissed Mary's crown.

Julien came earlier than the others for dinner. "How is Maman?" he asked Mary.

"I think you'll be surprised." She reported the afternoon's happenings. "After the session with the hairbrush, she said her arm was very painful and took a quick nip of laudanum. But she didn't go to sleep. She's fuzzy, but she's holding on. When I came downstairs she was berating Valentine because she couldn't find the earrings she wants to wear at dinner."

Julien clasped his hands to his chest, his way of expressing emotion. "I'll never be able to thank you adequately, Marie."

Mary eyed him dispassionately. "Don't get carried away, Julien. This afternoon may be a fluke, a once-only thing. In case it isn't, I want you to understand certain conditions I have to insist on."

"Anything you need, Marie, anything you want."

Mary's nape tingled. She rubbed the sensation away. "There's no point in my playing the part of a Creole maiden, Julien. I've been on my own for too long, and the restrictions would drive me mad. I intend to go out alone if I want to, and I'll talk to whomever I choose. I have some interesting acquaintances among the tradesmen and craftsmen of the city.

"I also intend to keep my house in Carrollton. I'll make a reasonable effort to make my home here. But I may escape to my own house from time to time if I feel the need."

Julien looked unhappy, but he agreed to all Mary's conditions without arguing.

A little later, when the other family members arrived, Mary understood how hard Julien's acquiescence must have been for him. Everyone except Mémère was deferential to him as the male head of the family. Julien's word was law.

But not for me, Mary thought. My word is law for him. The nape of her neck tingled, and Mary recognized it for what it was. The thrill of power. The Baroness was right, Mary told herself. It is more exciting than love. Love never gave me anything but pain and helplessness. I'm in control now. It's infinitely better.

She was pleasant and polite to her newly found relations. But she didn't care whether they liked her or not. She had memorized the names; she even managed to attach the right name to the right child, although there were so many. The Sazeracs were a typical Creole family.

Julien's wife Eleanore was an attractive woman in her early thirties.

She was visibly pregnant and glowingly proud of the five little boys and two little girls she presented to "Cousine Marie."

Roland, Julien's younger brother, was father of four, stepfather to two. Diane, his wife, was a widow when he married her six years earlier.

Bertrand, the youngest brother, was still a bachelor at thirty-six. He was the easiest of them all to get along with. When Julien introduced him Bertrand kissed Mary's hand then tucked it in the crook of his arm. "Don't scowl so, brother," he laughed, "I'm going to take my niece on a get-acquainted stroll down the hall." He winked at Mary. "The whiskey decanter is on the sideboard in the dining room."

"It's too bad we're so closely related," he told her as they walked. "The word is that you're the heiress of the century. I'd be after you like a shot. Julien is stingy about allowances. Alas. All the single men in New Orleans will be dancing attendance on you, save only myself. What will I do for amusement without my friends?

"I'm not really a rotter, Marie, no matter what you may hear. I just like a good time, and I don't much like children. That makes me an outcast in the family. Outside the family I'm considered a remarkably nice fellow. I hope you'll think so too."

Mary assured him she would.

In fact, Mary didn't think about him at all. She was occupied with too many other things.

In the days and weeks ahead Mary learned more and more about the pleasures of power. She took Mémère to Madame Alphande's shop, sat with her in the private sitting room, and sipped coffee while Madame extolled the virtues of the workmanship in the gowns she made. Mary didn't say a word. Anne-Marie Sazerac knew nothing about her granddaughter's ordeal in the Alphande workroom. "Why in the world was that Alphande woman so nervous, Marie?" she asked when they left.

"I don't know, Mémère," Mary said. She could easily imagine Madame Alphande's despair when so many potential thousands of dollars walked into her sitting room then walked out again.

Just wait, she promised her former employer silently. You'll squirm a lot more before I'm through with you.

A few days later she watched from across the street when a battery of policemen arrested Rose Jackson and nailed a poster on the door of the luxurious mansion that housed her brothel. "Closed," read the sign.

"This confiscated property is for sale through the offices of the Municipal Council."

At her request, Julien had said a few words to a few people. Julien would do anything at all at her request. Mary was almost moved by his happiness at every small step his mother took toward returning to the world.

Each day Mémère spent a little more time doing things with Mary, a little less in her laudanum dreamworld. She was firm about social protocol. "You haven't been presented yet, dearest Marie, so we must refuse all invitations for you that come from strangers. Only family entertainments are acceptable until autumn next, when your Season will begin." But the network of family included hundreds of cousins and aunts and uncles at varying degrees of remove. Virtually everyone in Creole society was related to everyone else. Mémère herself was one of nine children; each of her brothers and sisters had from four to twelve children; she had more than fifty nieces and nephews. Most of them had large families, too. Mary didn't even try to keep them straight. It was simply enough to call everyone cousin. And safe. The odds were that there was a connection somewhere.

You wanted a family, she reminded herself. You've no right to complain if it turned out to be so much bigger than you ever imagined. The daily outings with Mémère to take coffee and cakes with Cousine This or Cousine That would have been less tiring if another half dozen Cousines hadn't come to take coffee and cakes with Mémère later in the same day.

Mary was grateful that it would soon be June. Most of the cousins left the city in the summer.

She was grateful, too, that Bertrand's bachelor friends couldn't start paying attention to her until she was formally presented to society. She wasn't ready for that. She didn't know that she ever would be ready.

Three letters came from Valmont. Mary returned them unopened. And tried not to wonder what was in them.

She didn't know yet how she'd avenge herself against Val. Rose Jackson and Madame Alphande were easy to blame and easy to punish. But the rage and hatred she felt for Valmont Saint-Brévin demanded a far greater retribution. And it had to be her vengeance, at her hands. By her power.

Mary often thought about Michaela de Pontalba during those early weeks of testing her strength in her new role as the Sazerac heiress. She felt the shocked glances when she was seen without chaperone on the street or was observed laughing and talking with the vendors and ragpickers at the Market. The Baroness had shocked New Orleans, too. And enjoyed doing it. Almost as much as Mary did.

When June came the Vieux Carré emptied. The silver tray on the table in the hall was piled high with cards left by the cousins. "P.P.C." was written in spiky script on the corner of them. "Pour Prendre Congé," it was a formal goodbye, "To Take Leave," until autumn, when fresh cards on the tray would announce that their owners had returned to the city.

"Why don't you and Maman go to the lake, Marie?" Julien suggested. "We own a very pleasant hotel there. You'd have the best rooms, and the other guests are always people we know."

Mary suppressed a shudder. She'd had enough cousins to last her for a while. "Maybe later, Julien. Mémère wants to redecorate the house before autumn. She's planning several receptions during the season. I think we'd both enjoy seeing to curtains and paints more than a vacation at the lake."

Julien was torn. "Of course, anything that interests Maman . . . but I have a responsibility to you, Marie. There's danger of fever in the summer."

"Don't worry, Julien. I've had yellow fever. It didn't bother me much." Julien's as foolish as Berthe Courtenay, Mary thought. I don't know why these people make such a hobgoblin out of a little illness. They probably swoon over measles.

She wondered briefly how Berthe was taking the scandal about Jeanne. At all the cousins' coffees there had been much whispering behind fans with eyebrows raised. Jeanne's name was linked with a notorious roué. Her behavior at the soirée dansante she gave had been outrageously indiscreet, everyone said. Mary hadn't been there to see it. Jeanne's invitation had been refused. A closer cousin was entertaining on the same night.

Mary felt sorry for Berthe. Jeanne was her life. She felt sorry for Jeanne, too. Society was her life, and she was going to be shunned if she didn't change her ways. In spite of the ugly fight about the house in Carrollton, Mary felt a loyalty to Jeanne. She had been Mary's friend, in her own self-centered definition of friendship.

Mary had no pity for Carlos. He was an enemy. She had seen him at a party and had been deliberately blind to his bow. His shamefaced embarrassment had made her neck tingle. She liked the sensation.

June fifth was Mary's seventeenth birthday. She asked her grandmother for a birthday favor. No party, no family. Just the two of them celebrating together. Mémère wept with mingled happiness and sorrow.

"You are a darling to want to be with me, Marie. Especially on your seventeenth birthday. Your mother was gone from me before she reached seventeen."

Mary kissed her. "I'm here now, Mémère. You take a nice rest this afternoon. Tonight we'll put on our fancy new gowns and drink champagne."

Mary went for a long walk that afternoon. She wanted to be alone. It hardly seemed possible that only a year earlier she was at the convent school in the Pennsylvania mountains. So much had happened in that year. She felt a need to look over who that schoolgirl Mary was, what this Mary had become, and where she was going.

She walked from the house on Royal Street to the Pontalba buildings. The shop was now occupied by a milliner. The tenants of the Rincks' old apartment were having their lunch at a table on their shady iron-framed gallery. Mary could hear the low murmur of voices. There were five new shops on the street level. Across Jackson Square she saw three other luncheon tables scattered on the gallery of Michaela's second building. The apartments and shops were gradually filling up. Good for the Baroness!

The parterre garden in the square was bright with flowers. A picnic was taking place under the shade of the trees in one corner. Mary thought of the expanse of mud that had been the Place d'Armes. Good for the Baroness again!

She went over to the levee and watched the organized chaos of the ships loading and unloading passengers and cargo on the batture. Then she followed the levee to the Canal Street docks and the gay row of Mississippi paddle wheelers with their gilt-edged lacy trim. She'd entered New Orleans there with Rose Jackson; Joshua had found her there when she was homeless and afraid.

Walking across Canal she used the leafy tunnel in the center park, the Neutral Ground. It was a good place for her, she mused. Half American, half Creole, just like her. Sometimes she longed for the sound of a voice speaking English. Just as she longed for the sight of a broken horizon, green mountains, and snow-crisped air. It was already hot in New Orleans, even in the shade of the avenue of trees. Temperatures had reached eighty-five in May. It felt like that or more today.

She crossed over to D. H. Holmes, the department store where she had bought her little chip bonnet and the brown fabric for her work dress. She looked at parasols, selected a blue one, paid for it with one of the gold coins in her handbag. It cost more than all the purchases she had made when she first shopped there. There's progress for you, Mary said to herself. She laughed softly when she stepped onto the banquette and opened the pretty extravagance to shade her from the sun.

Canal Street was always busy, regardless of heat, summer, natural disaster. Mary had to watch where she was going. On one corner she walked out into the street with the other pedestrians to detour around an excited cluster of weatherbeaten men waving leather pouches in the air. "Just back from California, I expect," she heard a man say to his companion. "That's the assay office where they buy gold. The barrooms'll be busy tonight. Gambling hells, too, and the houses of pleasure. New Orleans has got everything a body could ask for."

It does, Mary thought. She turned right at the next corner. There was no need to take the street cars up to Carrollton, to revisit the Irish Channel, as she'd planned. That bit of overheard conversation had said it all. New Orleans had given her everything she'd asked for. Mary the schoolgirl had come in search of a family that would envelop her and love her. She had found it, and so much more. Self-reliance. Adulthood. She had learned to take care of herself, to run a successful business, to survive the loss of innocence, to grow up. And, as a bonus, to speak French as well as anyone outside Paris could hope to speak it. Mary MacAlistair, seventeen on this day, June 5, 1851, was a very lucky young woman.

It was time for her to stop brooding over past injuries. She had come a long way; the journey was behind her. All the good and all the bad. Over and done with. Now it was time to look ahead.

She walked along Royal Street. Going home.

Everything looked different. Everything was different. The bank building she passed wasn't merely an impressive columned structure. It was her Uncle Julien's bank. That candle shop wasn't a shop only. Above it were the lovely old rooms where her cousin Narcisse lived. He was the son of Mémère's elder sister, long dead. On All Souls' Day she'd put chrysanthemums on her tomb next to the bouquet Narcisse laid there. With the flowers of all the other cousins and children and brothers and sisters. All the streets, all the houses, all the brick and stucco, all the pink and yellow and blue walls, all the wavy tiled roofs and funny chimney pots, all the iron gates and galleries and fences and balconies, all the cobblestones and bricks and mud and dust, all the flowers and trees and fountains and hidden courtyards, all the romance and mystery and ghosts of earlier ages, all, all, all New Orleans was hers, her home of the blood and the heart.

She belonged to it. It belonged to her.

She could spend the rest of her life getting to know its stories, its secrets, its delights.

Her footsteps became faster. She wanted to tell Mémère that she was happy to be her granddaughter. And that she loved her.

All of a sudden there was a downpour of rain, a characteristic New Orleans summer shower. Mary took shelter under the overhang of a deep balcony.

"'New Orleans has everything a body could ask for,'" she quoted to the black woman sheltering there with her. "All the houses even have umbrellas on them to protect people from the weather."

The woman looked at the rain with an expert eye. "Going to last a while," she said. She sat on the steps of the house to wait.

Mary sat down beside her. "I love this muggy old city," she said.

"Everybody that's got a soul in them loves New Orleans," added the smiling woman.

# 56

"You should know, Marie," said Mémère, "that we celebrate the feast day of one's saint with more festivity then the anniversary of one's birth. We will have a wonderful party in August, on Marie's Day."

"I think this is a wonderful party we're having now." They were dining on the iron balcony at a lace-covered table lit by candles in hurricane shades. Mary had planned it with the servants when she returned from her walk.

"I had a special reason for having our party here, Mémère. When I arrived in New Orleans it was dark. I looked up as I was riding along the street, and I saw a girl about my age at a table with her parents. I envied that girl so much.

"Now I feel as if I am the girl that I envied. Everyone should envy me. I have you, Mémère. I love you very much."

"My dear child. . ." Mémère was crying.

Mary took her hand. "Tears aren't allowed on my birthday, Mémère. Only smiles."

Anne-Marie Sazerac held Mary's hand to her wet cheek. Her smile was more beautiful than ever.

The coffee service was waiting in the drawing room after dinner. There was a square velvet case on the tray next to the pot.

"A gift for you, Marie," said Mémère. She opened the case.

It held a pair of bracelets. They were wide cuffs of gold studded with cabochon emeralds. "Marie-Hélène always wore them," said Mémère. "She liked to call attention to her extraordinary hands."

Mary looked at the portrait of her grandmother's grandmother. The bracelets were there. And the fan from the casket. She felt as if the portrait might come to life.

"What else did she do, Mémère? Did you know her? What was she like?"

"I remember her well. I was twelve when she died. She was so exciting. All my friends at the Ursuline school were wildly jealous of me because I had such a fantastic grandmother. She traveled all over the world; she spoke languages none of us had ever heard. She had been to Saint Petersburg, São Paulo, Alexandria, Delhi, Constantinople, everywhere. Her honeymoon voyage lasted five years. She and my grandfather came home to New Orleans with three children.

"He was exciting, too, but we children saw very little of him. He was a special adviser to the King of Spain, and he was often away for months on diplomatic missions."

"Why the King of Spain, Mémère? Why not the King of France?"

"Because he was Spanish, Marie. The King of France was nothing to him."

"Then why was he in New Orleans? It seems an odd place for the King of Spain to send someone."

"Marie, don't you know that Spain ruled New Orleans for longer than France did?"

"I can't believe it. Why don't people speak Spanish, then?"

"Because French is so clearly the better language. The Spaniards were absorbed by the French. Do you want to know about my Spanish grandfather or not?"

"Yes, please, Mémère."

"Very well. José Luis was his name. He came to New Orleans with the Spanish Army in 1769. He used to say that he saw Marie-Hélène from the deck of his ship with a telescope and blew a kiss at her even before he landed. We girls thought that very romantic.

"But of course it wasn't true. The army was in no mood to blow kisses. New Orleans was a French city. The people had been furious when they learned that King Louis, their king, had given them away to his cousin, King Charles of Spain. That was years before José Luis came. The French wouldn't accept the governors sent by Spain or the Spanish laws. They finally drove the Spanish governor away.

"King Charles sent a new governor. He was an Irish mercenary, Alessandro O'Reilly. He came with an armada of ships and two thousand soldiers. He executed the men who led the rebellion and made all the citizens of New Orleans swear allegiance to the King of Spain. They didn't have much choice. There were only about three thousand people in the city, including children, and a thousand of the three thousand were slaves.

"That's when Marie-Hélène's father and mother decided that their daughter had better marry a Spaniard."

Mary shook her head. "I think I like the story better about blowing kisses from the ship."

Her grandmother smiled. "It's a lovely story, I agree. And José Luis did say it. I heard him myself. You must remember both, Marie. The lovely story and the real one. You'll have children someday; the stories of the women who owned the casket are the inheritance of all of them, even though only the eldest daughter can own the treasures."

Mary looked at the painting again. "How did José Luis fall in love with her, then, if not through a telescope?"

Mémère laughed. "There's a mystery about that. Marie-Hélène told us that she took a document to the Cabildo, the government offices, to be notarized for her father and that José Luis asked permission to walk her home. By the time they reached her house, she said, he had proposed."

"You don't think that's true, Mémère?"

"I did when she told me, but I was very young. When I got older I wondered why a young woman would be allowed to go alone to a building filled with men. And why an important official would marry a girl of fourteen with poor parents and no dowry. But by the time I wondered, Marie-Hélène was dead. I couldn't ask her."

"You could have asked your mother."

"Not in a thousand years, Marie. My mother was the first child of the marriage. She wouldn't want to believe she was also the cause of it. It was certainly convenient that she was born while her parents were traveling."

"How naughty you are, Mémère. Is that what you want me to tell my children?"

"Not until they're old enough to hear it, my love. Then they have the right to make up their own minds. It's no kindness to tell your children only romantic tales, Marie. It can confuse them when they're facing the real world." Anne-Marie looked old suddenly.

"Tell me the other stories, Mémère. Marie-Hélène's treasure was the fan. Who did the gloves belong to, and the locket?"

"No more tonight, my dear. My head is throbbing. Ring for Valentine. I'd better go to bed."

Mary stayed in the drawing room with Marie-Hélène's portrait. She put the bracelets on her wrists, then held her hands against the painted ones. They were almost a perfect match.

"Thank you for giving me your bracelets," she said to her great-great-grandmother.

"Oh, no," she said to herself, "you never thanked Mémère. First thing tomorrow."

She sat for a long time in a chair facing the portrait. From time to time she looked down at the bracelets and her spider-fingered hands. She'd never be ashamed of them again.

Heat clamped down on the city as the June days went by. The heavy clouds were oppressive, holding heat near the earth, refusing to release the showers that might provide at least temporary comfort.

Mary had forgotten the degree of irritation and discomfort that prolonged hot, humid weather could cause. She began to regret the elaborate redecorating that she and her grandmother had scheduled for the summer months. She also began to worry about Mémère, who spent more and more time in her darkened room with damp cloths on her forehead and her medicine close at hand.

Valentine told Mary that her grandmother was always weakest in the summer. She needed laudanum to escape the difficulty of breathing the thick gutter-redolent air.

Mary went to see Julien at once. "You've got to take her to the country before she slides back too far to listen to us," she told him. "I can get her to go now, I think. Another week like the last one, and I don't know if I can do it."

"Eleanore and the children are at our house on the Gulf. We'll take Maman down tomorrow."

"You and Valentine can take her. I have to stay in town, Julien. We've made too many arrangements for the decorating. Someone has to supervise." Julien argued, but Mary was adamant. Once she began something, she had to see it through. She compromised about his concern for her being alone in the house. His younger brother Bertrand could move back to his old rooms to protect her and keep her company.

Mary was reasonably certain that Bertrand wouldn't be at home enough to get in the way of the decorators.

The following day she kissed her drug-dazed grandmother goodbye, with the promise that she'd join her as soon as the house was done.

Then she went home to start reshuffling the schedule of work. It could be done much more quickly now that Mémère's siesta time didn't have to be kept quiet. She got interested, then completely involved. She almost forgot the heat. It was exciting to go through swatches and samples; it made up for her loss of her house in Carrollton. She had reluctantly decided to rent it out when she realized that she had no time to take care of it, and she missed it. It was her handiwork.

Bertrand Sazerac was at the house more often than Mary had expected. He was unperturbed by the chaos of furniture being moved out and in, windows that were curtained one day and bare the next, painters and paperhangers on ladders and scaffolding above the normal routes from one door to another. Mary apologized for the inconvenience, but Bertrand just laughed. "Everybody needs some amusement, my dear. I suppose draperies and dresses are what you ladies do for fun."

What he did, Bertrand said, was what every Creole gentlemen did. Dropped in at coffee houses for a small black coffee and conversation with whoever was there; stopped by the Exchange to see how his shares were doing; looked in on the auctions in the Rotunda to talk with any friends who might also be looking in; visited the barroom for a drink or two and some lunch; went to the barber for a shave and hot towel and a manicure; went to his tailor, his shirtmaker, his bootmaker, his hatmaker, the shop that had the latest thing in canes and swords; took his fencing lessons, watched any good matches that were going; attended the theater, the opera, the cockfights and dog fights, the horse races in the spring season, the dinners and receptions and dances and balls in the Season; spent a little time at a house of pleasure from time to time; gambled. Mostly he gambled. At the private clubs for gentlemen only or in the better rooms of the public clubs or at the keno parlors that were in every section of the city. Gambling, Betrand assured Mary, was the principal occupation of every man in New Orleans.

"The fact is," he said, "I'm busy as the proverbial bee day and night. Even so, I'm one of the creatures known as 'fainéant,' 'do-nothing.' Just because I don't go to the same place every day to gamble, like Julien at his bank or Roland at his cotton brokerage. Never have understood it."

Bertrand generally ate dinner with Mary. Usually they had it in the courtyard, with the gate to the street open to invite any stray breezes.

One evening it invited Philippe Courtenay.

"I thought we were going to meet at Hewlett's for some faro," said Bertrand. "Sit down and have a coffee."

Philippe bowed to Mary. "Bonsoir, Mademoiselle MacAlistair."

Mary held out her hand. "It's good to see you again, Philippe. Don't be so formal, for goodness' sake. Sit down. And call me Mary as you used to."

Philippe shook her hand vigorously. "Good to see you, too, Mary."

"I didn't know you two were friends," said Bertrand. "Is this a romance I'm interrupting?"

"Certainly not," Mary said.

Philippe looked at his boots.

Bertrand chuckled. "I'll just go up to my room and get my cigar case." He left before Mary could object.

"I'm sorry, Philippe," she said. "Bertrand likes to tease. I hope he didn't embarrass you. Believe me, I don't for a minute think that you're here to court me."

"But I am," Philippe mumbled. He took a deep breath and his voice strengthened. "Look here, Mary, I've got to say this fast or I'll never get it out. So be quiet, please, until I finish.

"We got along fine last summer. I figure we could keep on getting along fine. Now that you're a Sazerac and respectable I can marry you. How about it?"

Mary studied his beet-red, agonized face. She felt a great temptation to tease him, but she resisted. "No, Philippe," she said.

"What did I do wrong? You're supposed to say yes."

"For one thing, Philippe, it's customary to say something about love."

"Hell, Mary, I like you. That's a lot better—I apologize for cursing."

"That's all right. And I like you, too. But I don't want to marry you. So that's that. Now tell me what you've been doing. Are you still at your uncle's plantation?"

"Just a minute, Mary. That's not that, yet. Let me tell you something. The minute everyone learned you were a Sazerac, my father told me to rush in and marry you, before anyone else did. Because you're going to be so rich. I told him to go to hell.

"He had put the idea in my head, though, and it wouldn't go away. Of marrying you, I mean. You know what I'm like, Mary. Women make me nervous with their simpering and twittering. You never did. I never thought about marrying you because it was impossible. I'm not rich enough to take a wife with no dowry. Plus everybody knows I'm a bastard, so I can't have a nobody for a wife. Now you're somebody and you're rich. I want you to marry me.

"But I want you to marry me because I like you. I'm not asking you because you're somebody and rich. I'm asking you because you're you. The other men who ask you aren't going to know or care who you are. They'll be after the Sazerac heiress.

"So you'd do better to marry me. Think about it." He leaned back in his chair, folded his arms across his chest, waited.

Mary thought. Then, "No. You're right, I'm sure. But no, thank you all the same."

"You're just being dumb, Mary. What is it? Have you set your cap for somebody else?"

"No," Mary said quickly. "I'm just not ready to get married. Maybe I never will be."

"When you get ready, will you marry me?"

"I don't know. Don't bully me, Philippe."

"I'll ask you again, later."

"Wait until the Season. Mémère is very traditional."

"All right. I'll see you at the opera. Where's old Bertrand? We've got a game set up for tonight." Philippe went into the house, calling.

Mary sat alone at the table, laughing quietly. The blossoms on the orange trees in the courtyard surrounded her with sweetness. The fountain reflected fragments of silver, the face of the moon in tumbling water. In the distance, someone was playing a guitar and singing a ballad.

So much for romance, she thought.

But she remembered what Philippe had said.

A few days later she was looking at fringes for the dining room draperies when she heard a familiar cry.

"May-ree!"

She turned in time to receive Jeanne's hug and kiss.

"Oh, May-ree, is it true that you're going to marry Philippe? I'm so happy. We will be real sisters, yes?"

"No, Jeanne, no. It's not true."

Jeanne pouted. "You're just being a secret slyboots, May-ree, I know it. Maman told me he proposed. You must have said yes. He's so handsome, and you flirted with him so at Montfleury. I know you love him."

"Jeanne, I am not going to marry Philippe. I haven't even been presented yet. I can't marry anyone." Mary spoke as firmly as she knew how, and in terms that Jeanne would immediately understand, to shut her up.

"Of course! You want to have all the beaux first. I'll be good, Mayree. Quiet as a mouse."

It had worked. Mary smiled. "How are you, Jeanne?"

"Wonderful. I am doing over my boudoir, as you see. All these laces, I just cannot choose." She grabbed Mary's arm. "Come with me, Mayree, to my house. You can tell me what I should do. You're so clever. We'll have a coffee and talk and talk, just as we used to."

There was an urgency in Jeanne's grasp and in her eyes. Mary went with her.

# 57

Mary had almost forgotten how Jeanne could rattle on without, seemingly, even needing to draw breath. All the way to her big house on Esplanade Avenue Jeanne talked about the dance she had given for Mary. How wounded she was that Mary didn't come, what a shame it was that Mary had missed it, what a beautiful party it was, who was there, wearing what, dancing with whom.

She kept it up until they were in her bedroom. Then she closed the door and bolted it. "May-ree," she said, "I have so much to tell you!"

Mary removed her bonnet and gloves and sat down.

Jeanne did indeed have a lot to tell. It chilled Mary's blood to hear it.

Jeanne was completely spellbound by Marie Laveau. She had her hair dressed every day so that she could see the Voodoo Queen and talk to her. She even manufactured discontent with her rooms and a need to redecorate them in order to stay in the city when everyone was going away for the summer. She couldn't bear to leave Marie.

Marie still supplied her with abortifacients; Jeanne now depended on her for other things as well. Oils and salves to keep her beautiful. Powders to put in her wine to make her sleep. Gris-gris for protection against sadness, illness, enemies, aging.

Jeanne was giving Marie her jewels, one by one, in payment.

Mary tried to interrupt Jeanne, to reason with her. Jeanne didn't need any of those things. She was young and beautiful and she had no enemies, no cause for sorrow or sleeplessness.

Jeanne didn't seem even to hear her. She talked on and on, growing more excited by the moment. Marie Laveau had granted her special favors, she said. She was permitted to attend voodoo ceremonies at Marie's house. She was an initiate. It was the most thrilling experience of her life.

"You must come, too, next time, May-ree. You're rich now. You can afford it. There are lots of white women there; you needn't feel afraid. I'll ask Marie for you if you may come. May-ree, you've never known anything so wonderful."

Mary stood up. "I've never heard anything so horrible. Jeanne, you must stop this. You're destroying yourself. You're acting like a crazy person. Marie Laveau is only a hairdresser. She's not magic. All this voodoo nonsense is nothing but a trick. You've got more sense than this. You're not an ignorant slave dancing in Congo Square."

Jeanne's eyes narrowed. "You're nothing but an American. You don't know anything. Marie knows everything. She reads my fortune. She warns me. There's a woman, a witch, who turned herself into an image of me. I've seen her. Marie told me where to look. I carried my gris-gris in my hand when I knocked on her door. She opened it, and I was looking at myself!"

Oh, my God, thought Mary. Cécile Dulac. Jeanne musn't know that she's her sister. She braced herself for Jeanne's next words.

"The witch took my image to steal Valmont Saint-Brévin from me. She's his mistress."

The name struck Mary like a hammer. She knew, she had known for a long time that Cécile was his placée. But she had managed to forget.

It's nothing to me, she said to herself, just as she had done when she first learned about it. She sank into the chair, despising herself for the weakness in her legs. She hadn't been prepared to hear his name.

"See!" Jeanne said, triumphant. "I'm right to listen to Marie. She knows."

"Jeanne, you mustn't. It's dangerous."

"I'm not afraid. I have gris-gris. I can buy more. Nothing will happen to me."

Mary felt sick.

"Marie's more powerful than the witch. She made a spell for me, May-ree, against her. And it is working. She's losing Valmont. He's going to marry a rich woman from Charleston. Philippe told me all about it. In July he's going to take his big ship to her home for the wedding."

"I'll be going away next month, Cécile." Val stretched his long legs out in front of the chair and poured another brandy.

"Yes, I know." Cécile sipped her coffee. "Bon voyage."

Val held his temper in check. Cécile's distant calm irritated him more every time he came to the Saint Peter Street house. She never spoke except in response to something he said. He knew no more about what went on in her mind and heart than he knew about the reasons for the wind. But he felt responsible for her.

"Why don't you let me send you to France, Cécile? I have friends there who would guide you. Your brother's there. You could have a good life, a good marriage, a home and family."

"We've talked about this before, Valmont. I don't want to go to France."

Val hesitated. He could take Cécile to Canada. His ship was at anchor in a small bayou near the plantation. Everything was ready for the trip. Runaway slaves were concealed at Benison, waiting. They had come from upriver and down, east and west, many more of them than he had envisioned. The news of the earlier successful voyage had filtered through the entire network of the Underground Railroad.

Perhaps the sense of freedom and purpose of the black community in Canada was what Cécile really wanted. But he didn't know. He didn't know anything about her. And, not knowing, he couldn't trust her. Too many lives were in his hands. He couldn't risk their safety.

He drank his brandy in silence.

Silence was always plentiful at the house.

When his glass was empty Val stood up and left without a word.

Cécile stretched like a cat, smiled. The day she was waiting for had almost arrived.

Val rode hard to the plantation. When he arrived, his horse was lathered and he was dripping with sweat. "Cool him down," he told a stableboy, handing him the reins. He slapped the horse on the rump. "Sorry, old boy. I had to get away from the stink of the city as fast as possible."

He dunked his head in the trough of water near the stables, shook it dry; it made him feel much better. He was whistling when he walked toward the house.

His butler Nehemiah came down the steps to meet him. The expression on the old man's face stopped Val in mid-song.

"Trouble," he said. "What kind?"

"Two more runaways, Maître. A man and a boy. They came two nights ago in a canoe."

Val clapped Nehemiah on the shoulder. "You shouldn't scare me like that. From your face I thought a patrol was here. We can find room someplace for two more."

"The boy's sick today. I put him in the hospital."

"Bad sick?"

"It might be the fever."

Val changed direction at once, turned toward the slave cabins and the small building near the chapel that they called the hospital. If the boy had yellow fever, the ship couldn't sail. No one knew how the fever was transmitted. But it was almost certain that it would spread. On shipboard there was no escaping the contagion, and anyone who had been near the boy might carry it.

He heard the sounds of grief and fear before he reached the building. Men and women were gathered outside, chanting, moaning, praying. Waiting for him.

A woman rushed forward. "He's dead, Maître. Not two minutes ago. He vomited black, then he died."

Vomit black with blood was the final phase of yellow fever.

Val jumped to the top of a wide tree stump. "Get some lye solution from the storerooms," he said, "and scrub out your cabins. We won't let Bronze John come to Benison. The ship will sail. Later than we thought, but it will sail, I promise you."

# 58

It was like a repetition of the week before. Mary and Bertrand were dining in the courtyard. Candles flickered on the table. Philippe Courtenay walked in without an invitation. Mary started to speak sharply to him, but Philippe didn't give her time.

"Mary, have you seen Jeanne?" He was nearly distraught. "Her maid doesn't know where she is. No one knows. Milly came to Papa's house looking for her."

"Calm down, Philippe. Jeanne's a grown woman, not a child. She's probably visiting a friend." Mary hoped she sounded believable. She couldn't help thinking of the rumors about Jeanne and of the scene in Carrollton. Perhaps she was meeting her lover somewhere.

Philippe took the chair Bertrand pulled out for him with a nod of thanks. But he spoke only to Mary. It was as if he were reading her mind. "I shook Milly until her eyes nearly fell out of her head. I'm sure she's telling the truth. Jeanne hasn't gone to meet a man. None of her good dresses are missing, and she didn't have her hairdresser in today. Milly confessed that there's a regular routine for my sister's indiscretions.

"Thank God Berthe is away. Papa is bad enough. It was all I could do to keep him from killing Milly."

Bertrand poured a glass of wine for Philippe. "Drink this. She'll show up. Mary's right. She'd probably gossiping her little heart out with some friend. Complaining about their husbands more than likely. Take a leaf from my book, Philippe, and stay a bachelor. No matter how charming the temptation." He raised his glass in salute to Mary.

Philippe groaned. "Her husband complaining about Jeanne is more likely. Graham has been in Baton Rouge on business. He's on his way home right now as far as we know. What's he going to say if he gets home tonight to find his wife missing? He's not blind. He's already hinted to Papa that he might return Jeanne and her dowry and get a divorce."

Bertrand delighted in scandal. "What did Carlos say?"

"He threatened to horsewhip Graham. He doesn't believe a word of the talk that's going around. He can't. It would destroy him to think that his little girl was less than perfect."

Mary had been wondering whether to tell what she was thinking. She decided that she had to. "Jeanne might be at her hairdresser's house,

Philippe. She's been there before, I know. The woman's name is Marie Laveau; she stages some kind of voodoo ceremonies."

"Marie Laveau!" the two men exclaimed in unison. Bertrand crossed himself three times.

"You've heard of her?" Mary asked.

"Bertrand," Philippe shouted, "do you realize what day this is? June twenty-third."

"Saint John's Eve," said Bertrand. He stood up so hastily that his chair toppled over with a crash. "I'll get my things."

"What are you talking about?" Mary demanded. "Where are you going? What is Saint John's Eve?"

Saint John's Eve, Philippe told her, was the most important night of the year for voodoo worshipers. Every year they met at a secret place on the shore of Lake Pontchartrain. Always a different place. Always secluded. There were always the curious who searched for it. Almost never did anyone succeed in finding it. And so horrible were the ceremonies that those who had seen them would never talk about it.

"We've got to go after Jeanne, hopeless or not," he said.

"I'm going with you," said Mary.

"Absolutely not." Bertrand was back.

They wasted time debating Mary's conviction that she would have more influence over Jeanne than they. While they were arguing, Carlos Courtenay came in search of Philippe. When he understood what they were talking about, he settled things. "What difference does it make who does what as long as we find her?" he shouted. "Philippe, go to the livery stable and tell them to saddle some horses. We'll follow you."

Mary had forgotten how much she disliked riding and how poorly she did it. It required all her powers of will and concentration to keep up with the others. She had no time to be frightened by the eerieness of the white Shell Road illuminated by the torch in Carlos Courtenay's hand. She even forgot her old anger at Carlos in her new anger that he was riding so fast.

When they reached the lake and turned into the swampy woods, they slowed to a walk. Then there was time for fear. The torch woke and frightened birds and unseen animals that bolted away, making sharp sudden noises in the darkness that surrounded them. Vines and Spanish moss, unseen, touched Mary's face, making her want to scream. Everything was hidden, unknown, menacing.

No one spoke. They were straining to hear sounds that might guide them. It was, Mary thought, like being lost in the dark woods alone, the terror of every childhood tale. She told herself that she was no longer a child. But the terror mounted with every slithering sound, every brushing across her face.

They blundered through trees and marshes for what seemed an eternity in a hell of nightmarish darkness. Then they entered a clearing. Mary saw stars overhead, felt space on all sides. She bit her lip to keep from sobbing with relief.

"This is futile," said Bertrand. "We could go on like this for hours without finding anything. The lake is twenty-six miles across; who knows how long the shoreline is, with all the bays and inlets? We need a boat. There must be light for the ceremony. We'd see it from the water. Follow me." He turned in the direction of the lake and plunged into the woods again.

"There's a trail," he called out after a minute.

It led to a dock. And a boat.

Philippe tied the horses to trees while Carlos forced the base of the torch into the shale alongside the water, to guide them when they returned.

"Thank God," said Bertrand. "I've found the oars."

They cast off, onto the warm, measureless waters, Bertrand rowing.

When he tired, Carlos took over.

Then Philippe.

Then Bertrand again.

Staying close to the dark shore, they moved steadily, quietly, the only sound the soft splash as the oars lifted from the water, bit in again.

Until, far away, felt more than heard, there was the beat, beat, beat of drumming.

It entered their bloodstreams when they were nearer, became the oars' rhythm, the in and out of their breath.

The shoreline bent; they rounded a promontory. Ahead were the leaping flames of giant bonfires, lighting the waters that reflected them, making the shadows behind them even darker than the night the flames held back. The beat of the drums was distinct now: Badoum, badoum, badoum, badoum. Incessant. Insidious. Mesmerizing.

Bertrand dug deep into the lake with one oar. "We'd best land and approach through the woods." His voice was calm, conversational. But the words fell on the accents of the drums.

• • •

The bonfires marked the corners of a huge clearing on the lake shore. A smaller fire burned in the center. On it there was a giant black iron cauldron. A low platform stood between the cauldron and the lakeside edge of the clearing. It held a table with a wooden box in the center of it.

The drum sound vibrated everywhere. Badoum, badoum, badoum, badoum, badoum.

The clearing was empty, waiting. In the shadows between the bonfires, shifting featureless forms made rustling, breathing noises, noises of anticipation and pent-up excitement. Badoum, said the air, badoum, badoum.

Mary grabbed hold of Philippe's arm. She needed something tangible, recognizable, human to hold onto. She had to force her feet to move toward the dreadful firelit emptiness.

Bertrand turned, held out his arms to stop the others. "We have to wait until we can see the people," he said. "Jeanne may not be here." His words quivered, their pitch high and thin. He moved each of them to a vantage point in the shadow of one of the trees that edged the clearing.

Mary put her arms around a thin trunk, rubbed her cheek against its rough bark. She wished she needn't stand alone. She could feel the drums through the soles of her feet, through the trunk of the tree, in the air that she breathed. Badoum, badoum, badoum . . . doum . . . doum . . . doum . . .

They were quickening, stronger, louder, more insistent. Mary let go of the tree, held her hands over her ears, but it did no good. The reverberations penetrated her very skin, pounded inside her head, her chest, her stomach. She felt as if the earth was shaking under her feet. She grabbed frantically for the tree trunk.

Another sound was added to the drums, this one fainter but piercing, high and eerie.

Then the shadows exploded. Men with gleaming black skin leapt from all sides into the clearing. Their bodies were nude except for red loincloths and strings of tiny bells tied around their knees and ankles. Their bare feet pounded the flattened grass in time with the beat of the drums and they turned, turned in tight circles, dancing, leaping, then dancing, bells ringing. They were everywhere, spinning, leaping, eyes and teeth flashes of white against dark skin, dozens of them, hundreds, red and black and white blurring together to the spinning, stamping, and drums and bells.

Women ran from the darkness, dancing, bare arms and heads and feet, bodies moving beneath thin white cotton shifts that clung to their twisting, sweaty hips and abdomens and swelling breasts and buttocks. One ran to the cauldron with a chicken flapping and fighting in her raised hands. She threw it into the bubbling liquid with a scream. Another followed her, then another and yet another and another, throwing living creatures, frogs and snails and birds and a yowling black cat, dancing and turning and leaping after each offering.

Mary tried to turn her head away, but she could not. She could only cling to the solidity of the tree.

Suddenly the dancing stopped, and the drums. The quiet was more terrifying than the sacrifices.

A woman strode into the clearing, into the quiet. Gold bracelets on her arms slid and struck one another, making a muted crashing that was unnaturally loud in the hushed clearing. She was wearing a fluttering garment made of red bandanas knotted together, held at the waist by a blue cord. Her black hair cascaded over her shoulders and down her back. Bright gold hoops in her earlobes glinted through locks of hair.

She stepped up on the platform, turned to face the silent dancers. Firelight was golden on her regal bronze face.

Mary drew in her breath. It was Marie Laveau.

The Voodoo Queen raised her arms. She spoke, as if to herself and the skies, the words a near whisper, but penetrating to the farthest corner of the clearing.

"L'Appé vini..."

Badoum, badoum. The drums began again. Mary strained to understand, but the language was only part French.

"L'Appé vini, le Grand Zombi." Badoum, badoum, badoum, badoum, badoum, badoum.

> L'Appé vini, le Grand Zombi,
> L'Appé vini, pou fé gris-gris!

The men and women in the clearing began to sway to the cadence, to chant with Marie.

"L'Appé vini, le Grand Zombi..." Badoum, badoum. "L'Appé vini, pou fé gris-gris!"

"Le Grand Zombi, Zombi, Zombi." The chanting grew louder, the drums more pronounced.

A man ran from the shadows to Marie's feet, his hands stretched to her holding a small white goat by its legs. The kid's thin bleating excited the chanting crowd, and they began to stamp their feet. "Zombi, Zombi, Zombi." The shouting melded into the steady beat of the drums.

There was a flash of reflected firelight on the knife that Marie Laveau lifted from the table behind her. She took the kid into the cradle of her left arm and plunged the knife into its throat. Blood spurted onto her breasts and shoulders. She held the sacrifice out; the kid's blood pumped into a bowl held by the waiting man below the platform. The stamping feet and swaying bodies were a single beat, single movement, staring at their queen.

Mary looked for Jeanne, but the light of the bonfires made all faces, all swaying bodies into one confused mass of flickering brightness.

Then there was a long, animal, wordless cry as if from the single throat of the swaying mass.

She saw that the Voodoo Queen was drinking from the bowl.

Marie Laveau moved quickly then. In one motion she put the bowl on the table, opened the box waiting there, held high the great, thick, twisting snake that was locked in it.

"Zombi! Zombi! Zombi!" The shouts were deafening.

Marie lifted her face, the lips wet with blood. Her body was writhing, feet together, immobile, hips and knees and waist and shoulders moving, undulating, mirroring the sinuous folding and unfolding length of the snake in her hands, as it slowly twisted itself around her body, slid across her bare shoulders and neck, brought its flat triangular head to her face. Its tongue flickered forward to her cheek, then to her chin, at last to her lips again and again until it had taken the last drop of blood.

"Aie! Aie! Voodoo Magnian!" Marie screamed. Her writhing grew more frenzied, matched by the drums, and she caressed the snake, holding its head to her throat, her breasts, while its coils moved over her legs, buttocks, quivering stomach, jutting pelvis.

"Eh! Eh! Bomba hé! hé!" she cried.

Canga bafie té
Danga moune de té
Canga do ki li!
Canga li! Canga li! Canga li!

The crowd took up the chant and the frenzy. "Eh! Eh! Bomba hé! hé!" The stamping, turning, jumping was wilder, faster, pierced by cries. The bowl of blood passed from hand to hand. Marie Laveau reached forward to the hands reaching for her. Her body was twitching, jerking, twisting. The drums pounded in furious crescendo.

She clasped the hand nearest her. Its owner leapt into the air with a scream of ecstatic pain, as if he had been seared by electric shock. He touched the hands nearest him, and a woman screamed.

The power was passing from the snake-god Zombi through his queen to her people. From hand to hand in a frenzy of touching, screaming, leaping, dancing. Until the clearing was a sea of dervishes spinning to unconsciousness.

A man fell as if dead, then a woman, another woman. The dance continued, trampling them.

Mary crouched at the foot of the tree, trembling with fear and with the surging of her blood, driven by the heartbeat racing to match the drums.

She looked for Philippe, Bertrand, Carlos, but they were hidden as she was.

Then she saw Jeanne.

Her shift was torn, one breast exposed. It was streaked with blood; stains blotched the corners of her mouth. She whirled past the trees, and Mary could hear her laughing, more growl than laugh, an inhuman sound.

Branches crashed as Carlos Courtenay lunged forward, fell under the weight of his son. "No, Papa," Mary heard. "They'd tear you apart."

"Jeanne," Carlos cried. A hand muffled his voice.

Mary could hear the noise close by, beneath the drums and mad cries of the dancers. Bertrand and Philippe dragged Carlos back from the firelit edge of the clearing. "Don't look," they urged him.

Don't look, Mary told herself. But she could not turn away.

"I must," Carlos groaned.

Marie Laveau was dancing alone, the snake-god back in its cabalistically marked cage. She had become Zombi, with the god's power and the god's unearthly boneless undulation. Her arms and hands slithered over her body, tearing off the red bandanas, throwing them into the flames, until she was naked, beautiful, shining with sweat. "Canga li!" she cried, "Canga li!"

"Canga li!" the cry rose from hundreds of throats. First one, then ten, then forty loincloths were thrown into the bonfire; naked black and brown men jumped high, bells ringing, flaunting their virility. Their arms seized gyrating female bodies and flung them to the ground.

"Canga li!" In an instant the dancing changed into an orgiastic scene of horror. Naked men and women crawled on all fours, howling, biting, ripping away cloth, grappling, copulating, savaging the bodies nearest, indiscriminate of age or sex or color. Mary saw Madame Alphande, and Mademoiselle Annette, and the Creole matron from the house opposite her grandmother's.

Jeanne's laughter ran out close by. Then her exquisite pale body ran past, tumbled over a heap of dark forms and burrowed into their midst, shouting, "Me, Me, Me!"

A different laugh came from the woods behind Mary. Cécile Dulac walked gracefully by Mary's hiding place. "Michie Carlos," she said. "Are you enjoying yourself? I brought Mr. Graham to keep you company."

# 59

Mary stayed in her room for two days after the horror of Saint John's Eve. She didn't want to look at anyone, man or woman, black or white. She wanted to forget what she had seen, what she had felt, what she had dreamed when at last she was safe, she thought, in her own home, her own room, her own bed.

You can't hide forever, she told herself at the end of the forty-eight hours. You have to face the world.

No, I don't, she answered herself. I can run away. At least for a little while.

She tucked the most recent letter from her grandmother into her handbag and went to talk to Julien at his office.

The following day she was on a boat on her way to Julien's summer house on the Gulf. "Mémère keeps begging me to come," Mary had told him. "I can arrange to go for a week."

Julien encouraged her to go. He knew from Bertrand what had happened on Saint John's Eve. Mary's haunted appearance told him the effect it was having on her.

Mary had never imagined that water could be as beautiful as the greens and blues and turquoises of the Gulf of Mexico. "I think I must be dreaming," she exclaimed to her grandmother.

"It's like a dream come true for me, Marie, having you here. I've missed you."

"I've missed you, too, Mémère." To Mary's surprise her automatic response was largely true. When she wasn't drugged, Anne-Marie Sazerac was very good company. Mary never tired of hearing anecdotes about her mother's childhood or about the lives of the myriad cousins who lived or had lived in New Orleans.

Mary had also discovered that her grandmother was really the one who made the big house on Royal Street operate smoothly; even when she was incapacitated by opium, the slaves' loyalty and affection made them do their best work so that her comfort was assured. When Mémère went away, rivalry and dissension and an impulse to test Mary's strength brought one servant after another to her, asking for decisions, for preference, for indulgence. She was always uncomfortable when talking to the servants. She was unable to shed her abhorrence of slavery, and they made her feel guilty just by being there in the house.

She'd be glad when the hot days were done with and her grandmother came back to the city.

"You'll be pleased with the house, I think, Mémère. The decorating is almost done. Let me tell you about the man I found to repair the gold leaf on the ceiling medallions..."

Throughout the long lazy afternoons Mary and her grandmother rocked in the big chairs on the wide breeze-swept porch overlooking the water, sometimes reading, sometimes talking, sometimes lost in private thoughts. Mémère had commandeered the afternoons as her own, the porch as her own place. "I adore my grandchildren," she said, "but not all day long."

Mary quickly learned what made Mémère say that. Julien and Eleanore's seven children ranged from Paul, fourteen, to Auguste, two. Even though she was only three years older than Paul, Mary felt old and exhausted after a morning with the children. She welcomed her grandmother's invitation to share the serenity of the porch.

One afternoon they talked again about the casket's treasures. Mary asked if the glove had belonged to her mother.

"Oh, no, my dear. Your mother's fingers were just like anyone else's. That's why your hands were so astonishing to me. I was sure that the family trait had vanished, that my mother was the last. All the Maries had them, before me. Probably that's why the first Marie that we know about came to New Orleans. She might have simply been poor, and, without a dowry, unable to marry. I prefer to believe the story that's been handed down in the family. It says that she was the first to have the long little fingers and that she was suspected of being a witch. People believed in witches in those days."

Some still do, Mary thought, remembering Jeanne's hysteria. "So Marie Duclos came to America. What happened here?" She urged Mémère to speak. She didn't want to remember anything more about Jeanne.

"She married one of the King's soldiers; that's what she and the other casket girls were sent to do. France had sent women before the casket girls, but most of them didn't marry. They didn't want the hard life of mother and wife in a new colony. Instead they kept on with the profession that had sent them to the prisons where the King's men found them to start with. They were prostitutes. And thieves.

"They must have laughed at the casket girls. I sometimes wonder if any of the casket girls joined their ranks. Tradition doesn't tell us.

"Anyhow, we know that Marie Duclos didn't. She married a foot soldier named André Villandry, and they had fourteen children, of whom five lived to adulthood."

Mary was shocked. "Nine of her children died? Why? That's terrible."

"Children have always died, Marie, and it's always terrible. They die at birth, in epidemics, in accidents, for reasons that have no name. The Marie who owned the glove was the third baby to be named Marie. The two previous died in infancy. Our Marie was called Jeanne-Marie. She was born in 1732. New Orleans was barely fourteen years old.

"They called the city squares 'islands' then because whenever it rained the ditches that separated them filled with water and made islands of them. There were planks from one to another for bridges over the deep water in the streets. Planks on the sides of them, too, to walk on over the mud. They were the first banquettes. There were no more than five hundred people in the city, including children and slaves. I suppose that everyone knew everyone else even more then than now. It's said that there were fewer than a hundred houses, and they were hardly more than huts.

"But the Place d'Armes was there. And a church, and a convent for the Ursuline nuns. The sisters civilized Louisiana. They were nurses, teachers, most of all optimists. Can you imagine? In the middle of mud and rain and floods and hurricanes, they cultivated mulberry trees with their medicinal herbs. Then they raised silkworms and taught young women how to harvest the silk and weave it into fabric for dresses.

"I digress. We were talking about Jeanne-Marie's glove. She must have been about ten years old when a truly incredible man was sent from France to be the new governor. He was the Marquis de Vaudrieul. His wife, the Marquise, came with him. Also a regular retinue of courtiers. They acted as if the mud-brick governor's house was Versailles. They brought shiploads of furniture, silver, mirrors, carpets, clothing, wigs, cosmetics, even a state carriage with a matched team of four white horses. The Marquise and her lady-in-waiting would ride in it through the streets whenever the mud wasn't too deep, nodding graciously to the ordinary women who were tending their vegetables and chickens and pigs and children in the plots of land outside their homes.

"Naturally all the young girls, including Jeanne-Marie, wanted to be like the Marquise instead of like their own mothers. She wasn't very happy when her soldier father betrothed her to a tanner. Giles Chalon was a good match. He was a good tanner, and there was always a market for leather. His wife would never want for food or shelter. Unfortunately he had lost one eye in the war with the Indians that was going on. And, of course, there's nothing that stinks worse than a tannery.

"Nevertheless, marry Giles she did. She must have made him happy. She gave him five sons and five daughters. And to please her, he moved the tannery away from their cottage when the Indian wars finally ended, and he made her a pair of gloves fine enough for a Marquise."

"That's a charming story, Mémère."

"All the women of our family have had charm, Marie. Remember, the daughter of Jeanne-Marie Chalon was my grandmother, Marie-Hélène, of the portrait in our drawing room. It must have pleased her mother greatly when her daughter became far more elegant than the Marquise de Vaudrieul."

Mary was stunned. She hadn't made the connection. It seemed impossible that the woman in the painting had even been anything other than a great lady.

"Did Marie-Hélène become too elegant? Did she look down her nose at her parents?"

Mémère laughed. "You still have a lot to learn about families, my child. Marie-Hélène's father was given a contract to supply all the leather goods for the Spanish Army in Louisiana. Naturally he made a fortune without ever again touching the skin of an animal. He built the big house your cousin Christophe lives in. Christophe's father was my uncle Laurent, Marie-Hélène's elder brother. He was a government official. Her other brothers and her sisters' husbands were well taken care of, too."

Mary held up her hands. "Stop, Mémère. I get miserably confused when you start rattling off the uncles' and cousins' names."

"You'll learn, Marie. It just takes time."

"I'll never even learn all the names," Mary moaned. Julien came down from the city for the celebrations on July Fourth. Seventeen relations came with him, all cousins to one degree or another. Mary watched with admiration approaching awe while Eleanore calmly supervised the details of arranging food and bedding for her unexpected guests. Cots, hammocks, cribs, pillows, linens, and a quick rearrangement of her children's allotted sleeping places gave everyone a place to stay for as long as he or she liked in the six-bedroom cottage.

Julien also brought fireworks. Old and young ate watermelon on the beach while the sun set, then exclaimed noisily as rocket after rocket soared into the dark sky and scattered colorful new stars across it. Other people at other cottages were celebrating the same way. For more than an hour there were fireworks as far as the eye could see.

Mary thought about the previous Fourth of July and the fireworks then. What a happy change to be here in the midst of her family instead of alone, terrified, on the city street among shouting, menacing strangers.

The curly head of a cousin was silhouetted against a burst of red light, and she remembered Valmont Saint-Brévin coming to her aid the year before. He was like a knight of old. How could she have known how cruel his heart was? She concentrated on the beauty of the evening before the surge of anger and hatred could spoil it for her.

The next morning Julien invited Mary to walk along the beach with him, leaving the others behind. "I wanted to talk with you before I made any decision, Mary. I have a recent letter from the director of the rest home where Celeste is. He's of the opinion that some time with her family might restore her to normalcy. Eleanore is willing to have her here. There'll be a trained companion from the home, of course.

"But I won't authorize the visit if you're against it. Celeste injured you beyond forgiving, I know that."

Mary smiled at him. "Don't worry, Julien, you can do whatever you think best. I was already planning to go back to New Orleans with you on Sunday. I've been here a day longer than I intended, and I'm longing to see the new curtains hung in Mémère's sitting room.

"Besides, there's no newspaper down here. I confess, I've been missing the installments of *Ange Pitou* in *The Bee.* The poor doctor hero was in terrible trouble when I left him."

Bertrand was delighted to have Mary home again. "My dear niece," he said solemly, "I almost torched the house a minimum of ten times. The painters you hired positively lurk outside my door. First they make tremendous crashing noises when they set up their ladders. Then, when I open my door to shout at them, they try to paint me a most bilious shade of green."

"I am sorry to have deserted you that way, Bertrand. I needed to get as far away from Lake Pontchartrain as I could. That was a ghastly evening."

"That it was. We should never have let you go with us." His eyes were bright with the joy of new scandals. "The Courtenay-Graham marriage is being annulled. Who can guess what it's costing poor Carlos. One never sees him anywhere any more. They say he's a broken man. Berthe has taken Jeanne on retreat at a convent in Mississippi. I hope she made sure the walls were high."

The look on Mary's face made him stop talking. "Forgive me, my dear. I forgot she was a friend of yours. I'll tell you something more cheerful. I saved all copies of *The Bee.* You can have a good wallow in the chapters you missed."

Alexandre Dumas's hero was still in trouble. Even more complications afflicted the brave man in chapter sixty-four than had surrounded him in chapter fifty-six. She enjoyed her breakfast coffee more every day, happily sharing the doctor's printed tribulations before tackling the real difficulties of persuading the painters to try just one more time to mix a little more blue into the green paint for the upstairs woodwork.

On July sixteenth, the fictional doctor's troubles suddenly became insignificant. The *Bee's* headline was a single word: EPIDEMIC.

Two hundred people had died of yellow fever in the previous week.

# 60

Two. Hundred. People.

Mary couldn't believe it. She had had the fever herself. It was unpleasant, but not deadly. How could so many people die?

Perhaps they were all babies or little children. Jeanne's brothers and sisters had died of fever, she remembered. Little children.

She read the paper again, more slowly. People, it said, not children. She turned the page over, read the story in English. People, it said.

At that moment she heard Bertrand's voice, talking to one of the servants. Mary poured a coffee for him. He'd be able to explain.

"Bonjour, Marie. Is that coffee for me? Good girl."

"Bonjour, Bertrand. *The Bee* has the most astonishing story. I wanted to ask you about it."

"The fever, you mean? Yes, I know. Jacques came and woke me. He's packing for me now. How soon will you be ready to leave?"

"'Leave'? I don't want to go any place."

"Don't be ridiculous, Marie. Of course we're going to leave. If the newpaper is reporting an epidemic, it means that people have been dying from it for weeks. They always hush it up as long as they can. Everyone who can afford it will be getting out of the city. We've got to go now while we can still find transportation."

Mary could barely recognize this man as laughing, devil-may-care Bertrand. His hand was rattling his cup in its saucer, and his mouth twitched at one corner. He was terrified.

"Don't look at me like that," he half shouted at Mary. "You don't know what it's like. An epidemic isn't the usual summer fever that kills a couple of hundred immigrants. An epidemic kills everybody. I remember the last one, in '32. I was eighteen, a man, and Papa made me help. Julien and Roland, too. We had to go through the streets and carry the fallen we found there. To the hospital or to the cemetery. There were so many. Sick, revoltingly sick. Or stiff, covered with the death vomit, their black tongues hanging out of their mouths. It went on and on for months, I tell you. It was hell. Putrefying, stinking, filthy hell. We've got to go while we can. Pack some things. Or go without them, I don't care. We've got to go."

"Where to, Bertrand?"

"To the lake. Our hotel. They'll have to find room for us. But we've got to go now. Everyone else will be trying to get our rooms." His eyes shifted from side to side as if he were searching for a way out of the tranquil courtyard.

"There! Do you hear that?" Bertrand dashed toward the gate. "I knew it," he shouted. "See for yourself."

Mary ran to his side. On the street beyond the gate a carriage was driving past.

"We've got to hurry." He shook her arm. "Why aren't you packing?"

The street was quiet again.

"I'm not going with you, Bertrand," Mary said. "I've already had the fever. I'm not worried. And I've got too much still to do on the house."

Jacques came up behind them carrying two valises. "Here's your luggage, Michie Bertrand."

Bertrand looked at Mary, read the determination in her face, turned away. "Carry those for me to the railroad, Jacques. I'll be able to get a boat at the lake to take me to the hotel. If I hurry."

Mary watched her urbane, dapper uncle scurry away, his shoulders hunched as if to ward off a blow. He looked almost furtive.

She returned to her chair and read the Dumas serial. But she couldn't remember one paragraph while she was reading the next one. Bertrand wasn't a cowardly man. He had been as cool as ice in the terrifying expedition on Saint John's Eve. If the word "epidemic" had such an effect on him, it must be truly horrible. Maybe she was wrong. Maybe she should leave the city, too.

Then she heard the painters arriving, and she put the yellow fever out of her mind. Today they were definitely going to get the color right, or she'd tell them to paint the woodwork blue and be done with it. Of course that would mean that the curtains wouldn't look right. She'd have to use them in another room, maybe the small guest room on the third floor. No, the larger one would be better. But that would mean... She folded the paper and got to work.

It started to rain at midday. Mary was thankful. The shower would cool things off a little. Even with all the windows open the house was like a reeking, paint-smelling oven.

An hour later the rain was still falling heavily from a low gray sky. Mary let the painters go. Nothing would dry on a day like this. "But you be here extra early tomorrow," she told them. "Now that we've finally got the color right, I want to get it done."

They promised.

Mary took a coffee to the windows that opened onto the balcony. She wished the rain would stop. The balcony was her favorite place in the house. Whenever she could, she sat there for a few minutes, watching the street as if she were in a box at the theater. The street vendors were the actors, their songs the arias. She'd never tell anyone, but she liked mornings on Royal Street even more than the opera.

There were no street songs today. The rain was too heavy. The only sounds were the pealing of church bells and the rumble of wheels on cobblestones. And the rain.

Mary was thinking about the rain and the wet paint in the hall. It was a long time before she realized that the bells and the wheels had not stopped. Not at all, for the entire time she'd been near the window. She put her empty cup on a table and stepped out onto the balcony.

She was soaked within seconds, but she didn't notice. She was staring, disbelieving, at the scene below. Carriages, buggies, carts filled the street as far as her eye could see. They were moving steadily, slowly, in orderly procession, stopping for traffic crossing Royal at corners, then resuming their dignified, unified escape from the city. While the churches tolled the funeral bells.

For the first time Mary believed that Bertrand knew what he was doing. Everyone else seemed to be doing the same as he.

Her heart thumped. I should go, too. They know something I don't. I'll be the only person left in New Orleans. Panic made her slam the windows shut, lean against them to hold the danger away.

Then she was ashamed of herself. You're being a ninny, Mary MacAlistair. And making a puddle on Mémère's best rug to boot. What did you see? Forty vehicles, at most fifty. About a hundred people running away.

Why, only a month ago *The Bee* was bragging about how big New Orleans has become. A hundred and fifty thousand population, it said. Even without the fifty thousand that it predicted would go away for the summer, that still leaves a hundred thousand. What difference does it make if a hundred run away? That's nothing in a big city like this. Naturally every single one of them chooses Royal Street for the route. There's only one other street in the Quarter that's paved, and it's always jammed with people on foot because of all the shops.

Mary ran to her room for dry clothes, then to the linen press for a towel to blot the rug dry. By the time she finished tidying the mess she had made, she was feeling pleased with herself for her calm good sense.

That night she could hear wheels still rumbling through the dark rainy street, even after she went to bed. She wondered for a terror-struck moment if she was being a pigheaded fool.

But then the cool air and the lulling sound of the rain slipped her from worry into a deep refreshed sleep. It was delicious not to be hot and sticky for a change.

The next day there was no reference to the fever in *The Bee.*

But the church bells tolled all day.

And the rain continued to fall.

Mary went out to the kitchen to talk to the servants. "You know what they're saying about the fever epidemic. Would any of you like to leave the city? I'm sure Monsieur Julien could arrange it."

All of them declined. "Black folks almost never catch it, 'Zelle Marie," explained Jacques, "and we're all city people."

I'm city people, too, thought Mary. She was reassured by the servants' calmness. Everything will be all right, she thought, if this rain will just stop so I can get on with the house.

Two days later the maid Michelle came back from the Market with a basket of provisions for the day's meals. She was laughing, shaking the heavy drops of water off her umbrella; then her face became blank with surprise, and she fell onto the floor.

Mary heard the crash and came running. The floor of the kitchen was strewn with the contents of the basket. White eggs, broken, with yellow yolks spreading. Greens spread like a fan. Two live chickens, trussed together at the legs, wings flapping.

A pomegranate was still rolling unevenly in a lazy zigzag toward the feet of the cook and the gardener. They were holding onto one another, cowering dangerously close to the open fire in the big chimney.

Mary knelt to help Michelle.

The maid's eyes were rolled back in her head. They were yellow.

Small trickles of blood seeped from her nostrils and open mouth. The tongue was black.

"Help me get her into bed," Mary ordered. "She has the fever."

The two servants only stared.

"Help me, I said." Mary put her arm under Michelle's shoulders, tried to lift her.

"I'll help you, 'Zelle." Jacques came from the hall, gently moved Mary aside, lifted the sick woman. "I got her."

"I'll go for a doctor," said Mary.

She ran out into the rain without umbrella, cloak, or bonnet.

Royal Street was empty except for the sheeting rain and the sound of the bells.

She remembered that a doctor's house was in the next block. Spattering water from puddles, tripping on uneven bricks, she ran as she had never run before.

She pounded on the doctor's door with the big brass dolphin-shaped knocker, babbled in English to the neatly uniformed maid who answered, repeated herself in carefully slowed French.

"The doctor just left," said the maid. She pointed to a carriage turning at the far corner.

Mary raced after it. She caught up with it four blocks later, ran alongside, beating on the door with her fists.

The carriage slowed, stopped.

"What do you want, young woman?"

Mary was panting. She could barely speak.

When she managed to make herself understood, the doctor opened the door and helped her into the carriage.

"The Sazerac house," he said to his driver.

Mary slumped in the corner, still trying to catch her breath.

Doctor Brissac introduced himself and then delivered a short, short-tempered lecture about Mary's reprehensible disregard for her own health. Soaked, chilled, exhausted, she would be the fever's next victim.

She assured him she would not. She had already had it. And she felt perfectly healthy. Her teeth chattered as she said it.

"You should have left town," Dr. Brissac scolded.

"Oh, I'm going to, Doctor. As soon as Michelle has recovered, I'm going to take the servants and go."

"You're too late, Mademoiselle. We have a hundred deaths a day now. That we know about. There are no longer any boats leaving the city because they're not permitted to land anywhere. And the only horses left are the ones that belong to us doctors. Or the undertakers. You're too late."

It was too late for Michelle, too. When Mary and Dr. Brissac reached the house, she was dead.

The doctor addressed Jacques. "Go to the undertaker Glampion; he may still have some coffins. Make haste."

He took Mary's hand. "You did the best you could, Mademoiselle. Be grateful for this: she went quickly. Some linger for hours or even days. And there is little we doctors can do to help them. If any more in your house come down with the fever, try to get them to Charity Hospital. All the doctors and nurses are there. There are too many sick for us to visit the houses. I must go. I was on my way to the hospital when you stopped me."

Mary tried to thank him, but he waved her words aside.

That afternoon she insisted on going to Michelle's funeral, although Jacques tried to wave aside her words just as the doctor had done. The dignified black man walked behind her, his outrage clear on his face. He considered Mary's behavior too bold and unladylike, an insult to the name of Sazerac and to his pride as the Sazerac butler.

Mary didn't notice Jacques's outrage; if she had, she wouldn't have cared. Someone had to care that Michelle was dead; someone had to be with her, to mourn her, to put flowers on her grave. Mary clutched the bouquet of roses she had gathered from the courtyard and plodded through the steady rain in the mud-mired ruts made by the undertaker's wagon. It seemed a very long way to the Spanish-built church of Our Lady of Guadeloupe on Rampart Street. She felt a simmering anger at the Church authorities who had built it two decades earlier so that they could ban funerals in the Cathedral. If there was a God, surely the dead deserved the shelter and comfort of all His houses, including the grandest.

The wagon halted its jolting, squeaking progress a full block before Rampart Street. Mary slogged forward to shout to the driver.

She stopped short before she spoke. There was an unbroken line of wagons, carts, carriages, and hearses ahead of them, each with its pitiful burden of the newly dead. The leather and wood and painted metal of the vehicles glistened wetly; the horses shook their heads to free them of the blinding rain; the quagmire that was the street was carpeted with muddy, crushed flower petals.

Mary turned her face up to the low gray sky and let the rain wash away the tears she could no longer hold back. She wanted to howl like a dog or a wolf, release her anger and sorrow and fear into the monotonous deep tolling of the church's funeral bell. But she knew it would change nothing.

Michelle's funeral consisted of a hastily muttered prayer and blessing and a sprinkling of holy water on her coffin. It remained in the wagon for the few minutes the prayers lasted. Then the haggard elderly priest motioned the driver to move on, gestured to the carriage behind them to move up.

The cemetery was only one square away. It was the same one that

Mary had visited with the Courtenays on All Saints' Day. Then it had been a place of freshly cleaned tombs, solemn festivity, sunlight on crisply scented white chrysanthemums.

Now it was wet, dirty, a Gehenna of mud and putrefaction. A white man in black hooded oilskin asked the driver the nature of his load. "Down there for slaves," he said, jabbing over his shoulder with his thumb. "You can't take the wagon. I can let you have two pallbearers for ten dollars each."

Mary had brought only five dollars with her, for candles and an offering, she had thought.

"We'll carry her ourselves," she told Jacques. She stared him down before he could protest.

They staggered under the load; the deep, churned mud sucked at their boots and made a thick, heavy layer of black mire on the bottom of Mary's skirts. But they did not drop the coffin.

The incessant tolling bell pained Mary's ears and skull. As they approached the burial site, the stench of decomposing bodies made her retch and gag. A woman came up to her. She was carrying a pail of vinegar and a basket of rags. The sharp acidic smell seemed cleansing amid the reek of death.

"One dollar for a soaked cloth, Mademoiselle. It's guaranteed protection against the fever."

"I want two," Mary said. "Give one to the man helping me." The woman dipped and wrung out two rags, put them on the coffin near Mary and Jacques.

"I can't reach into my pocket," said Mary; "please take the money out and put the change back in."

The woman extracted the gold piece, bit it, grinned with stained and broken teeth. Then she hiked up her skirt and ran through a deep puddle of muddy water, out of Mary's reach.

It made no difference. The smell of vinegar was worth all the money she had or ever hoped to have. She grabbed the cloth and held it over her nose and mouth when two graveyard attendants took the coffin away from her and Jacques. The butler, she saw, did the same thing. His black skin looked gray.

Then the attendants heaved the coffin up onto a teetering stack of other coffins. "What are you doing?" Mary shouted. "We want to bury that."

"This pile goes as soon as that one's finished," one man replied.

Mary held the cloth closer when she realized what he meant. Five yards away six men were dropping coffins into a shallow water-filled trench, throwing ballast stone on top of them to make them sink. Beyond them other men were digging a second trench.

She started forward to protest. Jacques took her arm and pulled her away.

"Let me go, Jacques. That's not decent. No tomb. No marker. It's inhuman. It's because those are dead slaves. I won't stand for it."

"'Zelle Marie, stop. Look." He turned Mary round. On the other side of the picket fence that divided the cemetery men were disposing of stacked coffins in the same hasty, barbarous manner. "Those are white dead," said Jacques.

Mary put the vinegar cloth in the pocket of her cloak when she was well away from the cemetery. The rain-wet air felt wonderfully fresh in her mouth. She stretched her legs as she walked along the banquette of Conti Street, and the exercise felt good.

She was alone. Jacques had gone back to the house after protesting the impropriety of her walking without a servant following. His perpetual disapproval annoyed Mary, but she was deeply moved by his loyalty to the family. She was on her way to Julien's bank; she wanted him to find a way to send the servants out of town. They had decided to go after the shock of Michelle's death.

All of them, except Jacques. "I can't leave Madame Anne-Marie's house," he said. "Somebody might take her things."

While Mary was picking her way across the morass of Dauphine Street, the rain stopped. She looked up and saw a patch of blue sky; it grew larger as she watched.

Immediately her spirits lifted. It will clear and everything will become normal again, she thought. Surely the epidemic must be nearly over.

She was terribly wrong. It had barely begun.

# 61

Julien agreed immediately to take the servants away. "I was going to come talk to you as soon as I finished clearing up here," he said. "I've got my carriage, and a wagon for the slaves. I'm taking everyone from my house, too. We'll all go together. I have to finish up some work here, then organize the move. I'll come pick you and your servants up after that. Say, seven o'clock. Thank God the days are so long. We'll be well along the River Road before dark. We're going to our cousin's plantation at St. Francisville. You'd better bring bedding and whatever food you have in the house, just in case. No telling how many refugees they're housing, and it could be useful."

Mary thanked him and left. Two men were starting to board up the windows of the bank. The sound of hammering overcame the tolling of the bells for a few moments, until she had walked halfway to the corner.

She hadn't intended to leave with the servants. Her sense of responsibility should equal Jacques's at least. But Julien's matter-of-fact attitude made her change her mind. If he was closing the bank and abandoning his house, there had to be good cause. For once in her life maybe she should listen to an older and wiser person. Mary sighed aloud.

The sound startled her. It was the only noise anywhere, except for the bells. She stopped walking, looked around. No one. No sign of life, not even a dog or a cat.

Mary shivered. It was as if everyone in New Orleans had run away. Or died.

She was on Bourbon Street, a street lined with impressive houses and centered by a quagmire of black shining mud.

Alone, unhurried, undistracted by the bustle and excitement that normally infused the city, Mary saw the beauty around her with fresh vision. Even the mud had a special beauty. Its dangerous gullies and ridges were curling, glistening shapes, like a length of black satin tossed carelessly down.

The watery sunlight made the housefronts opposite look supernaturally clear in every detail. The mortar between soft red old bricks caught and held the dilute, slanting rays of the sun, while the bricks shed them in a barely perceived glow of rose color. Painted stucco of other housefronts looked soft, powdery, their blues and ochers and grays gentle. Mary had never really looked closely before, not this way, not with the luxury of solitary undisturbed attention. She saw that each house had a door different from every other, windows unique in shape and placement, shutters or curved lintels or fanlights of unique beauty. All had iron balconies or galleries. They cast echoing shadows on the house fronts. Shadows of vines, of flowers, of arabesques, shells, leaves, trellises. Each beautiful in design, exciting in the contradiction of delicacy and strength, individual and particular. No house was like any other. And yet they created a single unified beauty, seemingly a solid variegated wall along the banquette, broken only by a few narrow iron gates, and the quietly idiosyncratic doors, veiled by the shadows of their overhanging, sheltering balconies.

So many different beauties, yet all combined without disharmony into one. It astonished her. How could she not have looked before now, and marveled?

Mary's return home was laggard. And thrilling. Block after block, she had the same experience. Looking. Seeing. Loving. Just as each house was different and yet part of a whole, so, too, each block was unique, yet unmistakably part of the whole that was New Orleans.

The emptiness of the streets ceased being ominous, became a gift to her, the gift of sight. She was ecstatic with the endless discoveries that the city gave her, and the many more held in store. She could look and look for the rest of her life and never exhaust the bounty of beauty.

She forgot, for the moment, that she would be leaving it all in a few hours.

On the single step to the front door of the house there was a plate of food surrounded by a circle of silver coins. Mary had seen several other doorsteps with the same arrangement. She assumed it was small, private charity, put there for poor, hungry victims of the epidemic, and she wondered which of the servants had done it. Jacques would never risk breaking one of Mémère's finest French porcelain plates. He would be harsh with whoever had done it. Mary didn't want to be uncharitable, but even less did she want a crisis of discipline in the house. They were all too nervous as it was.

She scooped up the coins, picked up the plate, carried them through the walkway to the courtyard. René, the gardener, was tying up some rose canes flattened by the rains. When he saw Mary he fell on his knees and covered his head with his arms. "No, 'Zelle, no!" he moaned. "Terrible trouble if you take away the offering for the Grand Zombi. Put it back. Put it back."

Mary's temper snapped. All the horror of Saint John's Eve had blurred during her time on the Gulf. Now it came back, strong, disgusting, horrifying. And René was trying to bring voodoo to the house. She emptied the food onto his head and threw the coins after it.

Then she marched into the kitchen with the dirty plate. "Wash this carefully and put it away," she ordered the cook. "When that's done, find all the other servants and tell them to get ready to leave. You're to carry your mattresses and sheets and all the food that you can pack.

"Tell René that he's to wash his head with laundry soap before we go. Maybe the stinging will make it clean inside, too. You only have an hour, so start working."

It was, in fact, only a few minutes after five. But Mary knew how slow the cook could be.

She repeated Julien's instructions for Jacques. "Are you quite sure you won't come with us, Jacques?"

"Quite sure, 'Zelle Marie... If I may disturb you, there is a person to see you. I had her wait in the hall."

"For heaven's sake. There's no place to sit there. And I have no time to receive guests. Who is it, Jacques?"

"A person," was all he would say.

Mary hurried to the house, ready to apologize to whatever cousin it might be. Perhaps another passenger in Julien's carriage.

She was in no way prepared to see Cécile Dulac.

Cécile didn't wait to be greeted. "You must come with me, Mary," she said. "Valmont needs you."

Mary's hand found a newel post for support. "There is nothing that I can do for Monsieur Saint-Brévin," she said. "Nor anything that I would be willing to do."

Cécile ignored Mary's harsh tone and her words.

"Valmont has the fever, Mary. He's delirious, and he's calling your name. He has been for hours. You needn't come, of course. But it would ease him and make his death less painful."

"'Death'? He's dying?"

"He may be dead already. I've been waiting for you for nearly three hours."

Mary turned, ran. "Jacques," she cried, "Jacques." He met her halfway to the kitchen.

"Jacques, tell Monsieur Julien I'm not going with him. And get the servants ready. I have to go out; I don't know when I'll be back."

She had imagined herself killing Valmont Saint-Brévin a hundred times.

She couldn't stand it if he was dead.

# 62

Cécile led Mary to the sagging gate of Marie Laveau's house on Saint Anne Street. Mary didn't know the house, but she knew it couldn't belong to the fastidious Cécile.

"What are we doing here?" she asked.

"Valmont is inside. Some of his friends brought him to me to nurse after he collapsed. I arranged for him to be brought here. I'll have no disease in my house."

Mary stared at Cécile as if she were a snake. Cécile was unperturbed. "Go in," she said. "You're expected."

"You aren't coming?"

"No." Cécile walked away, choosing her stepping spots carefully to avoid muddying her dress.

Mary pushed through the gate and the tangled greenery of the yard. The door to the house was ajar. She walked in, stopped, waited for her eyes to adjust to the shadowy dimness.

When she could see, she recognized the woman in the doorway across the room. She shrank away from the Voodoo Queen.

"He's in here," said Marie, turning.

Mary followed her.

Val was lying on a tremendous bed with carved spiral posts as thick as tree trunks. The bed was in the center of the small room, surrounded by tall iron stands holding bowls of burning oil. They made the room brighter than daylight.

Val was nude except for a strip of blue cloth across his loins and a white cloth across his eyes. His skin was yellow, vivid on the white sheet beneath him. He was stirring restlessly, limbs twitching, cracked lips moving, emitting a low, keening moan.

He's alive. Mary could think no further. She went between two lamps to stand near his head. Her hands trembled with the need to smooth his wet hair from his forehead, to moisten his parched lips, to comfort him in some way. To comfort herself by touching him. All the pain he had caused her, all the ugliness and cruelty were meaningless now. He was suffering, and it broke her heart.

"I'll take him to the hospital," she said. "My uncle has a carriage. 'll go bring it."

"You will not," Marie said. "The doctors would kill him with their urges and bleeding. I know better medicine than theirs. If he could est, his own strength would save him. But even with the sleeping drugs, e cannot stop exhausting himself this way. That's why I sent for Cécile nd told her to bring you... Speak to him. Tell him you're here."

Mary raised her fists. "He needs a doctor, not your snake-vorshiping mumbo jumbo. Let me pass. I'm going for the carriage." She unged at Marie.

Marie stepped aside, and Mary stumbled against the wall. Marie's trong hands caught her wrists and held her pinioned there. She spoke nto Mary's ear. "Quiet, you fool. He's disturbed enough without clattering from you. Listen to what I tell you.

"This man is my friend. I love him, and I am going to make him vell. If it can be done, I am the one who can do it.

"You can help or you can go away. But you will not take Valmont way from his only chance of living. I will kill you if you try. Believe hat."

Mary felt Marie Laveau's hot breath on her cheek. She tried to hink of a way to break free of Marie's grip.

Then she heard Val's voice. Weak. Pitiful. "Mary... Mary..."

She burst from Marie's grip. Or Marie let her go.

"Val. I'm here. I'm here." In an instant she was by his side.

"... Mary..." Val's hands were reaching, moving across his chest; e was too weak to lift them. "... Mary..."

She caught his hands in hers. Her fingers felt burned by the fever n his.

"... Mary... sorry... forgive... me..."

"I do, Val, I do." She raised his hands to her lips and kissed them gain and again. Tears poured from her eyes, and she moved Val's hands o her cheeks to cool his fever with her tears. "I forgive you," she said. 'Anything. Everything. It's all right. Only don't die, my love. Only ive."

He sighed, a long, long exhalation and relaxation. His legs stopped heir agitated jerking, and his arms became limp. His hands were suddenly oo heavy for Mary to hold. They fell from her clasp onto his still body.

"Val!"

There was a fleeting smile on his lips. Then they, too, went slack. A gush of bright red blood erupted from his nostrils onto his mouth and chin and neck.

Mary screamed. "He's dead." She tried to stop the blood with her hands, but it poured through her fingers.

Marie Laveau shoved Mary aside. She put her strong hands on Val's bloody throat. "Quiet, you fool," she said, her whisper as brutal as a shout. "He's asleep, a true sleep." She took a cloth from the bowl of water on a table near the bed and wrung it out. Then she washed the blood from his face and held the cool cloth against his nostrils until the bleeding stopped.

"Rest is what he needs," she said to Mary. "It's good that you came. Now we wash his body to cool it."

Mary wrung out another cloth and began. It was quiet in the room. She could hear that the rain had started again.

In the brightly lit curtained room there was no sense of day and night, no sense of time passing in the constant vigilance for the needs of the sick man. Marie Laveau showed Mary the low stools in a dark corner, and she sat there when Val was sleeping. Sometimes she dozed, her head resting against the wall, until a stirring from the bed or Val's cries wakened her. Once she woke and ran to him, but he was sleeping quietly. Then she realized that her rest had been broken by the absence of sound. The bells had stopped. She returned to the corner, thankful for the peace.

Marie Laveau entered and left the room silently. Sometimes she sat next to Mary. They talked in low tones, then, strange disjointed conversations broken by long periods of silence. Mary learned that Val had come to the city in search of a doctor for the fevered slaves on his plantation when the doctor who usually treated them refused to go to Benison a second time. The sickness had struck Val in the Exchange at the hotel.

She also heard a little bit about the long friendship by mail that bound Marie to him, and she envied Marie with a hot jealousy that shocked and shamed her. And made her admit to herself that she loved this man with all the strength that was in her. No matter what he had done or could ever do, she loved him. Not with her body alone, as she had told herself. She loved him with everything that she was, heart, mind, soul.

She sensed that Marie's love for Val was as great as hers, though different. And an indefinable kind of love grew between the two of them, as they worked together to save the life of the man they both loved.

They bathed his hot body to soothe his fevered tossing, washed away the blood that came from his nose and ears. Mary held his shoulders and head while Marie fed him broth or medicines; they moved quickly in unison to hold him when he jerked with violent spasms as his diseased stomach rejected the liquids. "A few drops stay with him," Marie said; "they will help." She washed the foulness from his body while Mary swabbed the inside of his mouth. Together they moved his weight from side to side and put clean linen on the big bed.

Mary never asked what was in the potions that Marie gave Val. They eased him, and that was enough. She would deal with the devil himself to save Val's life. She could hear the comings and goings of people in the other part of the house, heard voices black and white, words French and English, asking for medicines and gris-gris and spells against the fever.

She went out into the yard behind the house when she needed the privy or the refreshing cleansing of the rain on her stinking clothes and body. From the hallway she could see sometimes into the room where the voodoo altar stood. Black candles burned on it and small jars of colored powders with tapers in their centers. A statue of the Virgin Mary in bright colors and a crucifix of carved dark wood stood on each side of a bronze chest with grilled sides. Inside it a dry rustling noise told of twining serpents moving, always moving.

She didn't care. When all Marie's potions and spells failed to calm Val's agitation, her voice and her hand in his gave him rest. He needed her. Only her.

Hours after the bells stopped tolling, or perhaps days after, Mary heard a dull, reverberating explosion. The bowl of water she was holding dropped from her hands and broke on the floor. "What was that?" she whispered.

"Cannon," Marie replied. "They've moved cannon into the streets to fire at the clouds. They think it will break up the miasma that gives the fever." Her voice was heavy with scorn. "Next they'll start burning tar. Who knows why? It has never done any good before. They'll lie, the way they always do, tell the people that it will smother the fever. Liars. They stopped the bells for the dead, as if no one would know then that people are dying. Two hundred every day it is now."

Mary couldn't comprehend such numbers. "But not Val," she said.

"Not Val," said Marie.

One time he woke, clearheaded and conscious. Marie was feeding him, tipping a bowl against his lips while Mary supported him from behind. Val grunted, and his hands reached for the bowl, tilted it more. "I'm hungry," he said distinctly; he drank in loud greedy swallows.

Then the spasms of vomiting began, and he slid back down into coma.

"He will get well," said Marie. "Half stayed with him. Nourishment is what he needs, even more than medicines."

Later that day, or that night, or the next day or night, Val suddenly groaned loudly. Mary and Marie hurried from the corner. His groaning continued, louder, more urgent and pain-filled. Marie felt his cheeks, the pulse in his straining neck. "It's the crisis," she said, a rasp of fear in her voice.

His stomach heaved, muscles standing out in great knots. Mary could hear Marie's whispered prayers, added her silent pleas to them. Then a spate of noxious black matter pulsed from Val's body onto the white linen between and under his legs. The excrement was unspeakably foul. Mary staggered backwards, gagging.

"He will live!" Marie's cry was exultant. "It is not the vomit. His body has won. He will live." She grabbed all the wet cloths and started frantically washing Val's body. In seconds they were filthy. Marie threw them onto the bed. "Quick," she said. "Get more cloths from the kitchen. He'll wake soon. He should be clean."

Mary ran to obey her. She rummaged through cupboards and drawers, searching for the cloths. Then she heard Val's voice. It was weak but it was lucid.

"What the hell is that disgusting stink?"

Marie's voice was calm, warm. "That stink is you, Monsieur Saint-Brévin."

"Who is that? Get this thing off my eyes. Marie, is that you?"

"It is I."

"Is this your house? Why am I here? I don't remember anything."

"You've been sick with the fever. Now you're well."

"Help me up. I need a bath. And I'm starving."

Mary tumbled boxes onto the floor, frantic to find the cloths. He was conscious. She wanted to see him.

She heard Marie's laughter. "You're naked and in my bed, Valmont; why hurry to get up? You're where you've wanted to get for years."

Val's chuckle froze Mary. It was intimate, loving. "You don't understand," he said. "I must get up. I have to shed this stink. And I have to see to my ship." He was no longer laughing. "I must go, Marie. I have to . . ." He hesitated. "I have to go marry my rich Charleston beauty."

Mary doubled over in pain. She crept quietly from the kitchen to the rain-washed outdoors.

The sky was dark and low, the light murky. She couldn't tell if it was day or night because a great barrel of pitch was blazing on the corner. It lit the space around it while the thick rolling black smoke from the blaze darkened all the air beyond. Every corner had one. The cannon fire was irregular but constant, a dull "whump," as leaden as Mary's blasted heart.

She walked blindly through the dim deserted streets, choking on the fumes, holding her ears to protect them from the assault of the cannons, until she stumbled and almost fell. Then she felt along the walls of the dark houses beside her for guidance through the swirling smoke. She was crying. Whether the acrid smoke caused her tears or some more burning pain, she didn't know.

The creak of ungreased wheels stopped her at the next corner. She wiped her eyes with sooty fingers and peered into the billowing smoke to see what was coming. The rain intensified, substituting a new blindness for the old one. Mary didn't see the wagon until she could almost have touched it. It was an old wooden dray, heavy laden with a swaying, ghastly pile of swollen, decaying bodies. Limp arms hung over its edges, moving like pendulums of death.

Mary fell to the ground and covered her eyes. Wetness seeped into her skirts. She could hear her own jagged breathing and her teeth chattering with horror. The wagon passed on. From the next block she heard the driver's call.

"Bring out your dead."

It came again, fainter, when he reached the next block, and the next. Then there was only the thump of the cannons and the rain drumming on the bricks of the banquette.

Mary got to her feet and ran. She slid and fell in the deep mud of the streets, scrabbled on hands and knees to the sound footing of the next banquette where she could run again. The pitch barrels were beacons, their smoke a blinding torture.

When she fell against the door of the Sazerac house she was a sodden, blackened, screaming creature. Jacques opened the door a crack in response to her pounding.

"Jacques, Jacques, for the love of God, let me in. It's me, Mary MacAlistair."

The tall butler knelt, a lantern in one hand, a pistol in the other. He looked through the narrow opening at Mary's desperate eyes.

"My God," he breathed, "I thought you were dead." He laid lantern and pistol on the floor, pulled the door wide. "Come in, child. You're home now."

# 63

Mary tried to hide from the horrors beyond the walls of the house. She even drank some of her grandmother's laudanum to escape into sleep. But her vivid, Grand Guignol dreams were more terrifying than reality. And when she woke, the memory of Valmont was more agonizing than the dreams.

Busy, she said to herself, I must keep busy. She found the letter that Jacques had given her. Dr. Brissac left it at the house when she was away. "If you have a strong heart, we need you," he had written. "There are not enough hands to tend the sick at the hospital. Help us."

Mary wrapped a shawl around her shoulders and head and went out into the blanket of stinging smoke, and the incessant rain. Jacques made the sign of the cross behind her as she walked away.

The hospital was the greatest nightmare of all. All beds were filled, and all the mattresses on the floor between the beds and in the corridors. Sick and dying lay in corners, on the floor of the entry, on the steps leading to it. There was a thick effluvium of blood and vomit and death.

Mary wore a vinegar-soaked sponge strapped by a bandage under her nose and carried filled pans and dirty linens to the area set aside for washing. She helped bathe and turn the ill, wrap the dead in grave clothes. Ursuline nuns were the hospital's nurses. Their hollow eyes and worn faces gave testimony to their uncomplaining exhaustion.

There were other volunteer nurses besides Mary. She saw Mrs. O'Neill, her former landlady, but there was no time to speak to her. She must seem like a visiting angel, Mary thought, with her lilting voice and her memories of Ireland. So many of the sick were Irish. Recent immigrants were always the hardest hit, a nun told her.

Dr. Brissac spied Mary when he entered the big ward with two other doctors. "Come help me, Mademoiselle," he shouted. "I need someone who speaks French, and I don't want to take the Sisters away from their acts of mercy." Mary hastened to his side.

She learned that Marie Laveau had been right. The treatment of the sickness would kill any but the strongest. "Give me a lancet and a cup," he said. "I'm going to bleed this woman."

"But she's already bleeding, Doctor. Look at her nose."

"Give me the lancet, Mademoiselle, and the cup. When you become a man and a doctor, you'll be able to discuss treatment with me."

Mary took the tools from the case he had put on the floor. They were caked with dried blood. She tried to wipe them off on her apron. It seemed indecent to her to use them, like offering food on an unwashed plate.

"Hurry up, don't you see how many are waiting?" The doctor snatched them from her hands. He held the knife to the woman's arm then, with a practiced twist, opened her vein. The woman cried out in pain, although she was unconscious.

When the cup was full, the doctor gave it to Mary. "Dispose of this, then hold her while I give her a dose of medicine."

The woman kicked and fought, but Mary held her shoulders flat while Dr. Brissac forced her jaws apart and poured a thick dark liquid down her throat.

Then he moved to the next patient on the floor. "Give me the cup and lancet, Mademoiselle, and be quick."

"Don't cut me, Doctor," the patient screamed. "Merciful Jesus, hear my prayers. Don't let him cut me."

"Come hold this woman still, Mademoiselle."

Mary did as he ordered. She tried to speak soothingly to the terrified woman, but the woman's yellowed hands clutched at Mary's arms, and her blood-stained mouth babbled wildly, "Don't let him cut me, Miss, don't let him, don't let him." Her scream when the lancet entered her vein was horrible.

There were other screams as the other doctors moved swiftly from patient to patient, administering the best treatment they knew.

Mary was sickened by it. And by the callous treatment of the dead. The bodies were stacked like cordwood at the end of the ward. Of all the wards.

One of the nuns saw her staring at them. "It is terrible, but it's all we can do," she said. "There is a death every five minutes. A priest will bless them and pray for them before they're taken away."

At the end of the tenth hour, Mary could stand no more. "I'm leaving, Sister," she said. She pulled off her grimy apron and threw it onto the mountain of dirty linen.

"God bless you for helping, Mademoiselle." The nun went on to the next sufferer, to bathe, to pray for, to offer the comfort of her serene, worn face and familiar dark habit.

Mary never went back.

The following day she packed a basket with soap and vinegar and a half dozen sheets. A second basket held jars of the chicken broth Jacques had helped her to make the night before.

I don't have Marie Laveau's potion, she thought, but she said nourishment was most important. I can at least try.

She walked along the deserted levee to the Irish Channel. There were no boats at the docks, not even the rough-hewn keelboats and flatboats that usually made a wooden island two miles long. Abandoned cargo was rotting in the rain. A rat scuttled into an overturned harpsichord at the sound of Mary's footsteps. The twang of the strings made her jerk nervously.

Nearing Adele Street she saw two naked children playing in the swift-running water of the gutter. She approached them with a smile. "Hello," she said.

They splashed forward to meet her.

They were hungry, they told Mary, but their mother wouldn't give them anything to eat. She told them to go away because she was sick.

"Show me where you live," said Mary. "Maybe I can help your mother."

The mother was unconscious, yellow, fouled with blood and vomit, burning with fever.

No worse than Val, Mary told herself, and she set to work cleaning the woman and the bed. Then the room and then the house. She found scrubbing brushes and a pail in the kitchen. Also some potatoes and a piece of salted beef for the children. She sent silent thanks to Mrs. O'Neill for teaching her how to clean things and for the lesson that boiling water will cook anything sooner or later.

When the children were dressed and fed and their mother as comfortable as possible, Mary went on to the next cottage and the next and the ones after that, carrying her baskets and her strength and her knowledge that the fever could be cured.

Before the long rainy day was over she found a man and a woman who would help her. She taught them the little she knew; more important, she freed them of their certainty that the fever would kill everyone before it was over.

They promised to visit each house of the sick at intervals during the night, to bathe and feed the person or people in it. Mary promised to return the next morning with more supplies. There were ten patients.

Only ten, she thought bitterly; I could only help ten people, and help them very little.

When she was well away from the Channel she allowed herself to cry. Then she squared her shoulders and walked quickly through the rain and the mud to find the dead wagon. She had found thirteen putrefying bodies and wrapped them for burial.

Day after day Mary went to the streets of the immigrants to do what little she could. She became numb to horror. The dreadful plague was always before her eyes. In one two-roomed house there were twenty-six bloated bodies. In another an infant sucked the breast of his mother's cold corpse. She took child after child to the nearby orphanages, added sacks of food for the orphanages to her morning loads.

She despaired when the black vomit told her that her efforts had failed, wept with happiness when a cool forehead or foul loosened bowels signified success.

Her hands were raw from the strong soap with which she cleaned the cramped cottages, her eyes red from its fumes. But she kept her shoulders straight at all times, her person neat and clean, a smile on her face, no matter how profound her discouragement and fatigue. She knew that her confidence that the fever need not win was her most valuable service to the sick and fearful.

One afternoon there was a harrumph behind her when she was bathing an old man. Mary looked over her shoulder. Her smile when she saw Mrs. O'Neill was spontaneous and genuine.

"So it is you, Mary MacAlistair," said the widow. "I've heard talk, but I didn't believe my ears. When you've finished with Michael O'Roarke, him who should have been dead these ten years and more, come to my house. I'll give you breakfast and a hundred questions."

"Well!" Mrs. O'Neill exclaimed when Mary finished talking. "I never thought I'd agree with a heathen voodoo. But I do. I've seen it with my own eyes, a poor creature hardly sick at all saving the yellowness of him and dead after losing all his good red blood to the doctors' knives.

"What you've done here in the Channel hasn't gone unnoticed either, Mary. Now, I know my neighbors, and there's more than you would think sitting on their hands when they could be helping the sick. I'll have them working tomorrow. There may be some too squeamish to wash a yellow face, but there's none of them too puny to scrub a floor.

"You come to me tomorrow, my dear, and I'll show you how your good works can spread. No need to burden yourself with all the food, neither. You can help the orphans, but I'll fix the broth for the poor suffering yellows. I don't wonder but that a little cabbage wouldn't add a nice bit of flavor."

Within two days Mary wasn't needed any more in the Irish Channel.

She walked home slowly, aware of her exhaustion for the first time. She should be glad that the Widow O'Neill had taken over. More sick people were being tended, and there was a sense of community that heartened both the sick and the healthy.

She was glad.

But she felt unwanted and useless. And lonely.

What you need is some sleep, Mary MacAlistair, she told herself. Then maybe you'll have sense enough to stop sniveling.

But she was late getting to bed. When she arrived at the house, the door flew open. Mémère stood in the doorway, arms outstretched. "Marie, my darling, I've been watching for you. Embrace your old grandmother who's missed you so dreadfully."

Mary inhaled her grandmother's clean sweet lavender scent, felt the soft wrinkled cheek next to hers, and her despondency vanished. "You shouldn't have come back to the city, Mémère, but I'm so happy to see you."

"Don't be silly, Marie. I had to come back. Two days from now is our Saint's Day, and we must have a party."

A party amidst the death and despair; Mémère's lavender powder in the reek of burning tar; her light, fluting voice over the grim barrage of the cannons. "You're such a Creole, dearest Mémère," said Mary. For the first time in an eternity of desolation, she laughed.

Anne-Marie Sazerac's refusal to recognize the tragedy in New Orleans was like a magic wand waved over the house. When Mary woke the next morning it was to the delicious aroma of café au lait and beignets. Mémère's maid Valentine was by her bed with a breakfast tray in her hands. Dainty flowered porcelain, an embroidered pink cloth and napkin, a tiny silver vase of fresh roses were on the tray. Mary thought she had never seen anything so lovely in her life.

When she went downstairs after breakfast there were flowers on freshly polished tables in all the rooms and the piquant smell of lemon oil in the air. Mémère was sitting on a low stool with drawings spread in an arch before her on the floor.

"Bonjour, my love. What excellent mail was awaiting me. Come see the sketches from Paris. We must think about ordering the gown for your début. And a dozen others. You must have the best of everything for your Season. There's no dressmaker in New Orleans to match Paris, no matter what they say. Look, Marie, look what they're doing now. No more piles of crinolines. There's a kind of wire cage to hold the skirts wider than ever before. I shall get one, too. They must be very exciting to manage."

Mary's buried instincts of a seamstress were reignited. She crouched on the floor to study the drawings.

Later her grandmother insisted that they walk to the Market. "Wear a dark veil, chérie. Then if the smoke dirties your face, no one will know."

Mary tried to be gentle. "There's no one to see us, Mémère."

"Nonsense. There are always vendors at the Market, and it's the time of year for strawberries. I have a fancy for strawberries today."

She was right. There were black women with exquisitely arranged baskets of strawberries at the Market. And vegetables and flowers and bellicose crayfish and pearl-colored oysters. There were few vendors, and prices were ten times what they had been, but almost everything that had ever been sold before was for sale now. Madame Sazerac made careful selections and bargained eloquently for better prices, more appealing lagniappe. The vendors were delighted. They competed noisily for her attention. By the time she left, everyone was smiling broadly.

Opposite the Market there was a barroom. It was usually frequented by sailors from the ships anchored at the levee. Now its open doors revealed men of all classes drinking and shouting lewd suggestions at a heavily painted woman who was singing and playing a banjo.

"How awful," said Mary.

Her grandmother looked across at the rowdy scene. "Remember Marie, all the theaters are closed. People must be entertained. And I do like that song. 'Oh, Susannah' isn't it? Such a catchy tune, I think."

"I wasn't talking about the singer. It's that chalkboard outside the door. They're taking bets on how many people will die of the fever today."

Mémère shrugged. "Men will gamble, Marie, especially men in New Orleans. And people will die without the gambling making it happen.

Everything is a gamble to some men. They like it that way. What are Roland's cotton prices for crops not yet in the ground? And Julien's bank shares? My own father was a sugar planter. That's the biggest gamble of them all. An early frost and everything is lost in an hour."

Mary felt herself stiffen, managed to overcome it. There was only one sugar planter in the world to her mind, and she had to forget him. She concentrated on her grandmother's gay conversation.

"We must find the ribbons to decorate the dining room for our fête, Marie. And the special plate for the cake. Just because we are only two instead of the many Maries in the family that usually come, that's no reason to omit any of the festivities tomorrow."

Mary did her best to forget Val, to concentrate on Mémère's preparations for the party. But memories of Valmont haunted her. And questions. If she had stayed at Marie Laveau's house, if Val had seen her, would he have changed his mind about the Charleston heiress? He called for her, Mary. Why? Was it only to ask forgiveness? Why should he care, unless she meant something to him?

That evening after dinner she asked her grandmother for help. Not directly, not about her dilemma in particular. "What should I know about love, Mémère?" she asked.

Anne-Marie Sazerac looked at her with old eyes. She rested her hand on Mary's, stroked the long fingers. "You mean love between a man and a woman. I know more about such love than you might expect, Marie. I intended to talk with you before summer's end, before your début. I suppose this is as good a time as we will ever have.

"Go get your casket, child. There is something in it that I must hold in my hand when I speak about love."

# 64

Mémère ran her fingers across the blackened corner of the casket. "This happened the year I was born, 1788. The great fire. It burned practically the whole city, our home included. My mother loved to tell that story. She was carrying me, and like most first babies I was late to be born. She said that she ran back into the burning house to save the casket and the excitement made her labor begin. I was born in the Ursuline convent; it was just about the only building that survived the fire. Maman used to call me 'Firebrand' as a pet name."

Mary was enchanted. "I'm going to start calling you that, too. What a wonderful name. 'Mémère Firebrand.'"

Her grandmother laughed. "I want to see Jacques's face when he hears it. He doesn't like for any of us to be undignified, you know." She touched the charred box again, laughed again.

"I always wondered about Maman's memory. My younger brother Alessandro was born the year of the second great fire. He's six years younger than I. He's convinced that the fire story was really about his birth, not mine."

"Was your home burned then, too?"

"Oh, yes. I remember it. It was thrilling. We had to live in a tent on the levee for months. All my friends were there, too. It was like a gigantic picnic. We never thought of what it was like for our parents. It was after the two fires that my father decided to become a planter. He said the city was too risky to live in. That was the only thing I ever heard of that he considered too risky. He was the biggest gambler in New Orleans."

"What did he do before he became a planter?"

Mémère's eyes widened. "Isn't that odd? I don't really know. I guess he was a *fainéant* like Bertrand. He must have been just rich and charming. He had to be rich, or my grandparents would never have allowed him to marry my mother. And I can remember how charming he was. I adored him. So did Maman. Theirs was a love match, a true romance."

Mary inched her footstool closer to her grandmother's chair. "Tell me about it, Mémère."

Anne-Marie Sazerac stroked Mary's hair, and sighed. "It's a tale that should begin with 'once upon a time,'" she said. "My mother's name was

Isabella-Maria, and she was very beautiful, just as a fairy princess is supposed to be. When Marie-Hélène was presented to the King of Spain, Isabella-Maria and her brothers and sisters were there to see their mother at that moment of such great honor.

"Look at Marie-Hélène's portrait, Marie, and see how beautiful she was. And then imagine that in the great throne room of the palace all eyes were on Isabella-Maria in her simple young girl's frock and not on her beautiful mother in full court dress. That's how astonishingly beautiful she was.

"My grandfather was besieged by the grandees of Spain, asking for his daughter's hand in marriage. But Isabella-Maria would have none of them. Her parents didn't object. They were going to come home to New Orleans, and they didn't want to leave their beloved daughter behind, so far away.

"There was a tremendous reception for them at the Governor's House when they arrived home. Isabella-Maria met Antoine Ferrand there. They danced and they looked into each other's eyes and when the reception was over Isabella-Maria told her father that she had found the man she wanted to wed."

Mary sighed. "It's like a fairytale."

Mémère laughed. "But I've barely begun. The fairytale was their wedding. People in New Orleans still talk about it, though none of them were alive to see it. My grandfather lived in a great planation house outside the city, where the Americans have their houses now. The city was only the French Quarter then.

"A long allée of oak trees led to the house. Weeks before the wedding he sent all his slaves into the gardens and the woods to gather spiders and release them into the limbs of the oaks. The spiders spun their webs all through the trees, making a gossamer canopy over the carriage drive. On the day of the wedding Marie-Hélène and all her children went out in the early morning and blew gold dust from their palms onto the spider webs. Then the servants lay the rugs that had been ordered from Persia to cover the drive. The guests came to Isabella-Maria's wedding in their open carriages on a lovely day in May with the sunlight gleaming through the most delicate lace of gold onto the jewellike colors of the carpeted drive. And beneath her white lace veil the bride's dark hair was bright with flecks of gold."

"Magical," said Mary in a near whisper. "And they lived happily ever after."

"Yes, they really did. At the expense of everyone around them. Is the little pouch with a stone in it still in the casket?"

Mary opened the lid and removed it. She placed it in her grandmother's hand. Mémère's expression was harsh. She bounced the small leather package in her palm. "It weighs very little," she said, "but it cost two fortunes." She spilled the black arrowhead out onto the table.

"This was my father's lucky piece. It's a lodestone. And the pouch is made from the skin of a black cat. Powerful gris-gris. He gave my mother's wedding veil to a voodoo woman in exchange for it. That was after he had lost half his money at the gambling tables. This would change his luck, he was sure.

"So sure that he gambled more than ever and lost the rest of his money. My mother's jewels were sold, then the land she inherited when her parents died. Then the money her brothers gave them to live on was gambled away. The last thing he gambled on was the day the frost would come. He lost his crop of cane; he would have lost the mortgaged plantation and his honor, because he had terrible gambling debts. But he had one more thing to sell. My husband settled all of his obligations, including the mortgage. It was his gift to my father; my father gave him my hand in marriage.

"I was already sixteen when I was betrothed. The casket was mine. But my mother asked to change the contents. She had saved a bit of golden cobweb for her treasure. This lodestone was far more precious, she said. My father gave it up when he saw how desperately unhappy I was. He swore to her that he'd never gamble again.

"She believed him, of course. She always believed him. She blamed the voodoo lodestone, not him. She loved him.

"Two months after my wedding, he lost the plantation on the turn of one card. He went outside the gambling club and shot himself in the head. I didn't learn that until many years later. At the time his friends put up the money to buy back the plantation and they arranged things to look as if my father had been killed in a duel with an American who made a personal remark about my mother. She never knew the truth. She lived for another fifteen years, happy that hers had been one of the great loves of all time.

"There was enough gold in the cobweb to pay for my father's funeral."

Mary took her grandmother's hand in hers. "That's a tragic story, Mémère. I'm sorry."

Anne-Marie Sazerac squeezed her granddaughter's hand. "But it's romantic, my dear; we must admit that. And romance is a heady wine. The love affair that my parents knew was intoxicating to me. I saw their happiness together, and I envied it. I wanted to love and be loved like that.

"That's why I was so bitter when Papa married me to Jules Sazerac. I was young and Jules was old, thirty-three years older than I. I was giddy and Jules was severely aristocratic. He had escaped the Revolution in France and supported the restoration of the monarchy. I got involved with the Bonapartists in New Orleans. I even pawned Marie-Hélène's bracelets so that I could contribute to the cost of the ship the Bonapartists bought. We were going to rescue him from Saint Helena and bring him to a glorious sanctuary in New Orleans." Mémère's eyes were shining.

"It was very exciting, I must say. There were famous pirates here when I was young. Jean Lafitte had a veritable pirate kingdom on an island in one of the bayous. His chief lieutenant was a man named Dominique You, who was going to command the ship. We outfitted the ship with every luxury and did the same with a house on the corner of Chartres and Saint Louis streets where Napoleon would live."

Mémère giggled like a girl. "I remember there were little bees everywhere. All the drapery materials were embroidered with them, all the china painted with them, all the silver marked with them. It's a wonder the very walls didn't ooze honey. We didn't know what to do with all those bees when the word came three days before the ship was to sail: The Emperor was dead and so was our little adventure.

"The locket that I put in the casket has a bee engraved inside it. Very small and secret. The clandestine, conspiratorial atmosphere of the whole business was at least half the fun of it... Here, let me have it. The latch is concealed."

Mémère pressed a spot near the jeweled monogram and the locket flew open. Something fell out of it into her lap. She let out a small cry of dismay. Her fingers were careful, gentle, reaching for it. She held it out for Mary to see. It was a straw-like, stained lock of hair.

"I told you, Marie, that I knew more about love than you might expect. This is my souvenir of my great love. His name was Tom." Her voice was a caress. "Tom. Such a foreign, American name. Tom Miller.

"He was an American solider. Just an ordinary foot soldier, but to me he was extraordinary. I saw him first at the ceremony when the Americans took control of New Orleans. Everyone was there, all of them hating these barbarous new owners. New Orleans was French, had always been French, intended to remain French forever. No matter that Spain ruled her for most of her life. The Spanish had become Creoles, and that meant French. When we got the news that Spain had returned us to France, the celebrations went on, day and night, for over a week.

"It was a good thing, too, that we celebrated then, because while we were dancing, Napoleon was selling us to Thomas Jefferson. The tricolor of France flew over the Place d'Armes for only three weeks. Then the American army marched in and replaced it with the stars and stripes.

"We knew they were coming. The ceremony was all prepared. Every soul in New Orleans was in the Place d'Armes. It was less than a week before Christmas, the most festive time of year, but there was no joy in us.

"I was fifteen, and I hated the Americans more than anyone. Because of them there would be no gaiety, no more dancing that year. I scowled my fiercest scowl at that conquering army.

"One of the soldiers saw me and made such a hideous, childish, ugly face at me that I had to laugh. He laughed too, then. And I fell in love with him on the spot.

"He had eyes as blue and bright as a sunny sky, and hair the color of the sun. I'd never seen such a thing in my Creole life. He wasn't anything like the men and boys in my world.

"He found out who I was, I don't know how, and the next day he walked out to our plantation as bold as brass to see me. I was in the garden cutting greens to decorate the house; we couldn't be gloomy forever. He loped, the way Americans do when they're running, across the flower beds and picked me up, greens and all. And he kissed me full on the mouth. I'd never been so shocked—and so thrilled—in all my proper life.

"Papa was on the gallery. You've never seen anything move as fast as Papa did. He grabbed my soldier by the collar and me by my arm and, whoosh, I was flying toward the house while Tom was being booted off the property. That's when I learned his name. He yelled it out. 'I'm Tom Miller. Don't you forget me.'

"I never did. The next time I saw him was eleven years later, and almost Christmas again. I had been married for ten years, delivered five children, and buried two of them. And all those years I loved Tom Miller. I gave my husband obedience and duty, no more.

"Tom came back to New Orleans with General Andy Jackson to fight the British. England and America had been at war for over two years, and it had finally gotten around to us. The British fleet was on its way to capture New Orleans.

"We were scared to death. We had some pretty smart-looking militia. The uniforms were handsome, and so were the men. But they'd never been in a battle and there were only enough of them to fill out the guest list for a ball.

"General Jackson's army didn't make people feel much better when it arrived. There couldn't have been more than a couple of hundred men.

"For me, only one of them counted, and he counted for everything. I was absolutely shameless. I put on a dark veil and went to the barracks to find Tom. I remember, there was a big crowd of prostitutes outside, shouting their prices and their talents. I'd never even heard of half the things they were promising. But I stood there with them, like a strumpet, and sent a note in to Tom.

"When he came out, I threw back my veil and kissed him in full view of anyone that cared to look.

"He was a lot more sensible than I was. He put my veil down and walked me off real quick to a quiet spot on the levee. He gave me a real talking-to, about decency and responsibility and duty and marriage vows, because he was married, too. But the whole time he was scolding me, he was kissing me, until I was light-headed. And we made plans to run away together as soon as the battle was over.

"You must have heard all about the Battle of Chalmette, Marie. The whole city celebrates it every January eighth. The British had fifty warships and ten thousand of their finest soldiers. Jackson had two little schooners and a makeshift army of soldiers, Indians, militia, pirates, backwoodsmen, and volunteers from New Orleans, black and white and free men of color. They say there were under four thousand altogether.

"The battle started before daybreak and lasted about twenty-five minutes. When it was over there were twenty-six hundred British dead and thousands more wounded. The American casualties were thirteen wounded and eight killed.

"Seven and Tom Miller.

"I knew he was dead. We could hear the guns in the city. When they stopped so soon everyone waited with terror in his heart. Then a rider came with news of the victory, and the whole city rang with cheering. But not from me.

"I took a horse, stole it really, and rode out to Chalmette. Tom's body had already been brought from the field to rest under a live oak. I held his head in my lap and talked to him until General Jackson sent me home with an escort. He was the one who cut off the lock of Tom's hair and gave it to me. He was a kind man. I was glad when he became the President."

Mémère's voice had been soft and even; now she began to cry. Quietly. She was able to talk still, but her words were blurred.

"I ruined your mother's life because of Tom Miller, Marie, and my foolish, romantic heart. When she confided to me that she was in love with an American she had met only once, that she wanted to betray the sacred vows of betrothal and run away with him, I encouraged her to do it. I helped her. I wanted her to have what I had never had and always longed for. I thought your father was her Tom Miller.

"I should never have done it. Love, romantic love, isn't what makes a man and woman happy together. I was misled by my mother and father's marriage. I believed that marriage should be one long love affair, that kisses were the only thing that counted.

"After your mother died I went into a terrible melancholy. My husband took me to Europe. When we were on the ship, alone together, he talked to me as he never had in our thirty years of marriage. He was a severe man, but he had never been severe with me before. He always indulged me. Because he loved me and because I was so much younger.

"He'd always gotten me out of everything I got myself into. He bought Marie-Hélène's bracelets back after I pawned them. He fought and killed the only man who dared to mention my presence on the battlefield at Chalmette. He paid my gambling debts, too, because I liked to play for high stakes at whist.

"On the ship he told me that I had used up all his love and indulgence, that I had gone too far. Losing your mother was more than he could bear. I believe he loved her even more than I did, if such a thing is possible. He couldn't forgive me for helping her run away.

"'Anne-Marie,' he said, 'I have only a few years left to live. I want them to be as free of sorrow as they can be, and you have given me only sorrow in our thirty years together. You've never thought of me, only of yourself and your desires.'

"He said that he intended to stay in France, to die in the country of his birth. He would send me back to New Orleans alone. He'd take care of me and the children through his bankers. But he wanted never to see me again.

"A ship is the perfect place to learn oneself, Marie. There are no distractions, only the measureless sea and sky. I saw, at last, what I had done to this good, loving man. I had given him nothing. I had conceived his children with disgust and conspired with them against him. Not once had I wondered if he was happy; I was too preoccupied with my own unhappiness. I went over the years in my mind, remembering his many kind and thoughtful acts and words to me, finding none at all from me to him.

"I was ashamed, deeply, bitterly, miserably ashamed. I told him so.

"And his heart was so noble, so generous that he forgave me for thirty years of shamefulness.

"Jules lived for only six more years. They were sweet years for us both, sweet and yet sad, because the thirty that went before had been wasted. They, too, had sweetness waiting in them, but I wouldn't allow it to be born.

"So you see, my dear Marie, your Mémère has thought long and learned much about love. To be good it must build, not explode. Years make it strong, not embraces. Your mother paid a dreadful price for my mistakes. I hope that you will profit from what they have taught me.

"Fall in love if you will. That's why there are débuts and beaux. A certain arm around your waist in the waltz, a certain name on a bouquet of flowers will make your heart pound and your head spin.

"But when your uncles and I choose your husband, throw away the dance cards and pressed flowers you've saved. Cherish your husband and be grateful that he cherishes you. From that will grow the love that really matters."

Mémère tipped Mary's chin up, kissed her on both cheeks. Mary, too, was quietly weeping, moved by her grandmother's emotion.

"It's late," said Mémère, "and we must be rested tomorrow. It's Marie's day, our day. We shall be merry all day. I'm going to bed now. Don't stay up too late."

"I won't, Mémère." Mary knelt, hugged her grandmother. "Thank you for tonight."

"I love you, darling Marie."

"I love you, Mémère."

Mary did stay up, despite her pledge to Mémère. There was so much for her to think about. She put the casket's treasures on the rug in front of her and thought about the lives of the women who had owned them.

She knew the story of each of the things now, except for the Spanish moss in the lace handkerchief. Her mother must have added it to the box. It was, Mary supposed, her souvenir of New Orleans, her link with her home and her family.

Had she been homesick? Had she thought of the warm courtyard and the fragrance of orange blossoms when the first snows came in Pennsylvania? Had she regretted falling in love and running away?

Mary held the dry scratchy moss to her mouth to muffle the sound of her loud crying. How frightened she must have been and how lonely. Without her loving mother and father, her brothers and her cousins. Without New Orleans.

Had she known she was going to die, when the birth pangs started? So far from home.

Mary crawled to the small lace-draped altar in the corner of the room. "Forgive me," she sobbed, "for my pride and my lack of faith. Please, dear God, forgive me. And take my mother to your heart and give her happiness and peace in Your Heaven."

The votive candle flickered from her breath; the ivory Virgin Mary's outstretched arms and gentle face glowed in its warm golden light.

Mary whispered to her. "Please, Blessed Mother, let it not take too long for me to forget Valmont."

# 65

Mémère slept so late the next morning that Mary was distressed. Valentine told her not to worry. "Madame took some medicine last night, 'Zelle, that's all. Don't worry about that, either. Since you came, she's been taking less and less all the time. Last night she was upset about something and afraid she wouldn't sleep."

She suggested that she and Mary put up the Marie's Day decorations. It would be a happy surprise for her grandmother when she woke.

The broad blue silk ribbons were freshly ironed. Mary and Valentine attached the biggest rosette to the bottom of the dining room chandelier, then fastened the long streamers from it to the four corners of the table. Smaller rosettes decorated the sideboard and mantel and the tops of the tall gilt mirrors. Valentine tucked nosegays of pink rosebuds into their centers. Bouquets of pink roses went in the center of the mantel and sideboard, and a wreath of roses with silver-painted leaves went in the center of the table.

"The cake will stand inside the wreath," said Valentine. "Now we'll do the chairs, and everything will be ready." She tied a crisp blue bow to the top of Mary's chair while Mary did the same for Mémère's. The ribbon box was still half full.

"I'll just put this in the corner," the maid said. "There's no knowing how many people may decide to come for dinner."

Mary argued that everyone was out of the city because of the fever. The cannons were still firing, the tar barrels still burning, the dead wagon still creaking through the thick mud streets. And the rain never stopped.

Valentine repeated that there was no knowing. "Do you have a gift for your Mémère? There's special paper to wrap it in."

Mary did. It wasn't as fine as she wished, only some lace-edged handkerchiefs that she had bought months before and never used. All the shops were closed and boarded up. She wrapped them in the blue paper Valentine supplied, tied the package with white silk ribbon the maid gave her.

When the present was arranged with a spray of silvered leaves in front of Mémère's place at table, Valentine stepped back and surveyed the room. "Good," she pronounced. "It looks like Marie's Day."

"It's lovely," said Mémère from the doorway. "And a lovely surprise.

Thank you." She kissed them both. To Mary she said, "Bonne fête, Marie," and added another kiss.

She was dressed for the street, bonnet and gloves on, umbrella in hand. "Hurry now, get your things. We don't want to be late for mass. I especially like the altar flowers on Marie's Day." She had a newly cut rose pinned to her bonnet.

They made a distinctive little procession. Jacques held the big umbrella over Mémère and Mary from behind, while Valentine held one over her head and another over Jacques. At corners the umbrellas shifted from one to another as Jacques waded back and forth through the mud and foot-deep water carrying one woman at a time. By the time they reached the Cathedral they were all in laughing high spirits, feeling more than a little silly.

There were many more people in the Cathedral than Mary had expected. It was far from full, but she had believed the city empty. A hundred women or more were there in their bravest, albeit somewhat damp, finery. "Marie is an extremely popular name," Mémère whispered before she opened her missal.

Mary opened hers; she was relieved and happy to be reconciled in her heart with the Church that had always been such a major influence in her life. Especially for the Feast of the Annunciation, one of the most joyous of all the celebrations in the Church calendar.

The sermon added new reasons for happiness. Although the tragic epidemic was still with them, there was cause for thanks, said the priest. The numbers of the stricken were going down every day; there were now fewer than a hundred deaths every twenty-four hours.

Even the unprecedented unceasing rain was a blessing. There were many fires, and not enough firemen left alive to man the firewagons. The rain kept the fires from spreading, the city from destruction.

And the municipal authorities had granted special permission for the Cathedral on this feast day. The bells would ring a paean of joy and praise after mass was concluded.

The celebrants smiled in the shelter of their umbrellas, lingered on the wide banquette as they were used to do. The bells were an anthem of hope and normality. Even the coffee seller was there outside the door, her stove and fragrant coffee covered by a gaily striped tent.

Mémère darted from one friend, one cousin, to another, with Jacques skillfully maneuvering the umbrella above her head. Mary and Valentine laughed together while they watched.

When Mémère joined them, she joined in their laughter, also, even though she didn't know the cause. "I told you, Marie," she said, "that we would have a merry day. Come along now. We have to go buy the cake."

Mary sobered. "There are no shops open, Mémère."

"Nonsense. Vincent will never miss a Marie's Day. No one would ever buy so much as an éclair ever again."

She was right. The patisserie opposite the opera house was scrubbed and sparkling and door ajar. "Your lightest *massepain,*" ordered Mémère. "Wait. I'd best have two. I'm having a lot of guests for dinner."

"No way of knowing," murmured Valentine to Mary.

Massepain was a cake made especially for Marie's Day. When Mary saw it on its silver stand in the center of the table, she understood the planning behind all the room's decorations. It was a tall sponge cake iced in white, with *Bonne Fête* written on the top in blue icing letters, wonderfully curlicued. An open center held a pink rose with silver leaves.

While Mémère placed the blue-bowed cake knife to her satisfaction, Valentine tied bows on the backs of additional chairs. Mary wasn't even surprised when Jacques brought in two high chairs for trimming. Maries came in all sizes.

"I'm going to open my gift now," Mémère said, "and I want you to open yours, Marie. Usually all the guests bring gifts and I have gifts for all of them, but this isn't a usual Marie's Day."

She clapped her hands when she saw the handkerchiefs and vowed that her last one was in shreds and she'd been meaning to get some.

Mary couldn't respond to her grandmother's gratitude. She was overcome by the fragile beauty of the nightdress and peignoir Mémère had given her. They were made of white linen, as soft as silk, and embroidered with white butterflies above delicate woods flowers.

"I made those myself, for your mother," said Mémère. "I couldn't let them be destroyed with her other things. Now you can begin your trousseau with them."

"I've never seen anything so lovely in my life, Mémère. I don't know how to thank you."

"The look on your face speaks for you, my child. You make me very happy . . . There's the door. Quickly, put our gifts away before the guests come in. The paper and ribbon, too."

Mary ran up the stairs.

She came down by the back stairs. She could hear the twittering of female voices in the entrance hall. "They're here," she called to the kitchen.

"I'm not deaf yet," Jacques rumbled.

There were two major surprises at the festive dinner. One was that the two baby Maries never fussed or cried. The second was that the menu served was red beans and rice.

"I know it's not Monday," Mémère laughed. "I'm not in my dotage yet. But my Marie has an absolute passion for rice and beans. For her first ever Marie's Day I wanted her to have her favorite. For everyone else, there's an extra massepain to take up the slack."

Mary could feel the hot color in her face. She did full justice to the beans and rice anyhow. And to the massepain.

So did everyone else.

Perhaps the booming of the cannon reminded everyone that the beribboned room was an island of pleasure in the chaotic, desperate life and death of the city; perhaps Mémère's rediscovered happiness gave special joy to her friends. Whatever the reason, there was an extraordinary closeness, even intimacy, in the gathering. Women skilled in social chitchat instead spoke simply, and from the heart. About their fears, their hopes, their sorrows, their joys.

Mémère was the last to speak. She said how moved she was by the loyalty of them all, friendships that lasted through the ten long years that she'd been lost to them. It was right to mourn her husband, she said, but not for so long and not the way she did, withdrawing from the world and everyone in it. Finding her Marie had brought her back. She would never leave again. That was a promise. No, more than a promise, a solemn vow.

"I find that I like the world very much indeed. The Season is coming, with my Marie's début. I intend to put all your parties to shame with the extravaganzas I shall have. And when Marie marries, the wedding will make everyone forget my mother's golden cobwebs. Afterwards, I shall go to France for a respite from all the excitement. Just a visit. I love my home and my friends too much to be away from them ever again for too long."

The guests' goodbyes were emotional and prolonged. The babies howled protests at all the kisses they were forced to accept. A final burst of sound, and then everyone was gone.

"The cannons sound positively peaceful, don't they?" Mémère said, smiling. "Parties are always so much quieter when there are men, too." She kissed Mary. "Bonne fête, Marie."

"It was a bonne fête, Mémère."

"Yes it was. And tiring. I'm going to go to my room, take off my corset and have a good rest... Don't worry, child. I shan't need any medicine."

"I'll see you at supper, then. Rest well."

Mary went back into the dining room. She could start taking down the ribbons while Valentine was helping Mémère undress. She was on the library stepladder when Jacques came into the room and spoke to her.

"Jacques, I'm going to buy you a bell for you to wear around your neck. You walk too quietly. I nearly fell off the ladder when you said my name."

"There's a person who'd like to see you, 'Zelle."

"All right. I'm coming down. Who is it?"

"Not a person known to me, 'Zelle. A man of color. He's in the courtyard."

"In this rain? That's inhuman." Mary thought it must be one of the painters or paperhangers. Maybe the house would be finished at last, now that the epidemic was ending.

She was astounded when she saw her old friend Joshua.

"Come in this minute," she said. Then she laughed, repeated herself in English. "Sorry, Joshua. I've been talking French so long I forget there's anything else."

Joshua stood in the hall, dripping on the floor. Jacques was nearby, frowning.

"Does your butler know English, Missy?"

"Probably. He knows everything else."

"Then come outside, please, Missy. I need to talk to you." For the first time since Mary had first seen Joshua, he wasn't smiling. Mary took two umbrellas from the urn and handed one to him.

"I'm going out for some air," she said in rapid French, "and I don't want to be disturbed." She walked even more rapidly into the courtyard, across to its far side.

"What's wrong, Joshua? How can I help you? I'll do anything I can."

"This is a terrible chance I'm taking coming to you, Miss Mary. I believe I can trust you. Don't show me I'm wrong."

"Whatever it is, Joshua, you can trust me. I give you my word."

"You ever heard of the Underground Railroad, Missy?"

Mary's heart skipped a beat. She'd learned at the convent about it, its dangers. "Are the patrols after you, Joshua? Are you hiding a runaway? This house won't do. Let me think of some place."

"No. Not me," said Joshua. He put his mouth close to Mary's ear. Masked by the sound of the rain and the cannonfire he told her about Val's ship. The plantation doctor was suspicious, he said, when there were so many slaves in the hospital at Benison that he'd never seen before. He'd reported it to the authorities. Fear of contagion had kept them from investigating. Until now. Word had spread all along the secret network of the Railroad that patrols were going to Benison. Joshua had gone to warn him. Too late.

"Mr. Val's done set sail, Missy. Before they could get to him. But it's not over. The word is that they're going to stop him on the river, catch him with that big boat full up with niggers."

"But what can I do? Why did you come to me, Joshua?"

"There might still be time to stop him before he gets to the patrol boats. The runaways can get overboard, swim for it. Otherwise they gets jail and he gets worse. Trouble is, he don't know me. I'm just a worker on the Railroad. He'd never stop to my hail. I need you to come with me, Missy. Mr. Val's man, that Nehemiah, he say you the only one to ask."

Mary's mind worked faster than ever before in her entire life. Then, "I have to get some things," she said. "I'll only be five minutes, maybe less."

"You'll do it?"

"Of course."

Even while she was running to the house Mary was telling herself to stop. She was being a fool. Again. She was risking consequences she couldn't even name, as well as the ones she could: humiliation, rejection, scorn, ridicule.

She continued to run. Val needed her help.

She raced to her room, pulled the things she'd need from her wardrobe. Then she wrote a note for her grandmother.

Dearest Mémère.

I'm doing something foolish. I hope you'll forgive me. I believe everything you said about the best, real love. Yet still I'm running after Valmont Saint-Brévin because I love him too much to be sensible and sane. If you don't hear of me tomorrow, it means I'm with him on his ship on the high seas. I'll come home, I don't know when, but I will be back because I love you.

Mary.

While the ink dried Mary changed her clothes. Then she folded the note, ran to Mémère's room, slid it under the door, and dashed down the stairs. Jacques was standing by the door to the courtyard, glowering.

"I'm going out," Mary told him. "I left a note for Mémère." She opened her umbrella, ran out into the rain.

Joshua had a skiff hidden between some sodden bales of cotton on the levee. When they drew near, the men guarding it disappeared into the maze of abandoned cargo. It slid easily across the mud into the river, high from the month's downpours.

Mary was wearing her old brown work dress, holding a black umbrella. Joshua's dark shirt and pants were soaked; they were almost as black as his skin. Before the boat had traveled ten feet it was invisible in the rain and the tarry smoke that clung to the surface of the water.

Neither of them spoke, and the oars were wrapped. They moved silently and rapidly in the Mississippi's strong current. Mary thanked God that the fever had halted the traffic to New Orleans. Although it was not many minutes after four o'clock, in the rain and smoke it was almost as dark as night. If there had been boats in the river, they would almost certainly have hit one.

As they left the city behind, they moved out from the pall of smoke. Joshua turned his head with every pull on the oars, trying to see through the curtains of rain. But there was only water. Beneath them and on all sides of them.

"Better start bailing," he said quietly. "We're getting pretty heavy."

Mary found the big gourd dipper that was tied to the oarlocks. She bailed in rhythm with the oars. Her arm grew stiff.

And still no sight of Valmont's ship.

He got away, she thought. Thank God.

A moment later she heard Joshua's low moan. "They got him. He's dead in the water straight ahead. I'll take you back."

Before he could turn, Mary's urgent whisper stopped him. "Sssh, no, Joshua. I thought of this. There's still a chance." She told him her plan while they moved steadily nearer to Val's *Benison.* They could hear voices, but not words.

Joshua eased the skiff soundlessly alongside the stern of the ship. Mary held it there while he clambered up onto the deck. Then he threw down a rope, sliding down it with noiseless speed.

"Are you sure?" he whispered.

Mary nodded. She closed her umbrella, dropped it in the water sloshing in the bottom of the skiff, grasped the rope, and took a deep breath.

"Now," she said.

Joshua cupped his hands for her foot. Mary stepped up into them, holding the rope for balance. She released it when he tossed her up, caught it at the top of her flight through the rain. Her arms felt as if they were pulling out of their sockets when they took her weight.

I can't do it, she cried silently.

Then she heard a sneering American voice. "You expect us to believe that you're going off through a rain that makes your helmsman half-blind, plus in the middle of the hurricane season, all to do a little courting? You can do better than that, Mister Saint-Brévin."

Mary pulled on the rope with all her strength while her feet found purchase on the carved trim of the *Benison.* One step, up, two, four, and she could hook her leg over the rail.

"I'm up," she called softly. "Get out of here." She heard the muffled splash of Joshua's oars as she pulled herself onto the deck.

She ran into a sheltering overhang; her fingers moved like lightning as she ran, opening the buttons of her dress. Quickly, quickly, she pulled her arms out of the sleeves. Val was shouting about insults and over-reaching authority. She pushed the dress down over her hips and stepped out of it, kicked off her boots. Under the dress she was wearing the gown and peignoir Mémère had given her.

Mary could see into the helmsman's cabin now. He was loading a rifle under the cover of the chart table. She pulled the hairpins out of her chignon, ran her fingers through her hair as she edged along the outside of the cabin.

At the front corner she darted quickly to her left, stopping at the doorway. Now, Mary MacAlistair, she ordered, make it good. She stepped forward.

"Val," she cried, a querulous whine in her voice, "are you going to stand there talking to your friends all day?" She spoke in English.

Valmont's face when he turned toward her registered shock, then amazed comprehension. "Mary, I told you to stay below," he said clearly.

"You could have told me why we were stopping," Mary answered. "I was afraid Uncle Julien Sazerac had caught us. Who are these people? If this is your idea of eloping, to invite a bunch of people..."

The admiration in Val's eyes made her heart dance. The amusement in them made her look away before she gave in to the desire to laugh. The men from the patrol boat blocking the *Benison's* bow were red-faced from embarrassment. And nervousness. Julien Sazerac was too powerful to offend. If he ever knew that they had seen his niece with a negligée plastered to her naked body by the rain so that everything showed...

"My mistake, Mr. Saint-Brévin," said their captain. "I had no idea. I would never have..."

Val interrupted him with a clap on the shoulder. "How could you have known? We've been very clever. I'll just pretend this never happened. Of course I'll expect you to do the same, Captain. If I ever learn that there's any kind of talk about my wife, I'll expect satisfaction on the field of honor."

Mary ducked into the cabin.

"I'd be grateful for your coat," she said to the baffled helmsman.

"Mary, you were magnificent," Val said from the deck.

"Are they gone?"

"The last one's at the bottom of the ladder. I can pull it up now. Then we'll get under way."

Mary pulled the helmsman's coat more tightly around her. She was shivering from reaction.

When Val entered the cabin she started to babble. "Joshua, he's a friend of mine, told me that Nehemiah said to get me to help, and I had no time to think so I just said yes, and I didn't know if it would work but I couldn't think of anything else and... and... I'm so embarrassed I could die."

"Mary. Stop it. You just saved two hundred men and women and children from slavery. You also saved my life. You're fabulously brave and fantastically quick-witted. You should be proud, not embarrassed."

"Thank you, Val." She didn't know what to say or do. She looked miserably at her bare feet. Val stepped toward her, stopped. When he spoke, his voice was ragged. "I have so much to say to you, Mary, so many things to explain... Oh, hell, I've been such a fool. I don't know where to start."

Mary felt the beginning of an idea too much longed for to be true. She looked up at him. It was true. He loved her. The pain on his face was for the pain he'd caused her. The longing in his eyes was the same as her longing.

"Val," she said. She reached out her hand.

Then she was in his arms, and her shivering was warmed away.

*The author apologizes to historians and lovers of New Orleans for adding a yellow fever epidemic in 1851 to the actual ones that decimated the city in 1832 and 1853.*